The Brides
of Bella Rosa

RAYE MORGAN

BARBARA HANNAY

REBECCA WINTERS

MILLS &
BOON

First published in Great Britain 2013
by Mills & Boon, an imprint of Harlequin (UK) Limited,
Eton House, 18-24 Paradise Road, Richmond, Surrey TW9 1SR

THE BRIDES OF BELLA ROSA © by Harlequin Enterprises II B.V./S.à.r.l 2013

Beauty and the Reclusive Prince, Executive: Expecting Tiny Twins and *Miracle for the Girl Next Door* were published in Great Britain by Harlequin (UK) Limited.

Beauty and the Reclusive Prince © Harlequin Books S.A. 2010
Executive: Expecting Tiny Twins © Harlequin Books S.A. 2010
Miracle for the Girl Next Door © Harlequin Books S.A. 2010

Special thanks and acknowledgement are given to Raye Morgan, Barbara Hannay and Rebecca Winters for their contributions to THE BRIDES OF BELLA ROSA series.

ISBN: 978 0 263 90550 2
ebook ISBN: 978 1 472 00123 8

05-0413

Printed and bound in Spain
by Blackprint CPI, Barcelona

BEAUTY AND THE RECLUSIVE PRINCE

BY
RAYE MORGAN

CHAPTER ONE

"ENOUGH!"

Isabella Casali's cry was snatched right out of her mouth by the gust of wind that tore at her thick dark hair and slapped it back against her face. What a night she'd picked to go sneaking onto royal property. The moon had been riding a crest of silky clouds when she'd started out from the village. Now the sky had turned black and the moon was playing hide and seek, taking away her light just when she'd stepped on forbidden territory. Where had this sudden storm come from, anyway?

"Bad luck," she whispered to herself, squinting against another gust of wind. "I've got reams of it."

She knew she ought to turn and head for home, but she couldn't go back without finding what she'd come for—not after all she'd done to work up the nerve to come in the first place.

The grounds of the local prince's palazzo were famously said to be the stomping grounds for all sorts of supernatural creatures. She'd discounted it before, thought it was nothing but old wives' tales. But now that she'd come here and seen for herself, she was beginning to get the shivers just like everyone else. Every gust of wind, every snapping twig, every moan from the trees made her jump and turn to see what was behind her.

"You'd better hope the prince doesn't catch you."

Those words had made her smile when Susa, her restaurant's vintage pastry chef, had uttered them like an aging Cassandra just before Isabella had left for this adventure. Susa often had wise advice, but this time Isabella was sure she was off the beam. What had Susa said again?

"They say he patrols the grounds himself, looking for young women who stray into his woods…"

"Oh, Susa, please," she'd scoffed. "They've said the same thing about every prince who's lived in that old moldy castle for the last hundred years. The royal Rossi family has never been a very friendly bunch, from what I've heard. When you don't get out and mix with the citizens, you're bound to get a bad reputation."

She'd chuckled at the time, completely unconcerned, even though the royal grounds were the last place she wanted to venture onto anyway. Given a choice, she would have stayed home with a good book.

"But it's mostly because they're such a mystery," she continued, thinking it over. "I'll bet they're very nice people once you get to know them."

Susa raised her eyebrows and looked superior. "We'll see how nice you think he is when he has you locked up in his dungeon."

"Susa!" Isabella was reluctant enough to go on this mission without the older woman raising more reasons why she should just stay home.

"Besides, Papa has been sneaking in there to collect the *Monta Rosa Basil* we need for years and, as far as I know, he's never seen a royal person there yet. I don't believe a word of it."

Her father, Luca Casali, had discovered the almost magical properties of this fine herb years before and it had transformed his cuisine from average Italian fare into something so special people came from miles around just to get a bowl of exquisitely cooked pasta topped with the steaming tomato-based sauce Luca had come up with.

The special recipe and the herb were a closely held family secret. Only a few knew that the delicious flavor came from a plant that could be found only on a hillside located on the estate of the royal Rossi family in Monta Correnti.

For years, her father had gone once a month to collect the herb. Now he was ill and could no longer make the trip. It was up to Isabella to take up the mantle as herb-gatherer, reluctant as she might be. She'd decided she might have less risk of being caught at it if she went at night. She was a little nervous, but fairly confident. After all, her father had never had a problem. She told herself calmly that she would do just fine.

But that was before the storm came up, and the moon disappeared, and the wind began to whip at her. Right now, every scary rumor seemed highly plausible and she was definitely looking over her shoulder for marauding royalty.

Earlier, when the sun was still shining, she'd thought it might be interesting to meet the prince.

"What's he like, really?" she'd asked Susa. "When he's not enticing young women into his bedroom, at any rate."

Susa shrugged. "I don't know much about him. Only that his young wife died years ago and he's been sort of a recluse ever since."

"Oh." Isabella thought she'd heard something about that a long time ago, but she didn't remember any details. "How sad."

"They say she died under mysterious circumstances," the woman added ominously.

"Are there any other kind in your world?" Isabella shot back.

Susa gave her a superior look and turned away, but at the same time Isabella was remembering what Noni Braccini, the restaurant cook who had taught her most of what she knew about Italian cooking when she was a young girl, used to say.

"Nothing good could happen in a place like that." She would point a wrinkled finger toward where the old, crumbling palazzo stood and mutter, "Bats."

Isabella would look at her, nonplussed. "Bats?"

She would nod wisely. "Bats. You don't want bats in your hair."

Isabella would find herself smoothing down her own wild tresses and agreeing quickly, with a shudder. "No, no, indeed. I don't want bats in my hair."

And that was about all she knew about the prince in the castle. Of course, there was the fact that the essential herb grew on a hillside on castle grounds.

Noni had died long since, but Susa was still around to give dire warnings, and she'd said matter-of-factly as Isabella was going out the door, "When I was a girl, it was common knowledge that the Rossi prince was a vampire."

"What?" Isabella had laughed aloud at that one. "Susa, that's crazy!"

"He was the grandfather of this one." The older woman had shrugged. "We'll see, won't we?"

Isabella had laughed all the way to her car, but she wasn't laughing now. It wasn't just what Susa had said in warning. There were plenty of other old stories swirling in her head. Her childhood had been full of them—tales told in the dark at girlfriend sleepovers, stories of blackbeards who captured women and held them within the castle walls—vampires who roamed the night looking for beautiful victims with virgin throats—seducers with dark, glittering eyes, who lured innocent girls into their sumptuous bedrooms. Suddenly they all seemed too plausible. She was half regretting that she'd come to this frightening place at all, and half angry with herself for being such a wimp.

"Come on," she muttered to herself encouragingly. "Just a bit further and we'll get this done."

After all, how bad could it be? Even if she did run into the prince, he couldn't possibly be as wicked as Susa had painted him. In fact, she remembered seeing him once, years ago, when she was a teenager. She'd been visiting a hot springs resort area a few hours from the village and someone had pointed him out. She'd thought him incredibly handsome at the time—and incredibly arrogant-looking.

"The old royalty are all like that," her friend had said. "They think they're better than the rest of us. It's best to stay out of their way."

And she had, all these years. Now she was rambling around on royal grounds. The quicker she got this over with, the better.

Just a little further and she would find the hillside where the special basil grew, pick enough to fill the canvas bag she'd brought along, and head for home. Of course, it would help if she could see more than three feet in front of her with this stupid flashlight that kept blinking off.

"Oh!"

Her foot slipped and she almost tumbled down the hill. At least the problem with the flashlight was solved. It *did* tumble down the hill, and over a ledge, and into the river. Even above the noise of the wind, she could hear the splash.

Isabella wasn't one to swear, but she was working up to it tonight. What a disaster. What had she been thinking when she'd decided to come here all alone in the middle of the night? She'd known she was just asking for trouble.

"I just wasn't made for this cloak-and-dagger stuff," she muttered to herself as she tried to climb higher on the hill. All she wanted was to find the herbs and get out of here. She hated doing this. She dreaded getting caught by guards…or the prince. Or attacked by vampires—whichever came first.

The wind slashed through the tops of the trees, howling like a banshee. Lightning flashed, and in that same moment she looked up and saw a figure all in black atop a huge horse, racing down on her.

Time stopped. Fear clutched at her heart like a vise. This was too much. The dark, the wind, the sight of danger crashing toward her—had she taken a wrong turn somewhere? Suddenly, everything was upside down and she was terrified. Without a pause, she screamed at the top of her lungs. The sounds echoed through the valley, louder and louder, as lightning cracked and thunder rolled.

That lifetime of scary stories had set her up to think the worst. Every story flashed through her soul in an instant. She was shaking now, panic taking over, and she turned to run.

She heard him shout. Her heart was in her throat. She was dashing off blindly, startled as a cornered deer, and she heard him coming up behind her. The hoofbeats sounded like thunder striking stone, and his shout was angry.

She was in big trouble. He was going to catch her. She couldn't let that happen! She had to run faster…faster…

She couldn't run fast enough and she couldn't get her breath. Her foot slipped, wrenching her balance out from under her. She started to slide down the steep hill. Crying out, she reached to catch herself on a bush, but it pulled right out of the ground. Suddenly, she was tumbling toward the river.

She hit the water with a splash that sent a spray in all directions. She gasped as the icy water took her in. Now she was going to drown!

But she barely had time to reach for the surface before the strong arms of the man in black had caught hold of her and she was pulled instantly from the racing water.

He had her. Stunned by the cold, shocked by what was happening, she couldn't find her bearings. Disoriented in the moment, she realized dimly that she was being carried toward the horse, but she was a bystander, watching helplessly, as though from afar. For now, it seemed there was nothing she could do to resist.

Later, she was mortified as she remembered this scene. How could she have succumbed so quickly to the overwhelming sense of his strength like that? She'd just suffered a shock, of course, and that had pretty much knocked her silly, but still... As she remembered just how much the feel of his strong, muscular arms seemed to paralyze her reactions, she could do nothing but groan aloud in frustration. How could she have been such a ninny?

But in the moment, she was spellbound. The moon came out from behind the clouds, turning the landscape silver. Trying to look up at his face, all she could see was his strong chin, and the smooth, tight cords of his sculptured neck. And still, she couldn't seem to make a move.

This was crazy. He was just a man. Nothing supernatural at all. Just a man. A man who had no right to carry her this way. She had to assert herself, had to let him know what he was dealing with. But before she could get a word out, she found herself thrown up onto the horse and the creature who'd captured her was rising to mount behind her.

And finally, with a lot of effort, she found her voice.

"Hey, wait a minute!" she cried. "You can't do this. Let me go!"

Maybe he didn't hear her. The wind was making a riot in the tops of the trees. At any rate, he didn't answer, and in seconds the horse was galloping toward the ancient, forbidding structure looming at the top of the hill, and she was going along for the ride. She hung on for dear life. She could hardly breathe. She heard the hoofs clattering on the cobblestones as they neared the entrance. Huge lanterns lit the entryway. And then they came to a halt and he had dismounted and pulled her down as well.

She swayed. For a moment, she was confused and couldn't find her footing. His hands gripped her shoulders from behind, holding her steady. She turned, wanting to see his face, but he kept it from her.

"This way," he said, taking her by the hand and leading her up to the huge wooden door.

"No," she said, but her voice was weak and she found herself following along where he led, even though her soggy running suit was sticking to her legs, the heavy jacket flapping against her torso, the running shoes sloshing with every step. She was a mess. She hated to think what her hair looked like.

Somewhere on the grounds, a pair of dogs began to howl. Or was it wolves? Her heart was thumping so hard she could hardly tell. The roll of distant thunder added to the menace in the air. The lanterns made eerie shadows and her gaze rose to take in the sinister spikes at the top of the castle wall.

She shuddered. Was she dreaming? Or had she ventured by mistake into one of this area's old-fashioned legends? Was she on her way to the dungeon, as Susa had warned?

And if this was a story, was this man who'd scared her and then saved her the hero or the villain?

"Both," said a little voice inside her.

She shook her head. It didn't matter right now. She needed him. She had no one else to turn to.

The front door creaked open as they approached. She caught a glimpse of a man as old and craggy as the walls, his features exaggerated by the lighting. A wizard? She shrank back against her companion, automatically turning to him for protection despite everything. He hesitated for a moment, then put his arm around her shoulders and let her curl herself up against him. After a second or two, his arm actually tightened around her.

Isabella was still too dazed to know what was really going on. She was wet, she was cold, she was in the courtyard of a forbidden palazzo, and a man she had momentarily thought might be a vampire—well, just for a second or two—now had his arm around her. What was more, his arm felt darn good, as did the rest of him. In fact, she didn't think she'd seen a man in a long time that appealed to her senses quite as much as this scary and yet comforting man did right now.

She'd pretty much decided men and romance and things of that nature weren't going to be a part of her life. Too much trouble, not worth the effort. And here she was, responding to this scary man like a cat to cream. Maybe she was just an adrenaline junky after all.

"We're almost there," he told her helpfully.

That surprised her. Were vampires usually this considerate? She didn't think so. But maybe he was just calming her fears to make her more amenable to manipulation. Or maybe she'd seen too many horror movies in her time.

She sighed and closed her eyes, wishing she could get

orientated. She wasn't used to feeling so helpless, as though her muscles couldn't really respond. But maybe that was because her mind didn't seem to be working at all. She was so tired. Maybe when she opened her eyes, this would all fade away and she would be home in her own bed....

Prince Maximilliano Di Rossi looked down at the woman who was clinging to him and frowned. He was surprised that she'd turned to him for protection the way she had, but he was also surprised at his own reaction to her move. His first impulse was to pull away, to reject all contact. That was his way, the style he'd been living with for the last ten years. The only people he allowed near him were those who had always been closest to him, a few people who had known him since childhood—since before the accident. He never had other visitors. He'd been stepping out of character even to bring her here.

But something in the easy, open way she'd clung to him had stirred old memories. She was shivering and turning toward him as a lover would. Something deep inside him hungered for this. It had been so long since he'd held a woman in his arms, since he'd felt that warmth, that contrast between his own hard body and the soft, rounded responsiveness of a woman. He'd thought he might never feel it again. And yet, here it was, like a gift out of the blue.

But not for long. He knew she'd been trying to see his face and he'd been keeping it averted. Once she really saw him in full light, any instincts for touching him in any way would dry up like summer rain on a hot pavement.

With a cynical twist of his wide mouth, he turned and led her into the palazzo through the tall, heavy wood door. Their footsteps echoed down the long empty hallways. Someone coughed. He looked up. There stood his man,

Renzo, in his nightclothes and dressing gown, and wearing what appeared to be a pair of aging woodchucks on his feet. He looked sleepy and ridiculous, but definitely alarmed at the same time.

"Nice slippers," he commented wryly, cocking an eyebrow.

"Thank you, sir," Renzo responded, shuffling his feet and looking slightly abashed.

Max paused for a moment. He knew he could very easily hand over this piece of womanly baggage to the individual who had been his combination valet, butler, and personal assistant most of his life. Hand her over and turn his back and walk away and never give her another thought. He knew very well that Renzo would take care of everything discreetly and efficiently. Doing just that would fit the pattern of his life, the way things were done around here. He made a move as though to do it. He could see that Renzo expected it. How easy it would be to follow through.

And then he glanced down at the woman. She was still turning to him for refuge. She'd reached for him, given herself into the comfort of his arm, pressed her beautiful young body against his as though she was trusting that he would keep her safe. Something moved inside him—and that was dangerous. Just looking down into her gorgeous thick, tangled hair, he could feel his emotions stirring in a way he didn't need.

And still, he didn't leave.

Later he told himself it was nothing more than a typical impulse of the male role of guardian, the same he might have had for a puppy or a kitten that needed his attention. Despite his background, despite his guilty past, the urge to safeguard those smaller and more vulnerable rose in him and he'd followed his instincts.

But for once, he wasn't convinced. No, there was something about this woman—something threatening. He knew he should walk away and leave her to Renzo to deal with.

But he didn't do that.

Looking up, he shook his head at his man. "I'll handle this," he said, shedding his long black cloak and dropping it on a chair along the side of the room. He was going to see to her himself.

At the same time he realized what this meant. He was going to be forced to go against habit and his recent tradition. He was going to have to do something he almost never did these days. He was going to have to turn and let her see his face.

Renzo looked alarmed. "But, sir—" he began.

The prince cut him off. "Notify Marcello that I would like him to join us in the Blue Room," he said.

Renzo blinked. "Excuse me, sir, but I think the doctor is asleep…"

"Then wake him," Max said crisply. "I want him to take a look at this young lady. She's had a fall."

"Oh, my goodness," Renzo said faintly, but he didn't leave the room. Instead, he cleared his throat as though to say more, but Max wasn't listening. He was steeling himself for the moment that was about to come.

He knew his hesitation would seem strange to others. Most would let anyone see their face at any time. After all, it was the side they showed to the world, the representation of just who they were.

But he wasn't like everyone else. His face was scarred, horribly damaged and ugly to see. It couldn't represent him, because he wasn't like that inside. But it was all he had, and therefore it was something he avoided showing to strangers.

To turn and let her see his face would be a serious step for him. Still, he was going to do it. He was impatient with himself for even wavering. It was time he got over this weakness. He would turn and let her see just what she was dealing with. And he would hold his gaze steady so that he would be forced to take in every ounce of the shock and horror in her eyes. It was best to stay real.

"Come this way," he told her brusquely, turning to stride down the hall. She almost ran to keep up, holding onto his hand as though she would be lost if she let go. The huge portraits that lined their path were a blur, as were the long, aging tapestries that hung from the walls. He swept her into a room lined with heavy blue velvet drapes. The embers of a dying fire were smoldering in the large stone fireplace.

"Sit down," he said, gesturing toward an antique Grecian couch. "My cousin Marcello is a physician. I want him to take a look at you."

"I can't," she said, shaking her head and looking down at herself. Everything about her seemed to be dripping. "I'm filthy and muddy and wet. I'll ruin the upholstery."

"That doesn't matter," he said shortly.

She raised her dark gaze and cocked her head to the side, trying to see more than the left half of his face. Was he joking? This was one of the most sumptuously embellished rooms she'd ever been in. Not what she was used to, but most people she knew didn't do much decorating in velvet and gold leaf.

"Of course it matters," she responded, beginning to feel some of her usual fire returning. "I may not look like much right now, but I've got manners. I know how to act in polite company."

"Polite company?" He gave a little grunt, not even sure himself if it were partly a laugh or not. "Is that what you're expecting? We'll have to see if we can muster some up for you."

He was pacing about the room in a restless way and she turned to keep him in her line of vision. She was pretty sure she knew who he was by now. After all, she'd seen him all those years ago at the hot springs. If only she could get a full view of his face she would know for sure, but he seemed to have a talent for keeping in the shadows.

"You're making me dizzy," she said, reaching out to steady herself with a hand on the back of an overstuffed chair.

He grunted again, but he didn't stop moving. She watched nervously, wondering what he was planning to do with her. Luckily, he didn't seem inclined to lock her in a cell, so Susa was wrong there, but she supposed he could call the police and have her arrested if he wanted to. This was his castle and she didn't belong here.

She watched and waited. She liked the way he moved. There was a controlled, animal strength to him, and every action, every turn, presented with a certain masculine grace. And yet there was the sense of something more to him, something hidden, something leashed and waiting. He was new to her, unpredictable. Once again she realized that she was in a presence she didn't know how to handle. That made her heart thump.

Stopping to look out into the hall, he muttered something she couldn't quite make out, but it sounded slightly obscene.

"What's the matter?" she asked, tensing as though to be ready to run for it.

He started to turn toward her, then stopped. "My cousin is taking his own sweet time about it," he said evenly. "I'd like to get this over with."

"So would I," she said, her tone heartfelt. "Listen, why don't I just go and—?"

"No," he ordered firmly, glancing at her sideways. "You stay right where you are."

That put her back up a bit and sparked a sense of rebellion in her soul.

"Much as I appreciate your warm and welcoming hospitality," she began with a touch of sarcasm, taking a step toward the door, "I think it's time—"

"No."

He took a step closer and his hand shot out and circled her wrist. "You're staying right here until I permit you to go."

"Oh, I am, am I?" Her lower lip jutted out and she pulled hard on his hold but he wasn't letting go. "Your rules are on the medieval side, you know. These days one doesn't take orders from another person unless they are being paid money."

He pulled her closer, his face half turned her way. "Is that what you're after?" he asked harshly. "Is it money you want?"

"What?" She stared up at him, shocked by the very concept. "No, no, of course not."

"Then what do you want here?" he demanded.

She swallowed hard. Somehow this didn't seem to be a good segue into asking for monthly access to his hillside. "N...nothing," she stammered.

"Liar."

She gasped. He was right but she didn't like hearing it. "You...you wouldn't understand," she stammered senselessly. "But I meant you no harm."

He gave a sharp tug to her wrist, pulling her up close. "Harm." He said it as though it were a pointless word. "All the harm's been done years ago," he added softly.

She winced at the bitterness in his voice. It was clear something about his life just wasn't going well. The gloomy, bleak atmosphere was only reinforced by his dark attitude.

Negative people usually turned her off but there was a lot more here than a bad mood. She felt it like a vibration in the air, and her heart began to beat just a bit harder.

He felt her pulse quicken under his hold on her wrist and he knew what he had to do. Slowly, very deliberately, he turned and faced her, the light from the lamps and the fire exposing his horrible scars.

Was it pride that kept him from showing this to anyone who didn't know him intimately? Was it conceit, arrogance, egoism? Was it really that hard to think that his face, which had once been considered quite handsome, was now so repellent, people turned away rather than be forced to look at him?

It was probably all those things. But he'd known from the start there was something deeper and harder to face than that. He knew very well there was a large measure of guilt mixed into his motivations. His scars were retribution for his sins, but, even more painful, they were his own fault. That was the hardest thing to live with.

He'd spent years now, hidden away, traveling in limousines with tinted windows, moving anonymously from one house to another. It was a strange, lonely existence, and he was sick of it. But in order to change things, he would have to get used to people seeing his face, and he wasn't sure he could do it. Or that he deserved to.

But tonight, he wasn't going to dodge anything. It was high time he accepted his fate and learned to live with it. He was going to stare directly into her huge blue eyes and read every scrap of emotion that was mirrored there. No more avoidance. His jaw tightened and he steeled himself. And then he presented himself to her, scars and all.

Her eyes widened as she took in the totality of his face. The shock was there. He tensed, waiting for the disgust, the wince, the hand to the mouth, the flood of pity, the eyes darting away, looking anywhere but at him. He'd seen it before.

The only mystery was—why did he still let it bother him? It was time to harden himself to it. And so he stood his ground and met her gaze.

But things weren't going quite as he'd expected. The quality of her surprise was somehow different from what he was used to. No curtain of instant distance appeared, no revulsion, no reserve tainted her manner.

Instead of dread, instead of a cold drawing away in repugnance, a warm, curious light came into her eyes. Rather than pull away, she was coming closer. He watched in astonishment as she actually cocked her head to the side, then reached out for him.

He didn't move as she edged closer and touched his face, her fingertips moving lightly over the scar, tracing its path down his cheek and into the corner of his wide mouth.

"Oh," she said, letting it out in a long sigh.

But there was no pity. Maybe there was a hint of sorrow. But other than that, only a touch of confusion along with much interest and curiosity. It seemed almost as though she'd found a wonderful piece of statuary with a tragic flaw that deserved a little exploring. And she felt no inhibitions in doing exactly that.

CHAPTER TWO

ISABELLA was moving in a haze of unreality, as though she really had stepped into a fairy tale. She saw the jagged, fascinating scars, the tragic flaw that split his face in two and made her heart ache with compassion, but there was so much beside that. There was power and presence in the man, and, even more, there was overwhelming beauty in him. His shirt was open, exposing the tanned skin of a hard, sculptured chest, and his wonderful male heat filled her with a strange sense of longing that scared her more than anything else had—and at the same time it tugged at her with an impossible attraction.

He reached out as though to steady her, his hands gentle yet firm on her shoulders, and she felt herself melt into his touch, wanted to lean closer yet. She had a sudden, wild desire to press her lips to the pulse she could see beating hard at the base of his throat. She stared at it, irresistibly drawn.

But she recoiled in time, shocked at her own impulses. What next—was she going to offer herself to the man outright? She gasped softly, then began to think she ought to pull away. Ought to—but couldn't quite summon up the will.

Max couldn't have been more amazed if she *had* kissed him. The moment crystallized in time, her body arched toward his, her fingertips on his face, his heart pounding, his gaze locked on hers. Something twisted in his chest and he realized he was holding his breath. He was feeling something new and strange and he didn't like it at all. But she'd touched him. No woman had done that since the accident. No woman had wanted to. That lit a fire inside him he hadn't known he was capable of feeling. Whatever else this young woman was, she was unique in a way he'd never seen before. She didn't make him feel like a freak. He savored the moment.

And in the same instant he became aware that Renzo had come into the room at last and was now lurching forward as though he was prepared to push this woman back away from his prince. It all seemed to be happening in slow motion. And it all seemed to be so very beside the point, but it had to be dealt with, and so he did.

Turning to block Renzo's ridiculous protective lunge with the position of his body, he pulled the young woman up against him and out of Renzo's reach. Looking down, he sank into the clouds in her dark eyes, searching for the mysteries they might contain. She seemed to hold worlds he'd never visited deep inside her. Those worlds were suddenly the most interesting places he'd ever had a glimpse of. He suddenly found it very hard to pull away from her gaze. Or maybe, the truth was, he didn't want to.

Who was she? Where had she come from? Should he get away from her as fast as he could—or should he find a way to keep her here? He knew what his instincts were telling him. But he knew from experience that his instincts could lie.

Renzo still hung at his shoulder. "Sir…"

It took Max a moment to respond. He was still looking deep into the young woman's eyes. "I thought I told you to get Marcello," he said without turning.

"But, sir…" Renzo was blinking rapidly, obviously upset by this strange behavior.

"Go."

Renzo averted his gaze, bowed deeply, and gave in. "Very well, sir." Turning on his heel, he left the room.

And at the same time Max's sister, Angela, appeared in the opening. She took in the scene and her eyebrows arched even higher than usual.

"Well, Max," she said, starting into the room at last. "Who's this?"

The sound of her voice snapped them both to attention as though a spell had been broken. They turned to look at her. She came closer, circling and gazing with wonder at the two of them.

"Where on earth did you find her?"

Max drew in a sharp breath and stepped away from Isabella as though she'd suddenly grown too hot to touch. She reached out to steady herself against the back of the couch, not sure if she was reacting to general dizziness, or to the man himself. She was still in a muddle, but at least her head was clear enough by now to fully understand whom she was dealing with. After all, if you trespassed on a prince's property, you were likely to run into the prince at some point. And maybe even a princess or two.

"I found her wandering around down by the river," this particular prince was saying. "The dogs were loose and I was afraid they might attack her." He made a gesture and looked down at Isabella, still swaying next to the couch, then back at his sister. "I must have startled her. She fell down the hill."

Angela nodded, looking her over, then glanced sharply at Max. "Right into the water, I see."

"Yes."

"And you…you rescued her?"

His hands curled around the back of a chair and gripped so hard his knuckles were white. "Yes, Angela. I rescued her." He turned to stare at his sister with a measure of hostility.

"I see." She stared back, but looked away first, looking Isabella over again. "That still doesn't tell me who she is."

He turned to look at her, too, his large dark eyes dispassionate. All sense of a special tension between them seemed to have melted away.

"True," Max agreed. "Nor what she was doing on the property." He hesitated, then added, almost to himself, "And so close to the river."

Isabella drew herself up. Now that she was coming back down to earth, she was getting tired of being treated like a rather stupid child and talked about as though it didn't matter if she understood or not. For one trembling moment, she'd actually thought she and this man had a special connection of sorts, something quick and searing that was going to change her life. But now she could see that she'd been fooling herself—as usual.

First he'd terrified her, then beguiled her with his tenderness and his scarred face. Now he was acting as if she were a wet cat who shouldn't have been let inside. The disappointment she felt was real. She noticed he was avoiding her gaze again, turning his head so that the scarred side was hidden by shadows. Her chin rose and she looked at them both defiantly, her pride returning.

"My name is Isabella Casali. I help my father Luca run the restaurant in the square. Rosa? Perhaps you've eaten there."

Angela gave a careless shrug. Dressed in a flowing robe, she'd obviously been preparing for bed when the sounds of Isabella's arrival had drawn her back downstairs. In her mid-thirties, she had a cool, blonde beauty that was slightly marred by just a touch too much arrogance for comfort.

"I know it though we've never eaten there." Her smile was perfunctory. "We will have to try your food someday."

Isabella was surprised. Everyone ate at Rosa. "You've never had anything from our restaurant?" Isabella asked, incredulous.

"No."

She looked from the handsome woman to the incredible man. Despite her newfound annoyance with him, she had to admit he was a striking figure with the sort of presence that demanded more than simple respect. Tall and muscular in a slender way that bespoke strength along with graceful movement, he was the sort of man you couldn't take your eyes off once you'd seen him. And that scar…she'd never seen anything like it before.

"Perhaps my aunt's restaurant, Sorella, is more to your liking," she commented. "She has things that are very international and trendy. It's right next door to Rosa."

He shook his head. "We have our own cooks," he said simply. "We don't eat in restaurants."

Her head went back. That certainly put her in her place.

"Oh," she said faintly. "Of course."

"I'm sure we can make an exception," Angela said with a wave of her hand, giving her brother a look as though to remind him to be polite to the little people. "To complete the introductions, this is Prince Maximilliano Di Rossi, who owns this palazzo, and I am his sister, Angela. If you live in Monta Correnti, I'm sure you know that."

Isabella didn't answer. It took a moment to get all this in focus. Of course, she'd known there was a Rossi prince living here in the castle from time to time, but, except for stories and the one sighting at the springs, she'd never actually given him much thought. He wasn't a regular presence in the village or around the countryside, so if she'd ever known his name, she'd forgotten it long since.

When she'd been young, there had been a Prince Bartholomew who had lived here. If she remembered correctly, he'd had a beautiful film-star wife who had seldom come here with him, and three teenaged children who had come occasionally. She'd seen them every now and then, but they were years older than she was and she hadn't paid much attention. The family hadn't mixed with their neighbors then, either, and no one knew much about them. The castle on the top of the steep hill was dark and imposing and pretty scary-looking, which was part of the reason legends about strange goings-on there were rife. People tended to give it a wide berth.

She thought now that Prince Bartholomew must have been this prince's father.

"And that brings us back to the question of why you were on the grounds," Max said coolly. "Since you live here in the area, I'm sure you understand that you were trespassing."

Isabella's chin rose again and she looked at him defiantly. "Yes, I know that."

He shrugged extravagantly, a clear response to her bravado. "And so…?" he asked, pinning her down with his direct gaze.

She drew her breath in sharply. She was caught, wasn't she? What could she do but tell him the truth?

That meant talking about the unique basil that grew on his hillside, and she really didn't want to do that. Very few people knew the identity of their special ingredient and they had kept it that way to discourage copycat trouble.

"If I could patent the *Monta Rosa Basil*, I would do so,"

her father was always muttering. "Just don't talk about it to others. We don't want anyone to know where we get it. If others started to use it, we would be in big trouble."

"No one else would make sauces as good as yours, even with the basil," Isabella would respond loyally.

"Bah," he would say. "It's our secret. Without it, we're doomed."

So she didn't want to tell the Rossi family what she'd come for. But now, she felt she had to. Besides, there was very little chance that they would care or tell other chefs anything about it. So she tried to explain. "I...I came because I had to. You see, there is a certain herb that only seems to grow on the southern-facing hill above your river." She shrugged, all innocence. At least, she hoped it was coming off that way. "I need it for our signature recipe at the restaurant."

"You *need* it?" Angela sniffed. "That's stealing, you know."

Isabella frowned. How could she explain to them that stealing from the prince's estate was considered a time-honored tradition in the village?

"I wouldn't call it that exactly," she hedged, but Max gave a cold laugh, dismissing her excuse out of hand.

"What would you call it, then?" he demanded.

She shrugged again, searching for a proper term. "Sharing?"

She looked at him hopefully. He looked right into her eyes and suddenly a hint of that connection that had sparked between them before was hovering there, just out of reach.

"Sharing?" he repeated softly.

She nodded, searching his eyes for signs that the coldness in his gaze might melt if she said the right things, but there wasn't much there to give her hope.

"Doesn't that require the consent of those 'shared' with?"

"I…well, you could give your consent," she suggested. "If only you would." She was still held by those huge dark eyes. Her heart was beating quickly again, as though something were happening here. But nothing was. No, she was sure of it. Nothing at all.

"Never," he said flatly, his gaze as cool as ever. "Never," he said more softly. "The river is too dangerous."

She stared up at him, captivated by the impression of energy she sensed from him. It felt as though he had a certain sort of power trapped and controlled inside him, just waiting for a release. What would it take to free him? Could she do it? Did she dare try?

When Angela's voice, saying goodnight, snapped her out of her reverie again, she had to shake herself and wonder just how long it had lasted. For some reason, she felt almost as though she knew him now. Almost as though they had always known each other. Not friends, exactly. Maybe lovers? Her breath caught in her throat at that brazen thought.

But Max was hardly thinking along those lines himself. He obviously wanted to get on with it. "If you'll just take a seat," he began impatiently, but his sister, halfway out of the room, turned back and let out a rude exclamation.

"She's soggy," she stated flatly.

Exactly what Isabella had said herself, but somehow the way this woman said it carried a bit of a sting. She bit her lip. Why was she letting these people play with her emotions like this? She was out of place here, in way above her head. She needed to leave. Quickly, she spun on her heel and started for the door.

"I'll just get out of your way," she snapped, glancing at the prince as she tried to pass him. "I should be getting home anyway…"

His hand shot out and curled around her upper arm. "Not until Marcello takes a look," he said, pulling her a bit too close. She gasped softly, then shook her head, ready to object. But the prince's sister beat her to the punch.

"As you can see, her condition is unacceptable," Angela said briskly. "We need to get her cleaned up before she sees Marcello." She made a face in her brother's direction. "It will only take a moment. I'll run her under a quick shower and have her back here in no time."

She gestured toward Isabella as she might have toward a servant. "Come along with me," she ordered.

Rebellion rose in Isabella's throat. She was beginning to feel like Eliza Doolittle in *My Fair Lady*. Shades of the little peasant girl being cleaned up and prepared to meet with her betters. No, thanks. She didn't really care for that role. It didn't suit her. She'd considered the options and decided against it.

She was regaining her bearings and beginning to feel a bit foolish. She'd been caught red-handed, so to speak, and deserved to get a little guff for it. But this was getting out of hand. After all, if the man didn't want her on his property, why didn't he just let her go? Why had he forced her to come back here to the house? She was certainly in a wet, bedraggled condition, but still...

"Why don't I just go?" she began, turning toward the door again.

"You have no choice in the matter," the prince said calmly. "For the good of all, you need to be clean and dry."

"But—"

"Go with my sister," the prince said. His voice was low and composed, but something in it made Isabella look up, surprised at how coolly he could give an order that made you want to do exactly what he said. "You fell on our land, into our river. We are responsible for your condition. It's only right that we make you whole again."

That didn't make any sense at all. She'd been trespassing, not visiting. But somehow she found herself following Angela down the hall. She looked back. The prince was watching her go, half leaning against the couch, his head lowered. For some crazy reason, that made her heart lurch in her chest. She turned away quickly and followed where Angela led, but the shivers his look had given her lingered on.

Max stayed where he was, listening as their footsteps faded down the hall, staring into the darkness where she'd just been. He was drawn to her and he hadn't been attracted to a woman for a long, long time. A picture of his beautiful wife, Laura, swam into his head and he closed his eyes as though to capture it there. Instead, it melted away and another face drifted into its place.

His eyes snapped open and he swore softly. This girl, this Isabella, was nothing like Laura. Why would he see her in his mind's eye? It was ridiculous to even begin comparing them. She was just a girl from the village. She meant nothing to him and never could.

Slowly, his hand rose until he touched the scar on his face. He wanted to feel what she had felt with her fingertips. What an odd young woman. Oddly compelling. Her reaction had been different from that of anyone he'd ever met and it still puzzled and intrigued him. Had she seen something no one else had? What had she found that had interested her that way? Had anything changed while he hadn't been paying attention?

No. Same old face. Same old scars. Cursing softly, he jerked his hand away and turned toward the fire. For a moment, he almost hated her.

And why not? She represented the world he'd given up almost ten years ago, the world he had to deny himself. He'd done a damn good job of keeping that world at bay. Now it seemed to have come looking for him. For his own sanity, he knew he had to resist its temptations. This dark, gloomy palazzo was his reality. There was no other way.

Isabella looked around her as she emerged from the steamy shower. It was an antiquated room with antiquated plumbing, but luxurious in an old-fashioned way, with high ceilings and a huge claw-footed tub in the middle of the room. She dried quickly and then stepped before a full-length mirror to check herself for damage.

What she saw made her gasp, then laugh softly. The area around her right eye was looking as if she'd smudged it with soot. A black eye! How was she going to explain that to her customers? She groaned, then began to check out the rest of her body. There was a large painful bruise on her hip and a rather deep cut on her right leg, just below the knee. Most of the blood had been soaked up by her running pants, but there was still some seeping out. Other than a few places that felt a bit achy, that seemed to be it.

Turning, she looked at the clothes Angela had set out for her—a lacy cream-colored sweater and tan stretch pants. They were very close to things she might have picked for herself, so she put them on without hesitation, covering her still bleeding wound with a wad of tissue.

"Are you decent?" Angela called as she was combing and fluffing her hair. She came in after Isabella invited her, handing her a bag with her wet clothes.

"Here you go. Marcello ought to be with Max by now. They'll be waiting in the Blue Room." She yawned. "I'm going back to bed. Goodnight, my dear."

"Wait." Isabella turned and hesitated, then went ahead and asked, "What happened to his face?"

Angela stared at her for a long moment before answering. "There was a terrible car accident. It was almost ten years ago, the same night that…" She stopped herself and shook her head. "It was a very bad accident. For days, we were sure that he would die."

Isabella frowned, taking that in. She had a feeling there was more to it than that. There was a weird, moody undercurrent to everything that went on here. She wanted to know more, but she could hardly ask many questions now.

"But he survived."

"Obviously. But his face…" Throwing out her hands, she turned away. "He was quite handsome, you know," she said softly.

Isabella shrugged. "He still is."

She turned to stare at Isabella. "You think so, do you?"

"Oh, yes."

Her eyebrows rose. "Well…" she said significantly. But she made a face and turned away. "Goodnight again, Isabella," she said, beginning to bustle out again. "I'm sure Max will make sure you get taken home safely once Marcello has given you his stamp of approval."

That sense of rebellion rose in her again, but Isabella thanked Angela as she left the room, then finished up making herself presentable. And all the while she was wondering how she could get out of this ancient stone building without running the gauntlet of the prince and his cousin. She was fine. She didn't need the attention of a doctor. And she especially didn't need to run into the prince again.

What she did need was the delicate and very special herb she'd come for. But she had to be realistic. Tonight was not her night. She would have to come back another time. Still, was that going to be possible? Now that she knew about the dogs…

Never mind. She would think about that later. Right now, she just needed to get out of here without seeing the prince again. She took one last look in the mirror. Her black eye was getting worse by the minute. In fact, half her face was now somewhat red and a bit swollen. She groaned. How was she going to hide this from the world?

And then it came to her—she was getting a small hint of what it must be like to be the prince with his vivid scar. She sighed softly as she thought of it. At least she knew that she would be healing soon.

Staring at her own face, she thought of how she'd touched him, and she gasped at her own reckless audacity. What on earth had possessed her to do a thing like that? And why had he stood for it? She must have still been groggy from the effects of the dunking she'd taken and the wild ride through the night on horseback. It really wasn't her habit to go poking at people's faces like that.

What had Susa said about him? That his wife had died, that he'd been something of a recluse ever since. Maybe that explained his cool, brooding manner. She shook her head and turned away. This was certainly a strange night and she was finding herself doing all sorts of strange things she'd never done before. It was time she got out of here.

Grabbing the bag with her clothes, she made her way quietly into the hall. She knew which way to turn for the Blue Room, so she took the other path, moving quickly to get away from where she might be seen.

Another sharp turn down a darker hallway and she found herself in the huge, cavernous kitchen. A night-light glowed at the end of the room, giving her just enough light to find her way. She stopped a moment, turning and admiring all the pans and cooking equipment hanging from hooks along the walls. Just the sheer size of the place was impressive. It was three or four times as big as her kitchen at the restaurant. What she could do with a situation like this!

But she didn't have time for dallying, so she took it all in with one sweeping glance, then picked a door that looked as if it might head outside. She pulled it open quickly, stepped through and suddenly she was falling again— right into the arms of the prince.

CHAPTER THREE

ISABELLA screamed. Screaming was getting to be a habit, it seemed. She didn't think she'd screamed this much at any time in her life before. But she couldn't help it. Running into this strong, scary man in the dark just sent her over the top every time.

He held her for barely a second before she jumped back away from him. Still, at the same time she was re-coiling and cursing her own continuing bad luck a traitor-ous part of her was entertaining the temptation to let herself relax in his arms again, to press her cheek against his chest and listen for his heartbeat. The moon was out again, sending beams in through a window just over their heads. What could be more romantic than to wrap herself in his arms and…?

Fanciful nonsense, of course. None of that could happen or would happen. She hadn't had such silly daydreams since she'd been a preteen and had been mooning after a boy named Romano Puccini. Bad things usually followed when you let your emotions run away with you. At least, that had been the lesson she had learned that long-ago summer.

"That's the second time tonight you scared me out of my wits," she told him accusingly.

"And that's the second time tonight I found you sneaking around where you shouldn't be," he shot back at her.

She tossed her hair, hooking the mop of it behind her ear with one quick swipe of her hand. "That's only true if you are the one who gets to set the rules of where I may or may not go."

He moved closer. Even in the dark, she could see the outline of his scar clearly. It was a slash of silver across his moonlit face. Eerie…otherworldly…and somehow alluring.

"And why wouldn't I set the rules?" he said firmly. "It's my house, remember?"

She looked up into his eyes. They seemed to glow in the dim light. "But you forget—I'm only passing through."

"Trespassing through, you mean."

Well, she had to give him that one. Suddenly she was so very tired.

"You know, I…I just want to go home." There was a quaver in her voice that she regretted, but, still, it was only the truth.

He took her hand, still looking down into what he could see of her face. "We all want things we can't have."

The hint of desolation in his voice hit her hard and stopped her from taking offense. An unexpected wave of sadness swept over her. She wanted to reach for him, to help him somehow. But then she remembered—he was the prince. What in the world could she do to comfort a man like this?

"Come back to the Blue Room and let Marcello take a look at you," he ordered, beginning to lead her that way. "After all this, we might as well go through with it." He glanced down at her as she walked beside him. "Then I'll have someone drive you home."

She sighed. She hated to admit how tempting it seemed to just follow wherever he led. She was going to have to work on that. A little strength of character—a little more confidence in her own strength—that was what she needed.

"My car is…is down by the south wall." She flushed as she said the words. Oh, how guilty she sounded.

When he replied, he sounded bemused, but satirical. "So you drove yourself out from the village, parked along the wall, and then what? Did you vault over?"

"Not quite." She hesitated, but she didn't want to tell him that she'd sneaked in exactly where her father had been sneaking in for years. Only her father had the good sense to do it in daylight, and he'd never been caught.

"Not going to say, are you?" he said, sounding cynical again, as though he really did consider her an outlaw in his world. "You're going to keep it a secret. That way you can keep your options open for sneaking in again." He tugged on her hand, leading her around a sharp corner. "But I would advise against that, Isabella Casali. I think we'll have to let the dogs patrol twenty-four hours a day from now on." He glanced back at her. "I don't want you anywhere near that river."

That surprised her. She would have expected him to say he didn't want to risk any more interruptions to his own life and peaceful existence, not to her welfare. But maybe she was taking his words too kindly. Of course, that was exactly what he meant. After all, if she got hurt, he would have to deal with it. Still, there was something in his tone when he mentioned the river that gave her pause.

He stopped just outside the door to the Blue Room and stared down at her. For the first time the light was good enough for him to see what had happened to her face.

"My God! *Maledizione!*" His hands cupped her face, tilting it up so that he could see it fully. "You seemed a little bruised before, but this…"

"It's okay," she said, gazing up at him in wonder. He was so close. The sense of his male presence overwhelmed her. For a few seconds, she felt a wave of emotion sweeping away her common sense, and suddenly she wanted his kiss more than she'd ever wanted anything else in her life.

And that in itself was like a splash of cold water on her face. What was she thinking? She wanted to turn away so that he wouldn't read her guilty secret in her eyes, but he was staring so hard, from so close.

"I…I'm okay."

"It's hard to see something so fresh and lovely marred this way," he said as though it really did pain him. His voice was cool and it was evident that this was a philosophical problem and nothing to do with him personally. But at the same time his gaze ranged over her face as though he were memorizing every line, every dimple. "You're just so… so…" His voice faded without saying the word, whatever it was meant to be.

And then he kissed her. Like a moth to the flame, he couldn't stay away. It was a light kiss, barely a touching of his lips to her forehead, right above her blackened eye. She gasped as she felt him, but at the same time she knew he'd done it in a strange way as though to erase the damage, make it go away. He seemed to have an obsession with avoiding harm. That had to be it. It didn't feel personal. His gaze still looked as hard and cold, his bearing was still just as arrogant.

But still—he kissed her.

"Is this going to take much longer?" said the deep, masculine voice of a tall man standing in the doorway, cutting into the magic of the moment. "Because I could go back to my room and get a few winks in and you could call me down later."

Isabella gulped in dismay, but the prince only straightened, giving his cousin a brief look of outraged dignity. It was obvious their relationship was maintained with a closeness that was disguised by a lot of good-natured mockery.

"Isabella, this is Marcello Martelli, my cousin."

"I'm pleased to meet you, Isabella," Marcello said, shaking her hand briskly. "This shouldn't take too long, nor be too painful."

Marcello was young and very handsome. In fact he looked very much like what she assumed Max would look like without the scar. She couldn't help but give him a big smile in answer to his friendly greeting. Here he was, barefoot and in jeans and a T-shirt—looking for all the world like any of the young men she knew in the village would look if you knocked on their door after midnight. He had the ruffled hair and the sleepy eyes as well.

"You fell into the river, I hear," he said, leading her in to sit on the antique couch. His gaze flickered back and forth between her and Max as though he didn't completely buy it.

"Yes," she told him earnestly.

"But luckily Max came along in time to…to rescue you."

She turned and looked at where the prince was standing back in the shadows just in time to see him turn away as though angry at what his cousin had just said. She frowned. Why would he do that? Did he realize what a part he'd played in creating her unfortunate incident? Maybe he needed a reminder.

"Is that the way he tells the story?"

Marcello grinned at her. "How do you tell it?"

She gave Max an arch look sideways. "Here's how I remember it. I was strolling along on the hillside when suddenly something that looked like a dark avenging angel came galloping down on me and I ran for my life. My foot slipped. I tumbled into the river." She shrugged. "A simple tale, really," she said.

"And all Max's fault," Marcello said with a knowing look.

Her eyes widened in mock innocence. "Of course." She glanced back at where Max was pacing, but she couldn't see his face.

"Here's what I don't quite get," Marcello was saying as he looked through his black bag for supplies. "What was it about Max that terrified you enough to start running?" He looked up at her. "Instead of just holding your ground and stating your case, I mean." He gave his cousin a mocking look. "He doesn't seem all that scary to me."

Yes, that was the slightly embarrassing element in all this, she had to admit. Should she tell him the truth? Would he laugh? Or think her a little looney? She glanced at Max again and his haughty reserve gave her the spark she needed to go on.

"I'm sure you know about the legends attached to this castle," she said. "I've heard them all my life."

Max stopped, though still in shadows. "What sort of legends?" he asked gruffly.

She hesitated, knowing he was going to scoff. "Well, the usual," she began, starting to wish she hadn't brought it up.

"I know what she's talking about," Marcello offered. "Village people love to think of their local prince as a modern day Casanova, seducing women and humiliating men." He gave his cousin a quick grin. "And you've got to admit we've got a few rakes and degenerates in the older branches of our family tree."

Max shrugged and turned away, and Isabella bit her lip, then added something in a very soft voice.

"Vampires," she said.

They both turned back to her. "What?"

Her chin came up and her eyes sparked. "Vampires," she said more forcefully.

They gaped at her and she went on quickly, before they could begin to laugh.

"There are plenty of rumors that your family has included vampires. I know it's crazy. I'm just saying…"

Max turned away again, shaking his head.

"It was partly the way you came crashing at me in the middle of a storm," she continued, raising her voice so that he couldn't ignore her. "Like something dropped from a thundercloud. And on horseback!" She shook her head. "I thought…I thought…" She bit her lip and wondered if she really should tell them this.

"Yes?" Marcello leaned forward, unmistakably interested. "What was it you thought?"

She narrowed her gaze and put steel in her spine. "I…I thought Max was a vampire. Just for a second or two."

There. She'd said it. She looked up at where Max was standing and wished she could see what his eyes were revealing at this very moment. It was difficult to tell his reactions and that was driving her crazy.

"Are you serious?" Marcello was another matter. His response was no mystery. "A vampire?"

She tossed her hair back and tried to explain, addressing Max directly, even if he wouldn't do the same to her.

"Well, it was a logical conclusion to draw. After all, you came galloping out of the forest, dressed all in black with that cape and everything. The setting was perfect for it with the moon hidden behind clouds over your shoulder. From where I was standing, it was like something right out of a vampire movie."

Max didn't move.

Marcello's mouth was holding steady but his gaze was rife with amusement.

"Isabella, I think you've got it wrong," he said carefully, as though teaching a lesson. "This is the Italian countryside, you know. As I understand it, vampires live in Transylvania. Am I right?"

Of course he was right, but she wasn't going to admit it so easily. "Oh, so you think an Italian can't be a vampire?" she demanded.

He shrugged grandly and almost rolled his eyes. "What do you think, Max? I'd say chances are slim."

Max didn't answer, but she wasn't giving up. She shook her head and threw out her arms. "They say there are vampires everywhere."

"I see." Marcello was laughing at her again. "How many have you met yourself?"

She gave him a quick, sideways look. "Well…not many, I will admit."

He nodded wisely. "Interesting."

His attitude was really beginning to annoy her, but even worse was the way the prince stayed silent through it all. She wanted some reply, some indication as to how he felt about the things she was saying, and she was getting nothing at all.

"So you actually haven't had a lot of experience with vampires."

"Max is the only one so far," she said tartly.

And that got the reaction she was after. Max swung around and came in front of her very much like the man who had swooped down upon her on horseback, bringing with him all the sense of power he seemed to carry with him, very much like that cape he'd worn.

"Miss Casali," he said icily, staring down at her, his full

scars exposed. "I may be many things, but I am not now, nor have I ever been, a vampire. If I start feeling a sudden craving for human blood, you'll be the first to know. Until then, drop this nonsense."

She swallowed hard, looking up at him. "Okay," she said in a small, soft voice. His gaze held hers for only seconds, but it made its mark. She felt as though she'd just had a wild ride on a roller coaster and her insides were still in flight.

"Marcello?" he said pointedly, then turned back to pace the shadows.

His cousin moved in to start his examination of the patient and, for now, all bantering ceased. He started with a look at her black eye, and what he saw had him shaking his head in dismay. "Ice will help the swelling," he told her after he'd checked to make sure there were no cuts or outright abrasions involved. "But the bruising will seem to go on forever. And there's really not much you can do about that."

There wasn't much he could do about her bruised hip, either. He tested her reactions and pronounced nothing broken. But the cut on her leg was deep and he decided a few stitches were in order.

She sat back obediently and didn't talk back. Her mind was swirling with emotions and reactions to the prince and to his fascinating life and home. What was she doing here? It was more than obvious she didn't belong. But she wouldn't have given up this chance at a taste of another sort of world for anything.

Max paced, then slumped into a chair and watched, feeling restless. He was torn. He wanted her out of here as quickly as possible. She disturbed everything about his life. And at the same time, he couldn't take his eyes off her. She was bad news, but it was a sort of bad news it seemed he hungered for. Having her here made him remember the old days, when Laura was still alive and they traveled and held parties on the terrace and lived the life of international socialites, attending shows and meeting famous people and competing in yacht races and attending fabulous dinners in exotic locations. Their life together had only lasted a year and a half, but it had been an enchanted existence, a life of pleasure and comfort such as most people could only dream of.

It seemed almost too indulgent now, as he looked back on it. Maybe that had been the problem. Maybe they had taken things too much for granted. Maybe they had been too happy. Sometimes it seemed the fates wouldn't allow too much happiness.

Isabella laughed at something his cousin said and he frowned, holding back the curt comment that came to mind. He seemed to remember a time when he might have been as good at the give and take as Marcello was now. But that time was gone. He didn't expect he would ever get it back. Still, it was interesting to watch this playing out before him. It was so unusual to have a stranger among them.

She'd dropped into his world out of nowhere and she would soon go back to whence she came. But she was an anomaly and, with her bruised and swollen face, he almost felt as though they had something in common. That was ridiculous and he knew it. He was alone in his own private hell and no one else could understand what this was like. It would be best to get rid of her as quickly as possible.

Isabella knew he was watching her and his interest sparked a warm fire in her chest, a fire that was spreading and beginning to create such heat it scared her. It wasn't that she was unused to male attention. She'd had that all her life.

She was a beautiful woman, her features wide and sensual. She knew some men considered her extremely sexy. She'd never understood that. She didn't feel very sexy. Most of the time she just felt as though she had too much to do and too little time to do it in. Men just sort of got in the way.

But men liked her. Still, she had a sharp tongue at times and didn't suffer fools gladly, or any other way. Over the years, there had been very few men she'd thought were worth the effort.

Just recently her friend Gino had railed at her, accusing her of being cold and heartless. That had cut her to the core. He'd asked her to go with him on a weekend trip to Rome and she'd turned him down. In his disappointment, he'd charged her with living for her own immediate family and no one else.

"All you want to do is run this restaurant and make your father happy. You'll never have children. You'll be content to be an old maid, clucking like an old hen over your aging chicks, those worthless brothers and your old, sick father."

She could dismiss Gino with no effort at all, but his words didn't fade away quite so easily. The things he'd said echoed in her mind all the time lately. Was it true? Was she really so wrapped up in her little family that she'd lost the knack of feeling like a desirable woman? Would she never have room for a man in her life? What if he was right? What if there was something wrong with her?

But the things she'd been through tonight were relieving some of those doubts. She was all right. She could relate to men, on the level of friendship at the very least. Marcello obviously liked her and they got along famously.

And Max… He'd kissed her, hadn't he? It had been a light, gentle gesture of healing, but still… A kiss was a kiss. Even in her ugly, bruised condition, he'd felt a pull in her direction. And she'd felt it too.

And that was just the problem. She couldn't remember when she'd felt such a thrill at a man's touch. It had been years. But was there any promise there? Of course not.

Come on, Isabella, she chided herself a bit sadly. *He's a prince. You work in a restaurant. So what if there seems to be a sensual connection that flares between the two of you every time your eyes meet? He may find you amusing for the moment—though evidence of that is pretty skimpy— but there is no way anything real can happen between the two of you. So you might as well forget it.*

Marcello finished up giving her stitches and began to pack his equipment away in his little black doctor bag. He and Max talked back and forth for a moment, and then the prince said something that chilled her.

"We're going to have to beef up security around here," he was saying, not even looking her way. "I don't want anyone near the river."

She turned to look at him. Whenever the river was brought up, there was some undercurrent of emotion that she couldn't quite pin down. What was it about the river that had so spooked this family?

"The dogs don't do the trick?" Marcello said.

Max shrugged. "The dogs can't be everywhere all the time. And they have to sleep. They're dogs."

Marcello grinned. "That they are. Have you thought of hiring guards?"

"No." He flashed a warning look at his cousin. "You know I can't do that."

Marcello shrugged with resignation. "Of course."

"We'll put in an alarm service, with cameras. We'll get state-of-the-art security going around here. No one will be able to slip through the cracks again." He shrugged. "We should have done it long ago."

Isabella sighed. That meant she wouldn't get a second chance. What was she going to do? Hire James Bond? It didn't seem likely.

Marcello headed back to his room to get some sleep. Isabella felt a flutter of nerves at being alone with Max again, but he treated her with distant politeness, making her sit closer to the fire to dry her hair while he dispatched poor Renzo off to get her car and bring it up for her. And then he began to pace the room again, staying as far away from her as he could manage.

Her conversational gambits seemed to have dried up with Marcello out of the room. She fluffed her hair in the warmth of the fire and racked her brain for a subject as the silence between the two of them got louder.

"I like your cousin," she said at last, risking a quick look his way. "And I appreciate the medical attention." She threw him a quick smile and made an attempt at a light joke. "You treat trespassers well around here."

He gave her a piercing look, then turned back to stare into the fire. She noted he was getting less and less protective of the right side of his face. Did that mean he was getting less self-conscious? Or that he cared less what she thought?

"Yes," he said at last, speaking slowly. "Marcello is my friend as well as my cousin." He glanced her way. "He and I once looked very much alike," he added softly, almost as though musing to himself. "People took us for brothers."

She nodded. She could tell that, despite the scar. "He's very handsome," she said before she thought, then colored slightly as she realized how he might take that.

He glanced at her, eyebrow raised, but didn't say anything. She didn't speak again right away. She wanted to. She wanted to tell him his own face was so much more interesting than his cousin's. It had all the beauty Marcello

had, but it had something more—character, history, a hard
and cruel story to tell. Just what that story was, she didn't
know, but there was passion there, and mystery, and heart-
break. It was a face for the ages, a map of human tragedy,
a work of art.

The more she thought about it, the more she realized she
preferred it. In fact, she found it beautiful in a rare and
special way. But she couldn't say those things—could she?
He would think she was flattering him, perhaps even trying
to get something from him.

"You are both very handsome," she said at last, feeling
a bit brave to say that much.

He shrugged, looking away. "My face is what it is. It is
what I made it. My burden to bear."

She sat back, biting her tongue and wondering if she
dared say any of the things she was thinking. He was wonderful to look at. Didn't he realize that?

Or was it her? Was she strange?

That was a loaded question and she didn't want to answer it. But she had to say something.

"You know what I think?" she began. "I think you
should come to my restaurant. You need to get out and…"

He swore softly but it was enough to stop the words in
her throat. "You don't know what you're talking about," he
told her roughly. "You don't have a clue."

Of course she didn't. She knew that. But he didn't have
to be so rude. She was only trying to help.

She bit her lip, considering the situation. For some
reason, when he ordered her about, she often found herself
wanting to do what he said. It was time to nip that in the
bud. He was beginning to think of her as a pushover, wasn't
he? Sure, he was a prince and she was a nobody—but that
didn't matter. She'd never been the amenable one in any

relationship. Why let it get started now? She had to fight this drift toward subservience. Rising from her seat on the couch, she faced him with her hands on her hips, her head cocked at a challenging angle.

"I thought I should let you know that I don't really think you're a vampire," she said as an opening.

He nodded, looking at her coolly. "I was pretty sure about that all along."

"But you do have cruel tendencies," she said, looking at him earnestly. "Listen, about the herbs I need from your hillside—"

"No." He said it with utter finality.

She pulled her head back, startled by his vehemence. "But…"

He held a hand up to stop her in her tracks. "If keeping you off a dangerous hillside is cruel, I'm a monster. Sorry, but that is the way it is."

"But—"

"No. You're to stay away. And that's final."

He rose as if to add emphasis to his words. She looked up at him and swallowed hard. He looked tall and stern and unyielding, and his shoulders were wide as the horizon. There was no humor in his face, no softness at all. His scars were vivid and his hard eyes made the breath catch in her throat and her heart beat just a little faster. Just that quickly she was back to being a timid petitioner, and he was once again a prince. His gaze met hers and held. She couldn't say a thing.

And then, breaking the spell, Renzo appeared.

"The young lady's car is here, sir."

The prince turned and nodded.

"Thank you, Renzo."

It was very late. The grandfather clock in the hallway

was chiming the hour. A part of him wanted to accompany her down to her home. Gallantry would suggest it. But practicalities, as well as common sense, forbade it. Not to mention the fact that he just plain couldn't do it. So he merely nodded to her, staying back away so that he wouldn't be tempted to repeat anything as silly as a kiss.

"Renzo will show you to your car," he said shortly. "Goodnight." She opened her mouth to say something, but there was no time. Turning on his heel, he went back into his dark and lonely palazzo, leaving her behind as though that was the main purpose. She sighed, feeling suddenly cold and lonely. Renzo showed her to her car and she drove off toward her home and restaurant in the village with a sense of frustration. But she knew very well that her life had been changed…changed forever, even if she never saw him again.

CHAPTER FOUR

"WELL," Susa said the next morning as she began to mix the dough for the large cake pans that sat waiting. "How's the prince?"

Isabella turned bright red and had to pretend to be looking for something in the huge wall refrigerator in order to hide that fact until things cooled.

"What prince?" she chirped, biding her time.

Susa's laugh sounded more like a cackle. "The one who punched you in the eye," she said, elbow-deep in flour. "Don't say I didn't warn you."

Isabella whirled and faced the older woman, wondering why she'd never noticed before how annoying she could be. "No one punched me. I...I fell."

"Ah." Susa nodded wisely, a mischievous gleam in her gray eyes. "So he pushed you, did he?"

"No!"

Isabella groaned with exasperation and escaped into the pantry to assemble the ingredients for the basic tomato sauce that was the foundation of all the Casali family cuisine. Let Susa cackle if she felt like it. Isabella wasn't going to tell her anything at all about what had happened. Pressing her lips together firmly, she set about making the sauce and pretended she didn't know what the older woman was talking about.

She couldn't discuss it yet. Not with anyone. She wasn't even sure herself what exactly had happened. Looking back, it seemed like a dream. When she tried to remember what she'd said or what he'd done, it didn't seem real. So she washed the clothes the prince's sister had loaned her, sent them back to the palazzo, and heard nothing in return. She had to put it behind her.

Besides, she had other problems, big problems, to deal with. She'd been putting off thinking about them because she'd assumed she would go to collect the *Monta Rosa Basil* and all would be well—or at least in abeyance. Without the basil, she was finally facing the fact that the restaurant was in big trouble.

Luca, her father and founder of Rosa, had gone into a panic when she had told him a sketchy version of what had happened and then tentatively speculated what life—and the menu—might be like without the herb.

"What are you talking about?" he demanded, looking a bit wild. A tall, rather elegant-looking man, in Isabella's eyes, he radiated integrity. Despite the demands he tended to put on her, she loved him to pieces.

"The old prince said I could come any time."

That was news to Isabella. She'd had no idea there was any sort of permission granted, and she had to wonder if it wasn't just a convenient memory her father had embellished a bit.

"Well, the new prince says 'no'."

"The new prince?" He stared at her. "You've talked to him?"

"Yes. A little."

He frowned. "No, Isabella. Stay away from the royalty.

It's no good to mix with them. They think they can walk all over us and they do it every time."

"But, Papa, if I'm going to try to get permission to—"

"You don't need permission."

She sighed. There was no way she was going to make him understand that the circumstances had changed.

"I'll go myself," he muttered. He tried to rise from his chair and she hurried to coax him back down.

"Father, you will not go anywhere," she said fretfully.

"Don't you understand how important this is? The *Basil* is our family's trademark, our sign of distinction. Without it we are just like all the others, not special at all. It's who we are, the heart and soul of our cuisine and of our identity. We have to have it."

She was feeling even worse about this than before. "But, Papa, if I can't get it any longer…"

He shook his head, unable to understand what the difficulty was. "But you can get it. Of course you can." His tired blue eyes searched hers. "I've never had any trouble. I go in right at sunrise. I go quietly, squeezing through the chink in the wall, right where I've entered the grounds since I was a young man. A short hike past the river and up the hill, and there it is, green leaves waving in the breeze, reaching up to kiss the morning sun." He kissed his fingertips in a salute to the wonderful plants that were the making of his reputation.

Then he frowned at her fiercely. "If you can't manage to do such a simple thing, I'll do it myself, even if I have to crawl up that hill. I've never failed yet."

That was it. She was a failure. She sighed. "The dogs never came after you?" she asked him, feeling almost wistful about it.

"The dogs are only out at night."

"Not anymore," she said sadly.

She left him pounding his walking stick on the tile floor and grumbling about incompetence, knowing she couldn't let him attempt the task. The climb up the hill would kill him in his current condition. She had to find a way.

Everyone knew there was a problem. The situation was getting desperate. Her father had let things go too long. They were losing customers and had been bleeding money even before this latest problem. To make matters worse, there was some nonsense about a permit her father had never bothered to get. Fredo Cavelli, an old friend of her father's and now on the local planning commission, had come by a few times, threatening dire consequences if the paperwork for a permit wasn't cleared up. The trouble was, she wasn't sure what Fredo was talking about and her father tended to do nothing but foam at the mouth and accuse Fredo of jealousy and double-dealing instead of taking care of the problem as he should.

It seemed to Isabella that control was slipping away. Without the special ingredient that set their sauce apart, there would be very little reason for anyone to choose their restaurant, Rosa, over the others operating nearby. She was desperate to get a handle on all these problems and get things back on an even keel.

Something had to be done.

She knew what it was. She had to go back there.

Just thinking about it made her shiver. She couldn't go back. The prince had explicitly ordered her to stay away. And for once in her life, she was not really ready to challenge that.

Odd as it seemed, he was so different, so separate from her way of life, that he threw her off balance in a way no other man had ever done. She was used to being the feisty one, the girl who didn't accept any nonsense from men, the one who could take it, deal with it, and serve it right back. A handsome face didn't bowl her over. Charm made her suspicious. The tough-guy act completely turned her off.

Isabella was a hard sell on every level. Life had made her that way. Though she looked happy and carefree to most who knew her casually, there was a thread of dread and unease in her soul that she'd come by naturally.

Her mother had died when she was three years old, leaving her the only female in the family. Her father and her two brothers immediately turned to her for everything. At the age of five she was already taking care of everyone else, in the family home, in the play yard, and even in the restaurant. People in the village called her "little Mama" as she scurried past on one errand or another. She was always in such a hurry to make things right for her little brothers, it seemed she never had time to have a childhood of her own.

But her unease and wistfulness were born of more than just too many responsibilities too early. There were uncertainties in her family background, half-remembered scenes from childhood, secrets and lies. Her mother's death, her father's sometimes mysterious background, the reason her baby brother Valentino carried his daredevil act too far, the reason her brother Cristiano felt he had to jump off cliffs to save lives—all these things and more created a shaky foundation for a calm, peaceful life.

Isabella had a recurring nightmare where her family restaurant began to sag, first on one side, then the other. Going outside, she would realize the building had been sitting on a sand dune and the sand was beginning to drain away. Frantically, she tried to shore it up with her hands, pushing the sand back, working faster and faster. But it was no use. The building sank into the sand as though it were water. Inside she could see her father and her brothers trying to get out. She tried to call for help, but she couldn't make a sound. Helpless, she watched them disappear beneath the surface. And that was when she woke.

"You've obviously got a savior complex," Susa told her the one time she'd confided in the older woman. "Get over it. You can't save these people. We are each our own worst enemy."

Susa's words weren't very comforting. In fact, they weren't even very helpful. So she never told anyone about her dreams again. But she thought of them now as she tried to analyze what had happened last night.

As much as the dream unnerved her, misty memories of her night at the castle unsettled her even more. Had he really kissed her forehead or had she just wished so hard that she'd dreamed it? Had she really told him she'd thought he was a vampire for a few shattering seconds? Had she really reached out and stroked his scar as though she had a right to touch him? It didn't seem credible and it made her blush all over again.

She hadn't been herself last night. And that was one reason she hesitated to try to go back. What would he cause her to act like if she actually got in to see him again?

Meanwhile she had to deal with losing customers, losing money, and Fredo Cavelli coming by to threaten that he would have Rosa's closed down for good if her father didn't come up with some obscure piece of paper.

"He thinks he can order me around because he bribed the mayor to put him on the planning commission," Luca would scoff whenever she tried to talk to him about it. "I'm in compliance in every way. He can't run me out of town.

He's just jealous because the little ice cream store he tried to run fell apart in a month. I won't give in to his rubbish."

She shook her head and walked away, unsure of how threatening this business really was. She had more problems than she had time for, so she let it go. Meanwhile, several times a day, her gaze wandered toward the hills, searching out the mist-shrouded tower of the castle, just barely visible toward evening, and she wondered what Max was doing in his lonely sanctuary. Was he out riding again? Did he ever think of her? Or had he been so glad to be rid of her, he'd erased her from his mind?

Max was on horseback, surveying the river in the twilight magic that hovered over his land, just after sunset. His sister had gone home, his cousin was about to leave for Milan, and his life was about to get back to normal. Boring, monotonous normal. Still, it was a relief.

This was his favorite time of day, and the only time he found he could come to the river without feeling unbearably sick inside. And he had to come to the river, if only as an homage to Laura. For the first few years after her death, he hadn't been able to come here without tears flowing freely.

"I'm sorry," he would cry into the wind, brokenhearted and in agony. "I'm so sorry."

And he was convinced that Laura had been here then. She'd heard him. Later, he would often talk to her for hours, and she responded with a breeze, or a leaf that might sail over his head. He could hear her laughter in the river as the water bubbled over the rocks. She'd felt so close, he could almost touch her.

As the years went by the talking began to fade away, but he still came. And now, he didn't talk anymore. He didn't feel her here as he had before. Maybe she'd lost interest. Maybe she'd forgotten him. Or maybe his emotions just weren't strong enough to break through the barriers any longer. He didn't know what it was that had silenced their conversation. He only knew it felt stilted and awkward to try to talk to her now. But he came anyway. She deserved that much, at the very least.

Tonight he was here in part out of a guilty conscience. His head had been full of the Casali girl for days and he couldn't seem to shake the thoughts away. He needed to fill his soul with his wife's image again.

He looked into the swirling water of the river, very near where that water had taken her from him.

"Laura," he said aloud, passion behind every word. "I miss you so."

He listened hard. He tried to let himself join the flow of the evening breeze. He tried to feel whatever was in the atmosphere and draw it in. But it was all a failure. She wasn't there. Heartsick, he turned his horse and headed back home.

Isabella had tried to figure out somehow to handle the declining basil supply problem in other ways, but the harder she tried, the more the answer seemed to elude her. As far as she knew, the prince's estate was the only site where the herb could be found. If she wasn't allowed to enter his gates, how was she going to get the supply she needed?

She spent hours poring over the Internet, trying to find where else the herb might grow, and, when that didn't yield fruit, trying to find a substitution. She tried a few candidates in a couple of dishes. People noticed.

"There's something different about this *Fruta di Mare*," an old friend of the family asked right away, frowning as though she'd found a bug in her meal. "Have you changed your recipe?"

"What are you doing that's different?" another asked, face twisted with displeasure.

And then she overheard a pair of regular customers whispering to each other. The phrases she caught included, "This place used to be so good, it's really gone downhill lately," and she knew she was in big trouble.

There was no choice. She had to go back.

But how?

She was still agonizing over that a day later when a surprise visitor came through the doors of the café. The late afternoon sun made a radiating halo around him and for just a moment she was sure it was the prince himself. Her heart began to pound in her chest. She'd never felt such a lurch to her system before. The room tilted and for a beat or two she was sure she would pass out. But in those same seconds she realized it wasn't the prince at all, but his cousin, Marcello, and the pounding began to fade.

It took a minute for her to catch her breath. Even as she greeted him warmly she was clutching her heart and wondering what on earth was the matter with her. She really couldn't imagine. The prince was just a man. Nothing special. Particularly. She'd known men before and even liked a few of them. Not many, but a few. She quickly steadied herself and managed to smile at Marcello.

"Welcome. I'm so glad you decided to come try us. Please sit right here and let me bring you some wine."

She pulled out a chair at the table best situated with a view of the square in one direction and the distant mountains in the other.

"Order whatever you like," she said cheerfully. "It will be our pleasure to—"

"Whoa, slow down," he said with a laugh, raising both hands as though to defend himself from the onslaught. "I didn't come for free food. I'm on my way home to Milan, but I wanted to come by to see how my patient is doing."

"Patient?" And then she realized he meant her. "Oh, I'm fine. As you can see, I still have a black eye, but I've been told I look better this way, so it's not a problem."

He made a face at her lame joke, but went on. "And your stitches?"

"Oh."

"I'd like to take a look and see how they are healing."

She glanced around the restaurant. It wasn't packed by any means but half the tables were filled with people she'd known all her life. Every one of them was watching with rapt attention.

"Too public?" he asked as he followed her train of thought. She threw another quick look at the audience, then turned with a toss of her head.

"Let them talk," she said blithely. "TV is mostly reruns this week. They need some fresh entertainment."

He laughed and followed her to the storeroom where he looked her over and quickly pronounced her healing nicely. They chatted in the kitchen for a few minutes. She enjoyed being with him, but wasn't sure how to deal with that. He was so good-looking, but it was as if there was a special ingredient missing—just like the Rosa sauce without the *Monta Rosa Basil*. The prince had an element of fire in him that she found lacking in his cousin. There was no doubt about it—something about the Rossi prince appealed to her like no other man she'd ever seen.

"I want to ask you a question about your cousin," she told him at one point, a little hesitant. She knew it was going to be a touchy subject.

"Shoot," he said casually, cradling the glass of golden wine she'd poured for him.

"It's about his scars. I understand he was badly injured in a car accident. Is that true?"

Marcello nodded.

She frowned. "Why doesn't anyone seem to know anything about it here in the village?"

He shrugged. "People like the Rossi family have ways of keeping things quiet," he said. "And there were certain elements about that accident they didn't want the world to know about."

She drew her breath in. "Like what?" she asked.

He smiled. "Sorry, Isabella. That is not something I'm at liberty to talk about."

She leaned back, disappointed but intrigued. What could it possibly be?

But she had a more important question. How could she get his cousin to let her back on the royal property?

"If I could just talk to him," she said, searching Marcello's eyes for ideas. "If I could just explain how important this is."

He shrugged, draining the last drop of golden liquid from his glass. "Go on over and confront the lion in his lair," he suggested with a casual gesture appealing to the fates.

She scrunched up her face, a picture of doubt. "I don't think I'd better do that. I don't think that would really work. Besides, how would I get in?"

He shrugged again and straightened from his place at the counter. "Your call."

She sighed and gave him a significant look. "If only I had the number for his mobile."

"Ah." He bit back a grin, his eyes sparkling with laughter. "You're not the first to hint around for that number."

She leaned closer, trying to look persuasive but not sure how to do that with a man like this. "I'm sure you know what it is."

He nodded, looking her over with barely leashed pity. "I do. And I'm sworn to secrecy, just as you'd expect."

"Oh." She straightened and frowned, her heart sinking. "I'm not allowed to tell anyone."

She nodded, feeling tragic and hopeless. "I was afraid of that."

He looked as tragic as she felt. "I'm sorry. It would be a betrayal of trust for me to tell you what it is."

She nodded again, leaning against the tall counter with her chin in her hand. "I understand," she said sadly.

He reached past her to take a pencil from a cup full of them. "It's a fairly easy number to remember," he said as he pulled a piece of paper from a stack of them on the counter. "I think I could probably recreate it right now, just doodling here." And he began to do just that. "But I would never tell you what it is."

Her eyes widened. Had he just done what she thought he'd done? "Of course not," she said faintly, hope rekindled.

They chatted for another few seconds. Isabella was on tenterhooks but she studiously avoided looking at the paper in front of him, which he was filling with doodles. Still, she noticed out of the corner of her eye when he turned to leave and crushed it into a ball. Very deliberately, he tossed it into a nearby trash can.

"Take care, Isabella," he said. Giving her a big smile, he winked and headed for the door.

She waited until he was out of the room, then whirled and grabbed the paper from the trash can. She pressed it flat against the counter, and there it was—a telephone number, the figures embellished wildly, but still legible.

Just the thought of calling it sent her pulse soaring. Thanks to Marcello, she had what she'd wanted, a connection to the prince. Now, how was she going to work up the courage to use it?

Max jerked upright when he heard his mobile chime. For just a moment, he wondered what the noise was. He'd only heard it a few times before. Almost no one had his number, and those who did usually called on the landline or sent him an e-mail. He frowned as he fumbled through his stack of books and papers, looking for the blasted thing and ready to bark at whoever was calling and interrupting a good idea flow he'd got into on this lazy, sunny afternoon.

His frown deepened as he realized he didn't recognize the caller's ID. Probably a wrong number. He dropped the phone back onto his desk and turned away, ready to let it ring itself silly. But it didn't stop and he swore sharply and reached for it again, prepared to turn it off. But this time something about the caller ID caught his attention. He hesitated. Why not give it a try? After all, what could it hurt? With a grimace, he clicked on and put it to his ear.

"*Ciao*."

There was a soft exhalation of breath and a feminine voice said, "Is this Max?"

He blinked. "Yes. Who's this?" But in a flash, he knew.

"Isabella Casali. I…we met the other night when I…"

Letting his head fall back, he closed his eyes. He really didn't need this. Life as he'd grown to know it was boring but placid. Not too many highs and lows—if you didn't count the midnight agonies of a guilty conscience. And then, this woman had inserted herself into his sphere. And it came to this—just the sound of her voice did strange and mystical things to him.

"I remember," he said gruffly. "How did you get this number?"

"It wasn't easy." She hesitated, then went on. "Listen, I don't mean to be a bother, but I need to talk to you."

His hand tightened on the small device. "It's that damned basil, isn't it?"

She sputtered for a few seconds, then got herself together again in time to be coherent. "Well, yes, it is. You see, this is a matter of such importance—"

He stopped her with a rude word. He was angry with himself, angry with her. The way she'd barged into his life a few nights before had affected him more than he wanted to admit. He told himself it was just her femaleness that had sent him into a tailspin for a couple of days.

It could have been any woman, anyone at all. Despite everything, he did feel a real lack of the feminine presence in his life. He missed having someone around who put flowers in a glass and plunked them in the middle of the table at breakfast. He missed the flow of shiny hair spilling over a smooth, silky shoulder, the soft pout of red, swollen lips, the cheerful voice that sounded like sunshine, the way a pair of breasts filled out a sweater and pulled the fabric in that tightly entrancing way that just knocked him out. All these things shouted femininity to him. Having a woman around made daily existence softer, more colorful, more dramatic. He missed that.

But such things were part of a life that was closed to him now. Finding Isabella on his property had just brought that home to him and made the loss fresh again. He needed to forget all about her.

And he'd managed over the last few days to practically obliterate her from his consciousness. He'd done it deliberately, piece by piece, setting up work schedules and exercise routines that demanded more of his attention and time, until he fell exhausted into bed at night and slept like a drugged beast. He'd done everything he could think of to make his life new and challenging in order to keep his mind from going where he didn't need it to go.

Now here she was with her provocative voice and her urgent requests, stirring up things he didn't want stirred. That made him angry, even though a part of him knew that the anger was a direct attempt to stave off temptation.

"Tell me the truth," he demanded. "How did you get this number?"

She drew her breath in. "I found it."

The sheer audacity of that answer took him by surprise and he nearly laughed out loud. But he held it back and managed to ask with a straight face, "Where?"

"In the trash."

He shook his head. Did she really think he was going to buy that one? "Isabella, please. That doesn't make any sense."

She sighed. "Life doesn't make any sense. Hadn't you noticed?"

"Don't try to throw sand in my eyes with ridiculous philosophical musings," he warned her, thoroughly annoyed. "This is a very basic problem. It doesn't need an esoteric response. You found my number. I want to know how so that it doesn't happen again."

"I've told you the truth," she insisted, sounding earnest. "It was in my trash."

So she wasn't going to tell him. That only strengthened his convictions. If she couldn't respond truthfully to a simple question, he didn't need her complicating his life any longer. Best to cut all ties as quickly as possible. Prolonging this would only make things worse for him and his peace of mind.

"I don't know how you got this number," he told her gruffly, "but it hardly matters. I'll get it changed right away."

She drew her breath in. "All so you can avoid any calls from me?" she asked, her voice sounding shocked.

"Yes," he said stoutly.

She didn't understand. But that was for the best. If she ever tumbled to the truth—that she affected him as no one else had in years—his situation would be that much more precarious.

"Why do you hate me?" she asked, aghast.

"I don't hate you." He groaned softly, closing his eyes. "That's just the problem," he muttered under his breath.

"What?" she said.

He gritted his teeth and expelled a long line of swear words in an obscure dialect, just because it made him feel better. This woman was driving him around the bend. And that was odd. He didn't remember trouble like this with women that he'd known before…before Laura. He'd always had friends and casual relationships. It seemed he'd lost the knack for free and easy dealings with the opposite sex.

Of course, Laura's death and the accident that had scarred him had changed all that. For over a year after it had happened, he hadn't been able to speak to anyone, even family members. He had waited to die, wishing for it. When that didn't happen, he began to realize he was going to have to go on without her and without his face. And that was a problem. He didn't have much appetite for it.

It had taken a long time, but slowly he had let others in—but only his immediate family and a few close friends. Most other friends had probably decided he must be dead himself. He didn't really want them around and that had become obvious.

And no strangers. Never strangers.

Yet, once he'd opened up to his closest family members, he'd begun to see that there were still things he could do with his life, even if he didn't go out into the world as before. Today, he had a relatively active professional life, thanks to the computer and the Internet. In the old days, he would probably have been locked away from all human commerce, but with the modern conveniences of semi-anonymous communication he was able to do quite a bit without having to come face-to-face with the people he interacted with. Mostly, he still only saw people he'd known all his life.

"That's because you're a coward," his sister maintained wryly during one of their frequent arguments.

He didn't take offense. She was probably right. Though he told himself he didn't want to inflict his savaged visage on others, that was only a part of it. He didn't want to see the reaction in the eyes of strangers. There was a certain vanity there, he had to admit. But he knew what the world wanted from him, and it wasn't his scarred face.

He'd been through the fickle reactions of the public at large before and he knew very well how cruel they could be. His mother had been a beautiful film star. During her twenties and early thirties, people had flocked to see her films. She'd been in demand everywhere.

But unlucky genetics had been her downfall. She had lost her looks early. Even as a young boy he'd understood how the media had begun to rip apart her image as she had disappointed them. It almost seemed they took it personally that she wasn't the beauty she once had been. As though she'd wasted their time and now would have to pay the price. He had been ten years old when she had taken her own life.

Yes, he knew what the public was like. And he didn't see any reason why he should go out of his way to be accepted by them again.

But Isabella Casali was another matter. He couldn't seem to put her off in a distant box the way he knew he ought to.

He came back to the conversation, knowing he needed to create a plausible alternative to her accusation of him hating her. "I hate talking on the phone," he supplied quickly. "It's not just you," he added.

Despite everything, he didn't want to hurt her. She was quite adorable and didn't deserve it. This was *his* problem, not hers. If only he could explain to her… But that was impossible. "I don't like talking to anyone."

"Oh."

She still sounded downhearted and that made him wince. Silently, he told himself to man up. He had to remain firm. It was the only way.

"Well, I won't keep you much longer," she promised, sounding wistful. "I just have one thing to talk to you about."

He knew what that was. There was no point prolonging things. "The answer is no," he said evenly.

"But you don't know——"

"Yes, I do. You want permission to come in and scavenge my river valley hillside for your precious basil herb. And I won't allow it. Case closed."

He could almost hear her gulp and he grimaced. He hated doing this. He could see the look she probably had in her huge blue eyes and it killed him. But he couldn't weaken.

"Please hear me out——"

"No, I won't allow it. It's too dangerous."

It was her turn to make that sound of exasperation. "Dangerous? What's dangerous about it?"

"You fell into the river, didn't you?"

"Yes, but that was because it was the middle of the night and you scared me."

He nodded. "Exactly. These things are always...accidents." He should just hang up and he knew it. He tried. But somehow, it just seemed too cruel.

"Why?" Her voice sharpened, as though she'd suddenly found the hint of a chink in his argument. "Why are you so sure I'll get hurt? Has anyone actually been hurt in that river?"

His throat choked shut for a moment. This was something he couldn't talk about. He closed his eyes for a moment and took a deep breath to steady his resolve. The consequences were too risky to gamble with.

There was a part of him, in a deep, secret place, that halfway believed there was an evil force lurking by the river, waiting to trap another woman—especially one that he had some affection for—and pull her under the water as well. There was another, more rational part of him that contended the evil force was his own sense of guilt. Which side was right? It wasn't worth putting it to the test.

"Isabella, I forbid you to go anywhere near that hillside. And the river. Stay away."

"But—"

"Promise me." His voice was harsh and stern. He had to make sure she didn't feel she could come on her own.

She swallowed hard. He could hear the effort she was making but that didn't matter. He steeled himself. It had to be done.

"All right," she said at last in a very small voice. "I'll stay away. At least I'll stay away until I can find a way to convince you—"

"You're not going to convince me. I'm changing this number, remember?"

"But, Max..."

He winced. Hearing his name in her voice sent a quiver through him, a sense of something edgy that he didn't like at all. Given a little time, it would chip away at his resolve, bit by bit.

"Goodbye, Isabella," he said firmly.

She sighed. "Goodbye."

Her voice had a plaintive quaver that touched his heart, but he hung up anyway. He had to. Another moment or two and he'd have been giving in to her, and that was something that couldn't happen.

This entire connection had to end. He couldn't afford the time and emotional effort involved in maintaining a relationship, even on the phone. He had work to do.

But returning to his research was hopeless at this point. Instead, he rose, grabbed his towel and headed for the fully equipped gym he'd had built into half of the whole ground level of the building. It was obvious he was going to have to fight harder to push Isabella Casali out of his system.

CHAPTER FIVE

ISABELLA fought back tears of frustration as she clicked off her phone connection to the palazzo.

"There go any hopes of a career in negotiations," she muttered to herself. "Turns out I'm not any better at that than I am at breaking and entering."

Hardly a surprise, but disappointing anyway. What now? Giving up wasn't an option. One look at her half-empty restaurant told her that. She was going to have to find another way. But how? She'd promised him she wouldn't go near the hillside or the river and she was going to keep that promise, much as it hurt.

But there had to be a way to breach those high walls in a more effective manner. Someone in the village had to have dealings with the palazzo. It didn't make sense that they would import everything from Rome. Slowly, carefully, she began to ask around. At first all she got were blank stares.

And then, finally, she hit pay dirt of a sort. Much to her surprise, the man who delivered seafood to her restaurant every morning also made a stop at the Rossi palazzo once or twice a week.

"Only on Tuesdays and Fridays," he told her chattily,

wiping his hands on his big white apron. "Wednesdays are out. It seems to be the day off for the staff, such as it is."

"Really?"

"Oh, yes. I made the mistake of showing up on a Wednesday once. I couldn't even get in the gate. I had two pounds of Chilean sea bass go bad over that little error."

"Do you ever see the prince?" she asked quickly, afraid he might escape before she got all she needed to know from him.

"The prince?" He shrugged. "I don't think so. I usually deal with an old fellow who tries to get something for nothing every time." He chuckled. "The place is like a mausoleum. You'd think it was full of old dead ancestors, but somebody seems to have an appetite for salmon and scallops."

And so, a plan was born.

The gap in the stone wall that surrounded the Rossi estate was still there. No one had filled it in—and that was lucky. Without this little piece of access, her plan would never have worked at all.

And so the following Wednesday, Isabella squeezed through and then stood very still in the warm noon sun, listening as hard as she could. The wind was quiet. The water was a distant babbling. And once the pounding of her heart quieted down, she could tell the guard dogs didn't seem to be loose. There wasn't a sign of them.

She bit her lip, tempted to race up the hill and gather basil as fast as she could, then race back again. But she knew that was no solution. And such an action certainly held no honor. Much as the prince scared her, she had to confront him about this and do things openly and honestly.

He'd told her not to come here. She had to change his mind—not steal from him. Taking a deep breath, she started up the hill toward the castle.

It was a long climb and she was carrying a heavy back-pack with supplies—her special sauce pan, her favorite olive oil, the tomatoes that would form her base—and a small container of all that was left of the basil supply for her restaurant. She was going to go for broke and cook for the prince. It was pretty much the last idea she had left.

All the way, she kept expecting to hear someone shouting for her to go back. That didn't happen and she found some shade once she'd reached the top of the hill. There were no cars in sight, and not a sign of life anywhere. The castle looked just as old and moldy, but a lot less intimidating in the sunlight.

A few minutes of rest and she began to work up the nerve to go on with her plan. She knew where the cook's entrance was. She would use that first, hoping to find things unlocked. Once she was inside, she knew exactly what to do next.

She scanned the windows as high as she could look. There was no telling where his rooms were, no way to know where he hung out during the day.

Her fingers trembled a bit as she reached for the latch on the kitchen door, and she paused for a moment. Closing her eyes, she muttered a quick plea. This had to work. He had to understand. He was a prince, but he was also a man and she was counting on that basic humanity to come through for her in the end.

And whatever chance there was, she had to take it. She had no choice.

Max stood with his eyes closed and savored being bombarded by water. He'd just had a grueling workout in his gym and the water pouring over his naked body was creating a special kind of ecstasy. Every aching muscle sang with relief. Every body part relaxed with delight. Every nerve, every fiber, came together in rapt happiness.

He would have to pay for this someday. Maybe at the gates of heaven. This was pure self-indulgence and he was probably wasting water to boot, but he let it go on and on, gushing through his thick hair, making small silver rivers over his tanned shoulders and through the dark thatch on his chest. It felt so damn good. He was pure appetite today, appetite for pleasure.

And what the hell? It was his birthday.

It was his birthday and no one had remembered.

That was okay. In fact, it was exactly as he wanted it to be. He hated people making a fuss. What was a birthday, anyway? Just a day. Nothing special. All the celebrating was just a pretence that something had actually happened, something had actually changed, a milestone had been set down. And actually, it was all much ado about nothing.

A memory floated into his mind, how his birthday had been when Laura was still with him. She'd slipped out of bed early in the morning and taken little gifts and hidden them all over the castle. It had taken him the entire day to find them all. How she'd laughed when he'd looked in all the wrong places. He could almost hear her musical voice now.

But he shook it away. Thinking of Laura was still too painful. Would there ever come a time when he could remember her without that dull, hopeless, agonizing pain of guilt in his gut?

Finally he was ready to put a stop to this and get on with his day. He turned off the water and stood there for a moment, feeling the mist around him turn into clear air, the warmth turn into refreshing coolness, the moisture evaporate on his skin. For some reason his senses seemed especially acute today. He was feeling things he never noticed, hearing birds outside, feeling a breeze, enjoying the rays of the sun that came in through the open window. As usual, he avoided looking in the mirror while he dried himself with a huge fluffy towel, glancing out the window at the beautiful day instead.

"There's no place like Italy," he murmured to himself. "And in Italy, there's no place like Monta Correnti."

He stretched in the warm sunlight, smelling the clean scent of his soap. And…something else.

He stopped, frowning, and sniffed the air again. There was something else in the wind—or, more likely, wafting up from the kitchen. Someone was cooking. How could someone be cooking? There was no one here. Even Renzo was gone, making his weekly trip to see his daughter an hour's drive away.

Was it his imagination?

No, it got stronger. Garlic, tomatoes, olive oil, and something else.

It was a wonderful smell. A slow smile began to transform his face. It seemed someone had remembered his birthday after all and had come back to surprise him. It had to be Renzo.

Much as the old sourpuss tended to be a dour figure, he had his moments. Max pulled on a pair of jeans, suddenly in a hurry to find out what was going on. He turned to the stairway, bounding down, barefooted and shirtless, feeling happier than he'd felt in a long time. Funny how the fact that someone had remembered his birthday after all seemed to buoy him. He was smiling as he pushed in through the swinging doors to the kitchen.

"So you did remember my birthday after all," he said, and then he stopped dead, shocked to the core. It wasn't Renzo who turned to greet him.

"You!" He stared at her. "How did you get in here?"

Isabella was opening her mouth, and as she did so she thought she had words to say. But somehow they never made it out past her lips. For the moment, she couldn't speak.

It was all too much. She was startled by the way he'd come barging into the room, but, more than that, she was stunned at the beauty of the man she saw before her. His bare chest, his strong shoulders and muscular arms, the way his worn jeans rode low on his hips, revealing a tanned stomach that was smooth and tight as a trampoline canvas, all combined to present a picture of raw, candid masculinity that took her breath away.

"Oh! I…I…"

His jaw was hard as stone and his eyes blazed. "What the hell are you doing here?"

"Uh…" She gestured toward the stove. "Cooking?"

His head went back. That part was obvious. He was tensed, every muscle hardening, as though ready to pick her up physically and throw her out onto the front walkway.

"That's not what I mean," he said through teeth that were close to clenched.

"I know. I know."

She shook her head, trying to clear it. She'd never responded to a man like this before. She was swooning like a young girl in the sixties at a Beatles concert. She had to get a grip.

But something about him had hit her hard, right in the emotions. He had come barging into the kitchen and as she'd turned to greet him she'd seen this beautifully sculptured image of a man, backlit by the golden light coming in from the high windows. Michelangelo's creation in the flesh. She had that feeling she sometimes got when her favorite tenor reached an impossibly high note and held it forever. She even had tears stinging in her eyes—he was just so beautiful.

She turned from him and leaned against the counter, her hand over her mouth. Staring into the red sauce bubbling on the stove, she fought for stability. What was she going to do? She couldn't seem to stay sane around this man.

And she had to. This was not what she'd come for. She didn't want to be mesmerized by his male appeal. She had a case to make and she had to stay on her toes to make it. But somehow sanity and the prince didn't seem to go together well.

Too bad, she told herself sternly. *You've got to do this right.*

Taking a deep breath, she turned back to face him. Resolutely, she lifted her gaze and stared at him hard.

"Okay, here's the deal," she said, and somehow she managed to sound strong. "You are denying me access to something I need in order to survive. Something my family traditionally has had access to. We have to find a way to compromise on this."

He stared back at her. She was looking up at him, her eyes very wide, and he realized he hadn't even thought to shield his face from her gaze. Here he was in broad daylight with none of the protective shadows of the other night. And there she was, staring straight at him. And yet, once again he felt no overwhelming need to turn away as he felt so often with others. Her gaze was open and natural. She might be scared of something about him, but it wasn't his face.

But it was *her* face that drew his attention. He took a step closer and reached out to take her chin in his hand and tilt her head so that he could examine her. And then he swore softly.

"Isabella, you still have a bad bruise," he said, a touch of outrage in his voice as he studied her black eye.

"Oh," she said, blinking rapidly. "Yes, I've been told it will take a while to fade."

He swore softly, shaking his head, then pulled away from her and looked at the items she'd spread out all over the kitchen.

"You're going to have to pack all this up and get out of here," he said tersely.

She took a step back away from him. She knew he was angry at finding her here. What confused her a bit, though, was why her black eye seemed to make him even angrier. As though it were her fault or something!

"Why?"

He looked back at her. "Because, once again, you're trespassing. You're going to have to go."

She shook her head. She wasn't going to be bowled over so easily. She lifted her chin. "Not until you try the sauce."

A look of surprise flashed in his dark eyes. He turned to glance at the brew simmering in the pot. "Is this your special sauce ?"

"Yes."

He turned back and met her defiant eyes.

"I don't want to try your sauce, Isabella. I'm sure it's a fine sauce. But, no matter how good it is, it won't change anything. The special quality of your sauce is not at issue here. It's the access to the hillside, and I can't allow you to go there."

He was like a stone wall. Her hope began to flag.

"Max, please." She winced and drew back a bit. "Don't you understand?" she said, trying hard to be calm and reasonable. "I have to go there."

He shrugged as though he just didn't care. "I'm going to go and finish dressing," he said dryly. "I expect you to have cleared out by the time I get back."

He began to turn away.

Isabella cried out. "No!"

He hesitated and looked back, and in that same moment a furious Isabella, all tossed hair and flashing eyes, got between him and the doorway before he realized what was happening.

"You listen to me," she demanded, jabbing a finger against his naked chest. "It wasn't easy doing this. It wasn't easy coming all this way and climbing the hill with all these supplies, or finding the right time to come here when I would be able to get in, and preparing myself and putting together a proper case to make to convince you. You can at least pay me the respect of hearing me out."

He grabbed her hand to stop the jabbing and ended up holding onto it. "Why should I hear you out? Your problems have nothing to do with me."

"Yes, they do," she insisted, trying to free her hand from his grip. "You own the hillside where the basil grows. That herb is the linchpin of my family's existence. Without it, our restaurant is over and my father's lifework is in ruins."

She finally yanked her hand away and jabbed him again. "You will listen," she demanded, her eyes fierce.

Max hadn't been around many people for a good long time, but he'd always had a knack for understanding a lot about human psychology. One thing he knew was that, faced with someone who was almost overwrought with passionate intensity, the worst thing you could do was to laugh. It drove the person crazy and it made you look like a jerk. He knew it was all wrong. Not to mention, if your goal was to calm the person down, it just plain didn't work very well.

But he couldn't help it. She looked so cute. Her curly hair was flopping down over her huge eyes and her cheeks were bright red and her lips looked lusciously swollen. And she was so earnest.

He started to try to answer her, but the words didn't come out right. What did come out was a choking laugh, and once it got started he had a hard time getting it stopped again.

Laughing. It was something he never did. As he tried to analyze it later, he decided it was a release of sorts. He'd spent so long being so tense, so filled with anguished guilt, and Isabella had reached into his life and pulled aside the curtain, letting in a ray of sunshine that helped open the floodgates to emotions he had kept bottled up for too long. But once those gates had opened, it was hard getting them closed again.

She stood back, stunned, her blue eyes bewildered. Next she was going to look hurt and he knew it. He didn't want her to be hurt. He had to stop that. He had to tell her, had to explain…

But he was laughing and, for the moment, all he could do was reach for her and fold her into his arms.

"How dare you?" she cried, struggling against him.

"Hush, hush," he was saying, stroking her hair and leaning down into the crook of her neck to drop a kiss on her tender skin, his lips lingering a moment or two too long. His whole purpose was to calm her down, of course, and to reassure her that he wasn't laughing at her. Not really. But her neck was so inviting and her skin tasted so sweet and he found himself dropping more kisses than he'd ever meant to, dropping them lightly at first, then with more and more intensity, letting his tongue flicker on her skin.

"I'm sorry, Isabella," he murmured against her warmth, still racked with humor. "I don't mean to laugh. It's not that I'm laughing *at* you. Honestly, I'm really not…"

"I hate you!" she cried, still trying to break free. "You're mean and arrogant and—"

"No," he said, finally getting control of the laughter and pulling up to look at her. "No, listen…"

She shook her head and her hair flew around her face. There were tears in her eyes. His heart melted at the sight.

"Oh, Isabella," he said gruffly, full of regret. "No, I didn't mean to laugh."

Her lower lip was trembling. He cupped her face in his hands. She was beautiful and he moved purely by instinct. She had a spirit that had to be soothed, a mouth that had to be kissed. There was no stopping it. Nature had taken over.

CHAPTER SIX

UNPLANNED passion like this was taboo, unacceptable—and, once ignited, completely irresistible. Max's lips touched Isabella's once, twice, and then again, as though he'd suddenly developed a raving hunger for the taste of her, and then the moist warmth of her mouth was there, open and inviting and his kiss grew in sweet, silky intensity. And he was lost in the moment.

It was hard to know how long the kiss lasted. When he finally revived, feeling like a swimmer coming up for air, she was trying to push him away and murmuring, "No, no. I didn't come here for this."

He pulled his face back, but his fingers were still tangled in her hair. He looked down at her and shook his head almost sadly.

"Neither did I," he told her, his gaze ranging over her pretty face. It took all his strength to keep from kissing her again. "But I won't say I'm sorry it happened," he added, his voice husky with the lingering sense of how tempting she was.

Their eyes met. He saw wonder there, and questions. She was a woman who deserved more than he was allowing her. He groaned, then shrugged in bittersweet surrender.

"All right, Isabella. I'm ready to sample your sauce and hear your entire presentation."

Suddenly her face was shining. "That's all I ask," she said, blooming like a flower that had just found the sun. "Just give me half an hour."

He nodded, reluctantly smiling at the picture she made. "You've got it. Hit me with your best shot." He gave her a warning look. "And then I will tell you 'no' and send you home again."

She nodded happily. "I'll convince you. You just wait."

He released her slowly, wishing he could pull her back into his arms and hold her again. Somehow he doubted her cooking was going to captivate him more strongly than her kisses had.

He went back to his room to put on a shirt and she got busy cooking the pasta. She'd actually talked him into hearing her out. She could hardly believe it.

The fact that he'd kissed her didn't mean a thing, she told herself. It had thrilled her and she was still tingling. Her heart was racing, skittering around like a happy bird in her chest. But she knew she shouldn't have let it happen and now she had to get over it. She had work to do.

But she also knew that she would be remembering how her cheek had felt against his naked chest for the rest of her life. The smoothness of his skin, the strength of his arms, the sound of his heartbeat, had sent her into a tailspin. She had to push those thoughts away, save them for later, or she wouldn't be able to do what she'd set out to.

He was more beautiful, more manly, more exciting than any man she'd ever known, but, still, she hadn't let it completely drag her under, and she was proud of that. She'd been the one to pull away. And she had definitely not come here scheming to use any feminine wiles or anything of the sort. The kiss hadn't been planned by either of them and it didn't count.

At least, she hoped it didn't. Because she wasn't going to let it happen again. She couldn't.

Taking a deep breath, she nodded. Never again. That was the route to ruin and she was too smart to go that way. She had something to accomplish here, and she got down to it.

Max sat at the head of the long mahogany table that had been in his family for over two hundred years. Before him lay a mat of ivory lace that was set with heavy sterling silver flatware in an exceptionally beautiful baroque pattern. Two crystal goblets of wine had been added, one reflecting a golden hue, the other taking in sunlight and translating it into a deep, rich, royal red. There was a silver fingerbowl as well, deeply engraved with a bucolic scene, and a fine, creamy-white, linen napkin.

He surveyed it all and shook his head, wondering how she'd found everything so quickly. It had been almost thirty years since he'd seen these pieces laid out this way—when his mother was alive.

It came to him that he ought to do this more often. Just seeing these things here, touching them, brought up feelings of attachment, memories of ancestors, connections to his family and his past that he didn't think about often enough. It all touched a chord deep inside him, a link to eternity.

He swallowed his smile quickly as Isabella entered the room. Sunlight slanted in from the tall windows that lined the space, setting her dark hair aflame with golden highlights. Her cheeks were red from time over a hot stove and she was carrying a steaming pot with hot pads protecting her hands. As she approached, the scent of something extraordinary filled the room.

He shook his head. As he watched her a sense of her beauty overwhelmed him, despite her bruised eye, and he felt an intense need to hold her again that filled him with an aching regret.

How had he gotten here? It was insane. Over the last few years, he'd lived his whole life to keep people away. Isabella had somehow crept right through his barriers and found the center of his being in ways no one else had done. He wasn't really sure how she'd accomplished that, but he knew she had. And he knew he had to resist it.

She turned an impish smile his way as she placed the pot onto the trivet in the middle of the table.

"There you are," she told him, ladling the sublime sauce out into a porcelain bowl, which she'd already filled with freshly made pasta. "I hope you'll deem this fit for a king," she said with another grin. "Or, at any rate, a prince."

He looked down into the bowl. The sauce was the color of a late summer sunset and swimming with beautiful vegetables he couldn't name. "It smells wonderful."

She nodded and didn't waste time on false modesty. "It tastes wonderful, too."

He managed to maintain a skeptical look, just for dignity's sake. "We'll see."

And he began to eat.

She was right. The sauce filled his mouth with a feeling like ecstasy. He'd never had anything quite like it. Amazing how one little herb could make such a difference.

"Well?" she asked, watching him like a hawk.

He looked at her. He could hardly keep his eyes off her. She was so alive, so vibrant, so expressive. There was something real about her, something basic and decent and appealing in a new way. He felt a pull toward her, a definite attraction, something he couldn't deny.

But how could that be? She was so different from the wife he had loved so much. The woman he still missed so much.

Laura had been blonde, ethereal, slender and light as a bird. She had looked very much in life like the angel she had surely become since. But this woman was very different—full and round and earthy. And, to his eternal regret, he ached for her right now as he'd seldom ached for a woman before.

He looked back down at the bowl, avoiding her bright gaze. It was insane to let her stay. He had to get her out of here before he lost control and did something crazy.

The worst of it was, it was quite evident that she had not come here to seduce him at all. She was dressed modestly in a simple peasant blouse and full skirt. There was no cleavage showing, no revealing exposure of skin. She was honest and straightforward and she wasn't playing games. He liked her for that. It showed a certain respect for him and for the dilemma between them. The fact that he could detect the beauty of her body beneath all the swishing fabric was beside the point. She wasn't using it as a trump card— even though she probably sensed it wouldn't be hard to do.

Resolutely he lifted his gaze and met hers.

"*Magnifico*, Isabella," he told her. "This is spectacular. I can fully understand why your cuisine is famous and people come from miles around to enjoy it."

She brightened with happiness at his words. "You've heard of it, then?"

"Oh, yes," he admitted.

She radiated joy. "I knew once you tried it—"

"And I understand how important it is to you," he interrupted before she could have a chance to make assumptions his admission didn't quite warrant. "But that doesn't change the danger that you would face every time you went across that divide above the river." His hand swept out in a royal gesture. "If I had a house full of servants, I could have one of them go and harvest the weed for you. But at present, Renzo and I live here alone. There is no one to help out."

Isabella bit down hard on her lower lip, keeping herself under tight control. His constant emphasis on the danger of going near the river was clearly overstated and there had to be a reason for it. She was pretty sure it had something to do with the death of his wife. What had happened that had made him so sure the place wasn't safe for her? She wanted to know, but she didn't want to push him. A horrible vision of tractors mowing down the hillside if he got annoyed enough did the trick.

Back to the plan.

"We can talk about that later," she said quickly. "Right now I just want you to enjoy this."

He gave her a faint, reluctant smile, his eyes glowing. "I do, Isabella. More than you know."

She flushed. It was odd to watch how he still tended to turn his face away from her, as though trying to keep her from seeing the scars. No matter what he did, he looked gorgeous to her. How could it be otherwise when he was blessed with those huge, emotional dark eyes and that wide, sensual mouth?

He looked like a poet, she decided. A poet with a tender, sensitive soul purposefully disguised by his muscular form and his harsh, cynical manner, all protected by a wall of ice to keep the world at bay. She knew about his physical scars. What had hurt him so deeply that he couldn't be free? That was the mystery he carried with him.

"Tell me about this place," she said, leaning forward on her elbows as she watched him eat. "Did you grow up here?"

"Pretty much." He took another bite, savored it, and sighed with pleasure, then went on. "My father tended to drag us all over the continent, staying at one property after another. He was quite a gambler, you see, and he was always looking for another game. But when I was young we spent a lot of time here. I would ride my pony all over these grounds."

"Mmm. And you didn't fall into the river?"

His face darkened. "That is not a matter to joke about," he said curtly. "Our river is a dangerous place. We didn't realize how dangerous at the time." He looked at her face and winced. "I should have caught you before you hit the rocks."

She marveled at him. He seemed to think it was his job to save the world—or at least all females that came within his purview. That was too big a role to take on for any man. She wished she knew how to tell him so. Instead, she shrugged.

"It will heal. It will be gone in no time at all."

He heard her blithe words but they didn't placate him. He couldn't help but feel that the water had almost claimed another victim that night. If he hadn't been there to grab her...

He shook his head again and swore softly.

"And as you grew older?" she asked. "Did you still stay here often?"

He pushed away thoughts of the river and let himself look back instead. "Not as often. My mother died when I was young and, after that, I went to live with my aunt, Marcello's mother."

"I'm sorry," she murmured about his mother. She hesitated to tell him they had something in common. Was she being presumptuous? Never mind, she told him anyway.

"I lost my mother early, too," she told him. "I can hardly remember what she looked like."

"Where were you sent to live?" he asked.

She shrugged. "I stayed right where I was. Someone had to take care of my father, and my two little brothers."

He stared. "Surely you were a little young for that."

She smiled. "Yes, much too young. But we didn't have a choice. We didn't have the money or the other 'properties' like you did. We made do."

His face twisted. "You mean, *you* made do. But at least you had your family around you."

She looked up, surprised. "Where was your father?"

He gazed at her coolly. "He was despondent. My mother's death hit him hard." His gaze darkened. "We didn't see much of him after that."

"But you had your sister."

He shook his head. "Not really. She went to live with another aunt. I had a pretty lonely childhood when you come right down to it. You were lucky to stay with your family, even if it did mean you ended up being the support for everyone." He smiled at her. "That was the way it was, wasn't it?"

She frowned, feeling bad for him. At least she had her father and had benefited from his love and counsel all her life. She didn't know how she would have made it without that. Hearing about his experiences gave her a new perspective on what family could mean to a child.

"But I soon went away to school in Switzerland," he continued, "and then to university in England. And then... then I married."

The young wife he'd lost tragically. Should she say anything? She wasn't sure, so she murmured condolences again, and he brushed them aside.

"Never mind all that," he said crisply, looking at her over the rim of his wine glass. "Tell me more about you, Isabella. Tell me about your hopes and dreams and how many young men you've been in love with."

Here was the opening she'd been waiting for.

"Exactly what I planned to do," she told him cheerfully. "Well, not counting the boyfriends. They shall remain nameless, if you don't mind." She made a face at him. "But while you're finishing your meal, I'm going to give you a small background about my family and our restaurant." She gave a little bow. "With your permission," she added pertly.

He waved a hand her way, his attention back on the delicious food before him.

"Carry on," he said kindly.

"Thank you." She settled into the chair that faced his. "First about my father. His name is Luca Casali. His mother, Rosa, started a restaurant here in Monta Correnti after her husband died and left her with a young family to support. She used a special recipe she got from a secret source, and her food was well received."

He looked up with a slight smile, his gaze skimming over her face. He liked the way she talked. She was so animated.

"So you are from a restaurant family from the beginning, aren't you?"

She scrunched up her face a bit. "More or less. My father and his sister, Lisa, took over my grandmother's restaurant when she died, but they don't get along very well, so they split up. My father had a roadside stand for years before he moved to our current location. My aunt still runs Sorella, which is basically my grandmother's place updated for modern times."

She pulled a scrapbook out of her bag and put it on the

table, close to his mat. She'd put it together, using the computer to blow up pictures that would illustrate her family history and help Max understand what Rosa, and the special herb, meant to them all.

"Here is a picture of my father as a young man when he had the food stand on the Via Roma. And the next picture was taken when he was finally able to open a real restaurant, the place we call Rosa, after my grandmother, the culmination of all his hard work."

Max turned and leaned forward, taking the book from her and frowning at the first picture she'd turned to.

"This is your father?" he asked.

"Yes. Luca Casali."

He nodded slowly. "I remember him. He used to come here when I was a child."

Isabella stared at him. This was the first she'd heard of such a thing. "Here? To the Rossi palazzo?"

"Yes." He looked at her, noting an element or two of resemblance to the man. "I think he cooked for us occasionally."

She suddenly felt a bit smaller than before, reminded that she was from a different world than the one this man was from.

"Oh," she said, looking around the cavernous room and trying unsuccessfully to picture her father here. But she took a deep breath and went back to her story.

"Here is a picture of my aunt Lisa. Do you know her, too?"

He looked at the picture and shook his head. "No. I don't think I've ever seen her before."

For some reason, that was a huge relief to her.

"Good," she muttered, turning pages. "Here are my brothers, Cristiano and Valentino."

Max nodded, his interest only barely retained. "Nice-looking young men," he murmured, looking back at what was left of his pasta.

"*Very* nice-looking young men," she corrected. She was crazy about her brothers. "They are both away. Cristiano is a firefighter. He's in Australia right now, helping them with their terrible brush fires. And Valentino is a race-car driver. He's always somewhere racing around trying to challenge death at every turn."

He raised his head in surprise at the bitterness of her tone, and she smiled quickly to take the edge off it.

"So neither one is here helping run the restaurant," he noted.

"That's what my father has me for," she maintained stoutly. "But I do wish they would come home more often."

"Of course."

"And finally, here is a picture of Rosa as it was two months ago, when we still had a plentiful stock of the basil. See how crowded it is? Doesn't everyone look well fed and happy?"

He laughed softly at her characterization. "Yes," he admitted. "I see what you mean."

"And here is the restaurant now." She plunked down a picture of the half-empty room and threw out her hands to emphasize how overwhelming the situation was. "Without the basil, no one is happy anymore."

He groaned, turning his head and refusing to study that last picture. "Isabella, I get the point. You don't have to rub my nose in it."

"It seems I do." She gazed at him fiercely. "I want you to understand how important this is. How it means everything to my father."

"And to you."

"To me?" She pressed her lips together and thought

about it. Hearing his words surprised her, but what surprised her even more was that he might be right.

For years she'd chafed at being the one everybody depended on, the one who had to stay behind and help with the restaurant while her brothers went off in search of adventurous lives and her cousins went off to explore places like England and Australia. Isabella was the one who stayed home and kept the flames going. Sometimes it didn't seem fair. She'd had daydreams about leaving a note pinned to her pillow and slipping out into the night, getting on a train to Rome, flying to Singapore or Brazil, or maybe even New York. Meeting a dark, handsome stranger in an elevator. Talking over a drink in a hotel bar. Walking city streets in the rain, sharing an umbrella. All scenes snatched from romantic movies, all scenes folded into her momentary fantasies. What seemed hopeful at first eventually mutated into melancholy as it aged.

And lately, even those dreams had faded. She'd been as wrapped up in finding ways to save the restaurant as her father was. So maybe Max was right. Maybe it did mean everything to her, too.

"Maybe," she said faintly.

What did it mean when you gave up your dreams? Did they grow mellow and rich, like fine wine, warming you even as they faded? Or did they dry up and turn to powder that blew away with the wind?

"Maybe."

Snapping back into the moment, she looked at Max, trying to see if he'd come around yet. She grimaced lightly. It certainly didn't look like it. Those gorgeous dark eyes with their long, sweeping lashes were as cool and skeptical as ever.

She sighed. He'd finished eating and he'd finished

looking at her scrapbook and listening to her point of view. She had only one weapon left in her arsenal. Slipping away, she hurried back to the kitchen where she pulled a large portion of a beautiful tiramisu out of the refrigerator. Rummaging in a drawer, she found a candle, which she lit and put atop it. She smiled with satisfaction, then carried it back out into the dining room, singing *"Tanti auguri a te,"* as she went. She stopped, put the blazing pastry down before him, and added, *"Buon compleanno!"*

He was laughing again, only this time it was with her, not at her.

"How did you know it was my birthday?" he asked her, letting her see, for just a moment, how pleased he was.

She shrugged grandly. "You told me."

He frowned. "When?"

"It was the first thing you said when you came into the kitchen, before you realized it was me instead of Renzo."

"Oh, of course."

He looked into the flame as though it fascinated him. She watched him. In the afternoon light, his scar looked like a ribbon of silver across his face. She wondered if it gave him any pain. She knew it gave him heartache. And because of that, it gave her heartache, too.

"Make a wish and blow out the candle," she told him.

He looked at her and almost smiled. "What shall I wish for?"

She shook her head. "It's your wish. And don't tell me, or else it won't come true."

His face took on a hint of an attitude, teasing her. "Okay. I know what I'm going to wish for."

She knew he didn't mean anything by it; still, the implication was there, hovering in the air between them. She felt herself flushing and turned away, biting her lip.

"Go ahead. Blow it out. I won't watch."

"Why not?" He blew out the small fire and picked up a fork. "Anyone can watch. It's not much of an event, you know."

He broke off a bit of the pastry onto his fork, and, instead of taking the bite himself, he waited until she'd turned back and then popped it between her lips and left it there.

"Hey!" She ate it quickly, half laughing. "That was for you. I ate enough of it myself when I was making the thing."

He stopped, staring at her. The tiramisu was a thing of beauty, the dark of the coffee flavor and the cocoa topping a striking contrast to the light-as-a-feather, rich, creamy layers. It was a mystery to him how anyone made such a thing, and the thought that she had created it on her own was a revelation. Her talents were legion, it seemed.

"You made it yourself?"

She nodded. Yes, she had, thinking of him the whole time and warding off Susa, who'd wanted to take over.

Max shook his head as he studied her face, searching her eyes, sketching a trail of interest along the line of her chin. "You made me that delicious pasta and you made me my birthday dessert with your own hands." His eyes seemed to glow with a special light and his voice was so quiet, she could hardly hear him. "What can I do for you in return, Isabella?"

She met his gaze and held it. "You know what I want," she said, almost as softly as he had spoken.

He stared into her eyes a moment longer, then his face took on an expression she couldn't translate into anything but regret. Looking down, he began to eat and he didn't speak again until he had finished.

"Thank you," he said simply. "I appreciate this."

She waited. Was he going to relent? Was he going to

tell her she could have another try at his hillside? She waited another moment, but he didn't seem to have anything else to say, so she sighed and rose, beginning to clear the plates away.

"I suppose I'd better get all this cleaned up," she said, wondering if she'd actually made any impression on him at all. "I'm sure you have people coming over to help you celebrate tonight."

He looked up at her with a frown. "I don't see visitors. Not ever. I thought you understood that."

She stopped, staring at him. "Not anyone?"

"No. Not anyone."

Her blue eyes betrayed her bewilderment. "Why not?"

He sighed and threw down his napkin, then said in a clipped tone, "I think that's self-evident."

She sank back into her chair and gaped at him. She remembered suddenly what Susa had said about his having lost his young wife years ago. She'd implied that the pain of losing her had brought on his lonely existence, but surely there was more to it than that. "You mean, because of your face?"

He merely stared at her, confirming her suspicions.

"But…" She choked, unable to comprehend his motives. "Why would you let something like that ruin your life? You need people around you, you need…"

She stopped before she said something ill-advised. He needed love. That much was obvious. He needed a woman, someone to care for him and make him happy. Every man needed that.

But did she have any business saying such a thing? Of course not. Especially since she needed a man just as badly, and look how she'd been unable to take care of that little problem for years now. She didn't even have the excuses he had. So who was she to talk?

But she couldn't leave the subject alone.

"If I were like you," she said, pointing to her own injured eye, "I would have hidden myself away and we would have had to close down the restaurant for the last week and a half."

He half smiled at her characterization and he looked at her black eye almost affectionately.

"Did you get any reaction from your customers?"

"Of course." She stared at him again. He was a prince, rich and probably famous in certain circles, powerful, with resources she could only dream of. So how had he let this happen? How had others around him let it go this far? How had he become such a recluse, and how could he stand it for so long?

"I get plenty of reaction," she continued slowly, "lots of double takes, people turning back to have another look at me. Then I get the opposite, people who notice, then look away quickly as though thinking I must have been beaten up and would be embarrassed if they acknowledged seeing the evidence of it."

He nodded, recognizing the experience from his own ventures out into the world.

"I even have little children making fun of me in the street." She tossed her hair back with a defiant snap of her head. "But who cares? That's their problem."

He gazed at her in complete admiration. She was a tough one. She could handle what life threw at her in ways he didn't seem capable of. But there was so much more to his situation that she didn't know about. "Our conditions are not comparable," he said.

She shook her head. "Maybe not to the degree, but the basics are very much the same."

He frowned, beginning to feel a bit of backlash against

her attitude. "You don't understand." He glanced at her, then away. "You don't know why this happened."

She leaned forward, her elbow on the table, her chin in her hand, ready to hear, ready to understand. "So tell me."

His gaze darkened. For just a moment he saw it all again, the trees rushing past his window, the huge old bridge standing right in his path, the flash as they hit, the flames, the fire, the horrible sound of metal against concrete. They said no one should have lived through that crash. And there were times when he'd cursed his own powers of survival.

Looking up, he spoke dismissively. "No."

Her eyes widened. "Why not?"

His own eyes were as cold as they'd ever been as he turned to gaze at her again. "It's none of your business."

He was right, of course, but she drew back as though he'd slapped her.

"Oh."

She rose again and turned toward the door. He'd hurt her with those words, with that manner. She'd thought they were becoming friends and he'd shown her just how far from that they really were. She was not allowed into his real life. Of course, what had she expected? This was a cold, cruel world, after all.

"I'll just get out of your way, then," she said stiffly. She walked firmly out of the room, waiting at each step for him to call her back. But he didn't say a word.

It only took her a few minutes to get her things washed up and ready to go, but she banged the pots a bit more than necessary. She was angry. There was no denying it. After all she'd done, all she'd said, and he still didn't understand!

She was packing her supplies away in her backpack when he came into the kitchen again. She looked up hopefully, but his eyes were still cold as ice.

"Where did you park your car?" he asked.

She went back to putting her full attention on what she was doing, stuffing the last of her utensils into the bag. "Don't worry about me. I can take care of myself."

He erased the distance between them and took her chin in his hand, forcing her to look up at him. "I've told you I won't have you wandering around the grounds on your own," he reminded her sternly. "I'll drive you to your car."

A captive, she stared back at him without saying anything. She wasn't fooled. He wanted to see where it was that she was sneaking in. Good thing she'd parked a distance away from the chink in the wall. If he was going to find her secret, he was going to have to survey the wall himself, brick by brick.

"I'll do fine on my own," she said again.

"I'm going to drive you. I brought my car around while you were cleaning up."

Slowly, deliberately, she pushed his hand away from her chin. "If you insist," she said coldly.

His mouth twitched, but he managed not to smile at the fierce picture she made.

"I do," he responded. "Shall we go?"

He helped her carry her things outside and there was a slinky little BMW Roadster.

"Nice car," she allowed, refusing to meet his gaze.

"It's a beauty, isn't it?" he agreed, stowing her things behind the seat and holding the door for her. "It seems like something of a waste. I almost never get to drive it."

"Why not?"

He shrugged. "The only place I go is to my home on the coast, and I travel in a limousine for that."

"With darkened windows. I know." Susa had told her all about it. "All so others won't see your face?" she asked, troubled by such a denial of life.

"There's more to it than that," he said, sliding behind the wheel.

"Of course. And it's none of my business." She stared out the side window.

He twitched and gave her a look, then started the car and eased it out onto the driveway.

"I don't know why you think you should be let in on every little aspect of my interior life," he said gruffly. "Believe me, the nuances are not all that interesting."

She whipped her head around. "I didn't ask just because I was snoopy," she said indignantly. "I actually care—" she stopped dead, realizing what she was saying "—uh...about you," she ended softly and lamely, looking away again as quickly as she could.

He didn't answer. As they cruised down the two-lane road he wondered why her admitting that she cared sent warmth careening through his system. It wasn't as though women hadn't cared for him in the past. What made her so special?

"Is that your car?" he asked as they closed in on a silver-blue compact sitting by the side of the road.

"That's it," she admitted.

He pulled up behind it and frowned as he studied the wall of his own property. "This isn't where you go in," he noted.

She flashed him a triumphant smile.

"You're right. This isn't it."

She began to gather her things for her great escape, slipping out of the Roadster and reaching for her bag before he had a chance to get out and help her.

"Bye," she said, not meeting his gaze and turning for her car.

"Hey." He got out on his side and followed her. "Wait a minute."

Throwing her bags into the backseat of her car, she

turned to look at him, though she was poised to jump behind the wheel and race off.

"What is it?" she asked guardedly.

He stood facing her, his legs wide apart, his hands hooked on the belt of his jeans. For a moment, he seemed lost in the depths of her eyes. Then he shrugged and looked almost bored with it all.

"I think I've come up with a way for you to get your precious herb," he said casually.

Her jaw dropped and her eyes opened wide. "What? How?"

"It's simple really."

"You mean you'll trust me to go alone?"

Darkness flashed across his face.

"No, of course not. I've told you, I will not allow you to go there unattended."

"Unattended?" Her frustration was plain on her face. She obviously felt they were just going around in circles. "But who would be available to go with me?"

He shrugged, his head cocked at a rather arrogant angle. "I'll do it," he said.

For just a moment, she wasn't sure she'd heard him correctly. "What?" she said. But she could tell he meant what he'd said by the look on his face. Joy swept through her. "You!" And then spontaneous happiness catapulted her right up against his chest.

"Oh, thank you, thank you!" she cried, throwing her arms around his neck and kissing his cheek again and again. "Thank you so much!"

He laughed softly, holding her loosely, resisting the impulse to take advantage of her giddiness.

"Can we go right now?" she cried, looking as though she could fly all the way on her own.

"Today it's too late," he said sensibly. "Come tomorrow."

"Yes." She knew he was right. "Yes, I will."

He stroked her temple with his forefinger, smoothing back the tiny curls that were forming at her hairline. "And when you come tomorrow, you can drive in the front gate."

She stared at him, clutching his arm. "How am I going to do that?"

"I'll give you the code."

That took her breath away. "Why would you do a thing like that?"

His gaze was cool, yet intimate. "Why not? I trust you." For now, it suited him that she have the code, and that was that. He gave her a quick, quirky smile.

"Besides, I can change the code any time I decide I don't want you to have it any longer."

There were tears in her eyes. She'd been so downhearted and now she was so happy. "Why are you being so good to me?" she asked emotionally.

His smile faded. He gazed deeply into her eyes and winced a bit from what he saw there. And then, he told her the truth.

"Because I care about you, too," he said.

CHAPTER SEVEN

"YOU'VE been to see the prince again." Susa's tone was quietly jubilant, as though she'd just won a bet.

Isabella turned and glanced at her sideways. "How did you know?"

Susa smiled and looked superior, mixing gelatin into the whipping cream as a stiffener, preparing for the fabulous desserts she would be concocting that evening. Very casually, she shrugged.

"I know many things."

Susa was like a member of the family. After Isabella's mother died, it was Susa she often turned to for those familiar motherly things that she needed. It was Susa who taught her how to act with the customers, how to say, "Please," and, "Thank you," and look as if you meant it. When Luca was putting her into jeans and plaid shirts as though she were a little boy, Susa taught her how to wear frilly dresses. She had a lot to thank the woman for. But Susa could be annoying, all the same.

Just like family.

Her silver hair was set in neat curls around her head, augmented by tortoiseshell combs. She looked ageless and infinitely efficient, which was just exactly what she was.

Looking at her, Isabella had a flash of appreciation for the woman. Without her, they couldn't run this restaurant these days. If nothing else, she was completely loyal. And very good at making pastries.

Isabella stared at her for a long moment, then sighed. "Someone told you, didn't they? Someone who saw me driving up there."

"Perhaps. Or perhaps I saw it myself." She threw out a significant look. "I've told you before, I have the gift."

Isabella rolled her eyes, turning back to her garlic press.

"I just want to warn you to be careful," Susa said after a long pause."

Isabella nodded. "Everyone is warning me to be careful."

"You need a warning." Susa looked up sharply. "You're reckless. You trust people too much and you get hurt."

Isabella tried to keep her temper. "I also eat too many sweets and stay up too late watching old movies. We should put up a chart with all my vices on it, so everyone can see."

It was Susa's turn to roll her eyes and Isabella bit her lip, regretting that she'd spoken sharply.

But the woman wasn't chastened. "Just a word to the wise," she said crisply. "In the first place, stay away from the prince. But if you must go to see him, stay away from water." She got up from her seat and headed for the washroom.

Isabella stared after her, then jumped up and followed her to the door.

"What are you talking about?" she demanded.

"Oh, nothing." Susa disappeared into the washroom.

"Susa!"

Isabella began to pace impatiently, waiting for her to return. Whatever she was hinting at, she had to know her reasons. There was no doubt something was still bothering Max about his wife's death. And there was no doubt he was overly worried about that river. She would see how much Susa knew—or thought she knew—and then try to find out the truth on her own.

Susa came back out, smiling happily, knowing she had rocked Isabella's world.

"Well?" Isabella demanded. "Tell me what you mean by that water crack."

Susa shrugged. "That was how his young wife died. She drowned right in front of him."

"What?" Isabella suddenly felt breathless. "Why don't I know about this?"

"The family kept it quiet." Susa touched her arm in something close to sympathy. "There were whispers, but no one knew for sure what had happened." She shook her head. "But signs were not good."

Isabella regained her equilibrium and frowned, beginning to get suspicious.

"Why would you know about this if nobody else does?"

"I told you." She pointed to her own temple. "The gift," she said, her eyes widening.

"Susa!"

She smiled like a cat with a secret. "And also, I know because my cousin was working there, up at the castle, at the time."

That put a little more credence behind it, Isabella had to admit. Susa seemed to have relatives working everywhere. Isabella shook her head. She supposed that was all a part of having "the gift."

"So tell me everything you heard," she demanded.

Susa shrugged, starting toward the refrigerator. "I know she drowned in the river, right there on the estate. The two of them were there alone. There are those who think…" She raised her eyebrow significantly.

"No!" Isabella cried. She was furious, but she had a deep, sinking feeling in the pit of her stomach all the same. "I don't believe that for a minute."

Susa shrugged. "You never know."

But Isabella knew very well that Max could never have hurt anyone. Could he? Of course not. It was inconceivable.

Susa had no more information, but she'd said enough to send Isabella into orbit. This news was all she could think about. Her heart thumped as she went over this possibility and that probability. She wanted to run to Max, to see if he knew about these rumors. But how could she bring something like this up? Impossible. And she knew without a doubt that he wouldn't want to hear a word about it.

Still, it made her crazy to think of people suspecting him. She ached with it, wanting to defend him even though...

Even though she didn't even know if anything Susa said was real or just wild imaginings in the woman's mind. Slowly, she calmed herself. There was really no point in letting herself get so worked up when she didn't even know if any of this was true.

She looked at the clock. In just eighteen hours, she would see him again. Thinking about it, she felt a strange tingling spread from her chest down her arms to her fingertips, and that was when she knew she was letting herself make too much of this—and it was time to come back to earth.

The whole thing was a mistake and Max knew it. Sitting in his darkened library, he sipped from his third glass of aged port and pondered what he was going to do about it. A wood fire flickered in the stone fireplace. The huge old house creaked with its antiquity and echoed with its emptiness. He was alone—just the way he wanted it to be.

So what had he been thinking when he'd told Isabella

she could come back here? He knew very well her presence would begin to eat away at everything he thought he'd settled years ago. He needed to be alone. He didn't deserve anything else. What he'd done when he'd allowed his wife and the baby she was carrying to die in the river was an unforgivable crime. He would never be able to pay off that debt. It would take the rest of his life just to begin paying.

Closing his eyes, he fought back the doubt that had begun to tease him lately. He'd been sure all along that his scarred face was a judgement of fate, that it was a part of his punishment, that it helped to keep him in the private prison where it was fitting and appropriate that he be. For years he'd been—not content, exactly, but resigned.

Now Isabella had fallen into his life and that was a temptation in itself. He wanted her. He wanted to be with her. He wanted to be happy.

Was it really so wrong to want that? Could he resist all that Isabella had to offer him and his life?

"Laura," he murmured, shaking his head. "Oh, Laura."

If only he could feel that she was still there with him, he knew he could be stronger. As it was, he was going to have to count on his own sense of honor.

"Honor," he muttered darkly, and then an ugly, obscene word came out of his mouth and anger boiled up inside him. Filled with a surge of rage, he threw the glass against the fireplace. It smashed into a hundred pieces with a satisfying crunch. Watching the broken shards of glass fly through the air, he felt his anger dissipate just as quickly.

He could only do what he could do, but he would resist. That was the life he had made for himself. He was stuck with it.

* * *

Max was waiting for Isabella as she drove up to the front entry of the old castle. She assumed he'd been warned by a signal from the gate she'd had no trouble opening with the code he'd given her. His shoulders looked incredibly wide in a crisp, open-necked blue shirt. His smooth-fitting chinos accentuated his athletic form, giving her a tiny bubble of appreciative happiness for just a moment. But something about his stance and the way his arms were folded across his chest told her he was bound and determined to get the two of them back on a cool, polite trajectory and away from all the warmth they'd managed to generate between them the day before.

Uh oh, she thought as she slid from behind the wheel, her heart beating a little faster.

Surely he wasn't going to change his mind about the basil. She gave him a tentative glance, then reached into the backseat to get the basket of sandwiches she'd made for the trip to the hillside. Before she could turn with it, he was there, shaking his head.

"How did I know you would bring a picnic lunch?" he said wryly. "Better leave it here. I don't think it's a good idea."

She looked at him blankly, clutching her basket and not sure what the problem was.

"This isn't an outing, Isabella," he said coolly, his dark eyes shadowed. "It's a job to be done. Let's get on with it."

"But, the sandwiches won't keep out here in the sun and—"

"Give your basket to Renzo," he said.

She turned, surprised to see that the older man was standing there with his hand outstretched. Gingerly, she handed him her basket and tried a small smile. The man gave her a small smile back, and that helped a bit.

Turning, Max began to stride toward a fence that ran along part of the long driveway where two horses were saddled and ready to go. She hurried to follow him.

"You do know how to ride, don't you?" he asked over his shoulder.

Did she? She swallowed, looking at how big both beasts were.

"I've been riding a time or two," she admitted reluctantly, remembering one successful trip around the lake and another painful excursion in the mountains when she was younger.

But she was pretty sure she could do it. Given a choice, she would rather have walked with him all the way. But he was obviously in a hurry today. That was disappointing. But at least the trip was still on. She ought to be grateful for that.

"Don't worry, Mimi is gentle as a lamb," he told her, reaching out to stroke the downy nose of a gray mare with a black, silky mane. "She'll treat you right." His face softened as the horse nuzzled into the palm of his hand with clear affection. "Won't you, girl?"

Isabella watched, surprised to see him show such open emotion so effortlessly. That made her wonder what he'd been like before the accident that had scarred him. Had he been happy? Carefree? Had affection come naturally to him? Somehow she thought so. What a blessing it would be if somehow she could help him get that life back.

She bit her lip, knowing how ridiculous that thought was. She had no business thinking it. His life had nothing to do with her. Hadn't he even told her so? But as she watched him gently stroke the beautiful horse, she found herself wondering if the touch of his hand was as gentle when he stroked a woman, and she flushed.

And then it came to her in a flash of intuition—this had

been his wife's horse. Of course. And that made her even more nervous about riding

But the mounting went fine and soon they were trotting slowly out of the yard and onto the fields of the estate, she on Mimi and Max on the stunning black stallion he had been riding the night they'd met. Very quickly, she began to feel at ease, as though she were an experienced rider herself. Mimi was the perfect mount for a greenhorn such as she was.

The day was gorgeous, bright and breezy and full of promise. They were riding over territory she'd never been through before, rolling hills and green meadows. And then they came over a rise and below them spread an ancient vineyard with grape stakes as far as she could see.

She pulled the horse to a stop and made an exclamation of surprise as she looked at the limitless plain of struggling grape plants.

"What is this?" she asked him.

He leaned forward in the saddle and gazed at the expanse of it with one hand shading his eyes.

"This was once the Rossi vineyard," he said, his voice even and emotionless. "It supplied grapes for our small family winery, an enterprise that lasted for a couple of hundred years." He paused, then added dispassionately, "It was abandoned almost ten years ago."

"Abandoned? Why?"

He didn't turn to meet her gaze, and for a long moment, he didn't answer. Watching him, she suddenly realized his neck was strained, as though he were holding something back, something painful. Her breath caught in her throat. She wanted to reach out to him, to touch him, but she didn't dare. So she waited, and finally he spoke.

"I'm sure you know that I was married when I was younger. And that my...my wife died." His voice almost choked, but he went on firmly. "At the time it happened, everything stopped. Life stopped."

Turning, he stared into her eyes as though he was forcing himself to do it. "I mean that literally. All the workers were sent away, except a bare skeleton crew to keep the place from completely reverting to the wild." His eyes seemed to burn. "And I've never seen a good reason to bring any of them back." He stared at her a moment longer, then looked away. "It's better this way."

She shook her head. *Better for whom?* she wanted to say. But who was she to tell him how to live his life?

"It seems so lonely," was all she dared put out. "And such a waste."

He shrugged again. "There are plenty of vineyards in Italy," he said, giving his horse a snicker that started him moving again. "One more or less won't make a difference."

She sighed. So he thought she was talking about his grape plants? Well, maybe she was. But she'd meant a lot more than that. A waste, indeed.

They crested another hill and found a small forest barely protecting a group of small stone buildings.

"What's that?" she called to him, pointing at it.

He turned and looked, then grinned at her. "The family crypt," he said. "Want to see it?"

"Oh! Yes."

He helped her dismount and they tied the horses to a gate, then walked slowly into the little glen that held his ancestors' graves. The garden was overgrown, but not completely shabby. His caretaker had kept it decent, if not pristine. There was a small pond with tiny flashing fishes darting back and forth, a rose garden and a marble chapel. And behind them all was a larger, brooding stone building that had served as a mausoleum to the Rossi family through the Middle Ages and beyond.

Isabella loved it. The place seemed like a secret, enchanted garden, full of history and family stories. But what was most stunning to her as she rounded a corner was a life-size marble statue of a half-naked man with a sword held at the ready guarding the entrance. Carved at the base of the marble was the name Adonis Salviati Di Rossi, 1732-1801.

Isabella gasped, hands to her mouth, then whirled to face Max, who was right behind her.

"It looks just like you!" she cried.

He tried to keep a solemn face and raised one eyebrow cynically, but his pleased sense of humor was hard to hide. It shone from his dark eyes and along the lines that framed his wide mouth. This statue had been a source of teasing and torture for him in his younger days. His friends and cousins had called him "Adonis" and joked about reincarnation and ghostly presences. In fact, Isabella hadn't been the first to call him a vampire. His childhood playmates had done it as well.

He'd forgotten how much he hated it then. Now, it just seemed amusing.

"How would you know?" he challenged her. "You're not really sure what I look like at all."

"Oh, yes," she said, no doubt in her mind. "I know exactly what you look like."

She said it with such firm confidence, he looked at her, bemused. He felt so comfortable around her. Whenever he looked into her eyes, all he saw was a candid sort of joy in life. He hadn't believed her when she'd first told him she didn't see him as ugly. But ever since, he hadn't been able to detect one sign of anything negative in her eyes, and he'd definitely been looking for it.

Still, he had to remember that she represented nothing but peril to him. She appealed to him, emotionally, physically, temperamentally—in every way possible. He wanted to be with her. He wanted to hear her laugh. He wanted to feel her in his arms. There was no denying the fact that she made him happy—happier than he'd been in years.

Happier than he had any right to be.

And that was the danger. He had no business dragging her into his private limbo of a life. He would do what he could to help her with her herbal requirements, but that was all. Once he had her supplied, she would be on her way and he wouldn't see her again. Ever again.

At least that was the way he'd planned it. Now that she was here with him, it seemed almost impossible to think of losing her. She filled a need and a hunger in him he hadn't even realized he still had.

And so, she was dangerous.

He followed as she explored the mausoleum, chattering happily as she looked into everything, finding all she saw wonderful and interesting. And he wished...

But what the hell was the point of wishing? The more you wanted out of life, the less you got. He was through with wishing. There was a job to be done here and that was all he was prepared to do.

Over and out.

Isabella knew she was talking too much, but she couldn't help it. The day was so nice and the man she was with was so mesmerizing, she was bubbling with joy just being with him.

And yet, she knew he was troubled. She could sense it in his silence and in the look in his dark eyes. As they got back atop their horses and began the last leg of their trip to the hillside, she ached to help him, if only she knew how.

But that was silly, wasn't it? He had everything he might want; all he had to do was order it up and it would be there for him. What could she provide that he couldn't get on his own?

Right behind them in the little courtyard was the evidence of a life that was one of a long line of important people involved in important events. Ordinary people such as she was didn't find their ancestors memorialized in tombs like this. Here was history, a background to the story of her area. She was a spectator. He was a star of the show.

"What's it like being an Italian prince?" she asked him at one point.

He shrugged and gave her a look. "You know very well it's an honorary title these days. The monarchy was abolished in 1946."

"But you're still a prince. You still have a special place in history."

"Bah," was all he would say.

She smiled. The fact that her own father had been a part, though small, of that background was fascinating to her. She'd wanted to ask her father about his visits to the palazzo in the old days from the moment she'd got home from her visit to Max the day before.

For some reason, she still hadn't told him that she'd met the prince. She wasn't sure why she was hesitating, but something told her he wouldn't necessarily be pleased. So her approach was less direct than usual.

She'd found her father trying to practice using a walker and she'd watched for a while, giving him advice as he'd grown more and more impatient. His ex-friend Fredo had been to see him again and put him in a rotten mood.

"Now he's threatening me with health violations," he grumbled. "Me! I've always had the cleanest kitchen in the village. And yet he dares to call me a violator!"

She got him calmed down and made him sit in his chair to rest, then brought him a cold lemonade and perched next to him, ready for the inquisition.

"Papa, tell me," she said, trying to sound casual. "How did you first know about the *Monta Rosa Basil*? When did you first find it?"

He sat back and slowly he lost the tense look around his eyes as he went into the past with a dreamy look on his face.

"As it happened, I was catering a picnic for the old prince, Prince Bartholomew, and his family, on the top of the hill, just above where the basil grows. I did more catering on my own in those days. I took every side job I could just to keep afloat. Money was very tight. There was hardly enough income to keep my stand going and I had to make some painful sacrifices just to survive." She nodded encouragement, though at the same time she wondered if he didn't see that they were close to being in that position again right now.

"There was a young maid who worked for the prince's family. She showed me the herb. Made me pay a forfeit for some silliness or other by eating a leaf. I put it on my tongue, and I immediately knew it was something I'd never tasted before. At first I thought it strange. But I couldn't get that taste out of my mind."

Isabella nodded. Everyone was the same, instantly in love with the magic.

"So the next time I was on the grounds, I went to that hill again and picked some of the herb, took it home and tried it in some recipes." He snapped his fingers in the air. "Instant success. Everyone loved it."

How exciting that must have been for him. She smiled, loving him. Growing up without a mother, she'd always felt extra close to her father. His happiness was hers, sometimes too much so.

"Did they have a lot of parties in those days?" she asked, curious to know everything she could about Max's upbringing.

"Yes. Whole caravans of people would come from Rome or from Naples and stay a week."

She shook her head with wonder. "Why don't I remember any of this?"

"These things ended when you were a young child." Luca sighed. "After Prince Bartholomew's beautiful wife killed herself, the parties never resumed. In fact, he began to spend all his time in Rome after that."

"Killed herself!" She sat up straighter and stared at her father. He had to be talking about Max's mother. An icy hand gripped her heart. "What happened?"

"I don't know the details. They said she jumped from a balcony." He shook his head. "Poor thing. She was a film star, you know. She worked with Fellini and Antonioni. She was quite good. It was a tragedy."

What a series of tragedies in Max's family if all these stories were true. First his mother commited suicide, then his young wife drowned. And what about his own accident, the one that had done such damage to his face? She still didn't have the details on that.

It was no wonder he had troubled eyes as they rode across his estate lands. He'd come by them naturally, it seemed. She looked over at him now and found him looking back at her.

"Just a little further," he called to her from the back of his horse.

She nodded. "Your grounds are so beautiful. You should do something with them."

He looked out over his hills. "You think so? What do you suggest?"

She wanted to throw out her arms to encompass it all. "I don't know. You should share this with the world. Maybe put in a hotel, a spa, a destination resort."

He turned to look at her again, grinning. "Isabella, what a middle-class mind you have. Must everything make you money?"

"No, but…"

She flushed, realizing he was teasing her, and she dropped her defensiveness and returned to a light-hearted mode.

"Hey, it's the money-making middle class that makes the economy hum for everyone," she reminded him. "Let's have none of your upper-class arrogance."

"The idle rich," he muttered dismissively.

"Exactly."

But she was laughing.

"You think I'm lazy, don't you?" he said, as though it was a revelation to him.

"Not at all. I just think you don't have an eye out for profit. The spice of life."

He shook his head. His eyes were warm. For the moment, his troubled look had faded. "Tell me this, Isabella," he said. "You've said your restaurant was in trouble because you couldn't get the best ingredients. Is this going to make that big a difference? Will all be well now?"

She hesitated, tempted to fudge the truth a little. This was such a subject of frustration for her. But when she looked at his face, she knew she could never be less than frank with him.

"No," she said simply. "All will not be well. My father

is a wonderful man and a good cook, but he can't run a business to save his life. We are in big trouble financially, and in all sorts of other ways. I'm not sure we'll last much longer no matter how much good food we cook up."

He nodded. From what she'd told him and a few things he'd heard from Renzo, he'd had a feeling that was the case.

"Maybe your father should let you take the reins," he said dryly. "You are the one who seems to have a passion for business."

That brought her up short, but she realized, very quickly, that he had a point. She had the instincts, though not the training. If only Luca would give her a chance…

"So what could I do to make a profit?" he asked her. "Besides turning my ancestral estate into a…what did you call it? A destination resort." He gave her a mock glare. "Something, by the way, that I would never do."

She took his question quite seriously. "Well, to begin with, you could renovate your vineyards. How about that? Wine sells very well these days."

He was laughing at her. It was obvious he wasn't taking this as seriously as she was. "Isabella, Isabella, what about the nobility of the grape?"

She made a face. "Nobility is a pose," she said. "Something that looks nice for special occasions, but is shed in a moment when it's no longer working for you."

He threw back his head and laughed aloud. "I can see you have big plans for me. What in particular?"

"I was thinking after seeing your abandoned vineyard…" She hesitated. Did she really want to tell him her thoughts? But why not? If not now, when?

"Well, you could hire my friend Giancarlo. The way some people restore businesses that have been run badly, he restores vineyards. I'm sure he can get you up and running in no time."

He gazed at her as though he wasn't sure just how seriously to take what she was saying. "So I can sell my grapes?"

"Why not? Or how about your own winery? With a tasting room? Then you could run tours from the village. People love to tour wineries. A little wine tasting, a small bistro on the premises…"

He was laughing at her but she didn't care. "You could run my restaurant," he said with a grin.

"Thank you." She made a pretend curtsy from the saddle. "I'd love to."

What a great idea. She fairly shivered with excitement over it. To think of running a restaurant for Max! Of making the special sauce for tourists who would come from far and wide…

But she quickly brought herself back down to earth. It was a pipe dream and she knew it. He refused to come face-to-face with strangers. He wouldn't even let vineyard workers on his land. How could he stand to have tourists? It wasn't going to happen.

They crested another hill and there below them was the field where the basil grew. She leaned forward in the saddle and sighed with relief. She'd had a dream during the night that she'd arrived here only to find the earth scorched and not a plant in sight. At least that hadn't happened.

But that dream had cast a pall on her morning. She'd thought of it with dread as she was preparing the picnic lunch to take with her. Was it a sign? Should she be prepared for the worst?

Susa had raised an eyebrow at the preparations, but didn't say a thing. Isabella ignored her and packed sandwiches in a basket and stowed them in her little car.

"Where are you going?" her father called from the doorway.

She hesitated. Should she tell him? Dashing back to give him a hug, she whispered in his ear, "I think I will have the basil with me when I return. Say a prayer for me." And she kissed his leathery cheek, turned and hurried off before he had time to question her further.

And all the time, she'd wondered if the basil would even be there once she made her way to it. Now she knew. It was here all right. And she was going to take as much of it as she could.

CHAPTER EIGHT

ISABELLA slid down off the horse and began to collect the basil, snipping leaves with little scissors she'd brought along with her. Max dismounted as well, but he stood back, watching her, and when she glanced up she noticed that all his good humor had fled. In fact, he looked ill at ease.

This was the place he considered too dangerous to let her visit alone, but she still couldn't really understand why. The hillside looked quite benign. The river was racing past below, and she knew how he felt about the river, but even if she started to slide there were plenty of places where she would be able to break her fall. No, she didn't get it. The place seemed fine to her.

The only problem was, the basil was not quite at its peak and there was only a limited amount she could harvest at the moment. She was going to have to discuss this with him and ask to come again in a week or so. Was he going to allow it? She had no idea.

It did seem all his warmth had evaporated and all he wanted to do was hurry up and get her to finish up and head for home again. Looking at his face, she decided to deal with her problem later.

"Okay," she told him at last, tying her two large bags together. "I think I have enough for now."

He nodded, handing her Mimi's reins and helping her aboard, then turning to mount his own horse. Isabella turned to look at him, and as she did the reins slipped from her hand.

"Oh!" She started to lean down to get them again, but the bags full of basil began to fall and she had to grab for them instead, stuffing them under a strap to hold them tightly secure.

And in that moment, something went wrong. She was never able to pinpoint exactly what happened, but something frightened the sweet, gentle horse who had been so pleasant all day, and suddenly she turned into a different animal.

"Max!" Isabella cried, grabbing handfuls of mane in order to keep from falling. "Stop her!"

Mimi wasn't waiting around to see what Max would do. She neighed in an alarming way and shot off toward the river.

"Max!"

Isabella hung on for dear life. The water was straight ahead.

"No, Mimi!" she cried, seeing another dunking in her future, at the very least. Closer and closer—the river looked inevitable. Then, suddenly Mimi veered away, racing along the bank, into the trees.

In a moment, a small clearing appeared, and a beautiful waterfall, and Mimi came to an abrupt stop. Too abrupt. Isabella sailed right over her head and landed in the brush. Mimi seemed to understand exactly what she'd done and decided not to stick around and find out what her punishment would be. Instead, she took off again, this time with an empty saddle.

Isabella moaned, pulling herself out of the brambles and seeing Max arrive just too late.

"At least I didn't get wet this time," she commented shakily, then stopped dead as she saw Max's ashen face. He leaped from his horse and grabbed her, looking her over as though he expected to find broken limbs and gaping flesh wounds.

"Are you all right?" he demanded harshly. "Isabella, are you okay?"

"I'm fine. I think." After all, she hadn't had time to take an inventory. "I'm okay, but poor Mimi…"

He swore in a way that would have sent chills down Mimi's spine if she'd heard him. "Never mind that damn horse. You could have been killed."

"But I wasn't."

"No, but…" He took her by the shoulders, searching her face, then looked over his shoulder at the waterfall with such a look of dread, it took her breath away.

"What is it, Max?"

She put her hands flat against his chest, staring into his face. And suddenly, she knew.

"Is this where…?"

He looked at her as though he'd never seen her before.

"We have to go," he said curtly. "We have to get out of here."

"Oh, Max."

He turned toward the horse and swung up, pulling her up in front of him just as he had that first night. His face was like stone but she could feel the tension in him and see it in the cords of his neck. His dark eyes were filled with pain and a pulse was beating at his temple. She saw all this and didn't dare say a word. Just before they started off, he looked back toward the waterfall and the anguish in his face sent her reeling. Here, obviously, was the core and crux of his torment. This had to be the place where his young wife had died.

They rode hard back toward the palazzo, but after a few minutes the horse swerved into another direction and she realized he was taking them to the Rossi cemetery instead. They arrived and he lowered her, then dismounted himself. Without a word, he turned and strode off into the courtyard. Biting her lip, she followed, though she wasn't at all sure she was welcome.

At first she thought he was heading for the little marble chapel, but he turned into the flower garden instead. Turning, he waited while she joined him. Her heart beat like a drum as she looked into the desolation in his eyes.

"Isabella, I'm sorry. I…I think you've probably guessed why I was upset near the waterfall. I just need a few minutes to unwind. If you could wait out by the chapel…"

"You want me to go and wait for you?"

"Yes. Please."

She was already shaking her head. "No," she said. "No, I won't go."

He stared at her as though he wasn't sure she understood. "Isabella…"

"Max." She grabbed his arm and looked up into his tortured face. "I think you should talk about it. I think you should tell me…"

"No." He pulled away from her touch. "I don't talk about this. Not to anyone."

"That's why you must," she insisted passionately.

He began to back away, but she wouldn't let him go. "Max, don't you see? You need to talk about it. You've probably been holding it all inside for ten years. You have to talk." Tears filled her eyes. Taking his arm again, she shook it, not sure what else she could do to convince him. "Tell me about her. What was she like?"

He stared down at her. "Laura?" he asked softly.

"Yes," she said. "Tell me about Laura."

He turned woodenly and slumped onto the garden bench. She slipped in beside him, taking his hand in hers.

"What did she look like?" she asked gently.

"An angel." His voice was gruff as gravel and he cleared his throat. "Blonde hair, light as a feather. And so fragile…" His voice broke.

Isabella squeezed his hand. "You loved her."

"Yes." He nodded. "I loved her from the moment I saw her." His voice was getting stronger. "She was good and kind and so very loving. Our life together was like a fairy tale. We were so happy."

Isabella nodded as he went on and on about his wonderful wife. His pain was clear in his voice and it was agony just to listen to him. But it was also good. She needed it, too. She wanted to understand him.

"When we found out we were going to have a baby," he said at last, "we thought life couldn't get any better."

A baby. Isabella blinked hard and looked away. She hadn't realized Laura was pregnant. That only made it all so much worse. Her heart already ached for him, now it broke in two.

"Our favorite place to have a picnic was by the waterfall," he was saying. "But we shouldn't have gone that day." His voice was almost a monotone now. "I'd been up most of the night before trying to solve a problem with the accountant. I was dead tired. But Laura had been planning a special celebration and I didn't want to disappoint her. So we went, and we toasted the baby that was on the way, and we ate Laura's special croissants that she had just learned how to make." His voice was suddenly choked. "And then we lay back on the blanket, wrapped in each other's arms. And the next thing I knew, I was opening my eyes and she was gone."

His hand was gripping hers tightly now, so tightly she could hardly stand it, but she didn't complain.

"I looked around. I couldn't imagine where she could have gone. And then I saw a bit of her dress floating in the water." A shudder went through him and he pulled his hand away from hers, leaning forward, his face in his hands. "I was in a frenzy. I pulled her from the water. Her foot had been stuck between two stones. I was so sure I could make her breathe again. I tried and tried. But it was too late. She was dead." His voice was harsh now, harsh and grating. "Gone forever."

And then his shoulders began to shake and she knew he was releasing his grief at last.

He blamed himself. She'd seen it in his eyes, in every fiber of his being, as though despair and regret were all he knew. He blamed himself and it was so unfair. How could she get him to see that?

She stayed beside him, very quiet, until she could sense he would accept a bit of comfort, and then she touched his back, rubbing her hand softly up and down.

"I'm sorry," she murmured. "Oh, Max, I'm so sorry."

He rose slowly and turned toward her, his face ravaged. "Don't be sorry for me," he said coldly. "I don't deserve it. I let her die. I let them both die."

She gasped. "Max, how can you say that? You were asleep."

"Yes. Exactly. I was asleep. I should have…" His voice faded.

"See? You can't even say what you should have done. You couldn't help it. Accidents are called accidents because no one means for them to happen."

He was shaking his head, looking at her with haunted eyes. "I should have saved her."

She searched her mind for some way to get him to see this from another perspective. "Should your father have saved your mother when she jumped from the balcony?" she said a bit wildly, and then clamped her hand over her mouth, realizing she didn't know enough about the incident to use it this way.

But to her surprise, he didn't seem to notice that. He answered directly. "He couldn't have done anything. She was alone at home when it happened. How could he have stopped that?"

Isabella threw out her hands. "And Laura was alone when she went into the water. You weren't there. You were asleep." She shook his arm again. "Max, you couldn't help it. It's not your fault."

He looked doubtful, but she could tell he was beginning to mull that over. She shook her head.

"At least you talked about it," she said.

He gave her a sardonic look. "Quite the junior psychologist, aren't you?" he said, but there was no animosity in his voice. To his own surprise, he did feel better. Not much, but a little better. Maybe.

And she could see the truth in him, in his face, in his attitude. She was glad she'd risked everything on pushing him to talk. For now, it seemed to have worked out for him. There was so much guilt, so much self-doubt in his heart. And for her, there was so much new background that she knew about him. No matter what she learned, everything only made her regard for him grow. Her father and Susa were wrong. She was glad she hadn't stayed away from royalty after all.

There was just one thing that still nagged at her. She didn't know the details of the crash that had taken his face, the accident no one seemed to know anything about. That was still a mystery.

* * *

"You're going to have to ride with me again," he told her as he led in the stallion, and she nodded, thinking what a contrast this was to the other night in the dark.

"It's way past noon," she fretted. "Now don't you wish we'd brought the picnic I made?"

He nodded, feeling a touch of chagrin. Looking at her, he realized what a fool he'd been. He'd thought he could keep her at arm's length if he only tried hard enough. Now he knew that wasn't going to happen. Though he couldn't see how anything real and lasting between them could work out in the long run, for now, when she was near, he was going to live in the moment. No more pretending, especially to himself.

"I'm hungry as a wolf," he admitted.

She grinned up at him. "I have a solution to that. There's a place very near here we can get the most wonderful food."

"What are you talking about?" he asked suspiciously.

"Do you know the little stand by the reservoir? Where the Spanish family sells tapas?"

His face cleared. "Yes, I've driven past it."

"And you've never been tempted to stop?"

He half smiled down at her. Her lively interest in everything was contagious. "Actually, I have, but…"

She put a hand on his arm. "We're going there."

That was going a little far. "What? Who's going where?" He thought she understood he didn't do things like that.

"You and me. We're going to go have some of his delicious tapas. You'll thank me for this."

He stood where he was, shaking his head and looking stubborn. "Isabella, I don't think…"

"Oh, Max, please." She hung on his arm and looked adorably hungry. "It's just outside your walls. We'll go out the gate and we'll ride up and you can stay outside, under the trees. I'll go in and order the food. There are tables along the water." She made her face even more appealing. "At this time of day, we'll probably be the only ones there. You won't have to come face-to-face with another soul. I'll do that part."

He was still frowning but she could see he was going to bend. "I don't know."

"Yes, you do." She gave him her most playful smile. "You know very well you need this. You want it." She pulled on his arm. "Come on."

He gave in. He couldn't help it. To do anything else would seem churlish right now. He helped her up in front of him on his horse and they made their way through the gate, to the outside of the estate. This was territory he hadn't traveled in years, except to rush past in his limousine. There was something freeing about just venturing this far beyond his own walls.

The tables on the rise above the river were completely empty. He sat at one of them and she went in, bringing out a wonderful collection of small, delicious items, including prawn croquetas and chopped pork empanadas and sautéed artichokes. Señor Ortega trailed behind her carrying two bottles of cold beer, and Max tensed, waiting for the man to react to his scars. Maybe Isabella had warned him, but he showed no sign of noticing a thing, chattering on in his Spanish-accented Italian about how they should come back tomorrow because he was planning to make the best tapas ever seen in these parts and if they didn't return, they would miss that.

He smiled and nodded at the man, who turned back to the little stand, still talking as he went.

"Señor Ortega is a friend of my father's," Isabella told

him comfortably. "Someday he'll have his own full-size restaurant, just like we do."

The food was wonderful and the beer was ice-cold. They ate and talked and even laughed a bit together as though they'd known each other forever. Whenever she stopped to think about it, Isabella felt a glow. She could hardly believe they seemed so good together. She'd never known a man like this before.

They finished up and walked the horse back to the estate gate.

"You see?" she told him. "That wasn't so bad. You need to get out more and be a part of this area. After all, this place is yours. Your ancestors owned all this land and developed the village originally, didn't they? You can't just walk away and pretend it has no connection to you."

He rolled his eyes and made a gesture with his hand meant to show that she talked too much, and she laughed.

They stopped while he used his code to open the gate. It creaked out of the way, giving them room to enter, and she looked up and down the length of what she could see of the long stucco wall.

"I can't believe you have this wall around your whole huge property," she said. "It must be miles and miles long."

"And it took years and years to build it. About four hundred of them."

She sighed, feeling the history and the romance of it all. "And now the wind and rain and everything else is working hard to tear it back down again," she noted wistfully.

"Yes." He steadied his horse and helped her mount. "Just like that Robert Frost poem about there being something that does not love a wall," he added as he came up behind her and settled her into a comfortable place in front of him. "Nature abhors a wall more than it does a vacuum."

She nodded, relaxing against him and feeling his arms come around her waist with a sense of warm pleasure. "Maybe you should work on tearing down some of your walls," she murmured.

He groaned. "How did I know you were going to go in that direction?"

"Because you know you need to do it."

His voice hardened a bit. "I'm not going to be lectured by you," he warned her carefully.

She caught her breath. She certainly didn't want to put him off, but, still, he needed to begin to live a real life, and if she didn't help him do that, what good was she to him?

"Oh?" she said, deciding to use a humorous tone to help defray resentment. "Then who *will* you let do the lecturing?"

"No one."

His voice was firm, but not angry, and she risked going on with it.

"You see? That's your problem right there. You need other people in your life. You need to be with others, talk to people, hear some new opinions on things, new experiences in life. You're alone too much."

He shrugged. "I have the Internet."

"The Internet!" She turned to try to look him in the face. "That's like interacting with robots."

"They're not robots." He actually sounded a bit offended that she would say such a thing. "They're real people on real computers. I'm not quite the hermit you think I am."

She shook her head. "You can't see the people, you can't judge their emotions. You can't see their truth."

"Truth," he scoffed.

"Real life is better," she insisted stubbornly.

He was silent for a moment, then he said, softly, "Real life can be painful."

She drew in her breath. "Yes." She wished she could turn and hug him. He was holding her, but loosely, impersonally. It was odd to be so close, and yet so far apart. "Pain is like rain. You need it to grow."

He made a sound that was derisive, but with a touch of amusement that let her know he wasn't taking offense to all her philosophizing.

"Too much rain floods out life," he said, making it sound as though he were trying to bring in his own words to live by to stand against hers. "What then?" he challenged her.

"Then we learn to tread water," she shot back.

He laughed softly. "Don't worry about me, Bella. This is my lot in life. I can handle it."

She loved that he'd used that affectionate nickname for her, but she wasn't sure she liked the way his thoughts were tending otherwise.

She didn't know what he meant. Was he expressing a fatalistic acceptance of his scars, or was he saying he could rise above that if he wished? She wanted to know, but she wasn't sure she wanted to ask him to explain. So she was silent for the rest of the ride back to the castle.

They found Mimi grazing peacefully in the yard outside the kitchen with only about half the basil left under the strap that held the bags. Her wild ride to get home again must have sprayed it across the landscape.

"What a shame," Max said, a smile in his eyes. "It looks like you'll have to come back tomorrow and do this all over again."

She turned to look at him. He reached out and touched her cheek with the palm of his hand. She covered his hand with her own as she searched his eyes.

"Shall I come back?" she asked him, wanting to make sure.

He nodded. "Yes," he said.

She smiled at him, thinking of all they had been through today, and her heart was full. There were no words she could use, not right now. So she did the only thing she could think of. And in that moment, she would have done anything for him.

Reaching up, she took his face between her hands and kissed his mouth. He started to pull away at first, but she didn't let him go. She kissed him and held him close and used her body to tell him what she couldn't say with words. In a moment, he responded, curling his arms around her and kissing her back.

When she finally drew back, her eyes were swimming with tears, but his were smiling.

"Isabella," he said softly, holding her chin in his hand as he looked into her eyes with something close to affection. "How did you so quickly become the sunshine of my life? Without you, I live in darkness. I only wish…"

He didn't say what he wished, but she thought she knew. He wished she were just a little different. He wished he were just a bit more free to act on his inclinations. She wished those things too, and her heart broke a little just because reality was so cruel. But, for now, she was happy just to be with him. It was all she needed.

Isabella's joy in the day faded quickly once she got back to the restaurant. Her father was waiting for her, his face creased with worry.

"Where have you been?" he demanded.

"I…Papa, I've brought back basil." She lifted the bag to show him. "We'll be able to use it again right away. I…"

"You've been with the prince." He said the words as though she'd destroyed herself and her family's reputation in one fell swoop and there was no turning back.

"What?"

She tried to laugh at his serious attitude. It was so completely over the top and something she'd never expected from him. But he was obviously sincere. This sort of anguish just floored her.

"Papa, it's all right. He's allowing me to continue to harvest the leaves and he's helping me...."

Luca waved away her explanations. "I've heard all about it. I know you've been seeing him. And we all know what that means."

Her head went back. She didn't deserve this. Anger shot through her veins. Here she'd practically turned her life inside out in order to get the desperately needed ingredient, and when she returned in triumph, no one cared.

"Yes, I've been seeing him," she retorted. "But I don't think it means what you seem to think it does."

He turned away, muttering curses and complaints and she stared after him, more angry than she'd been in ages. She was not one to dwell upon resentments, but she was feeling some now. After all she'd done for her family, after all her sacrifices and delayed dreams, she didn't need payment—but she certainly could use a little acceptance and compassion. After all, she was very likely falling in love with a man she would never be able to have for her own. And all because she was trying to save the restaurant. A little family support would be helpful.

"You didn't tell me," he said, turning back. "Why didn't you tell me?"

"Because..."

That was a question. Why hadn't she told him? She usually told him everything. Now that she thought about it, she could see that not telling him made it seem as though she were ashamed, and there was nothing to be ashamed about.

"I guess I didn't want to get your hopes up about the basil," she said, knowing that was lame.

"Oh, Isabella, my beautiful daughter."

His voice echoed with despair. He swayed as though he was about to fall and she hurried to help him stay upright, then gave him an arm as she led him back into the restaurant and through the kitchen where Susa was grating chocolate, into the little room behind where he could rest.

Once she had him settled, she came out and asked Susa, "What on earth is going on? Why is he so upset?"

She shrugged. "He has a point, you know. Nothing good can come from these liaisons with princes."

Isabella threw out her hands. "Sorry, but I beg to differ. Something good has already come from them."

She pointed to the bag of basil. Then her chin rose defiantly.

"And anyway, I like the man and he likes me. We have fun together. End of story."

Susa shook her head, not giving an inch. "That's what they all say when the relationship begins," she noted gloomily. "It's later when reality sets in like crows on the clothesline."

Isabella stared at the older woman. "You have no faith in me, either one of you." She threw up her hands. "Maybe I should just go. Maybe I should go back to the city and forget all about helping out here."

"Maybe you should," Susa said. "But for now, your father is worried about other things besides the precious feelings of his little girl. Fredo Cavelli has filed a formal complaint with the village board."

Isabella whirled, her anger forgotten. "What?"

That really was bad news. If the board actually accepted his complaint, there would be an investigation. They might have to hire a lawyer to defend their interests. And where would the money come from for something like that?

"Your father says he can fight this on his own," Susa said, shaking her head, when Isabella brought that up. "I say, God help us all."

Isabella sighed. You solved one problem and another jumped up to take its place. Happened every time. So what was she going to do about this one?

"First," she told Susa, "I'm going to write to Cristiano and Valentino to come home and help with this attack on our livelihood." Another flash of anger roiled through her. Why were her brothers never here to help carry some of this burden? "They should be coming home soon for Papa's birthday anyway."

"Are you planning a party?"

Isabella hesitated, then let herself relax a bit. "Of course. Just a family party, but we need to celebrate. Papa needs the moral support, if nothing else."

"I'll start work on a cake right now," Susa said, looking happier.

Isabella frowned fiercely, gathering strength. "Then I'm going to come in here and start a big vat of sauce for the evening dinner rush."

"Good." Susa nodded approvingly. "That'll show them."

Isabella laughed and gave the older woman an affectionate hug. "You better believe it," she agreed, and went off to do just that.

Despite everything, Isabella went to the castle the next day. She and Max rode out on horseback again. This time they took the picnic lunch she brought and spread it out on a cloth at the hillside. The sun was shining, the day was fresh and clear, and something seemed to be sparkling in the air.

For some reason, she found herself telling him about the unpleasant reception she'd had when she got home the day before. A little of her anger still lingered, and he could tell.

"It's because they love you," he told her. "They think they're protecting you."

"They think they're controlling me, you mean," she shot back.

"That too," he admitted. "But I'm sure they're worried about the restaurant and that colors their emotions." He looked at her sideways. "Have you considered taking out a loan to get you through this rough patch?" he asked.

Her heart skipped a beat. He was ready to offer a loan to her family. She could tell by his tentative tone. That was unbelievably generous of him and it warmed her. But she shook her head quickly.

"My father is already up to his chin in loan repayment bills," she told him. "He can't handle any more."

"Hmm."

He looked thoughtful and she smiled. Yes, she could easily fall head over heels for this man. Sadness still haunted the recesses of his eyes, but it didn't seem to dominate his spirit the way it had before. His smile seemed more genuine. And he laughed more. He was opening up to her more than she would have dreamed possible just a few days before.

And that was good, because Isabella had plans. She had ideas. She had projects swirling in her head. She wanted to tell him, but she knew she had to take it slowly so as not to scare him off.

Max had no plans at all. He was enjoying her and enjoying the day, and that was all he thought about. Little by little he began to realize she had more on her mind, but he didn't flinch. As she tentatively brought up the vineyard

and what a shame it was to let it go to waste he listened.
He was enchanted by her and her enthusiasms and he didn't
want to tell her that her ideas were crazy.

So by the end of the day, they had a compromise of
sorts. He would allow her to bring her friend to take a look
at the vineyard and give an estimate of what it would take
to bring it back into production. And he would give it a fair
consideration. Then she would bring more of her restaurant's wonderful famous sauce for him to have on his pasta
for his dinner.

She felt good about it. It was so obvious to her that he
was ready. She wouldn't be pushing if she weren't sure of
that. If what he really wanted was to be alone, that was his
choice. But she could tell he was ready to spread his wings.
All he needed was the space and the opportunity to fly.

CHAPTER NINE

THE next few days seemed to race by. Isabella went to the castle nearly every day on one pretext or another, and Max was just as complicit as she was in finding reasons she should be there. They seemed to mesh so well, and their interest in each other was new and still overwhelming. Max told Isabella everything he could think of about his childhood, and she still asked for more. Then he quizzed her about the village, about her brothers, about her father's past, about her childhood and her dreams as a young adult.

"I went to library school for a while," she told him. "I was actually thinking of a career in a big university library. I dreamed about going to live in the city, of being a part of the hustle and bustle, the lights and the excitement."

Her eyes shone as she talked about it and he smiled.

"What happened?"

She sighed. "My father got sick. My brothers were both gone, so I came home to help him."

He nodded. It was just what he'd feared. She was the one whose shoulders were supposed to be big enough to carry all the weight. And here she was, ready to take up his concerns as well.

He asked more about the restaurant and she filled him

in. Once she started, it was as if she'd opened the floodgates and she opened up about her worries for her father,
about the state of the family finances and how worried she
was about the haphazard way her father had managed
things. And finally, she even told him about the problems
with Fredo Cavelli.

Max frowned as he listened to all this. "Can he really
do any damage to your restaurant?" he asked.

She thought for a moment. "You know, I didn't think so
until very recently. He was always just an old grouch who
had a grudge against my father. But now that he's become
big friends with the mayor and managed to get a seat on the
planning commission, he's starting to make me nervous."

He listened sympathetically, nodding and asking intelligent questions at all the right times. And she realized he
was the first person she'd ever told all these things to.
Suddenly that seemed very, very significant to her.

"If it's money your father needs," he began.

"No," she said quickly. "You are generous to a fault,
Max. But my father needs more than money right now. He
needs his family to get together and help him."

Max nodded. "Now, that's up to you to handle," he told
her. "You're the one they will all listen to."

"What?" She couldn't imagine where he could have got
that idea. "No one listens to me."

He gave her a penetrating look. "They will if you let
them know how important the family is to you, and to
them. Try it. I think you'll be surprised." He squeezed her
hand. "And in the meantime, if your father has more trouble
with the board, I might be able to make a few phone calls
and pull a few strings myself."

She loved that he was offering, but couldn't foresee a
time when his help could really make a difference. He still

didn't leave the castle walls. But his other advice was sound and she took it to heart.

She marveled at how her life had changed in such a short time. Who would have believed that she would so quickly become so at home in the castle? And so very happy there. The place seemed to be timeless, ageless, forever. If only that could really be true.

To her surprise, Renzo had become an ally of sorts. She'd been straightforward with him from the beginning.

"You know what I'm trying to do, don't you?" she asked him one day while Max was on the telephone with a researcher he often collaborated with.

"No, miss." The man looked more like a walking skeleton every day. "Perhaps you should explain it to me."

Isabella took a deep breath and searched for the right words. "I guess I would say that I'm trying to find a way to get the prince to come out of his shell a little, to take part in the wider life of the community he lives in."

"Ah."

She couldn't read a thing in that reaction.

"He's been living here, away from everyone else, though wonderfully protected by you and his family, for almost ten years now."

"Yes, miss."

"Do you think it's been good for him?"

Renzo hesitated. "Well, I do think that a large part of him has healed over that time."

She smiled, relieved. She'd been so afraid he would take offense at what she was doing. "Oh, I'm so glad to hear you say that. So you agree with me that it is time for him to branch out a bit?"

She held her breath, waiting to see what his verdict was.

"Yes. Yes, I do."

She closed her eyes and laughed a little. "Thank goodness. I was afraid…"

"No, miss," he said stoutly. "I will help you in any way I can."

She took his hand and shook it vigorously. "Thank you, Mr. Renzo. Thank you so much."

"I've known him since he was a boy," Renzo continued solemnly. "He's a wonderful man, you know. He's suffered too much. He deserves more out of life than what he's been given so far."

"We agree on that."

He nodded. He didn't quite smile, but she had a feeling he never did. "I could see from the first that you were a good-hearted lady," he went on. "I just want to help."

It was such a relief not to have to fight against Max's oldest employee and closest companion. Just knowing that he was in her corner gave her courage and she didn't waste any time.

The very next day, she brought in her friend the contractor to take a look at the vineyards. Having been warned ahead about what to expect and how she wanted him to act around Max, Giancarlo did fine. His face did register a bit of shock when he first caught sight of the scars, but he quickly settled down and treated Max like anyone at all.

So far so good. Now to convince him that the large mentioned sum would be worth the effort in expenditure. Giancarlo put up a pretty good argument and Max promised to think it over. The contractor left and Max didn't seem unduly bothered by the entire process. She breathed another sigh of relief.

And when Giancarlo returned the next day with a wine expert, just to give Max more information, that meeting went just fine as far as she could see.

To her eyes, he seemed to be blossoming. Little by little, he was beginning to be able to accept others in a way he hadn't been able to do for so long. She told him as much that day as they sat out on the veranda and ate a simple lunch.

"I think you've developed a sort of paranoia by living alone for so long," she told him. "Most people are perfectly willing to accept people who are different, once they get used to it. It's the surprise that gets them at first. Then, when they realize it's only skin-deep, they are usually okay with it."

"You've made a detailed study of this, I presume?" he teased her.

"Sure," she shot back. "Live and let live is the motto of our age," she added with a flourish meant to overwhelm his doubts.

He shook his head and his mouth twisted with his signature cynicism. "You're dreaming."

She gave him a mock glare. "If so, it's a good dream. Why not join me?"

He shrugged. He knew what she meant. She was so set on his starting off on this project. "Tell me this, Bella, why does the world need a Rossi vineyard?"

She leaned forward, her eyes big. "It's not just that. You need to be a part of your community. And just think of the jobs you could provide. People around here could live better lives, all because of you."

He bit back a grin. "What if I don't care if all those anonymous people I've never met are getting jobs or not?"

"You should care," she maintained stoutly. "That's why you have to go out and meet them. Then you'll care."

He groaned, but he didn't tell her to stop planning.

She brought in plants to fill in a bare spot in the gardens at the mausoleum. She loved going there, loved looking at the statue that reminded her of Max. He went along with her and helped break up the soil. And he told her about his beautiful mother and how she'd loved this garden. And somehow he went on to describe how destroyed she'd been when the people had turned against her as her looks had faded.

"For some reason, when a woman is that beautiful, it becomes the most important thing about her," Isabella said, agreeing with him. "Nothing else she does, no matter how much genius it displays, is held to the same esteem."

He nodded, thinking of his mother. "The celebrity culture needs its routine sacrifices, and she was one of them."

Isabella put a hand on his knee and looked up into his huge dark eyes. She knew very well that what had happened to his mother had colored how he looked at his own loss of beauty.

"It's very sad, but you can't let it affect you."

He smiled down at her, but he knew she was right. It had affected him. And it was high time he reversed that process.

Later that evening, Isabella got up the nerve to ask Renzo a very sensitive question. She'd made dinner for the three of them and was in the kitchen, gathering her supplies and getting ready to head home. Max was off doing some research on the Internet.

"Tell me something, Renzo," she said, turning to find him preparing breadcrumbs from the leftover garlic bread for toasting. "I know the prince was scarred in an accident, but I don't know much about the details. Are you willing to tell me what happened?"

She watched his eyes to see how he would react to that question but he didn't give away any clues.

"Have you asked him?"

She shook her head. "He's never volunteered the information and I don't want to make him relive it if it's just too painful for him. But if you'd rather not say…"

Slowly, he shook his head. "I think it would be better if you talked to him about it directly, miss."

Sighing, she nodded. She knew he was right. Walking out onto the terrace, she looked up at the stars. She remembered the day he'd told her about how Laura had died. Could she really ask him to do this as well? It seemed she was going to have to.

Max came out to join her a short time later.

"Max, I need to know. About your scars…" She raised her hand and touched his face. "How did it happen?"

His hand covered hers. "Do you want the official story? Or the truth?"

She searched his eyes. His words were bitter but his gaze was clear. "Don't they say the truth will set you free?" she asked softly.

"They say a lot of things meant to sound smart that are nothing but hot-air balloons," he told her, thrusting his hands deep into his pockets. "Okay, Bella, you asked for it. Here goes." He tilted his head back as though searching for the Milky Way. "It happened the night Laura died."

Her heart lurched. She'd been afraid of that.

"I raced her lifeless body to the hospital, knowing there was really no hope, but praying some miracle might happen. They tried. They did everything humanly possible. But she…" His voice choked and he paused for a moment, regaining his composure.

She put her hand over her heart, aching with the pain he must have felt that day. She rocked back and forth, wishing she could take it from him somehow. But that could never happen. It was his burden to hold forever. All she could do was hope, in some simple way, to help him deal with it.

"She was still dead," he said as he went on, his voice

rough. "They couldn't perform miracles and I found I had no magic powers either. It was hopeless. I was hopeless. I had just let my wife and my unborn child die while I lay snoozing a few feet away."

He turned to look at her, his eyes burning. "The horror of that, the pain and the guilt, were just too deep to bear. As I drove myself home, I found myself going faster and faster. I couldn't think of a reason to slow down. I no longer had anything to live for. The rest of my life would be hell on earth. What was the point?"

"Oh, Max. You didn't…"

He winced. "I aimed straight for that tree. All I could think of was joining Laura." He looked at her again. "So now you know."

"Yes." She barely whispered the word. In trying to end his suffering, he'd only made his own suffering worse—but perhaps that was what he'd wanted to do. She nodded. It didn't really surprise her. But she felt such utter sadness. He'd made his own hellish prison on earth and now he didn't know how to break out of it. She didn't speak. Her throat was choked with unshed tears. But she understood better now. She knew he'd created his own special torture. He'd locked himself away here because he thought he deserved it. It wasn't just that he didn't like the way people reacted to his face—he thought of it as a punishment. He thought he deserved never to connect with the rest of humanity. It was his lot in life, his life sentence, and he had no right to try to overturn it.

No reprieves for the Rossi prince.

Finally, tears filled her eyes and she could cry. She tried to turn away, but he wouldn't let her. Gently, carefully, he took her into his arms and held her close. And she cried.

She cried for Laura, and the tiny baby. She cried for Max and his mountain of pain. And she cried for herself.

"Don't cry, Bella," he said at last. "I only got what I deserved."

And that only made her start sobbing all over again.

Finally, she pulled back and looked up into his face, half laughing, wiping away the tears.

"Look, I've ruined your shirt," she said, putting her hand over the wet spots and feeling his heart beating very hard beneath her palm, as though he'd been running, as though he were feeling…

Her own heart began to pump in response. And then she looked up at him, her lips parted, waiting.

He looked down and she could see the struggle behind his eyes. He wanted to kiss her as much as she wanted it herself. Why, oh, why was he fighting it?

It was a question that was bothering her more and more lately. She'd never felt anything this close to love before, not with any man. She wanted to tell him so. She wanted his arms around her; she wanted his mouth on hers. She wanted his kiss.

He'd kissed her the day she'd let herself into his house with her sauce for him to sample. The entire encounter had been unexpected and he hadn't been prepared. His defenses had been down. His kiss had been spiced with a wildness that he'd quickly leashed, but she had been able to sense it flowing just under the surface. He'd been so gorgeous with his naked chest and his wet hair. Her heart beat like thunder whenever she thought of it.

She knew he cared for her. She even knew that he felt a strong attraction. A connection of excitement arced between them every time their gazes met across a room. When he helped put on her cloak in the evening, his fingers lingered on the slope of her neck and she knew he was aching to let his hands slide down and cup her breasts. She could feel it. And still he didn't kiss her.

She turned quickly once, wearing a light and skimpy vest-top, and let her breasts brush against the hair on his bare arm, making her nipples harden beneath the cloth. He watched her do it and the chords of his neck stood out like a mountain range while the color of his eyes deepened almost to purple. He clenched his fists and she knew it was taking a tremendous effort for him not to reach for her.

But he didn't. The moment passed, and he turned away as though he couldn't bear to look at her any longer.

She knew what the problem was. He didn't foresee any possibility that their light and friendly relationship would last, or that it could turn into anything meaningful, and he didn't want to set up any expectations in her mind. She knew he was probably right, but when she was with him, she hardly cared. She just wanted to touch him, to kiss him, to glory in the feeling they had between them.

So she waited, her lips parted, her eyes dreamy, and practically begged him to bend down and take control.

"Isabella," he began, his voice slightly choked. *"Cara mia."* He was shaking his head.

"Max!" She grabbed his arm and glared up at him. "If you don't kiss me, I'm going to walk out that door and never come back!"

His dark eyes warmed and then he was laughing at her again. "Bella," he said affectionately, reaching up to rake his fingers through the hair behind her shell-like ear. "You're lying."

"You think I won't do it?" she demanded wildly.

He pulled her closer. "I know you won't," he said, his warm breath singeing her lips. "But this should seal the deal."

And he kissed her.

All her wildness dissolved at his touch. This was what she'd been waiting for—living for. His mouth on hers was hot and his tongue was rough and his arms were hard with masculine strength that took her breath away. She could feel his hunger and it sent a sense of relief through her. He wanted her as much as she wanted him.

She could let go. She could sink into this feeling without fear, and she did, opening up her soul as she opened her heart. Her fingers sank into his thick hair, pulling him up harder against where she was arched, trying to feel as much of him as she could.

With her mouth, her tongue, her hands, her body, she was telling him, *Here I am. Take me. I'm yours.*

His hard, beautiful hands slid down her sides to her back and then cupped her bottom, pressing her even closer into the refuge of his hips. He knew it would take only seconds to lose himself in the heat of her kiss and let it build into something more serious. The urgency he'd been keeping under such tight control was stirring and he knew just how dangerous that could be. He should pull back and let her understand what she was risking.

But he couldn't do it—not yet. He'd had dreams about how it could be with them, and to have her in his arms like this made it all seem so much more possible. As he explored her mouth, her skin, her ear, she seemed to melt at his touch, as though she were made to love him.

"Bella," he moaned, his mind foggy with desire. *"Cara mia."*

She murmured something but he didn't know what she was saying. He was lost in the vortex. In another moment, he would be over the edge. He had to turn this back. He pulled his head away, groaning from a place deep inside.

His vision was blurred, but she looked like a goddess, too tempting to resist. Still, he managed.

"Bella, no," he muttered against her ear. "We have to stop."

She sighed, but she didn't argue. She pulled back away from him so that nothing was touching, but then she leaned her face close again and kissed him. Lips to lips, heart to heart. How could he turn that away? They'd gone from sweetness to searing fire and back to sweetness again.

The kiss went on and on. If she had her way, it would never stop.

She knew it now—she knew he was hers, at least for the moment, and she was flooded with a feeling of lightness and joy, as though a thousand angels were singing a Beethoven chorus in her heart.

This was good. This was the way things ought to be.

But the beautiful singing ended abruptly, like a scratch on a record, when Max's sister Angela entered the room.

"Well, excuse me," she said, but she didn't go back out again. Instead, she stood where she was and waited for them to compose themselves.

"Angela," Max said, turning reluctantly and straightening his shirt and not looking the least bit uncomfortable. "To what do we owe this unexpected visit?"

"I don't know how it can be unexpected when I told you I was coming back here this weekend."

"Oh." He frowned. "That's right. There's been so much going on around here, I'd forgotten all about that."

"So it seems." She pretended to smile. "So nice to see you again, Isabella. I hope the restaurant is doing well?"

"Yes, thank you," Isabella answered, trying to play this as cool as Max was, but knowing she wasn't quite as unruffled as he. She'd finally got Max to throw away his inhibitions and really kiss her, and now this!

"Very good." Angela gave her brother a scathing glance. "Well, I'll just go unpack my things. It seems Renzo forgot I was coming as well." She started out the door, then looked back and said with a touch of amused irony, "I'm beginning to feel downright unwelcome." And just before she disappeared, she made a face that almost made Isabella like her.

"You'd better go," Max told her. He touched her cheek and looked as if he might kiss her again, but then he didn't. "See you tomorrow?" he asked, regret in his eyes.

"Of course," she responded.

But she was the one who harbored the most remorse. Something told her this kiss hadn't really started a trend, and it was going to be just as much of an effort on her part before she got him to do it again. If only he could believe in something good between the two of them. If only she could convince him it might work.

But even thinking that surprised her, because it meant she'd begun to hope—maybe a little too much? Time would tell.

Angela stayed for three days but Isabella only spent time alone with her once. She was polite enough, but she seemed very skeptical about Isabella's place in the scheme of things.

"I understand you're lobbying for some big changes around here," she said as they came face-to-face in the kitchen one morning.

Isabella lifted her chin. "Yes, in fact, I am."

Angela raised one sleek eyebrow. "We all know Max has been lonely for a long time. It wouldn't be difficult for a pretty young woman like you to cast a spell that led him into something he wasn't prepared for. Something totally inappropriate."

Isabella took a deep breath. Angela seemed to think she

could be cowed. How interesting. Angela was going to have to think again.

"I think you underestimate your brother. Of course he's as capable of a flirtation as any man, but he's as careful and cynical as any man I've ever known as well. He's certainly nobody's pushover."

Angela's eyes widened. "Of course not. I didn't mean to imply any such thing." She frowned. "But, Isabella, it's plain as the nose on your face. You two are crazy about each other right now. The air fairly sizzles between you." She hesitated and looked suspicious. "You're not…?"

"No. No, we're not."

She nodded, looking relieved. "Well, I'm sure you understand that his family will have a say in any major decisions he makes about his future."

Isabella blinked. Did she mean what it sounded like she meant? "Angela, if you're worried we're going to run off and elope or something, I think you can rest easy on that score. I have no plans to try to snare your brother."

Angela nodded skeptically. "Plans are one thing, the heat of passion is another."

Isabella was trying hard to hold her temper.

"I don't think you should worry. I understand that he has duties and responsibilities to a larger universe than the relationship he and I have together. A different universe than the one I come from. I don't have any fantasies on that score."

Angela nodded. "Well, I'm pleased to see you have a head on your shoulders."

Isabella smiled. "On the other hand, if Max decides to do something, I don't think you will have a hope in heaven of stopping him."

Angela winced, then gave Isabella a penetrating look. "Tell me this. Do you think you are in love with my brother?"

She drew her breath in sharply. She could be blunt, but that would be offensive. So she rounded the edges a little. "Honestly, that is not something I've been thinking about. Much, anyway," she added softly.

Angela's eyes flashed. "So you won't tell me one way or another."

Isabella finally let her anger spill out. "Angela, I don't actually think it's any of your business how I feel about Max. I owe you a certain regard and a certain common courtesy, but I'm not going to spill out the inner workings of my heart and brain for you to pore over. Those are mine alone."

Angela stared at her for a long moment, then, unexpectedly, she laughed.

"Good answer," she said. "And I like you the better for it."

And that was the end of that encounter.

They all breathed a sigh of relief when Angela decamped. It allowed them to go back to the comfortable atmosphere they'd had before she came and it gave Isabella a bit of room to try to convince Max he should renovate the vineyards.

"Just look at the majesty of all this," she said as they walked through a portion where the grape plants still had green shoots and looked recoverable. "Can you imagine what it would be like?"

"There's something to that," Max mused as they strolled along. "There is something rejuvenating about plants that lose their leaves and then come back like the phoenix to show off their glory again."

"The rebirth of hope," she agreed.

"Yes." He nodded, his head to the side thoughtfully, and she smiled. She was winning. She could feel it.

"Watch out." His arm shot out to protect her from a broken stake, and then he was curling her into his arms. "Isabella," he said warningly.

She laughed, pressing against him with sheer joy in the body contact. "I didn't do this," she protested. "It was all you."

He kissed her softly and let her go and she sighed, wanting more, knowing she was going to have to wait. "Let's sit here by this little rose garden," she said, shielding her eyes from the sun. "It's hot out here today."

They sat in the shade and looked out over the plants again. "Have you thought about the estimate Giancarlo gave you?" she asked.

He nodded. "I could buy a new yacht for what he wants," he said. "A racing yacht and a racing crew to go with it."

"Oh." She was disappointed. "Is it really too much?"

"Yes," he said. "Tell me this, Bella. If you had a lot of money, what would you use it for?"

She thought for a moment. He probably expected her to say she would throw it away on his vineyards. Or help the poor. Or some other noble gesture. But she had another project in mind.

She looked at him and wondered if she dared say it. Taking a deep breath, she prepared for the worst.

"Max, if I had enough money, I would hire the best surgeon in the world to do something about the scars on your face."

He stared at her, shocked. "What?"

She reached out for his hand. "Not because I want you to change," she told him quickly. "I've told you before that I think you are the most beautiful man in the world, and your scars only make you more precious to me. But I would like to see you lose them because I want you to stop punishing yourself. Ten years is long enough. You deserve a pardon."

Picking up her hand, he brought it to his lips and opened it so that he could kiss her palm. "I don't need a pardon," he said softly, looking up at her through her spread fingers. "*Bella mia*, I have you."

Her heart seemed to swell at his words. Were they only meant in play? She couldn't be sure.

"Tell me, Max. Have you ever looked into surgery?"

He shook his head. "No."

"I knew it. You haven't even tried."

"You're right."

"I've seen some amazing things done with—"

"No." He dropped her hand and looked almost stern. "I could never do that."

She searched his eyes. "Why not?"

He shrugged and looked away. "You said it yourself. This is my punishment."

His voice hardened as he turned back to look deep into her eyes.

"Bella, I slept while my wife and child died in front of me. Don't you think I deserve a little pain for that?"

"No." She was passionate about that. "No, not at all. You've had enough pain to last a lifetime."

Their gazes held for a long moment. Finally, Max tried to smile. "So you see, we disagree." His smile widened as he studied her pretty face and took up her hand again.

"Bella, Bella, you take these things too hard." He kissed her fingers, one by one. "Maybe I should get a mask like that fellow in *Phantom of the Opera*. Do you think that would suit me?"

She'd settled down by now and could joke with him if that was what he wanted.

"I don't know." She pretended to consider it, then looked at him sharply. "How well do you sing?"

He looked surprised. "Oh, you have to sing?"

"Sure. It goes with the territory."

They laughed together. It was good to laugh. Laughter

took some of the sting out of the pain. And Lord knew she was ready to do anything she could to do that for him.

"Okay, Bella," he said finally, dropping her hand again. "Call your friend Giancarlo. We'll see if we can work something out on renovating a portion of the field."

"Oh!" She threw her arms around his neck and kissed his cheek. "Oh, I'm so glad!" She stopped. "But wait, only a portion?"

He nodded. "For now, greedy little lady. We'll just take this one step at a time."

"Oh. Of course." She calmed herself down. Naturally he wanted to see how having a few workmen around worked out for him before he committed to a huge operation. It was only logical. She was just happy he'd decided to take this step at all.

"Okay." She sighed happily. "We'll do it your way."

He gave her an adorably crooked grin. "What other way is there?"

CHAPTER TEN

AFTER spending so much time with Max, Isabella finally had to admit that she needed to concentrate on just how much her own family was making her crazy. Everything should be going swimmingly. They had the herb again. People were flocking to the restaurant just as they had in the best days of the past. You would think everyone would be happy with that—but no. There was a constant drumbeat of concern for her relationship with the prince, from her family and from everyone else, too.

Everyone in town seemed to know about it now, and each and every one had to stick his nose into it and give her the benefit of his or her great advice.

"Isabella, don't you think it is time to get over this obsession with the Rossi prince? He's not for you. You know how these things turn out, every time. You may be happy with it now, but in the end he'll want another sort of woman, a woman he can marry, and you'll be stuck with the consequences of your time with him."

That trend of thought was the most annoying, because it was very difficult to answer. She could either get mad, or walk away. She usually did the latter.

Her father was the most troubling because she knew he really did care about her and was genuinely worried.

"Where are you going?" he seemed to ask every time she came near a door. "When will you be back? You're not going to go see *him* again, are you?"

She was very careful not to take too much time away from the restaurant. She knew he needed her help and she didn't resent that at all. In fact, she wanted to make him feel less anxious, if only she knew how. Talking didn't seem to do it. And she decided a lot of it was based on his worry about the threats from Fredo—and those were beginning to worry her, too.

"Papa, what does he have against you?" she asked him again and again. "Why is he doing this?"

"He worked with me when I first had my stand on the Via Roma. We argued. He went off to start his own place, which failed. For years he's claimed I stole his recipes. Even after he opened his ice cream store, he told everyone my success was due to his recipes."

"Does he have even a tiny, tiny justification for thinking that?"

"Not a bit. He never even knew where I got the basil. He's just a crazy, angry old fool."

But crazy, angry old fools could do a lot of damage.

She went to a planning committee meeting with her father. He was too weak to stand up and speak his mind, so she did it for him and the arguing got pretty heated for a while. Even after all that, she wasn't totally clear on what the issue was and she didn't have a good feeling about things.

"What is it that you want?" she demanded of Fredo at one point. "Do you want us to admit guilt? Do you want money? What?"

Fredo was sitting in his chair at the long table and giving her his evil look. "I want Luca to lose his business like I lost mine." That was all he would say.

"The problem is," her father said as they were walking home from the meeting, "now that he has the mayor's ear and a seat on the planning commission, he thinks he can put the screws to me." He shook his head. "At first I was wondering if your aunt Lisa might not be behind it all. But he's gone further than even she would now."

"Oh, Papa. Aunt Lisa loves you deep down."

"Hah!" He shook his head. "A lot you know about it."

Luca's sister Lisa was a very different type from plain, sweet Luca. Isabella knew her well, though she had a way of flitting in and out of life in Monta Correnti, despite having a very successful restaurant right next to the one her brother ran. Lisa also had a habit of bestowing different fathers on each of her three daughters, all cousins to Isabella. Scarlett, who was just her age, had been a close friend when they were young. But the two of them had been involved in some childish antics that had put a pall on their friendship and to this day their secret was like a barrier between them and they seldom spoke.

But her aunt Lisa did enough talking to make up for it.

"Well, I hear you're flying high these days," she said, meeting Isabella in the courtyard outside their respective restaurants.

Isabella decided to play dumb. "What are you talking about?"

"Running with royalty, they say."

She bit her tongue. She couldn't explain to Lisa how it had all come about, because that would be giving away the secret of the basil, something only a few people knew about. When you came right down to it, Lisa was the last person they would want to know. In many ways, she and Luca were in direct competition and had been for years. If Lisa found out about the basil, Isabella knew she would get her hands on it immediately and hire the best chefs from Rome to come try out new recipes. As if they didn't have enough trouble with declining revenue at Rosa as it was. If Lisa took over the basil and began to promote it as only she knew how, they would be sunk.

"I've always heard he's such a recluse he won't even allow tradesmen at the palazzo. But suddenly he's hobnobbing with our little Izzy." Lisa gave her a flippant look. "If I'd known he was so easy to get to, I'd have been out there to see him myself."

A flare of panic rose in Isabella's throat. What if she tried it? "What would you want to see him about?" she asked, frowning.

"I'd invite him to dinner, of course." Lisa smiled. She knew she'd hit a nerve. "Can you imagine the promotional possibilities? I'm surprised you haven't had him in to your place yet. But I suppose that's to come. Isn't it?"

She shook her head. She really had to head off this thinking at the pass if she could.

"It's not like that, Aunt Lisa. I've been doing some consulting with him. He has some projects he's thinking of tackling and I'm putting him in touch with local experts."

"Is he thinking of starting a restaurant? I can't imagine you know much about anything else."

That did it. Lack of respect from relatives was a deal breaker as far as she was concerned. If her aunt couldn't even pretend to have some deference for her, she was toast.

"You'd be surprised what I know about, Aunt Lisa," she said icily, turning away. "You might want to think about that before you get involved in things you don't understand." She looked back at Lisa. To her surprise, the woman was looking flustered. "I would hate to think certain rumors might come back to bite you where my cousins are concerned."

Lisa looked downright startled and Isabella had a twinge of guilt. She didn't actually have a lot of juicy rumors about her aunt, but she was pretty sure there were some out there. So let her stew!

"She's just so arrogant," she explained to Max later that day as they were riding out across the estate, heading for another feast of tapas at the Spanish stand outside the walls. "I can't abide that."

"Forget about her," he advised. "We have a long, lazy afternoon with no one else but each other. Let's enjoy it."

That sounded good to her. He was in a good mood because work had started on the vineyards and he'd actually gone down and done a bit of supervising. No one had blanched at his scars. No one had turned green and gone behind a tree to vomit, something that had actually happened to him once at a seaside resort. He was feeling pretty good about prospects for the future. Maybe he could have something of a normal life after all.

They tied the horses and he went to sit at a table overlooking the river, while Isabella headed for the stand to get the food. She went inside and greeted Señor Ortega. He began talking the moment she entered and she laughed because it was obvious he was going to go on talking even after she was out of sight. She picked out some spiced clams, some corn fritters, some fried black pudding, some stuffed mushrooms, and nice cold beer for Max. Señor Ortega fried up some special samosas for her, and as he did the most beautiful little girl came into the store. Tiny and small-boned, she had a halo of light curls that flew around her pretty face like a cloud of spun gold.

"This is Ninita," Señor Ortega told her proudly. "My first grandchild."

"I'm pleased to meet you, Ninita," Isabella said, shaking

the child's hand and getting a solemn smile in return. "What a beautiful child," she said sotto voce to the man behind the bar.

"Yes, she is my angel," he said. "Here, take this tray. You've ordered so much food, I'll help you carry it out."

"Can I help too?" Ninita asked sweetly.

"Of course, my darling," said the older man. "Here, you can carry the napkins."

They formed a small train, carrying everything to the table where Max sat waiting.

"We come bearing lots of delicious tapas," Isabella said as they approached. "And we have help from Señor Ortega's grandchild. Meet little Ninita. Ninita, this is Prince Max."

The little girl had been carefully carrying the napkins and now she looked up, eager to meet a real live prince. Her face registered her shock as she saw him. Isabella saw what was happening as if in slow motion. She knew she had to stop it. She tried. But it was too late. The little girl took in a loud, gasping breath, dropped the napkins and threw her hands over her face. Then she began to scream as though she'd seen something horrible. Turning, she ran as fast as her little legs would carry her, screaming all the way.

Max sat very still. His face was drained of all color. Señor Ortega was apologizing profusely, and Max tried to smile as he waved away the older man's regrets. But the gaze that met Isabella's horrified eyes was full of self-loathing. As soon as Señor Ortega went back into the shop Max rose from where he was sitting. Without saying a word, he strode toward his horse and mounted, and before Isabella could say anything at all he was gone, too.

She stood there, holding the tray, knowing something very terrible had just happened—knowing it was going to change things. Something deep inside her was clenched like a fist and she was afraid it was going to be a long time before that feeling went away.

It was over an hour later before Isabella found Max, sitting by the river in a part of the estate she'd never seen before. She slid off Mimi's back and went to sit beside him. But when she reached out to take his hand, he pulled it away, then looked at her with eyes as cold as ice.

"It's over, Isabella. Our idyllic interlude is done."

She stared at him, aghast. "What are you talking about?"

"I thought I could elude my fate, but of course I was wrong. My crime is advertised on my face. I can't escape. I may fool myself for a while, but in the end it comes back to haunt me."

"Max, don't talk like that. It was my fault. I should have prepared her…"

He swore. "Can you prepare the whole world, Bella? I think not."

"But, Max…"

"Isabella, can't you see?" He turned his dark, tragic eyes on her. "I can't do this. I can't go out and mix with the world if I'm going to make precious little girls scream. I don't have the right to do that to them."

Suddenly it was clear to her that she had misunderstood his entire mental state. She'd thought he was shrinking from the pain of seeing how people reacted to his face. But he was way beyond that by now. It was evident to her that his motivations were very different. He was trying to avoid giving pain to others by inflicting his very disturbing scars on them.

And what could she possibly do about that? She couldn't control what others thought when they saw him. She stared into the water and felt a wave of hopelessness that wasn't like her. She was done. She had no more ideas, no more plans and projects. She had tried. And now it was over.

Turning so he wouldn't see the tears in her eyes, she rose and went to where Mimi was tied. In a moment, she was over the ridge and out of his sight. And then she let the tears fall like rain.

She spent the next week working hard at the restaurant, trying to develop some ideas for her father, ideas that would help brighten up the place. She hadn't been able to generate much interest as yet, but she was determined to try harder. Something would come of it yet.

She hadn't heard anything at all from Max, but she hadn't been able to think of much else. She missed him. She needed him. She was so in love…why hadn't she realized that before? She'd been in denial. Now that she'd lost him, she knew it was true. She loved him with all her heart. But what could she do about it?

She heard he'd paid off the workmen and sent everyone home. There were to be no more Rossi vineyards. She also heard a group from town had gone out to talk to him about using the estate for a fundraiser for the Monta Correnti Beautification Committee. He had refused to see them. He was doing just what he'd said he would do—reverting to his normal life. And that had no room for her in it.

Could it really be all over so soon? It seemed so. It truly hurt to have finally found a man whom she knew she could love with all her heart and soul, a man whose mind and interests fit nicely into the scope of her own, a man whose touch sent thrills through her body and created an ache of longing where her feminine secrets lay—and then have to give him up this way. But her life, as usual, was a less than stellar existence.

Okay, now she was whining and feeling very sorry for herself. But didn't she deserve to? Yes—though she knew very well too much of that self-indulgence could ruin a good summer if she didn't watch out. She gave herself one more day to mope about and cry, and then she was going to move on and find a place for herself where she could count for something and make a difference.

There. Just making a plan made her feel so much better.

Unfortunately, life had made its own plans and they didn't take hers into account. She was sitting in the kitchen, shelling peas with Susa, when a young man arrived to serve Luca with a writ of failure to comply with a permit ordinance. The warrant stated that he had been deemed to be in noncompliance and, unless he paid an exorbitant fine, he would have to vacate the restaurant premises within forty-eight hours.

Isabella was numb as she read it over to her father again and he struggled to understand what it meant.

"It means we lose the restaurant," she told him, unable to think straight, unable to understand much of this herself. "There is a meeting of the licensing board in two days. Unless we pay the fine by then, we have to pack up and get out."

"No," Luca said, banging his cane into the floor. "Not one cent for those bastards!"

"But, Papa…"

"I'll never give in to Fredo's blackmail. Never."

There wasn't much point in arguing with him. They didn't have the money to pay the fine anyway. She sighed and made plans to attend the meeting. All she could think of was to plead their case with the mayor. Surely he wouldn't be so hard-hearted as to kick them out of their own restaurant, the only means of survival for their family!

But a little place in her head told her there wasn't going to be much hope.

"Once your luck starts to go downhill," Susa intoned gloomily, "it just doesn't stop until it hits bottom."

Could Susa be right? Isabella shuddered and turned her head away.

Max sat out on the veranda, staring into the sunset, his eyes clouded, brooding. He'd thought it would be effortless to slip back into his old life, but in actuality it wasn't. In fact, it was hell on earth. He'd had a certain peace before, but now that was ruined. It sort of reminded him of that old World War I song, "How You Gonna Keep Them Down on the Farm, After They've Seen Paree?" He'd found out, once again, what it was to have a warm and wonderful woman in his life, and without her he felt as if a limb had been removed. Twenty times a day he started to call her. Twenty times a day he caught himself in time.

This was very different from losing Laura. That had been so full of agonizing pain and deep, deep guilt, he'd felt as though he'd been torn apart by red-hot pokers nightly—and that had gone on for years. This pain had very little guilt attached to it. Lots of regret, but not much guilt. Laura had been the love of his youth. Isabella was the joy of his maturity.

Strangely enough, he hadn't felt very guilty about putting memories of Laura to one side while he went about the sweet torture of falling for Isabella. In a funny way, he'd actually thought Laura might approve.

But that was all over now. He felt like a man re-condemned to a life sentence in a cold, lonely prison after he'd had a taste of freedom. It wasn't pleasant.

He looked at the bottle he'd brought out with him. He'd thought he would spend an evening drinking away his sorrows. But somehow he'd lost his thirst. He knew very well the bottom of a bottle was its own special hell. He didn't need another one.

Renzo came out to see if he needed anything, then lingered a moment, and Max could tell he wanted to say something.

"What is it, Renzo? Spit it out, man."

Renzo coughed. "Sir, I thought I'd mention, I went into the village this afternoon to see Miss Isabella."

"What?" He turned to stare at the man. "What did you do that for?"

"She had left some cooking equipment that I thought she might be missing, so I drove over to drop it by the restaurant."

"Oh." He looked away. He shouldn't ask. He knew the rules. A clean break was the best way. No, he wouldn't ask. He drew his breath in deeply, and then the words came out as though on their own.

"How…how did she seem? Is she all right?"

"I don't know."

He sat up straighter. "What do you mean, you don't know?"

"She wasn't there. I talked to an old woman named Susa who works for Isabella and her father. She said the two of them were over at the town meeting room preparing for an important meeting where they will have to fight to keep those crooks who run the city council from taking their restaurant away."

"Oh, no." Max swore and shook his head. "On what grounds?"

"Something about forgetting to file a permit and the fine being too high to pay."

He nodded. "A put-up job," he said bitterly.

"I'm afraid so, sir."

"Poor Isabella." A slight smile curled his lip. "Good thing she's got spunk. I bet she'll be able to save things on her own."

"You think so, sir?" Renzo said doubtfully.

"Sure. She's amazing." He glanced at Renzo, then away again. "It will be interesting to see how she does it. Keep me informed any time you find out anything new. I want to know how this comes out."

"Very well, sir." Renzo bowed out, looking puzzled.

Max sighed. He knew Renzo wanted him to ride in to the rescue. Didn't he understand how impossible that was? If he didn't get it yet, he would soon. Because Max couldn't have done anything even if he'd wanted to.

Closing his eyes, he saw Isabella's perfect face, and he groaned. The image seemed so real. She was saying something, trying to get him to do something, urging him to get up off his chair and...

He couldn't quite catch what it was, but the image stayed with him into the night, and the dreams he had were even clearer. Isabella needed help. He woke up and stared at the ceiling. Did he have the nerve to do what it would take to help her? That was the part that bothered him. He wasn't sure he did.

It was late in the afternoon of the next day that he received a visitor he wasn't expecting. Of course, since he didn't receive visitors at all, anyone would have been a surprise. But this one was special.

Renzo interrupted him just as he was finishing up some Internet research.

"There's someone here who would like a word with you," he said.

"What are you talking about?" he demanded, wondering if the man had lost his mind.

Renzo hesitated. "Sir, I know this man. He is a very good man. He runs a small tapas stand—"

"Señor Ortega?"

"Yes. You know him, then?"

"Of course." Max frowned. What on earth could the man want? He thought for a moment. Really, it seemed silly to deny him a short visit. "Send him in," he told Renzo. "I'll be happy to see him."

Renzo looked a bit startled, but readily complied, and in another moment Señor Ortega was in the library and shaking Max's hand effusively.

"Thank you so much, your honor," he said, bowing at the same time. "I have a small favor to ask of you. If you would be so kind."

"Por supuesto," Max said, speaking in the man's own language. "What can I do for you?"

"Do you remember the little girl who was there the last time you and Isabella came to eat at my stand?"

Max stiffened. How could he forget? "Yes," he said, his jaw tightening. "What about her?"

"Do you remember that she had a bad reaction to your…" He made a gesture to indicate the scarring on Max's face.

Max stared at Señor Ortega. The man was talking easily about his scars, as though they were just a part of life, not something to be whispered about and avoided at all costs.

"Yes," he said slowly. "I remember."

"Well, she feels so badly about how she acted. She's so ashamed. She asks me every day if we will see you again. She wants to apologize."

Max found himself smiling. "She has nothing to apologize for," he noted dryly. "I'm the one who inflicted my face on her."

Ortega frowned as though he didn't understand and thought the translation in his head must be bad. "I have brought her here with me. If you would please allow her to come in and pay her respects…"

Max swallowed hard. This was crazy. Was Señor Ortega making the girl do this? Surely she hadn't really requested this on her own. "I'm sorry," he began. "I'm afraid I can't allow…"

But Renzo had already escorted the girl to the library and she was coming in the door at that very moment. Max braced himself. It wasn't that he was afraid she would scream again. He knew that wouldn't happen. But if he saw horror in her face, he didn't know if he could stand it.

She was so pretty, and so small. As she entered her huge eyes turned on him and he saw the involuntary widening as she took in his face. But almost immediately, her angelic smile took over, and he felt a sense of relief pour through his body.

"Your Highness," she said, with a pretty curtsy. "I am so sorry for scaring you away that day. I cried and cried but my grandfather said not to bother you with such trivial things. But I begged him to let me come to see you again. And here I am."

Max laughed aloud, suddenly as relaxed and happy as he'd been in a long, long time. Could it be that he really wasn't such a monster after all? Was there a chance that he could live a somewhat normal life? Why not? If precious little girls could get over his scars so quickly, why not challenge the rest of the world to do the same?

It was over. Isabella sank into her seat at the end of the table and felt as though she were collapsing like a spent balloon. Her father was sitting with his head in his hands and she wasn't sure if he was crying. Others at the table were shouting and arguing, but she knew there was no more hope. It was over. The beautiful little restaurant with the special sauces made with *Monta Rosa Basil* was no more. They'd come to meeting after meeting and the result continued to be the same. The mayor, as parliamentarian presiding over this meeting, had finally ruled that her family had to clear out the building in two days.

It was truly over.

Reaching out, she took Luca's hand.

"Come on, Papa," she said sadly. "Let's go."

He looked up and tried to smile at his daughter. "Valentino is coming soon," he said, his voice shaky. "Maybe he will think of something."

She bit back her bitter reply. No recriminations. Reality was what it was. Time to deal with it and move on.

She rose and held out a hand to her father. He looked up but hardly seemed to have the strength to reach for her help. It was truly a sad and hopeless afternoon.

But in that same moment, the double doors to the meeting room swung open abruptly, and a man burst into the room. The reaction swept through the hall like a windstorm. Isabella turned to see who it was, and then couldn't believe her eyes.

There stood a tall, strong, proud man with eyes as black as coal and a presence that made everyone in the room sit up and take notice. It took her a moment to be certain it was Max, because at first she wasn't too sure. There was no hesitation about him, no favoring the good side of his face, no reluctance to challenge the crowd with his standing, scars and all. He was here and he was going to make a difference. That much was obvious.

"Sorry I'm late," he said in a voice that thundered through the room. "I hear you are dealing with a property that I have some interest in, so I decided I'd better be here to help you make the right decision."

The mayor and some of the councilors, after gaping for a few moments, made obsequious gestures and offered their chairs and generally made fools of themselves, and Isabella watched in wonder. He was more regal, more beautiful than ever. Where had this confidence come from? Had it been there all the time and she just hadn't noticed?

Max refused to take a seat. Instead, he stood in the middle of the room where he seemed to be in command of everyone in it. He requested that the mayor read the findings to him, and then the ruling. He listened, frowning, and when it was over he said, "I'm sorry, Mayor Gillano, but I don't agree with your ruling. I have some interest in the restaurant, Rosa, and I want it protected."

Everyone gaped at him in bewilderment. He stared straight ahead at the mayor and went on.

"You see, I'm about to be linked to the Casali family when I marry Isabella Casali. And she in turn will be a partner with me in my extensive real-estate holdings in the village. I believe I hold the lease on the building where you operate your furniture factory, Mayor Gillano. And the apartment building that you manage, Mr. Barelli," he added, looking at the mayor's right-hand man. "Oh, and don't you rent your stables from me, Miss Vivenda?"

He addressed each council member in turn and it seemed his real-estate manager had arranged it so that he had dealings with every one of them.

"Once Isabella is my bride, she will assist me in deciding which leases we may have to break in order to fulfill some new plans we're working on for the village." His gaze swept the room, a slight smile softening the hard lines of his face. "I hope we won't be inconveniencing any of you, but that is always a risk, as I'm sure you are well aware."

The murmurs had a ring of panic to them now. Isabella stared in wonder. She wasn't sure what was happening. Why was Max saying these things? Marrying her? He might have asked first. But she didn't care. She loved watching him and the way he took charge without regard to his scars or how they affected anyone. He'd been born a prince, raised a prince, and he was finally letting his inner prince out.

But what was this business about marrying her? Was this all a ruse, or did he really have something in mind? Her heart was beating so loud, she had to concentrate to understand what he was saying.

"I'm sure this matter can be settled to the benefit of all of us if you will just rescind your ruling regarding the restaurant Rosa." His dark gaze touched every one of them in turn. "Surely the fine can be waived, in light of this new information."

There was utter silence in the room.

He smiled. "Good. That's settled, then. I expect to see the Casali family back over the stove at their restaurant by nightfall."

"Oh, I'm sure something can be arranged…" the mayor was sputtering.

"Oh, yes, indeed," others were saying, suddenly acting as though this had been their intention all along.

Isabella shook her head, her mouth open in astonishment. They all fell into place like bowling pins. The only angry face was Fredo's scowling in the background. But it seemed his wishes were no longer relevant.

Max turned to look at Isabella. She looked at him. Electricity flashed between them, and as though propelled by it, she rose and flew into his arms. He swept her up into the air, and right in front of everyone his mouth came down on hers and he kissed her as though this were going to be the last kiss in the history of the world.

"I love you, Bella," he whispered close to her ear. "I've found out I can't live without you by my side. Would a wedding fit into your plans?"

"Oh, Max," she sighed, holding him close. "I penciled one in long ago. You're right in step with the program."

"Good," he said, his dark eyes smiling into hers. "You're my conscience and my courage. I need you badly."

"I think you've got the courage all on your own," she responded. "The way you came in here, taking charge, ignoring what they might make of your scars—oh, Max, it was masterful."

"I would never have been able to do something like that if you hadn't started the process of making me face the world," he told her.

The others in the room were still squabbling like a herd of cats, but they were alone in their private oasis, right in the middle of it all.

"Let's get married soon," he said, kissing her again. "We're going to need a very, very long honeymoon."

"Don't worry," she said, laughing as she clung to the man she loved. "I've got plans."

EPILOGUE

MAX stood before a large fountain in a courtyard in Monta Correnti holding a goblet that contained a pinot noir of fabulous vintage. He held it up to the light, enjoying the color, anticipating how it would taste on his tongue. And his mind was full of Isabella.

"Here's to you, my bride-to-be," he muttered, knowing his voice would be covered by the sound of water in the large fountain he stood before. Still, he lowered it further to add, "And to you, my bride that was—my beloved Laura, and our treasured child. You will always be a part of me."

Closing his eyes, he murmured a soft prayer, then smiled as he heard Isabella's voice coming from Rosa, one of two restaurants that bordered the courtyard. She was arguing with her brother, Valentino, again. Those two were at it night and day, it seemed.

They had just finished a wonderful meal to celebrate Luca's birthday and Max had come outside to get some fresh evening air and savor the moment. He'd been happy to be invited to this small, family gathering. Luca seemed to be just about ready to accept that Max was going to marry his daughter.

That was not to say that he was happy about it. He was

very worried that Max would take his daughter away and he would have no one to help him with the restaurant. And in truth, he was right to be worried, Max thought to himself. Right now Isabella was determined to go on helping, knowing what dire straits the finances were in, but there would come a time when she would have to commit fully to him and their relationship. And then—darn right he would take Isabella away.

He turned to look at the other restaurant on the courtyard, Sorella, run by Luca's sister Lisa. Happy diners were coming and going. It was a very popular place. He had yet to try her fare. He would have to do it one of these days. Lisa was a very hands-off manager and her place was doing fine. Surely he and Isabella could hire someone good enough to allow Luca to hand over most of the management in similar fashion.

Glancing back at the Casali place, he saw that Isabella and Valentino were still arguing, but Luca was making his way out onto the courtyard as well—probably fed up with the squabbling. Max chuckled, but turned away and melted into the shadows of the area. He didn't want to get involved in any more Casali family discussions for now. He had a glass of wine to drink and his future happiness to ponder.

Isabella was shaking her head and glaring at her brother. She loved him to distraction, and yet the two of them hardly ever could see eye to eye on anything.

"I wish Cristiano were here instead of being stuck in Australia fighting the brush fires," Luca grumbled as he started out the door onto the courtyard. "He'd knock your two heads together for sure."

"Oh, Papa," Isabella said. "Don't let it bother you. It's as much a family ritual with us as anything." But she turned right back to Valentino. "You're just so stubborn," she said. "Why don't you just try staying here for a month? Papa would be so happy and—"

"Izzy, why can't you understand? I have a career to think of. I have to defend my position on the tour. I have to fight for every increment of success. It doesn't come easy."

"I can understand that you want to give racing your all, but there is more to life than work, work, work."

"Really? And when did you have this revelation, Cinderella? Remember when we called you that?"

But Isabella had suddenly realized they were alone. "Hey, where did everybody go?" she said, looking around.

"You chased them away with your constant nagging," he teased.

She turned, ready to be outraged, and saw the humor in his eyes. Reluctantly, she smiled back at him. "Okay, I'll leave it alone for now." She sighed, then regained a bit of energy. "Come on. We'll go out in the courtyard, too. It's cooler out there."

They stopped to pour out a glass of wine for each of them, then linked arms and went out into the darkening night. The area was filled with people milling about, but Isabella noticed her father across the way.

"There he is." She frowned, looking harder. "I wonder who that is he's talking to. I don't think it's Max." They started over. "Oh, it's Aunt Lisa," she said as they got closer. "They hardly ever even speak to each other. What in the world…?"

She was about to rush forward when her brother stopped her with a hand on her arm. "There's something about the intensity between them that makes me think we ought to take this carefully," he told her. "Let's go for the side approach. Here, through the bushes."

"I'll ruin my shoes," she protested, but she agreed. There was something odd about the posture between Luca and Lisa that made her want to take it slowly as well. She was naturally protective toward her father. If Lisa was being mean to him, she wanted to be there to take his side— whatever the problem might be. As they drew closer the voices began to be audible. Lisa was the first they heard clearly enough to decipher.

"And here it is, your birthday, and you don't even have your whole family around you, do you?" Lisa was saying, and it was loud enough that anyone who walked past could have heard it.

Isabella made a sound of exasperation and started to push her way out of the bushes to go to her father's aid, but her brother, looking uncomfortable, grabbed her arm again to stop her.

"Shush," he whispered near her ear. "Let's just get out of here."

"But…"

"You've never told them, have you?" Lisa said in a scathing voice. "Here I know more about their brothers than they do."

Brothers? Isabella and Valentino both stopped and turned back, peering through the dim light at their older relatives.

"Lisa, what are you talking about?" Luca demanded. "Have you seen the twins? Have you been to New York?"

His voice was suddenly high-pitched with emotion. Isabella and Valentino looked at each other and they both shrugged at the same time.

"Who are they talking about?" he mouthed to her, and she shrugged again, shaking her head.

"You are the one who should be going to New York, brother dear. You should acknowledge those children you had so long ago. Don't you realize you've left a huge gaping hole in the middle of your family? You've poisoned relations between your children forever with the actions you've taken. To send those poor little boys away like you did…"

"And why did I have to send them away? You do remember that part of it, don't you, Lisa?"

"Ridiculous."

"It was because you, my loving sister, refused to loan me the money to put food in their mouths. What was I to do? Let them stay here with me and starve?"

She waved a hand in the air. "That's all in the past. You need to take care of the present. You need to contact those boys and try to patch things up." She started to turn away. "Oh, by the way. You do know that Alessandro has a ranch in the West, don't you? And that Angelo is a big baseball star?" She tossed her head, just to show she despised him. "Just thought I'd catch you up on the family news. *Your* family news. Why don't you let the rest of them know about it? I'm sure they'd be interested."

And with that, she turned on her heel and sashayed back toward her restaurant. Isabella waited only a few seconds before bursting out into the opening and going to her father, who looked gray and shaken by the things Lisa had said. He slumped down onto a stone bench and she hurried to his side.

"Papa, what was she talking about?" she said, going down onto one knee before him and searching his face for answers. "Who are these twins she spoke of?"

He looked up at her and winced. "Isabella, Valentino, I have a lot to tell you about. Too much." He gave a heavy sigh. "It's true. I haven't been honest. I've been thinking about it a lot lately and I know I need to fill you in about it all."

"Tell us what, Papa?" She took his hand. "You can tell us anything. You know we love you."

His sigh was deep and heart-rending. "It's the twins. Before I married your mother I had another wife and we had two sons—twins. I haven't seen them since they were little boys." He shook his head.

She squeezed his hand and looked up. "Valentino?" she called, looking for her brother. But he was striding off into the night, as though he wanted almost anything more than to hear about these two new brothers. She stared after him, disappointed again.

She was shocked, but, in a certain corner of her heart, quite thrilled to hear she had two brothers she'd never known about. Though it was a complete surprise, she had to admit there had been hints over the years that there were mysteries in her father's past that she didn't know about. Now she had some confirmation of that. And already she was beginning to formulate the beginning sketches of how she was going to find those twins and bring them home.

That was one thing her aunt Lisa had said that was absolutely right. There did seem to be a gaping hole in the middle of their family. There always had been. She could see that clearly now. And family was everything.

"Max!"

Valentino had deserted her, but at least she could count on Max. She turned as he entered the clearing, reaching for him.

"Oh, Max, hold me," she said. She needed his arms around her. The sand was shifting under her feet again and Max might be the only anchor she had.

She quickly filled him in. "I have two new brothers. How do you like that? And I'm going to make sure they come home soon so we can meet them."

Max nodded, holding her as though he would never let her go. "Sounds like a plan," he said. "Families should be together whenever possible."

She sighed and sank into his embrace. She was so lucky to have him. She knew that her most important responsibilities would be to the new family the two of them would make together and she knew that he felt those ties as deeply as she did. But in the meantime, she needed to shore up her other family where she could. If only her brothers would recognize the truth in that, she thought as she and Max helped her father back to the restaurant, the world would be a better place, especially here in their beloved Bella Rosa.

* * * * *

EXECUTIVE:
EXPECTING TINY TWINS

BY
BARBARA HANNAY

Barbara Hannay was born in Sydney, educated in Brisbane and has spent most of her adult life living in tropical North Queensland, where she and her husband have raised four children. While she has enjoyed many happy times camping and canoeing in the bush, she also delights in an urban lifestyle—chamber music, contemporary dance, movies and dining out. An English teacher, she has always loved writing, and now, by having her stories published, she is living her most cherished fantasy.

Visit www.barbarahannay.com.

CHAPTER ONE

SHE was wearing white, for crying out loud.

Jack Lewis grimaced as the elegant figure stepped down from the tiny plane while clouds of red dust slowly settled on the airstrip. The same red dust covered his ute, his riding boots, and practically everything else in the outback, and yet Senator Elizabeth Green had chosen to arrive on Savannah cattle station dressed from head to toe in blinding, laundry-commercial white.

Her elegant sandals were white, her crisply ironed trousers, her matching linen top and even her floppy-brimmed hat. The only non-white items were her accessories—swanky dark glasses and a pale green leather shoulder bag that clearly held a laptop.

Where did she think she'd flown to? The flaming Italian Riviera?

Jack muttered a soft oath, audible only to Cobber, the cattle dog at his heels. 'I suppose we'd better go and say g'day.'

Shrugging off an uncomfortable sense of martyrdom, Jack set out across the stretch of dirt, moving with a deliberately easy amble, his faithful dog close behind him.

He was mad with himself for allowing his boss, an

eighty-year-old widow, to bully him into hosting this visitor. Kate Burton regularly tested Jack's patience by directing her business via long-distance phone calls from her top-price-tag retirement home in Melbourne.

'I owe Lizzie a favour,' Kate had told him breezily. 'She won't be any trouble, Jack. She just wants to rest up and take in the country air, and she needs to retreat from the public eye for a spell. You understand, don't you?'

After a lifetime of getting her own way, Kate hadn't given Jack the chance to protest that no, he didn't understand, that he was managing her cattle station not a hotel, that the mustering season had started and he was planning to join the team.

For her part, Kate made no attempt to explain why a high-profile senator, the darling of the Canberra media, was suddenly diving for cover in distant North Queensland.

Kate had left Jack with no choice but to send out the mustering team while he remained behind at the homestead. This morning he'd dutifully rounded up the horses grazing in this paddock, and he'd flattened the anthills that had popped up on the airstrip since the last time a light plane had landed here.

Now, as he approached his guest, she straightened her shoulders and lifted her chin—her very neat and determined chin.

Her shady white hat and dark glasses hid the top half of her face, but Jack sensed her surprise, as if he wasn't quite what she'd expected.

He was having the same problem—madly readjusting his assumptions. Up close, Senator Elizabeth Green was a bombshell.

He'd seen photos of her in newspapers, of course, and he was aware of her classic Italian good looks, but he'd expected the real-life version to be closer to Iron Maiden than Sophia Loren. Surely this woman was too soft and sensuous to be a federal politician?

Jack could see curves beneath her crisp white linen clothes—old-fashioned, reach-out-and-touch-me curves.

Her dark hair was tucked up under her hat, but silky wisps had strayed onto her nape, drawing his attention to her super-smooth, pale skin with a dusky hint of the Mediterranean.

As for her mouth…

Whoa. Her mouth was wide and full and soft and sultry, quite possibly the sexiest mouth Jack had ever met.

Her mouth moved. 'Mr Lewis?'

It took Jack a second or two to get his brain on the right track.

'Good morning, Senator.' He spoke a little too loudly. 'Welcome to Savannah.'

He wondered if she was going to offer her hand. Her big hat and sunglasses hid so much of her that he found it hard to pick up clues, but he sensed she was still checking him out, trying to make as many correct assumptions as possible.

When at last she offered her hand, it was cool and slim, her grip firm.

'I have luggage.' Despite the faint Italian accent, when the senator spoke she was Iron Maiden through and through.

Reassured that he knew what he was dealing with, Jack waved to the pilot. 'I'll get the luggage, Jim.'

In the hold, he found two large and perfectly matched green leather suitcases—*Louis Vuitton, of course*—and a matching leather holdall filled with books. When he hefted the strap over his shoulder, the books weighed a ton.

'I see you plan to do a little light reading,' he said, offering her a grin.

The senator gave a slight shrug, as if it was obvious that she'd have little else to do out here except improve her mind.

Reducing his grin to a resigned smile, Jack waved to the pilot, then picked up the suitcases. Hell, judging by the weight of them, she planned to move in to Savannah for six months. Or longer. Kate Burton had been vague about the length of this visitor's stay.

'We'd better get going before Jim takes off and creates another dust storm.' Jack nodded in the direction of his parked ute. 'The limousine's this way.'

Again, Senator Green didn't acknowledge Jack's attempt at a joke. Instead, she looked over at the vehicle covered in dust and then gazed slowly about her, taking in the wide and empty red plains dotted sparsely with clumps of grey-green grass, and at the sky, huge, blue and cloudless. Boundless.

A lone crow's cry pierced the stillness. *Ark, ark, ark!*

Watching his guest closely, Jack saw her take a breath as if she were bracing herself for an ordeal. He had no interest in her problems or why she'd come here, yet to his dismay he felt a faint pang of sympathy.

They set off for the ute and by the time they reached it—a matter of sixty metres or so—Senator Green's sandals were filmed with red dust and a faint red rim showed at the bottom of her pristine trousers.

Her mouth pursed with sour-lemon tightness as she watched Jack set her glamorous luggage next to bales of fencing wire in the tray back of his battered ute.

'Hope you weren't expecting anything too flash.' He opened the passenger door, saw dog hairs on the seat, and, despite an urge to leave them there, swept the seat clean with the brim of his Akubra hat.

'Thank you,' the senator said in a princess-speaking-to-the-footmen tone.

Jack wished he hadn't bothered.

'How far is it to the homestead?' she asked.

'Not far. A couple of kilometres.'

She nodded, but chose not to comment.

'In the back, Cobber,' Jack ordered, and his dog obediently jumped up beside the pale green luggage. 'And you'd better fasten your seat belt,' he told his passenger as he swung into the driver's seat. 'It's bound to be a bumpy ride.'

Lizzie sat in grim silence as the ute set off across the trackless ground. She was grateful that Jack didn't try to carry on a conversation, yelling above the roar of the motor. He seemed happy enough to drive while she clung to the panic handle, which she needed more to steady her nerves than because the ride was rough.

She needed to calm down, to throw off the alarming schoolgirl thrill that had flared inside her the instant she'd set eyes on Jack Lewis.

Good grief. It was ridiculous. Laughable. She hadn't felt such an instantaneous, unwarranted reaction to a man for almost a decade. She'd thought she'd developed immunity.

For heaven's sake. It was absurd and distressing to feel this fireworks-in-her-very-veins excitement at the sedate age of forty. It was a joke. She would put her reaction down to surprise. She'd expected Jack Lewis to be older, several decades older, actually.

After her conversation with Kate Burton, she'd had an image of the manager of Savannah as a mature and kindly, grey-haired man of the land. He'd be a little shy perhaps, as rural folk were reputed to be. Reliable, dependable, salt of the earth. A fatherly figure, possibly a bit like her dad.

Lizzie couldn't have been further from the mark.

Jack was young, younger than she was, for sure, and he had all the attributes of a hunky pin-up boy—height, fitness, muscles, glowing health. Throw in sun-bleached hair and sparkling green eyes and a smile that would melt granite, and the man was borderline dangerous.

The silly thing was, Lizzie had met oodles of good-looking men without going weak at the knees, but there was something else about this fellow, something elusive.

Perhaps it was the slow and easy way he moved. She thought about the way he'd approached her with a leisurely, loose-hipped stride, and the effortless way he'd hefted her luggage as though it held nothing but tissue paper. Even the way he drove was relaxed and easy— guiding the steering wheel with one hand, while his other hand rested lightly on the gear stick.

Sex appeal in spades.

No doubt the young women for miles around were all in love with him.

Good grief. She had to stop thinking like this. *Now!*

Jack Lewis wasn't her type. Not remotely. She was a federal senator, earnest and conscientious—busy, busy, busy. Everything about Jack—his lazy smile and his easy, laid-back body language—showed that his whole attitude to life was different from hers.

Of course, Lizzie knew she shouldn't react to superficial appearances. She'd learned early in her career that if she genuinely wanted to find ways to help people, she had to look below the surface. Things were rarely as they appeared. The truth was always hidden.

As a woman, she also knew that she had a bad habit of

falling for the wrong man. Twice in her life, she'd met someone she'd found instantly attractive. Twice she'd been burned, almost reduced to ashes.

Never again. With good reason—two very handsome reasons—she'd made a conscious decision to keep her private life a male-free zone. Men. Just. Weren't. Worth. It.

She'd been relieved to finally step off the dating-relationship merry-go-round, and she couldn't believe she'd wasted so many years trying to choose a life partner. Now she embraced the freedom of going it alone, just as her mother had. In fact, she was taking her independence one step further than her mother had.

The ute bounced and rattled over a cattle grid and Lizzie automatically placed a protective hand over the tiny bulge below her navel.

Her baby.

Hers and only hers.

The past three months had flown so quickly, and, according to the pregnancy books that Lizzie had studied in depth and learned by heart, her baby was already the size of half a banana. It would have tiny fingerprints now, and if it was a little girl, she would have about two million eggs in her ovaries.

'Are you OK?' Jack sent Lizzie a quick look of concern that took in the protective hand on her stomach.

'I'm fine, thank you.' She spoke brusquely. Tension made her brittle and she quickly lifted her hand and fiddled with a stray wisp of hair, tucking it under her hat.

The last thing she wanted was to draw attention to her growing baby bump. Kate Burton had promised not to mention her pregnancy to Jack, and Lizzie certainly didn't want to explain until she got to know him better.

Come to think of it, Lizzie couldn't imagine taking Jack

into her confidence. Surely there would be someone else at the homestead, perhaps a kindly housekeeper, who would be happy to indulge in heart-to-heart chats over a cup of tea. She should have asked Kate Burton more questions.

Looking out at the endless stretch of red plains, Lizzie felt her spirits swoop. She was planning to spend at least a month out here in the back of beyond. She needed the break, for the baby's sake, and for sanity's sake, and she surely needed to escape from the hound dogs in the press gallery.

If they caught a sniff of Jack, I'd be in trouble.

The isolation should keep her safe, however, and somehow she would cope.

She planned to keep busy, of course, staying in touch with her office in Brisbane and her parliamentary colleagues in Canberra via her laptop and her mobile phone— her *new* mobile phone, with a number that she'd only shared with a discreet circle of people she could trust.

In her spare time she would work her way through the supplementary reading matter she'd brought with her. She'd always complained that she never had enough time for reading for pleasure, although once upon a time she'd liked nothing better than losing herself in a good book.

She'd also imagined going for pleasant country walks, except this flat, parched land didn't look very inviting.

'Here's the homestead,' Jack said, pulling up at a gate and pointing ahead through the dusty windscreen.

It was a timber building, long and low, and painted white. It had a dark green, corrugated iron roof, and there were several smaller buildings scattered around it. Sprawled beneath the harsh outback sun, the collection of buildings made Lizzie think of a sleepy dog with a litter of puppies.

Jack sent her a sideways glance loaded with expectation,

and she realised she was expected to say something. But what?

There was no garden to admire, although the curving lines of stones cemented together suggested that there might have been gardens in the past. She supposed she would be comfortable enough here, but the house looked very lonely sitting in the middle of the flat empty plains.

She said, 'The house looks…very…nice.'

There was a glimmer of impatience in his glance. *What is his problem?*

'Do you think you could get the gate?' he asked, super-politely.

The gate?

'Oh-h-h…the gate.' Lizzie gave a shaky laugh to cover her shock. In Canberra, she had a swipe card that opened doors or gates in a split second, or her staff went ahead of her, smoothing the way. 'You'd like *me* to open it?'

He gave her a wry smile. 'It's sort of bush tradition. Driver stays at the wheel. Passenger opens the gate. So, if it's not too much trouble.'

This gate proved to be a great deal of trouble.

First Lizzie had to wrestle with the door handle, then she had to clamber down from the ute into several inches of fine red dust that once again covered her sandals and seeped between her bare toes. Finally, she spent an embarrassing age at the gatepost, wrestling with a heavy metal loop and a complicated piece of rusty wire.

Pride wouldn't allow her to give in, but she hadn't a clue how to get the thing open.

A deep and very annoying chuckle brought her whirling around. Jack Lewis had left the truck and was standing close behind her, grinning. 'I guess I'd better show you how it works.'

'I guess you'd better,' she snapped. 'This is the most ridiculous gate I've ever seen. What's the point of making it so difficult? Why can't you have a normal latch?'

'That'd be too easy. Even the cattle could work out how to open it.'

Her response was a disdainful sniff, and she watched him with tightly closed lips as he tilted the metal loop, and, with the swift ease of a conjuring trick, slipped the wire hook free, letting the gate swing easily open.

He winked at her. 'Did you get that?'

'Of course,' she said stiffly, unwilling to admit that she wasn't completely sure how he'd done it.

'Good-o. I'll take the ute through, and you can close it after me.'

'Wait!' Lizzie commanded as he headed back to the truck.

Jack turned super-slowly, an ambiguous smile lurking in his eyes.

Her shoulders stiffened and her chin hiked higher. 'You didn't show me how to close it.'

With a lazy shake of his head he ambled back to her, and she couldn't tell if he was smiling at her expense, or trying to be friendly.

Unfortunately, he stood too close as he refastened the gate, and Lizzie found herself distracted by the play of muscles in his tanned forearms and the deft movements of his brown fingers.

'You tilt it at two o'clock,' he said, showing her twice. 'Here, you have a go.'

Their hands brushed, making her skin flash with ridiculous heat, but at last she had the hang of it, and, of course, it was dead easy once she knew.

Back in the truck, they trundled on till they reached the front steps, and Jack retrieved Lizzie's luggage with the same easy economy of movement that she found so unsettling. This time she tried very hard not to watch.

At the top of the steps he turned to her. 'I guess you'd like to see your room first.'

'Thank you.'

'It opens off this veranda.'

His blue cattle dog curled in a pool of sunlight on the veranda, while Lizzie followed its master, carrying her laptop, and shamelessly watching the man from behind, noting the way his broad shoulders stretched the seams of his blue cotton shirt, and his faded jeans rode low on his lean hips.

Good grief, Lizzie. Give it a miss.

Jack turned through French doors into a large, airy room and set Lizzie's bags on the beige carpeted floor beside the big bed with old-fashioned brass ends and a soft floral spread. He watched Lizzie look about her, inspecting the pale pink walls and fine, white spotted curtains.

'This is the room Kate uses when she visits Savannah,' he told her.

Lizzie nodded. 'I could well believe that. It's just like Kate—comfortable, relaxing and no-nonsense.'

And you're damn lucky to have it, he thought. *It's the best room in the house.*

Lizzie looked at the painting above the bed, a watercolour of a flock of birds taking off against a soft pink dawn.

'Kate thought you'd like it in here,' he said.

'It's very kind of her to let me use her room. I do like it. Very much.'

OK. One hurdle over, Jack thought.

But then two vertical lines creased Lizzie's forehead. 'Is there an en suite?'

He shook his head, and took perverse glee in saying, 'The bathroom's down the hall.'

'Oh, right.' Lizzie lifted her limp shirt collar away from her neck. 'I don't suppose there's air-conditioning?'

'The ceiling fans are adequate. It's not summer. You'll be OK.' He pointed to the large, silky oak table next to the window with a view across the paddocks. 'Kate said you needed a desk, so I put this here for you.'

'Thank you.' Lizzie sent a final queenly glance around the room, then slipped her laptop bag from her shoulder and set it on the desk, giving the laptop an affectionate pat, as if it was her best friend—or her lifeline.

Then she removed her sunglasses and set them beside the laptop, and took off her big white hat, which should not, of course, have been a big deal.

But *hell.*

Jack's body reacted as if Lizzie had launched into a striptease.

She'd accidentally dislodged her hairpins, and her hair—thick, lustrous, shiny and as dark as midnight—spilled to her shoulders, and suddenly he was having difficulty breathing.

Which was probably just as well. If he'd been able to draw breath, he might have spoken, might have said something crazy, like telling her she was out-of-this-world beautiful.

Because—damn it, she was. She was stunning. Her eyes were the most amazing hazel, with flecks of earthy brown and mossy green stippled with gold. As for her face, framed by all that silky dark hair—

Jack could feel the muscles in his throat working over-time as he stood there like a fool, staring. At her.

Until she frowned, then looked worried. Nervous.

Somehow, he dragged in a necessary breath, and switched his gaze to the desk, forced his mind back to business. 'I—I believe you—you've brought your own Internet connection?'

'Yes.' Lizzie also took a breath, and she lifted her shirt collar again, pulling it away from her flushed skin. 'I—um—have a wireless broadband mobile card.'

'Sounds brilliant.'

'It's handy for travelling.'

She took another breath, deep and slow, then began to twist her hair back into a safe, neat, spinsterish knot.

Jack rammed his hands hard into the pockets of his jeans and looked about him—anywhere but at her. 'So what would you like to do? Unpack and settle in here? Or take a gander at the rest of the house?'

Lizzie hesitated, dismayed that her mind was so fuddled she found the simplest decision difficult. Given the amount of work she had to do, she should unpack her laptop and get started immediately.

'Perhaps you need a cuppa first,' Jack suggested slowly, almost reluctantly.

There would be a housekeeper in the kitchen. Someone sensible and cosy to provide a reassuring buffer between Lizzie and this disturbingly attractive, but highly unsuitable man. She found herself saying, 'Tea would be lovely, thanks.'

Once again, she followed Jack, this time down a narrow hallway and through a large living room filled with deep squishy lounge chairs and low occasional tables, with two sets of French doors opening onto a veranda. Casting a quick glance around the room, she gained an impression of casual relaxation and carelessness.

Cushions had been left in a tumbled pile at one end of the sofa, clearly for the comfort of the person who'd lain there watching television. Sporting magazines and empty coffee cups were strewn about, and an overturned beer can lay on the floor beside the sofa. The housekeeper was obviously as casual as Jack.

Lizzie thought fondly of her minimalist, twenty-first-century apartment and her super-efficient cleaning woman, and sighed.

They reached the kitchen.

'Pull up a pew.' Jack nodded to one of the mismatched chairs gathered around a huge, scrubbed pine table that had one end cleared, while the rest was littered with magazines, newspapers, an assortment of mail, a hammer, nails and a leather strap with buckles that might have been part of a horse's bridle.

To Lizzie's surprise, he went to the sink and filled a kettle, turned on the gas and set it on the stove.

Where was the friendly, pink-cheeked, country housekeeper, waiting with a warming teapot and a batch of scones just out of the oven?

'Is it the housekeeper's day off, Jack?'

He frowned. 'What do you mean?' His eyes narrowed as he sent a puzzled look around the shabbily out-of-date kitchen. 'Is there something wrong?'

With growing dismay, Lizzie watched him reach up to a shelf above the stove for a caddy of loose-leaf tea. He did it automatically, with the familiar ease of someone who'd done this a thousand times. 'You do have a housekeeper, don't you?'

Jack shook his head. 'No need. There's just me in the main house.' He sent her a wry quarter-smile. 'Kate said you wanted a retreat. She didn't say anything about luxury.'

'I'm not asking for luxury.'

Jack's eyebrow rose, but he spoke quietly, 'That's all right, then.'

He poured a little hot water into the teapot, swirled it around and then tipped it into the sink before he added tea leaves. Once again, Lizzie watched his hands—

strong, long and capable, with golden, sun-bleached hairs on the backs.

Damn. She shouldn't have been watching Jack Lewis's hands. She was over men. Twice bitten, permanently shy. Besides, Jack was much younger than she was—and she'd come here to escape, to retreat in peace and quiet: optimum conditions for a healthy pregnancy. Already, she felt agitated and edgy. It was Jack's fault. No, it was hers. She simply had to control her reactions.

Of course, if she told Jack she was pregnant, she would clear the air instantly. Such news would quickly kill that sexy sparkle in his eyes, and she might be able to let her hair down without the world coming to a standstill.

She could get on with her plan to relax at Savannah while her baby grew healthy and strong.

She opened her mouth, already tasting the words: *By the way, Jack, I'm pregnant.*

But suddenly she knew she wasn't going to tell him. She'd come to this outpost to avoid giving explanations about her pregnancy to a pack of hungry journalists. There was no need to tell Jack. Not yet.

Maybe later.

Maybe never. He was a stranger, after all, and Lizzie's pregnancy was none of his business.

Very soon, her hormones would settle down and this inappropriate sense of attraction would die a natural death.

CHAPTER TWO

'DO YOU do all your own cooking?' Lizzie asked Jack, forcing her mind to practical matters.

'Not usually. Most of the time there's a station cook, but I sent him out with the mustering team.' Jack poured boiling water into the teapot, replaced the lid and set the pot on the table with two blue striped mugs.

'Is there a muster on at the moment?'

He nodded. 'We always muster as soon as the wet season's out of the way.'

'Does that mean I've inconvenienced you?'

His shrug was a beat too late. 'The team can manage without me.'

'But you're the manager. Are you supposed to be supervising?'

His back was to her now and he spoke as he reached for milk and sugar. 'I have a satellite phone. I can stay in touch.' He turned, and his green eyes regarded her steadily. 'You should know that, Senator. After all, you'll be running the whole country from here.'

It was a not-so-subtle dig—and she realised that Jack probably resented her sudden arrival.

She said, 'I suppose you're wondering how a federal

senator can retreat into the outback without reneging on her responsibilities.'

'Not at all. I leave politicking to politicians.' Jack's face was as unreadable as a poker player's as he poured tea into a mug. 'Do you take milk? Sugar?'

'Thank you.' She helped herself to a dash of milk and half a spoon of sugar. 'I hope I haven't spoiled too many of your plans.'

'Most plans are easy enough to change.' Jack sat and, now that he was level with Lizzie, she was reacquainted with the superior breadth of his shoulders.

He looked across the table at her, trapping her in his steady gaze. 'That goes for you, too, Senator. No one's holding you here if you find that this place doesn't suit you.'

Something in his gaze set fine tuning-fork vibrations inside her. Quickly, she looked down at her mug. 'Please, you mustn't keep calling me Senator.'

'What should I call you? Elizabeth?'

'My family and friends call me Lizzie.'

'Lizzie?' Jack repeated her name without shifting his gaze from her face. 'Now that's a surprise.'

'Why?'

His mouth twitched as he stirred sugar into black tea. 'Seems to me, a woman called Lizzie is a very different kettle of fish from an Elizabeth.'

'Really? How?' As soon as the question was out Lizzie regretted it. It wasn't appropriate for her to show so much interest in this young man's theories about women and their names. And yet, she was desperately curious to hear his answer.

'When I think of Elizabeth, I think of the Queen,' Jack said.

'My mother would be pleased to hear that. It's why she chose Elizabeth as my name.'

'She named you after the Queen?'

'Yes. She named all her daughters after strong women. I have a younger sister Jackie, named after Jackie Onassis, and then there's Scarlett, named after Scarlet O'Hara.'

'Yeah?' Jack chuckled. 'No maternal pressure or anything.' He lolled back in his chair, legs stretched under the table. The man sure had a talent for looking relaxed. 'Your mother must be proud of you. A federal senator. That's a pretty big deal.'

'Yes, I'm sure she is proud.'

'But she still calls you Lizzie.'

Lizzie... *Cara*...

With a wistful pang Lizzie remembered her mother's tearful reaction to the news she'd shared just last week, when she'd flown back to Italy, to her hometown of Monta Correnti. Her mother's tears had been happy, of course, and accompanied by fierce and wonderful hugs.

Lisa Firenzi was thrilled that her eldest daughter was about to become a mother at last, and she'd been surprisingly OK with the unexpected news that her grandchild's father was an unknown donor. But then, Lisa Firenzi had never bowed to convention.

Like mother, like daughter...

Lizzie took a sip of her tea, which was hot and strong, just as she liked it, and she pushed aside memories of the end of her visit home, and the unhappy family row that had erupted.

Instead, she asked Jack, 'Why do you think Lizzie is so different from Elizabeth? What kind of woman is a Lizzie?'

Jack laughed out loud and the flash in his eyes was most definitely wicked. 'I'm afraid I don't know you well enough to answer that.'

For heaven's sake, he was flirting with her. She had to stop this now. She was most definitely not looking for any kind of relationship. Apart from the fact that she'd given up on men, she was pregnant, for heaven's sake. Besides, Jack was probably the kind of man who flirted with any available female.

Lizzie froze him with her most cutting glare. It was time to get serious. Really serious. She hadn't come to the outback for a holiday, and she certainly hadn't come here for romance. She had a stack of paperwork to get through and she should set Jack Lewis straight. Now.

And yet…she couldn't help wondering…who was she really? An Elizabeth? Or a Lizzie?

A small frown settled between Jack's brows and he stood abruptly. 'We should talk about meals,' he said. 'The pantry's well stocked and so is the cold room, but we're the only ones here to do the cooking, so—'

'We?' Lizzie interrupted, somewhat startled. 'You're not expecting me to cook, are you?'

He slid a sideways glance to the big country stove, then back to Lizzie. 'Excuse me, Senator. Perhaps you weren't aware that lesser mortals actually prepare their own meals?'

'Of course I know that,' she snapped, aware that he probably planned to call her Senator whenever he wanted to put her down.

Jack narrowed his eyes at her. 'Can you recognise one end of a saucepan from another?'

She rolled her eyes to the ceiling to show her exasperation, but, truth was, in recent years she'd been far too busy to dally with anything remotely domesticated. Admittedly, since she'd become pregnant, she'd been conscientious about breakfast—making a smoothie from yoghurt and fruit—but her PA brought her a salad from the deli for lunch, and her diary was filled with evening engagements—charity functions, political dinners, business meetings—so she often ate out.

On the few occasions she ate at home, the meals had mostly been takeaway, eaten at her desk with little attention to taste or texture. She couldn't remember the last time she'd eaten alone with a man in a private home.

'I don't have time for cooking.' Lizzie added a dash of ice to her tone.

Not in the least intimidated, Jack leaned his hips against a cupboard and eyed her steadily. 'Then you'll have to risk your digestion with my cooking.'

'Is that a threat?'

His eyes held the glimmer of menace. 'I guess you'll soon find out, won't you? Otherwise, you could go solo and make your own meals. No skin off my nose. Or we could take turns at the stove and share what we cook.'

'Share?' Lizzie set her mug down before she spilled its contents. She hadn't shared a house, taking turns in the kitchen, since her carefree university days.

Back then, when she'd shared a house and a kitchen, she'd also fallen in love. With Mitch.

Her mind flashed an unbidden memory of her younger, laughing self, teaching Mitch to test spaghetti by throwing it against the kitchen wall to see if it stuck. As always, he'd had a better idea, and they'd shared a spaghetti strand between their linked mouths, eating until their lips met. And then, of course, they'd kissed…and, quite probably, they'd gone to bed. She'd been so madly in love back then.

But it was such a long time ago.

'No worries.' Jack gave her a crooked grin. 'I'm no chef, but I guess I can look after the cooking. I hope you like steak.'

'Steak's fine,' Lizzie said, and then, to her astonishment, she found herself adding, 'but I'm sure I could brush up on a few old recipes.'

When Jack looked uncertain, she supplied her credentials. 'After all, my mother owns a restaurant.'

'A restaurant?' His eyes widened, suitably impressed. 'Where?'

'In Monta Correnti. In Italy.'

'An Italian restaurant!' Jack sent her an eye-rolling grin and rubbed his stomach. 'I love Italian tucker. I bet the talent for cooking runs in your family.' His grin deepened. 'And here I was thinking you were just a pretty face.'

As Lizzie unpacked her suitcases she refused to think about Jack Lewis. She especially refused to think about his throwaway line about her pretty face.

For heaven's sake, he was a young man, barely thirty, and she was pregnant and practically middle-aged, and she'd long ago learned to ignore comments about her looks.

Female politicians were fair game for the media, and from the moment she'd hit parliament journalists had paid far too much attention to her appearance, her dress sense, and her hairstyles. It had been beyond infuriating.

Since Lizzie's university days, she'd had her heart set on working hard to better the lives of ordinary, everyday Australians, but the reporters only seemed to notice what she was wearing, or which man she was dating.

There'd been one infamous photo, early in her career, of her coming out of a restaurant, arm in arm with a male colleague. Her hair was loose, blowing in the wind, and she was wearing a shortish skirt with knee-high Italian leather boots. The boots were dark red, and the photo had found its way onto the front page of every metropolitan daily in the nation.

"Boots and all" the headlines had announced. It was as if she'd dropped IQ points simply because she'd worn something sexy.

After that, Lizzie had chosen to keep her hair in a tidy bun and to dress sedately and she'd schooled herself to ignore the unwanted attention of the press gallery.

Jack's comment was no different. It was water off a duck's back.

Of course it was.

She concentrated on colour-coding her clothing as she hung it in the old-fashioned wardrobe with an oval mirror on the door. Her undergarments and nightwear went into the Baltic pine chest of drawers.

She arranged the ten good books she'd brought on her desk, and set up her laptop, checked that the Internet connection worked—yes, thank heavens—and downloaded a raft of emails from her office.

Out of habit, she answered them promptly, although she would have loved to ignore them today and to wander down the hall to the old-fashioned bathroom, to take a long soak in the deep, claw-foot tub she'd spied there. Just as she would have loved to take a little nap on the big white bed, with the French doors open to catch the breeze blowing in from the paddocks.

She couldn't slacken off on her very first day. It was important to prove to herself and to her colleagues that this month-long retreat would not stop her from working.

With business emails completed, Lizzie sent a quick message of thanks to Kate Burton, telling her that she'd arrived safely. She considered gently chiding Kate for not warning her about Jack's youth, but she decided that even a gentle protest might give Kate the wrong idea.

She also sent a quick note to her mother and another,

warmer message to her cousin Isabella in Monta Correnti, telling her about the move to Savannah.

During Lizzie's latest trip to Italy, Isabella had surprised everyone by announcing her engagement to Maximilliano Di Rossi. But to Lizzie's dismay, the exciting news had been rather overshadowed by the terrible animosity that flared up, worse than ever, between her mother and Isabella's father, Luca.

There'd been ongoing tensions between the two families for decades now, fuelled by the fierce rivalry between their restaurants, "Sorella" and "Rosa", which stood next door to each other in Monta Correnti.

Lizzie, however, had always been close friends with Isabella, and she was determined to keep in touch with her now as an important step in her plan to build bridges across the family divide.

In her private life and her public life Lizzie Green planned to become a stress-free zone…

And with her duties accomplished, the big white bed still beckoned.

Really, she found herself asking, what was the harm? She'd been fighting tiredness ever since she'd first become pregnant—and there'd been an embarrassing occasion when she'd nodded off during a senate enquiry into the cost of roadworks in new mining areas.

Now, she was here in one of the remotest corners of the big empty outback, amazingly free to adjust her schedule in any way she liked, and next to no one would be any the wiser.

After years of relentless hard work and a punishing schedule, the sudden freedom was scary.

But it was real.

Wow.

Yes, she really was free. Out here, no one would know

or care if Senator Elizabeth Green took a long, relaxing bath in the middle of the afternoon. There were no journalists lurking outside the homestead, and Lizzie was free to contemplate the miracle happening inside her.

As always, her spirits lifted the instant she thought about the tiny little baby growing in her womb.

She was so, so glad she'd gone along with her plan, in spite of all the worry, and the doubts voiced by her friends.

'A sperm donor, Lizzie? You've got to be joking.'

Her girlfriends hadn't understood at first, and Lizzie couldn't really blame them. For years it hadn't bothered her that she was the only woman in her circle of friends who was still single and babyless. She'd been almost smug, proud that she was an independent thinker, a New Age woman who didn't bow down to the pressure to follow the crowd. She was focused on a higher calling.

Unfortunately, the smugness hadn't lasted.

At thirty-eight pushing thirty-nine, almost overnight, something had clicked inside her. She'd been gripped by a sudden, deep and painful yearning for the precious, warm weight of a baby in her arms. Not a friend's baby. Not a niece or a nephew.

Her baby.

The longing had become so powerful it had pressed against Lizzie's heart, becoming a constant ache, impossible to ignore and she'd faced the alarming truth that her body was a ticking time bomb…counting down, down, down…to a lonely and childless future…

Of course, the lack of a potential father for her baby had posed a hiccup. The scars left first by Mitch, and several years later by Toby, were deep and painful. Still.

Even so, Lizzie had tried dating. Truly, she had tried. But all the decent guys were already married, and she wasn't prepared to settle for Mr Good Enough, and there was no way she would leap into a convenient marriage just to have a baby. Where was the morality in that?

Besides, Lizzie had learned at her mother's knee that a woman could embrace independence and single mother-hood with dignity and flair.

So she'd settled on a sperm bank, but it had taken twelve nail-biting months before a viable pregnancy was con-firmed. By that time, Lizzie had been so fraught and nervous that Kate Burton had kindly insisted that she spend some time at her outback cattle station, where she could enjoy being pregnant out of the spotlight.

Lizzie had accepted with gratitude.

She knew only too well that eventually there would be questions, and all kinds of fuss about the sperm-bank decision. People would say that she'd kissed her politi-cal career goodbye, but for now she wanted to give her baby its best chance to be born healthy. Already, she loved it fiercely.

After the birth, she'd find a way to continue her career and raise her child.

Lizzie Green always found a way.

But right now, on this sunny autumn afternoon, she was a forty year old woman, pregnant for the first time, and feeling just a little lonely. And more than anything she was tired.

So why shouldn't she take that bath? If for no other reason than because she needed to get rid of the gritty red dust between her toes. Already she could picture the soothing ritual of running water, adding a swoosh of the scented salts that Kate had left. A glug of luxurious oil, then sliding down for a long soak.

And then afterwards, why not a nap?

* * *

At six o'clock, Jack tapped his knuckles on the door to Lizzie's room to tell her that dinner was ready.

When there was no answer he cleared his throat and called, 'Senator Green?' And then, another knock. 'Lizzie?'

Still there was no answer, and he wondered if she'd gone for a walk.

He'd come to her room via the veranda, so it was a simple matter to lean over the railing to scan the yard and the home paddock, but he saw no sign of her.

Surely she hadn't wandered off? Damn it. Was she going to be a nuisance on her very first day here?

He supposed there was no point in searching elsewhere without checking her room first, so he stepped through the open French doors, and his heart almost stopped beating when he saw her.

Asleep. Like a modern-day Sleeping Beauty.

Jack knew exactly what he should do—turn smartly on his heel, march straight back out of the room and knock again loudly, and he should keep on knocking or calling until the senator heard him and woke up.

Pigs might fly.

No way on this earth could he move. His feet were bolted to the floor, and his eyes were glued to Lizzie as she lay there.

She'd changed into soft and faded low-rise jeans and a pale green, sleeveless top with a low neck and little ruffles down the front. The way she was lying, curled on her side, exposed a good six inches of bare midriff.

Hey, senator, you're not so bad when you're asleep.

Not so bad? Who was he kidding?

Sleep hadn't only stolen Lizzie's haughtiness; it had left her defenceless and vulnerable. Out-of-this-world sexy.

With the attention of an artist commissioned to paint her portrait, Jack took careful note of details.

The soft light filtering through the curtains washed her with warm shadows, highlighting the intricate pattern of fine veins on her eyelids, the dusky curve of her lashes, and her dark hair rippling like water over her pillow.

Her mouth was a lush, full-blown rose, and the scooped neckline of her blouse revealed a little gold cross winking between the voluptuous swell of her breasts. His hands ached to touch her, to trace the cello-like dip and curve of her waist and hip.

Even her bare feet resting with one pressed against the other were neatly arched and sexy.

Far out. He had to get out of here fast. This sleeping beauty might look like every temptation known to man, but he knew damn well that the minute she woke she would morph straight back into the officious and cold city senator. So not the kind of woman he'd ever get involved with.

Jack forced himself to take a step back. And another. Problem was, he was still watching Lizzie instead of where he was going, and he backed into a chest of drawers, sending a hairbrush clattering to the floor.

She was instantly awake, sitting up quickly, dark hair flying about her shoulders, eyes and mouth wide with shock.

'I'm sorry.' Jack threw up his hands, protesting his innocence. 'Don't scream. It's OK.'

She was breathing rapidly, clearly frightened and disoriented, but even so she clung to her dignity.

'I'm not in the habit of screaming,' she said haughtily, while she tugged at the bottom of her blouse with both hands in a bid to close the gap of bare midriff.

No, Jack thought wryly as he bent to retrieve her silver-backed hairbrush and set it on the chest. Of course she wasn't a screamer. She was too cool. Too tough.

'I was trying to call you from the veranda, but you were

out like a light,' he said, forcing himself backwards towards the door. 'I just wanted to let you know that dinner's ready when you are.'

'Dinner? Already?' She sent a hasty glance to the fading light outside, then frowned as she reached for the wrist-watch on the bedside table. When she saw the time, she let out a huff of annoyance. 'I've been asleep for hours.'

'Half your luck.'

Clearly Lizzie didn't agree. Already she was off the bed, shuffling her feet into shoes while tying her hair into a tight, neat knot. 'Your steaks will be overcooked,' she said.

'At ease, Lizzie.'

She went still and frowned at him and Jack wondered what she would do if she knew how amazing she looked at that moment. In the shadowy twilight, with her arms raised to fix her hair, her breasts were wonderfully rounded and lifted, and the luscious gap of creamy skin at her waist was on show once more.

Jack forced his gaze to the floor. It was clearly too long since he'd had a girlfriend.

'We're not having steaks tonight,' he said. 'There's a stroganoff and it's simmering away nicely, so you've no need to rush.'

'Stroganoff?' Lizzie's eyes widened. 'You're serving stroganoff?'

'It's no big deal.' Jack shrugged, and began to head back along the veranda, calling over his shoulder, 'I'll see you in the kitchen. No hurry. Whenever you're ready.'

In the meantime he would go chop firewood, although it wasn't yet winter. Or he'd make a phone call to his dentist and volunteer to have all his teeth drilled, even though they were cavity-free. Anything to take his mind off his sexy, out-of-bounds houseguest.

* * *

To Lizzie's surprise, the stroganoff was really good. The beef was tender, the mushrooms plump and sweet, and the sauce super-smooth and tasty. She found that she was hungry—ravenous, in fact, with a new interest in food that had begun when she'd reached the end of her first trimester. As soon as her morning sickness had stopped, her appetite had blossomed.

Along with her libido. Which no doubt explained the difficulty she was having keeping her eyes off Jack. She didn't understand how she could find a man who'd slaved over a kitchen stove so incredibly attractive.

Lizzie respected successful, career-driven men, powerful politicians, or business magnates at the top of the corporate ladder. An unambitious cowboy, who managed a remote cattle property for an imperious old lady, held no appeal whatsoever.

And yet…she'd never seen blue jeans sit so attractively on a man, and Jack's shoulders were truly sensational. As for the easy way he moved and the lively sparkle in his eyes…and his smile…

He made her feel girly and soft.

Clearly, pregnancy hormones had depleted her common sense and awakened her earthier instincts.

It was an unsettling problem, and it wasn't going away.

'This is an excellent meal,' she admitted, in a bid to keep her mind on the food. 'I'm impressed.'

From across the table, Jack accepted her praise with a nonchalant smile. 'Glad you like it.' He drank deeply from a glass of beer.

'I suppose it was just a little something you threw together?'

'More or less.'

Lizzie didn't return Jack's smile. Her enjoyment of the

meal was somewhat spoiled by her competitive instincts.
Already, she was wondering how she could match Jack's
culinary efforts when it was her turn to cook, and she
wished she could remember the finer points of her mother's
favourite recipes.

'I've heard that country folk are exceptionally resource-
ful,' she said. 'I imagine you're probably a mechanic, a
cook, a cattleman and a businessman all rolled into one.'

'Something like that.' Jack's green eyes narrowed.
'That's how most city people see us, at any rate. Jack of
all trades and master of none.'

Lizzie was surprised that easy-going Jack was suddenly
touchy. Clearly she'd hit a raw nerve.

Practised at calming touchy politicians, she said, 'A
senator has to be a bit like that, too. Economist one day,
social worker the next. You get to be a minor expert in one
hundred and one areas of policy.' A moment later, she
asked, 'Have you always lived in the outback?'

Jack took his time answering her. 'Pretty much. Except
for the years I spent at boarding school.'

'And did you grow up always wanting to work on the
land?'

This question should have been perfectly harmless, but
again it seemed to annoy Jack. Leaning forward, elbows
on the table, he twisted his glass between his hands. 'Did
you grow up always wanting to be a politician?'

'Oh—' Lizzie wasn't normally thrown by sudden about-
turns, but tonight she was off her game. She responded too
quickly, 'Not really. Politics was something I sort of fell into.'

Jack's eyes widened with understandable surprise.

Unhappily, Lizzie set her knife and fork neatly together
on her empty plate, sank back in her chair and let out an
involuntary sigh. Why on earth had she made such a reveal-

ing confession to this man? She gave a dismissive wave of her hand. 'Everything changed when I went to university.'

He sent her a teasing grin. 'Don't tell me that you fell in with the wrong crowd?'

'I suppose you could say that,' she replied icily. 'I met a group of hardworking, committed idealists.'

Jack pulled a face as if to show that he wasn't impressed. Then he rose, and took their plates to the sink.

'Well…thanks for dinner.' Lizzie stood, too. It was time to get back to the work she'd missed while she'd napped. 'The stroganoff was delicious.'

'Hey,' he called as she headed for the door, 'Don't hardworking, committed idealists help with the dishes?'

Lizzie's cheeks grew hot. She hadn't given dishwashing a thought. Now she imagined standing with Jack at the sink, side by side, chatting cosily, possibly brushing against each other while they washed and dried their dishes.

'I'll wash up when I cook tomorrow night,' she said, and, without another word, she made a dignified, if hasty, exit.

Instead of watching TV as he did most nights, Jack spent the evening in the machinery shed, tinkering with the old station truck. The brakes were dodgy and needed fixing, and he seized the excuse to stay well clear of the homestead, well clear of Lizzie.

Unfortunately, staying clear of the senator didn't stop him from thinking about her. He kept remembering the way she'd looked when she was sleeping, kept thinking about her mouth, and how it would taste if he kissed her.

When he kissed her.

He was an A-grade fool.

He should be remembering how the senator turned starchy as soon as she woke, and the snooty way her lush mouth tightened when he asked her to do a simple thing like help with the dishes. Elizabeth Green was light years away from the kind of girl he was used to. She didn't even belong on a cattle property.

He couldn't imagine why Kate Burton had sent her here. Surely she must have known that Lizzie wouldn't fit in?

Jack had lived in the outback all his life and everyone he knew, even the hoity-toity grazier's wives, pitched in to lend a hand. On a working cattle property, people pulled their weight with everything from opening gates and helping with the dishes, to cooking, gardening, caring for children, mending a fence, or joining the cattle muster. Jack could remember one occasion when his mother had even helped to fight bushfires.

If the senator thought he was going to run around waiting on her, she had another think coming. She'd waltzed onto Savannah at an extremely inconvenient time, and she certainly couldn't expect kid-glove treatment.

If he had his way, he'd bring her down a peg or two.

Problem was, even though Lizzie was out of place here, and even though she was bossy and citified and bloody annoying, she *was* incredibly sexy. Maddeningly so. Those lips of hers and those alluring curves were driving Jack crazy. Already, after half a day.

An entire month of her presence on Savannah was going to be torture.

If Jack thought it would work, he'd ignore Kate's request to play host to Lizzie, and he'd ring the contract mustering plant on his satellite phone and offer to trade places with Bill Jervis, his cook.

Bill was sixty, and a grandfather, and he could keep an eye on Lizzie Green as easily as Jack could, and he could prepare top-class meals for her every night. Jack, on the other hand, could be out on the muster with the stockmen. They had a difficult task, clearing three thousand head of cattle out of some very rough country, and his intimate knowledge of the Savannah terrain would be a definite asset.

The swapping scheme was beautiful in its simplicity. There was only one problem with it. Jack might be a good stockman, but he'd have a mutiny on his hands if he tried to deprive the ringers of Bill's cooking.

Which brought him back to square one—he had no choice but to stay put and to grin and bear Lizzie Green's presence here.

It was ten o'clock when he left the truck's innards lying in pieces on the machinery shed floor and went to the laundry to scrub off the worst of his grime. The laundry was a simple wooden lean-to attached to the back of the house—a very basic and functional bachelor affair. Tonight, however, it was filled with white linen clothes soaking in sparkling suds, and wispy bits of lingerie dangled from a tiny line suspended above it.

Jack groaned as the fantasies fuelled by those scant scraps of fabric caused a whole new set of problems.

CHAPTER THREE

THE strident laughter of kookaburras woke Lizzie. Disoriented, she lay still, staring about her, taking in the soft grey morning light that crept through an unfamiliar window. Slowly, she remembered her arrival at Savannah yesterday, and why she'd come here.

She smelled bacon frying, which meant Jack was up.

Dismayed, she washed and dressed and hurried to the kitchen. It would be her turn to cook dinner this evening and already the task was looming in her mind as The Great Kitchen Challenge. She wanted to catch Jack before he took off for some far-flung corner of the property, to ask him about the contents of Savannah's pantry.

He was still at the stove, fortunately, tending to a frying pan, and looking far more appealing than any man had a right to look at such an early hour.

He was wearing a blue cotton shirt, faded from much washing, and old jeans torn at the knee. His fair hair was backlit by the morning sun and his skin was brown and weather-beaten, and he looked astonishingly real, and vitally alive. Impossibly attractive.

But I don't want to be attracted. I can't believe I'm reacting this way. It's bizarre.

He turned and smiled, and Lizzie's insides folded.

'Morning, Senator.'

'Good morning, Jack.' Good heavens. She sounded ridiculously breathless.

'Hope you slept well?'

'Quite well, thank you.'

She cast a deliberately cool glance at the contents of the frying pan and suppressed an urge to enquire about Jack's cholesterol levels.

'You're welcome to share this,' he said.

'No, thanks.' She gave a theatrical shudder. 'I usually have yoghurt and fruit.'

'Suit yourself,' he said smoothly. 'The fruit bowl's on the table. Feel free to take whatever you like. I'm pretty sure Bill keeps yoghurt in the cold room.'

'The cold room?'

With a lazy thumbing gesture, Jack pointed to a door in the opposite wall. 'Through there.'

Good heavens. What kind of host expected his guests to hunt for their own meals? Lizzie was distinctly put out as he turned off the heat and loaded up his plate, leaving her to march into the huge cold room in search of yoghurt.

Admittedly, the cold room was very well organised, and she found, not only a small tub of biodynamic berry yoghurt, but the cuts of meat she needed for the evening's meal.

'I've made coffee,' Jack said, sending her a smile when she returned. 'And there's still plenty in the pot.'

'I'm afraid I can't drink coffee.'

His eyebrows rose high. 'You don't like it?'

'Not—at the moment.' The doctors had warned Lizzie to avoid coffee while she was pregnant. 'I'll make tea,' she said, guessing he was unlikely to offer. Then, 'So what are your plans for the day?'

'I'll be bleeding the brakes on the old truck we use to cart feed around the property.'

'Bleeding brakes? That sounds tricky.'

'It is, actually. I decided to give the truck an overhaul while the men are away, and I started last night, but the brakes are even worse than I thought.' His green gaze held hers. 'I'm afraid I'm going to need a hand.'

Lizzie frowned. 'But there's no one left here to help you, is there?'

Across the table, he flashed a grin. 'That's why I was hoping you'd offer to help.'

'Me?' Lizzie's jaw dropped so quickly she was surprised it didn't crack.

'I'd really appreciate it.'

Stunned, she shook her head. '*I* can't help you. I'm far too busy, and I don't know the first thing about trucks. I've never even changed a tyre.'

'You don't need to *know* anything. You just have to press the brake pedal a few times.'

Clearly, Jack was one of those people who thought politicians only worked when parliament was in session. Lizzie was used to colleagues who treated her heavy workload with due reverence, but Jack didn't give a hoot about her investigations into fairer private health incentives.

'I have a mountain of important documents to read through this morning.' *And I have to spend this afternoon cooking*.

'You could spare a few minutes.'

Shocked, Lizzie stared at him, angry at his lack of respect. That is, she wanted to be angry. She intended to be angry, but his naughty-boy smile was like sun thawing frost.

She heard herself saying, feebly, 'I—I suppose I might be able to spare ten minutes. No more.'

Which was how she found herself in the machinery

shed a quarter of an hour later, balanced on the front bumper of a rusty old truck, breathing in diesel, while she stared helplessly at a bewildering tangle of metal cylinders, knobs, pipes and rubber hoses.

'I have to get fluid through the system and air out of the lines,' Jack said.

'So what do I have to do?'

'I'll need your help just as soon as I've poured this fluid down the brake line.'

'Where's the brake line?'

'Over there to the right, next to the carburettor.'

Lizzie hadn't a clue where the carburettor was, but she couldn't help admiring the concentration on Jack's face as he poured the fluid, very carefully, not spilling a drop.

That done, he told her to hop behind the wheel, ready to work the brakes, and then he promptly disappeared beneath the truck.

Fine prickles darted over Lizzie's skin as she watched him. There was something so very earthy and unsettling about seeing a grown man—a gorgeous, broad-shouldered, lean-hipped grown man, no less—on his back, on the ground, easing himself under a mass of machinery.

Jack's head and shoulders disappeared first, and she found herself staring at his torso and legs...at the bare tanned skin showing through the tear in his jeans—not a designer tear, but a proper work-worn rip—at the battered leather plait threaded through his belt loops...and the very masculine bulge beneath the zip in the centre seam.

Her mouth went dry as she actually imagined lying there beside him, on top of him, under him, their bodies intimately entwined.

'Right,' Jack called. 'Press the brake down steadily with an even force.'

'Oh.'

Caught out, she had to scramble to get into the truck's cabin.

'OK,' she called, a flustered minute later. 'I'm pressing the brake now.'

'Sing out "down", when you've pressed it as far as it will go. And then take it off when I call "up".'

It wasn't easy to depress the brake fully. Lizzie had to sit on the very edge of the seat, but at last she called, 'Down!'

It was ages before Jack called, 'OK. Up!'

Relieved, she let the brake off, but then Jack called, 'Can you do that again?' And the process was repeated over and over, while he patiently tested and retested the first brake, and then the brakes connected to each of the truck's wheels.

She couldn't believe he'd dragged her all the way down here just to call out 'down'. The process took much longer than ten minutes, and she was angry about the precious time she was wasting…

And yet, to her immense surprise, she actually enjoyed the strange back-and-forth communication with his disembodied voice. She liked the sense of teamwork…and she had to admit that brakes *were* vitally important… Men's lives relied on them.

Besides…she kept picturing Jack on his back beneath the massive vehicle…kept remembering how breathtaking he'd looked down there.

Oh, no. Not again.

How could she be obsessing about a man who was at least ten years younger than her? A man who had no idea that she was pregnant?

It was all very disturbing. And surprising. This time yesterday she'd been chairing a last-minute face-to-face meeting to discuss the Renewal Energy Amendment Bill.

Today she was perched behind the wheel of a truck in an outback machinery shed, breathing in diesel fumes, and having a disjointed conversation with a man lying beneath the vehicle.

It was almost as if she'd been teleported to another planet. Finally, Jack shouted, 'OK, that's it. All good.'

Relieved, Lizzie scrambled down from the truck, and Jack slid out from beneath it, wiping blackened hands on an old rag. He jumped to his feet with easy grace.

'Thanks,' he said. 'I couldn't have done that without your help. You were brilliant.'

He was looking into her eyes and his smile was so genuine, Lizzie became flustered and dismissive. 'Don't be silly. It was nothing.'

Jack laughed. 'I suppose you're used to putting your foot down.'

Her smile stiffened. 'It's a very necessary part of my job. Now, if you'll excuse me, I must get straight back to that job.'

'By all means, Senator. I'll walk with you to the house. I need to make a phone call to Kate Burton.'

Walking with Jack hadn't been part of her plan. She'd been hoping to escape his knowing smile, and those ripped jeans, the rumpled shirt, and the smear of grease on his jaw.

As they left the shed and emerged into dazzling sunlight Jack asked in a conversational tone, 'So how long have you known Kate?'

'Oh, for quite a few years.' Lizzie couldn't help smiling. 'Kate's hard to miss. She's involved in so many organisations. Quite a mover and shaker. On the national board of several charities. She got me onside to help with funding for additional places in aged care.'

Jack grinned. 'That sounds like her cup of tea.'

'Actually, it was a tall order. We needed to increase the

budget for the aging by a third, but Treasury was blocking it. In the end I had to get support from both houses to allow the passage of a new bill. Kate was very grateful.'

'No doubt.' Jack's voice was strangely rough, and his mouth had twisted into a complicated smile.

'What about you, Jack? How long have you known her?'

He shrugged. 'Since I was a kid. She and my mother have always been friends.'

Lizzie expected further explanation, but they'd reached the homestead steps.

'I'd better let you get to work,' he said, moving ahead of her, taking the steps two at a time, then swiftly disappearing inside, and leaving Lizzie to wonder if she'd said something wrong.

In his study, Jack raked a shaky hand through his hair.

He picked up the phone, dropped it down again, paced to the window and looked out, shocked by the confusion churning inside him. He fancied Lizzie like crazy, but she was the last woman on the planet he should chase.

Why would he want to? It didn't make sense. Why would an outback cowboy even dream of getting together with a high-profile federal senator, who had the power to affect the course of their nation?

She wasn't remotely his type. She was ambitious, and driven. The kind of person he'd always steered clear of. Too much like his father.

Jack's stomach clenched tighter as he thought about his old man.

Ambition, boy. That's what you need. A man's nothing without ambition.

Sure, Dad.

To please his old man, Jack had chosen his life's goal

at the age of six. Together they'd watched Air Force training exercises—sleek, super-sophisticated monsters ripping across the outback skies—and Jack had decided that as soon as he finished school, he would be in the cockpit of a fighter jet.

To impress his dad, he'd spent his boyhood trying to excel in the usual outback activities, but no matter how many pony races or calf-roping events he'd won, his father had always found something to criticise.

Just remembering the boxing lessons he'd taken sent a wave of resentment through Jack. He'd never satisfied his old man. He was constantly criticised for not having the killer instinct, for standing back if an opponent slipped, or for holding back on a knockout.

He'd put up with it all, however, because he knew that one day he'd finally make his father proud.

Then he'd sat the recruitment exams. Jack had known he had the necessary co-ordination and fitness, and he'd scored good grades in the required subjects, so he'd gone into the final tests brimming with confidence.

He'd come out devastated.

He'd passed every section with ease, except the most important of all—the psych test.

The recruiting officers had been diplomatic, but Jack got the message. He wasn't cut out to fly their devastating weapons into battle. They wanted someone with a ruthless streak, with hard arrogance and a get-out-of-my-way attitude...

The kind of man his father had pushed him to be... The kind of man he could never be...

It had taken Jack years to accept this, and to finally be comfortable in his own skin. Now, his awareness of his strengths and weaknesses only made it plain as day that he and Lizzie were polar opposites. He had no doubt that she'd trampled on people as she scaled the heights of parliament.

She was pushy and powerful. She had to be. OK, maybe she was driven by an urge to help people, but maybe she was also just hungry for success.

Bottom line—they had nothing in common. He was a strumming guitar. Lizzie was the whole brass band. Why was he lusting after a woman like that? And why the hell couldn't he simply talk himself out of it?

By six o'clock, Lizzie was ready to crawl into bed. Instead she had to face a mountain of washing-up.

She was out of practice at this cooking caper, and she'd gone overboard, of course.

Inspired by fond memories of her Grandmother Rosa's ossobucco in a heavenly vegetable sauce, she'd thrown herself into the task. She'd been so sure it would be the perfect meal to impress Jack, so she'd hunted on the Internet for a recipe that closely matched her memories of Rosa's dish, and she'd followed it to the letter.

The first part hadn't been too bad. She'd already found the meat she needed in the homestead's cold room and she'd tied string around each ossobucco, then lightly floured them on both sides, but not around the edges.

While they were browning, she'd cut zucchinis, carrots, onion and celery—all of which she'd found in a surprisingly well-maintained kitchen garden at the back of the house.

With the casserole in the oven, however, Lizzie had begun on the special vegetable sauce that had made her grandmother's dish out of the ordinary. Four different vegetables—peas, beans, carrots and celery—all had to go into separate bowls of cold water and soak for half an hour. Each vegetable then had to be boiled in its own pot, then they were blended together before being added as a smooth sauce to the casserole.

Honestly, Lizzie knew it was ridiculous to go to such lengths for a simple evening meal with Jack Lewis. He'd managed to throw together last night's meal with a minimum of fuss, and he'd only used one pot, for heaven's sake. She, on the other hand, had used practically every saucepan and dish in the kitchen.

With too much to fit in the dishwasher she was still up to her elbows in detergent suds when she heard Jack's footsteps approaching.

'Honey, I'm home!' he called in a pseudo-American accent, rippling with humour.

She spun around, outrageously pleased to see him fresh from the shower, damp strands of dark blond hair flopping onto his forehead, and smelling of sexy aftershave.

He was smiling and he looked so genuinely pleased to see her that her heart seemed to tilt in her chest.

'How's the truck?'

Jack smiled. 'I took it for a test-drive this afternoon and it runs as smoothly as a sewing machine. The brakes are perfect.' He sent a curious glance to the stove. 'I'm faint with hunger, and that smells amazing. Is it Italian?'

'Yes.' Lizzie took a breath to calm down. 'It's osso-bucco.' *Oh, dear.* She sounded far too proud of herself, didn't she?

'Ossobucco?' Jack's eyebrows lifted. 'That's authentic. Did you have any trouble finding everything you needed?'

'Not at all.' She wondered how he could look at her with such thrilling intensity and discuss food at the same time. 'There are so many different cuts of meat in the cold room, and all sorts of vegetables in the garden.'

'All thanks to Bill,' Jack admitted.

'Is he the cook who's out with the mustering team?'

'The one and only.' Jack saw the huge pile of dishes in front of her. 'Hey, you knew you only had to cook one meal tonight, didn't you?'

Lizzie bit her lip. 'You weren't supposed to see this mess. I wanted it all cleared up before we ate.'

'But what have you been up to? Cooking for a whole week?'

'No,' she said tightly, turning back to the sink, highly embarrassed by the amount of mess she'd made.

Jack snagged a tea towel. 'I'll give you a hand.'

'No!' This time she almost snapped at him. 'Please, don't bother. I—I'll have these dishes done in no time. Dinner won't be ready for another ten minutes, or so. Why don't you go and—and—'

'Count kookaburras?' he suggested with a knowing smile.

'Watch a bit of television,' she supplied lamely.

Shrugging, he crossed the kitchen, opened the refrigerator and selected a beer. 'I'll feed the dog,' he said as he snapped the top off the beer.

Lizzie felt strangely deflated when he left the room. Lips compressed, she finished the dishes and set the cleared end of the table, took the casserole from the oven, and cut the strings from around the meat before setting it aside to rest.

When Jack wandered back, he was carrying a dusty bottle of red wine. 'I found this in the cellar. I thought your meal deserved something better than beer.'

Lizzie forced a smile.

'You'll join me, won't you?' he said, reaching into an overhead cupboard for wine glasses.

'Um…I'm not drinking alcohol at the moment.'

Jack's green eyes widened. 'This retreat of yours requires abstinence?'

'Yes.'

With a puzzled grin, he held out the bottle. 'But this is a great vintage, and it's Italian vino.'

'I'm sure it's lovely, Jack.' She forced lightness into her voice. 'But you can't tempt me to the dark side. I won't have wine tonight, thanks.'

He turned the bottle in his hands, frowning at the label. 'I don't want to drink it alone. Guess I'll stick with beer.'

'I'm sorry. Normally, I'd love a glass of wine, but I'm—'

The word *pregnant* died on Lizzie's lips.

Annoyed with the situation, she picked up a fork from the table and rubbed at it against a tea towel as if she were removing a spot.

'No worries.' Jack was as easy-going as ever.

But Lizzie *was* worried. She shouldn't feel bad simply because she hadn't told Jack about her pregnancy. He didn't need to know. It wasn't any of his business. Except…unfortunately, she knew there was another reason she was clinging to her secret.

Her news would kill the playful warmth in his eyes, and, for reasons that made no sense at all, she didn't want to break the bewildering thread of attraction that thrummed between them. She hadn't felt anything like it for ages. She didn't want to feel anything like it. She'd deliberately distanced herself from such feelings.

And yet, even though she knew this attraction was highly inappropriate, it was also spectacularly thrilling.

She set the casserole dish on a mat on the table and lifted the lid.

Jack let out a soft groan. 'This is too good to be true.'

'What is?' She was tense as a violin string. The flash of heat in his eyes seemed to scorch her, but it disappeared as quickly as it had come, and he offered her a lopsided smile.

'Beauty, brains and a talent for cooking. You're quite a package, Senator Green.'

'Don't be too rash with the compliments until you've tasted the meal.'

Using a serving spoon, she lifted two ossobucci smothered in vegetable sauce onto Jack's plate. The smell was the same rich and appetising aroma she remembered from her grandmother's kitchen, and even though the meat probably wasn't young veal, it was tender and falling away from the bones, just as it should.

With a sense of relief Lizzie sat down to eat, but she couldn't completely relax until Jack had taken his first bite. To her dismay, he sat staring at his plate.

'Is something wrong, Jack?'

'No.' He picked up his knife and fork and sent her another crooked smile. 'I wondered where these bones had got to.'

'These bones?' she repeated in horrified alarm.

Jack grimaced, clearly embarrassed, and he shook his head. 'Don't worry. It's nothing. Shouldn't have mentioned it.' Immediately, he began to eat. 'Mmm. Lizzie, this is amazing.'

'But what were you saying about bones?' She couldn't eat until she knew.

'Don't worry about it. I shouldn't have said anything. Just relax and enjoy the meal. You've gone to a lot of trouble and it's sensational.'

'But I shouldn't have used these ossobucci, should I?'

Jack dropped his gaze to his plate. 'Well, I've never heard them called *that* before,' he admitted.

'What do you call them?'

His eyes were apologetic. 'Shin bones. We—er—usually keep them for the dogs.'

Caro Dio. Lizzie clasped a hand over her mouth. Tears stung her eyes.

'Lizzie.' Jack reached across the table and touched the back of her hand. 'It's OK. The meal's fabulous.'

'But you wanted the bones for your dogs.'

She sniffed. It would be ridiculous to cry.

'I didn't realise you could make a meal out of tough old bones, and, heaven knows, the dogs don't need them. Don't give it another thought.'

Jack's eyes sparkled at her, enticing from her an answering smile.

'I suppose it serves me right,' she admitted. 'I was trying too hard.' She gave a shaky laugh and a roll of her eyes. 'All those pots and pans.'

'This meal is worth every one of them,' Jack said, tucking in.

Lizzie ate, too, and she had to admit that the food tasted very good, but she could have saved herself an awful lot of work if she'd cooked something simple like spaghetti.

Why was it so hard for her to remember that she'd stepped out of the political circus ring? She didn't have to compete any more. She was here to relax. To slow down. Loosen up. Let go.

As they ate Jack encouraged her to talk, but, while most people expected her to talk about some aspect of her political work, he wanted to know more about her childhood in Italy, and she found herself unwinding as she recalled those happy times.

Many of her memories involved her little sisters, Jackie and Scarlett, and when she let her mind roll back she could almost hear the echoes of their laughter bouncing off their neighbours' houses as they chased each other down the cobbled streets. She could hear their girlish squeals as they ran up the hill, brushing past bushes of rosemary, catching its scent in their skirts, ducking beneath thorny branches in the lemon grove.

She told Jack about the sky in Monta Correnti, the unbelievable deep, deep blue of hyacinths, and the buttery sunlight that fell on ancient stone walls as she walked to school, clutching her mother's hand. She told him about the tangle of wild olive trees on the mountainside, the winding paths rimmed with autumn crocuses, her grandmother's cat asleep in the ivy.

Suddenly, she realised that Jack was staring at her, no longer easy-going, or relaxed, or smiling, but with an emotion that set her pulses racing.

'So beautiful,' he said softly.

Lizzie swallowed a gasp. She was almost certain he was talking about her, but this attraction thing was getting out of hand. She found it undeniably exciting, but it was wrong. Misplaced. She shouldn't allow Jack to speak to her like this.

'Yes, Italy's beautiful,' she said, pretending that she'd misunderstood him. 'But Australia's beautiful, too. Every country's beautiful in its own way.'

By now they'd finished their meal, and Lizzie stood to take their plates to the sink.

With a wry half-smile, Jack stood, too.

To her relief, he didn't try to repeat his compliment.

'Thank you,' he said instead. 'That was a memorable meal.'

'I'm glad you enjoyed it. I really liked your stroganoff last night.' Lizzie set the plates in the sink. 'I thought men were supposed to be messy cooks but you tossed that meal together so easily, *and* you only used one pot.'

From the sink, she threw a glance back over her shoulder to see Jack's reaction to this admission, was surprised to find him looking sheepish.

'Maybe that's because I only had to reheat the stroganoff,' he said.

Lizzie frowned. 'Excuse me?'

Standing there, with his hands shoved in his pockets, he looked like a little boy caught out for cheating in a spelling test. 'Bill, the cook, left the stroganoff in the freezer. I just had to heat it up.'

Lizzie's jaw dropped. 'But you let me think you'd made it from scratch.'

He shrugged. 'I didn't actually say I'd cooked it, but you seemed so impressed and I was happy to leave it that way.'

'Jack!' She couldn't believe he'd tricked her like that. How annoying.

Jack sent her a teasing smile. 'I should have known you'd turn the meals into a competition.'

'But I didn't!'

'Of course it was a competition, Lizzie.' Jack was moving towards her now. Laughter shimmered in his eyes as he came slowly, easily, across the kitchen, closer and closer. 'You can't help being competitive.' His voice was slow, deep, and teasing. 'Your mother named you after the Queen, and now you have to be top dog in everything.'

'That's not true.' As protests went, it was very weak. Lizzie threw up her hands in frustration.

Jack caught her wrists and held them fast.

Her breath was trapped in her throat. He was holding her by her wrists alone, and yet she felt pinned against the sink by the sheer force of his sexy masculinity. Looking up at him with a kind of fascinated awe, she could see that he wasn't smiling now.

She recognised the serious intent in his eyes. She'd seen it before, in other men, and she knew he wanted to kiss her. Oh, heavens, Jack was so very attractive and she could feel herself weakening, but she couldn't allow it. She was pregnant, for heaven's sake.

Their situation was precarious—a man and a woman alone in the middle of nowhere with a dangerously simmering attraction. Lizzie felt poised on a tightrope, about to fall, but she had to cling to common sense. She couldn't afford this kind of complication.

'Jack, you're invading my personal space.'

'Are you objecting?'

'Most definitely.' She spoke in her steeliest senatorial tones.

The light in Jack's eyes died. He let her wrists go and took a step back from her. For tense moments neither of them spoke, but they stared at each other, unhappily aware that a thrilling but reckless opportunity had been offered and rejected.

'So,' he said quietly, 'what would you like to do now?'

'I have to wash up.'

'You've washed up. It won't take a moment to throw these few things in the dishwasher. What then? Do you want to watch TV?' His mouth tilted in a half-mast smile. 'I'm assuming you'd like to keep up with the news.'

Lizzie imagined watching television with Jack, pictured him sprawled on the sofa, jeans stretched tight over solid, toned thighs. She knew she would spend the evening checking him out, and then he would know for sure how impossibly attracted she was.

She should keep her distance, calm down, get her head

straight. The news of the world would have to wait. She could always keep up with it via the Internet.

'No TV tonight, thanks,' she said as she headed for the door. 'I need to catch up on my emails.'

CHAPTER FOUR

SHE'D almost let Jack kiss her.

She'd *wanted* him to kiss her.

She'd very nearly jumped into his arms.

Lizzie stood at the doorway of her room, looking out across the front veranda to the quiet paddocks and the silvery trunks of gum trees, shocked by how close she'd come to wrecking her careful plans.

She'd come to Savannah to escape the pressures of the city, mostly to escape the pressure of journalists who'd just love to discover her pregnancy and turn it into a scandal. Yet tonight she'd been on the brink of creating a hot, new scandal.

With Jack.

She could imagine the headlines.

'Senator's Outback Love Nest.'

'Senator Takes a Cowboy.'

She'd wanted Jack to kiss her. Heaven help her, she'd practically *prayed* for amnesia. She'd wanted to forget her political responsibilities, and to forget she was forty and off men, and that she *always* picked the wrong men anyway. She'd wanted to forget that she was only here for a few short weeks, forget that her focus was on becoming a mother to an anonymous man's baby.

She'd wanted to forget everything…except the sexy sparkle in Jack's eyes and the alluring promise of his lips.

How scary it was to know she was so hopelessly weak. After years of self-discipline and hard work, after carefully weighing the pros and cons of single motherhood, tonight she'd wanted to risk it all while she carried on like a reckless, hormone-crazed kid.

Thank heavens nothing had happened.

She had to look on that encounter as a warning, and to be forewarned was to be forearmed. Now that she knew she was susceptible to Jack she would be much more careful in future.

On the back veranda, Jack stared out into the black night, idly stroking the springy fur between Cobber's ears while his mind replayed the scene in the kitchen.

He'd been so close to kissing Lizzie. Her mouth had been mere inches from his. He'd been able to smell her skin and the hint of lemony shampoo in her hair. He'd been about to taste her.

You're invading my personal space.

Are you objecting?

Most definitely.

'What do you reckon?' Jack asked the dog softly. 'Was that a stinging rejection? Or a lucky escape?'

Lizzie dreamed she was a child again. Wearing a blue dress and sandals, legs brown and bare, she wandered along the familiar, cobbled streets of Monta Correnti where purple petunias spilled from sunny balconies and washing hung from lines strung between windows.

Wherever she went, she could hear the church bell ringing the angelus from the top of the mountain, and she felt wonderfully safe.

But then, in the haphazard way that dreams changed, Lizzie was in her uncle Luca's kitchen where dried red peppers hung in loops from the ceiling and an old timber dresser held glassware and thick, blue and white plates. The fragrant aroma of tomato sauce, rich with basil and oregano, drifted from a pot on the stove.

Her cousins, Luca's twin boys, Alessandro and Angelo, were there in the dream, too. The three of them were eating spaghetti from deep bowls, slurping happily.

The scene changed again to a hot summer's night, and Lizzie and the twins were lying on the terrazzo balcony of her uncle's house, hoping for a cool breeze, while they looked up through stone arched windows to the jasmine-scented moon.

Suddenly, Isabella burst into the scene, but she was an adult, crying to Lizzie that she didn't know about the boys, and demanding to know where they'd come from.

When Lizzie woke the dream still felt real, even though Alessandro and Angelo had left Italy so very long ago— so long ago that Isabella and Lizzie's sisters hadn't even known about them.

Most of Lizzie's memories of the little boys were vague, but she could clearly remember their shiny eyes and cheeky smiles. She could definitely remember being in trouble with her mother for visiting Uncle Luca's house, and she remembered later being given strict orders never to speak to the rest of the family about the boys. Lizzie had never understood where they'd gone and she'd almost forgotten about them until her recent visit home.

With a heavy sigh, she rolled over in bed, cringing as she thought again about the terrible row that had erupted during her visit to Monta Correnti.

She'd gone to Italy full of her exciting baby news and she'd been even more excited about Isabella's engagement to Max, but she'd left hurt and bewildered, struggling to understand why her mother had so suddenly and angrily exposed the long-held secret that Luca had kept from his children.

Lisa was full of her own news because she'd just come back from New York where she'd seen a photo in the paper of Angelo, one of the twins who was a baseball star now. But… But it seemed incomprehensible to Lizzie that her mother would choose Luca's birthday to reveal the dark secret he'd kept from his children. Of course, the sudden news of the twins' existence had blown the family apart, but Isabella had been hit hardest of all.

But now that she was fully awake, Lizzie tried to shake off the dream. Last night, she'd reminded herself that she'd come to Savannah for a break, to focus on her pregnancy and on the changes that lay ahead. And yet here she was, still finding something to worry about.

By the time Lizzie arrived in the kitchen Jack had already breakfasted and gone, so she ate quickly, and returned to her room, carrying her mug of tea, where she downloaded her emails and discovered a brief message from her mother.

I'm too busy as always, but the restaurant is doing very well, so can't complain. I hope you're looking after yourself, darling. Do remember to take your iron tablets.

Lizzie knew she shouldn't have been surprised by the message's brevity. She should be used to her mother's ways by now.

Still, Lizzie longed to hear news of peace between her mother and her uncle. Perhaps it was too much to expect the brother and sister to kiss and make up. Just the same, she was worried. And there was still no message from Isabella. She'd sent her cousin several emails now, but Isabella was yet to reply.

There was every chance, of course, that Isabella was extremely busy. She'd always worked harder than anyone else, taking care of her smaller brothers after their mother died. Even now, when she was engaged to a wealthy Italian prince, Isabella was still working hard in the family restaurant.

Given Isabella's devotion to her family, it was no wonder she'd been especially upset by the news of Alessandro and Angelo in America. And it was completely understandable that she'd resented the fact that Lizzie had known about her brothers all along.

Thinking about it now, Lizzie felt as if she were almost as guilty as her mother was, which was pretty silly. She'd been a child, after all, and she'd promised to keep the secret without understanding any of it.

A sudden knock on Lizzie's door interrupted her thoughts. She whirled around, saw Jack standing there, sunburned and smiling in his dusty work clothes, and she was overcome by another astonishing burst of pleasure, as if someone had lit a flame inside her.

'How are you?' he asked.

'Fine, thanks.' Was she grinning foolishly?

'I was wondering if you're madly busy.'

Normally she would have responded automatically that of course she was terribly busy, but this morning she recognised how much like her mother that sounded.

'Why do you ask?'

'I was hoping you could lend me a hand again. Another quick job. I need to get feed to the newly weaned calves, the ones not included in the muster.'

To Lizzie's dismay, his request had instant appeal. She

told herself it was because she felt motherly towards the weaned calves. 'What does it involve?'

'I was hoping you could drive the truck. It's only a matter of driving slowly along a track, and I'd be on the back pushing off bales of stock feed.'

'I've never driven a truck.'

'It's a standard floor gear shift.' Jack grinned. 'And it's perfectly harmless now.'

Her first thought was for her baby's safety, but she was sure Jack wouldn't put her in a dangerous vehicle. Then she thought about how slow this job would be for him if he had to do it on his own—stopping the truck, leaping out and climbing onto the back to push off a bale or two, then jumping down and driving on to repeat the job, over and over. 'When do you want to do this?'

'Late this afternoon? Say, about four o'clock?'

She refused to smile. 'All right.'

For the rest of the day, an uncalled-for tingle of excitement zipped through Lizzie every time she thought about her late-afternoon assignment with Jack. *It's only work. It's perfectly harmless.*

She worked steadily, lunching on a sandwich at her desk, but promptly at four o'clock, dressed in blue jeans and a long-sleeved, blue and white striped cotton shirt, which she'd jokingly thought of as her country-woman shirt, she met Jack outside the machinery shed.

The sun was already slipping to the west and it sent a pretty, coppery-tinged light over the bales of hay on the back of the truck. Feeling only a little nervous, Lizzie climbed behind the driver's wheel for a practice drive, while Jack swung into the passenger seat beside her.

To her relief, the truck's motor started first go, and when

she eased the vehicle forward there was only one kangaroo-hop and one teeth-clenching clash of gears before she got the hang of it and drove smoothly. Jack pointed the way via a dirt track that wound through paddocks of dry grass dotted with gum trees, and Lizzie drove on, appreciative of the quietness of the outback afternoon—the wide starch blue skies, the distant mauve hills and white-trunked gums, all bathed in soft, golden light.

It was such a very different world out here.

Having grown up in Italy, Lizzie still found herself marvelling at the sheer size of Australian properties. Savannah station was miles from Gidgee Springs, the nearest township, and it was a thousand miles from Brisbane, thousands more from Sydney, from Canberra and Melbourne.

Every so often they came to a gate, and this time it was Jack who got out to open them, and then close them behind her, but it wasn't too long before they reached the huge paddock with the weaned calves.

'OK. This is where I start dropping off the feed,' Jack said. 'All you have to do is drive on slowly and we'll drop a line of feed across a couple of kilometres.'

Using the rear-vision mirrors as guides, Lizzie watched him swing up onto the tray-back of the truck with his customary ease. She drove slowly, watching him framed in the mirror, with his shirtsleeves rolled back over muscled forearms, using his pocket knife to cut the twine on the big bales of hay, then tossing them to the ground, as if they weighed no more than sugar cubes.

Young cattle came from everywhere, head butting each other like schoolboys tussling in a tuck-shop queue in their eagerness to get at the fresh sweet hay.

Too soon all the hay was dispersed and Lizzie stopped

the truck, while Jack dismounted and got back in beside her. 'Well done,' he said with a smile. 'I'll make a country-woman of you before you're through.'

They exchanged smiling glances.

Jack said, 'You'll be riding a horse next.'

'Oh, no, I won't.' No way would she threaten her preg-nancy on the back of a horse.

Again, she considered telling Jack about her baby. After all, he was very friendly, and he'd managed to thaw her frostiness despite her best efforts to remain remote.

Perhaps she might have told him if she was confident that he wanted no more than friendship, but she couldn't ignore last night's close call, and the inappropriate, two-way attraction that seemed to be getting stronger every minute. There was enough tension beween them already without adding her pregnancy to the mix.

When they reached the homestead and climbed down from the truck, Jack was surprised that Lizzie didn't seem in any hurry to go back inside. Instead, she walked to the timber fence of the stockyard and leaned her elbows on the top rail, looking out across the plains.

The sun was low in the west now, tingeing the sky with pink, and a cool breeze stirred the grasses. Lizzie, in her blue jeans and striped shirt, looked amazingly at home in that setting. Her profile, softened by loosened strands of dark hair, was pensive as she looked out at the land.

Jack couldn't resist going over to her. 'A penny for your thoughts.'

'I was thinking how very peaceful it is here.' She lifted her face to the rosy sky and took a deep breath. 'Especially now, at this time of day. The light's so soft and the land's all lovely and dappled by shadows.'

'If you can't relax here, you never will.'

She sent him a rueful smile. 'Is it living here that makes you so relaxed? Is everyone in the outback easy-going?'

'Not everyone. My father certainly wasn't.'

'I've been wondering about your family,' she said. 'Are they still on the land?'

'No.' Jack's shoulders slumped and he leaned heavily on the rail beside her. 'I'm an only child and my parents split up years ago. Mum went to Melbourne to live with her sister, and my father died of a heart attack about six months later.'

'I'm sorry.'

Jack gave a dismissive shrug. 'Mum's remarried now, and very happy.'

'And you stayed on the land, working for Kate?'

The breeze caught a strand of Lizzie's hair, blowing it towards Jack. He contemplated catching it, letting it slide through his fingers like a satin ribbon, then he came to his senses and erased the thought, answered her question instead.

'I ended up here eventually, but it wasn't what I'd planned for my life.' He dragged his gaze from Lizzie and watched a bird circling high above them. 'My parents used to own a cattle property almost as big as Savannah.'

Lizzie turned to him, her face soft with sympathy. 'Is it too nosy to ask what happened?'

'We lost it thanks to my pig-headed father.' Jack grimaced. 'My old man argued with everyone—the local council, auctioneers, neighbours, bank managers. He completely ignored his accountant's advice, made a stack of rash investments on the stock exchange, and lost all his money. The bank tried to foreclose on the property, and Dad had a whale of a time, arguing and resisting.'

'Did they take him to court?'

Jack nodded. 'The trial dragged on for ages, but the old

man wouldn't compromise and settle out of court. He wanted a fight. Stubborn as a broken bulldozer. In the end—' he gave a shrug '—we lost the lot.'

'Ouch,' Lizzie said softly. 'That must have been terribly hard for you and your mother.'

'It was the last straw. Ended their marriage.' Jack's mouth thinned. 'Dad died six months later, still furious with the world and everyone in it.'

It was a terrible story.

Lizzie almost wished she hadn't asked. Jack's eyes had completely lost their usual sparkle and they'd taken on a haunted look, as if he was seeing ghosts that still troubled him.

Surely it was a miracle he'd come through such an unhappy time without losing his cheerful and easy-going temperament. She wondered how much it had cost him to retain the 'Jack-factor' that she'd taken for granted.

'At least you know you're not anything like your father, Jack.'

'I should bloody well hope not. I've gone out of my way to make sure I'm not even remotely like him.'

'So you ended up working for Kate instead,' Lizzie said to change the subject.

'I got involved with Savannah after Kate's husband died, and she had all sorts of trouble. Corporate cowboys tried to frighten her into selling this place for a pittance.'

'But you were able to help her?'

'I had to,' he said with an offhand shrug. 'Kate might be a tough old cookie, but at that time she was a grieving widow and she couldn't stand up to those thugs on her own.'

So, Lizzie thought as darkness crept over Savannah and they left the stockyard and headed for the house, Jack had deliberately chosen to be different from his dad. Mr Nice

Guy. But although he was easy-going, he wasn't a push-over. He'd proved that when he'd stood up for Kate.

Even so, Jack had chosen well to stay here in the out-back where the only stress came from the weather and the seasons and the market fluctuations.

The lifestyle here suited him. He would hate her frantic pace, and for the thousandth time Lizzie told herself she was pleased she'd called a halt to last night's kiss.

The little niggle of regret that squirmed in her chest would disappear in time. Surely?

'You can cook a mean steak,' she declared at dinner.

Jack sent her one of his trademark smiles. 'Just as well you like it. I don't have a very wide repertoire.'

'Doesn't matter. This will do me.'

The steak was cooked to perfection, blackened and seared on the outside and rosy pink in the middle, and the accompanying lettuce, tomatoes and radishes were won-derfully crisp, straight from the garden.

They didn't talk a great deal as they ate. Lizzie wondered if Jack regretted having shared so much about his family. He didn't seem particularly upset, but perhaps he was good at hiding his feelings beneath his easy-going exterior.

Or perhaps she was thinking about him far too much.

'Would you like ice cream for dessert?' he asked as he cleared their dishes.

'Oh, no dessert for me.' Lizzie patted her stomach, aware of the bulge below her navel that seemed to be grow-ing exponentially.

'It's chocolate-fudge ripple.' Jack sent her a cheeky wink as he opened the freezer door.

Her taste buds leapt. 'No, I really shouldn't.'

He shrugged. 'Your loss.'

Didn't he worry about triglycerides? She supposed he could offset his eating habits with plenty of outdoor exercise.

Watching Jack fill a bowl with rich creamy scoops of vanilla and chocolate, she folded her arms and resisted the temptation to lick her lips. To her surprise, when he sat down again he handed her a spoon.

'In case you change your mind.' A slow smile unravelled, lighting his green eyes. 'I'm happy to share.'

Share?

Lizzie flashed back to her student days with Mitch and the way he'd so easily charmed and enslaved her. She'd made more mistakes over guys since then, especially with Toby. Hadn't she finally learned her lesson? Shouldn't she reject such easy familiarity from Jack?

But she was ridiculously relieved to see him looking happy again, and, after all, what was the harm in a spoonful of dessert? Lizzie lasted almost no time— perhaps, oh, all of twenty seconds—before she reached across the table and took a spoonful of ice cream from Jack's bowl.

It was cool and creamy against her tongue and it tasted sinfully luscious.

'Good, isn't it?' Jack said, pushing the bowl closer.

'Mmm.' She helped herself to a second spoonful.

'Not quite as good as Italian gelato, I guess.'

'Oh, I think this ice cream could hold its own.'

Jack grinned. 'So you don't feel compelled to stick up for everything Italian?'

'Why should I? I'm half Australian. My father's Australian.'

'I guessed with a surname like Green that he wasn't Italian. Does he live in Australia or Italy?'

'In Australia. In Sydney.'

Jack looked as if he wanted to ask another question, but was holding back.

It seemed only fair to expand her story, after he'd told her so much about his family. 'My mother was a fashion model,' she said. 'She travelled a lot when she was young, and she met my father when he was a dive master at a resort on the Great Barrier Reef.

'And no,' Lizzie added, guessing the direction of Jack's thoughts. 'My parents didn't marry. My father stayed here in Australia and my mother went back to Italy. I lived with her, mostly in Monta Correnti, until I started university. By then, my father had a boat-building business in Sydney, and I wanted to study English literature, so I decided to come out here to study, to be near him and to get to know his family and his country.'

'He must have been pleased about that.'

'Yes, he was. Very pleased.' Lizzie smiled, remembering their wonderful, emotion-filled meeting. It had been such a shock to discover how very deeply her father loved her, and how much he'd missed her.

Jack was watching her closely. 'And you've stayed on,' he said, 'so you must have liked it here.'

'Yes,' she said simply.

She helped herself to one last spoonful of ice cream, tipping her head back and holding the icy sweetness in her mouth until it began to melt, slipping slowly, languorously down her throat.

Out of the corner of her eye she caught Jack staring at her, and the unmistakable desire in his eyes sent flames shooting under her skin. Ribbons of heat formed knots in the pit of her stomach.

Caro Dio. She reached for her glass of mineral water

and took a deep swig, and then another, draining it. 'I—I'll do the dishes,' she muttered, jumping to her feet.

Slowly, Jack scooped the last of the ice cream from the bowl and then even more slowly he licked the spoon. When he stood, at last, and came lazily towards her, she realised she hadn't done a thing about the dishes. She was still standing there, watching him.

He set the bowl on the sink and his arm brushed hers. Another flash of heat engulfed her. He didn't move away.

It was a breathless age before he said in a low, lazy drawl, 'I'm invading your personal space.'

'Yes.'

It was no more than a whisper. Tonight she couldn't dredge up the right level of frostiness.

Jack placed a hand on the bench on either side of her, trapping her against the cupboards. 'I'd like to stay here, Lizzie.'

No. No. No. No. No. This was where she had to tell Jack, *again*, to step back, to stop saying such things.

She tried to speak. Couldn't summon the words. Heaven help her, she was too enchanted by the gathering storm inside her, and, already, she could feel the heat of his body surrounding her.

Already he was touching her. His hands slid lightly up her arms. She was shivering. Melting. His arms were closing around her…while his lips explored the curve of her neck.

She closed her eyes, savouring the astonishing, sweet pressure of Jack's mouth on her skin.

There was no way she could stop him. It had been so long since she'd experienced this gentle intimacy. Too long. She could feel her skin smiling wherever his lips touched her.

Her skin grew greedy and she arched her neck, seeking

more. Jack obliged beautifully, letting warm, lazy kisses trail over her neck to her jaw, while his hands traced the shape of her shoulders through the thin fabric of her T-shirt.

At any moment now their mouths would touch, and all chance of stopping him would fly out of the window.

It was already too late.

She was filled with a sweet, aching need that deadened all thoughts but her deepening yearning to be touched and kissed… She was desperate for the moment when Jack's mouth finally reached hers…

When it happened, her lips were already parted.

Breathlessly, he whispered her name. 'Lizzie.' Just once, brushing the soft syllables over her open lips. Then his tongue traced the rim of her parted mouth, and her knees turned to water.

Jack caught her, and she was instantly lost, drowning in the perfect taste and smell of him, in the hint of sun-drenched outdoors that clung to his skin.

Everything about his kiss was perfect—the texture of his mouth, and his grainy skin, and the muscly strength of his body pressing against her.

She felt rosy and warm and insanely happy.

When Jack broke the kiss, she was devastated. She'd wanted it to go on for ever.

Clearly, Jack had much more control than she had. With one last gentle kiss on her forehead, he released her.

He smiled. 'You taste delicious. Of ice cream.'

'So do you.'

She was smiling goofily when, without warning, common sense returned like a cold slap. What on earth was she doing? How could she have been such a fool? The kiss was a mistake, and the way she'd responded was an even bigger mistake.

Jack would think she was available for further seduction. She wasn't available. She was here for a brief stay. She was years older than he was, and she was pregnant, while he was young and fit and virile.

'We shouldn't have let that happen,' she said.

Jack smiled easily. 'Of course we should.'

'But—' Her mind skidded and slipped as she tried to think sensibly. She couldn't start a relationship with this cowboy. The press would have a field day.

With an air of desperation, she said, 'We hardly know each other.'

Jack stared at her for long, thoughtful seconds. 'I suppose I should have asked if there's a man in your life.'

'Yes, you should have.' Lizzie knew she had to take control. 'We need to talk about this, Jack. To set some ground rules.'

When he didn't object she was relieved that he was being reasonable. Now that they'd broken the spell, she couldn't believe she'd let things get so out of hand without asking all kinds of questions. The kinds of questions nearly every sane man or woman asked before leaping into each other's arms.

But the questions were also the sort that would lead to informing Jack that she was pregnant, and already she could picture him reeling back with shocked dismay, could feel the chill of isolation as he retreated from her.

She knew it was appallingly wrong of her, but in that moment she wished they'd both stayed crazy for just a little longer.

CHAPTER FIVE

THEY went through to the lounge room.

To talk.

Jack still couldn't believe he was doing this, couldn't believe he'd pulled back from the most sensational kiss he'd ever known. He'd been a lost man, on the very brink of taking an Australian federal senator. Right there. In the kitchen.

Unless he was terribly mistaken, she'd been as swept away as he was. In another five seconds they might have been too lost in passion to stop.

Now, it was hard to be grateful for the inner voice that had urged him to remember why Kate Burton had sent Lizzie Green to Savannah.

She'd wanted Lizzie to be safe. Safe. In his care. She was in some kind of trouble and she'd been placed under his protection. He knew zero about her private life. Which meant he had no choice but to cool his heels, and his ardour, until he'd extracted satisfactory answers.

So, yeah. He'd let Lizzie talk, and he'd listen, and *then* he'd kiss her senseless.

As Lizzie took a seat in Jack's lounge room, she was sure she'd never felt more shaken or self-conscious. She was, of course, grateful for this reprieve. If she hadn't stopped Jack, she would have broken every single one of her relationship rules. But she felt bereft now, rather than thankful.

She also felt terribly exposed.

From the moment she'd decided to be a single mum, she'd been so careful to hold men at bay. Relationships simply weren't worth the pain.

Tonight, Jack Lewis had ripped through her defences. From the very first touch of his lips she'd been shameless, and even though she'd stopped him, she was certain he knew *exactly* how needy she was. Even though she was sitting primly with her ankles crossed, he could probably guess that he only had to reach out and touch her and she'd be scrambling down the sofa and into his arms.

Oh, for heaven's sake, get rid of those thoughts. Get over it.

At least Jack didn't ply her with questions the minute they were seated. Lizzie didn't want to discuss the men or lack of men in her life and she was grateful for the chance to sit in the lamplight, nursing a mug of peppermint tea while she gathered her wits. She had to work out how to warn Jack off, and, as they were still going to be living together, it had to be done nicely.

A practised tactician, she took the roundabout route. 'The silence out here is really quite amazing,' she said. 'I found it strange at first. In my apartment in Brisbane there's constant background noise—traffic, building construction, roadwork. Sirens blaring day and night.'

'I suppose you get used to the noise and you don't even hear it after a while.'

'That's true.' Lizzie turned to Jack. 'Have you spent much time in the city?'

He answered with a shake of his head, then he smiled.

'But I do enjoy the big smoke, and when I get there I make the most of it.'

'I suppose you paint the town red?'

His smile took a wicked tilt. 'Wouldn't you like to know?'

Actually, yes, Lizzie thought, dismayed. She was unbearably curious about the fun Jack got up to in the city, but no way would she admit it.

Jack looked annoyingly at ease now, sprawled casually at his end of the sofa, long legs loose and relaxed, his body angled Lizzie's way.

He was even able to smile. 'OK. You were going to tell me about the men in your life. Where would you like to start?'

'Actually, I don't think we should even begin, Jack. We should just accept that the kiss was a mistake and—'

'That's rubbish, Lizzie, and you know it.'

'What do you mean?'

'The kiss was fantastic and we're going to do it again.' Jack's eyes flashed emerald fire. 'Unless you have a damn good reason why we shouldn't.'

Lizzie looked away, afraid that she might blush.

'For example,' Jack said, 'it would be helpful to know if there's a boyfriend back in Canberra, or Brisbane, or wherever.'

After too long, she admitted softly, 'There's no one.'

'You're sure?'

'Of course I'm sure. It's not the kind of thing I'd forget. I—I haven't been in a relationship for some time.'

Surely Jack didn't need to know about Mitch, the first man who'd broken her heart, or about Toby, her banker lover who'd leaked their story to the press and almost finished her career?

She shot Jack a sharp glance. 'The question works both ways, Jack. What about you? Do you have a girlfriend?'

She held her breath, realising that she was far too interested in his answer.

'There's no one with a claim on me,' he said quietly.

It wasn't quite the unambiguous answer she would have preferred.

After a small silence, he said, 'So if there's no man in your life, what's the problem, Lizzie?'

She hesitated. After kissing him into oblivion, it wasn't going to be easy to explain that she didn't want a relationship.

'You've come here to get away from something, haven't you?' he said.

'Well, yes,' she admitted, grateful for the lead. 'Mostly, I wanted to keep away from journalists.'

'Any special reason? I thought politicians thrived on publicity.'

Of course there was a special reason, but Lizzie still baulked at telling Jack about her baby. She tried to picture sharing her news, going through the involved explanation and her reasons for choosing the sperm-donor option.

She had no idea how Jack would react. For some people, the whole idea of a single woman choosing an anonymous donor was too new, too confronting. Telling anyone about her pregnancy was like letting a genie out of a bottle. She never knew what kind of reaction she would get, but once it was out, it was impossible to cram it back. The damage was done.

Instead, she said, 'Unfortunately, journalists always target female politicians.'

'Especially the photogenic ones,' Jack suggested dryly.

Lizzie nodded. 'I'm afraid I've been called a bimbo once too often. It's beyond annoying. It doesn't matter how hard, or how seriously I take my job, journalists take one look at me and decide my head's full of chiffon and sequins.'

He smiled in sympathy. 'So how did you get into politics

in the first place? Was it really like you said? Something you sort of fell into?'

'Well…yes. It was…more or less.'

'Like Alice down the rabbit hole?'

She couldn't help smiling. 'Some people do say the PM looks like the Cheshire cat, but my story isn't nearly as interesting as Alice's.'

'I'm interested.' Jack's eyes burned, as if challenging her.

Lizzie squirmed. Any explanation would involve talking about Mitch. Then again, if Jack understood more about her, he might keep his distance.

'I think it started when I was very young,' she said. 'Way back when I was at school in Monta Correnti. My best friend's father was the mayor, and I used to go and play at Gianna's house. Her father wasn't home very often, but when he was, he was always kind and so much fun. Never too busy to talk to us.'

Dipping her head, Lizzie breathed in the scent of her peppermint tea. 'And I'd always hear grown-ups saying how wonderful Gianna's father was because he fixed our town's water and sewers, and helped the old people. The whole town loved him. I think he was probably my first inspiration.'

'But you chose Australian politics,' Jack said.

'Yes. When I started at Sydney uni, I was excited to discover how certain movements and certain ways of thinking could positively affect the world. I was full of noble aims—wanting to help people, to make the world a better place, to represent neglected viewpoints.'

She gave a self-conscious laugh. 'Then I fell madly in love with a politician.'

The mild amusement in Jack's eyes vanished. 'Who was he?'

Lizzie took another sip of tea. 'Have you heard of Mitchell MacCallum?'

'Of course.' Jack looked distinctly shocked. 'Don't tell me he was the one?'

Lizzie nodded. Even now, after all this time, saying Mitch's name out loud sent a chill chasing down her spine.

An awkward silence fell over the room, and Jack sat very still, frowning. She could almost see his mind working, thinking back through everything he'd heard and read about Mitchell MacCullum.

'This was well before the scandal,' she said.

'I should hope so,' he replied grimly.

So Jack had a very low opinion of Mitch. Lizzie wasn't surprised. Five years ago, the media had left little room for sympathy when they had exposed Mitch. He'd been married for years by then, and he'd been caught using his ministerial expense account to keep a mistress in a penthouse on Sydney Harbour.

Jack said tightly, 'Tell me more about MacCallum.'

She hesitated, but now that she'd started she might as well get it over with, so she took a deep breath and dived in. 'Mitch and I were both at Sydney University. Actually, we were housemates. There were five of us, sharing a big, old, tumbledown house in Balmain. He was a couple of years ahead of me, studying political science and economics. He was brilliant and charismatic, and I suppose you could say I became a kind of disciple.'

'A disciple who slept with the prophet.'

'Eventually.' A hot blush burned her cheeks. 'At first I simply spent hours in the university refectory, or in coffee bars listening to Mitch talk. He was incredibly articulate about human rights and international relations, and he championed all kinds of student causes. He was head of the student union, and a wonderful debater, so he was very easy to listen to.'

Jack looked as if he was going to say something, but changed his mind. He simply offered a thoughtful nod, like a journalist in a TV interview, and waited for her to continue with her story.

'After that, I started going to political rallies with Mitch. It all seemed very intellectual and idealistic and exciting, and when he graduated and decided to stand for parliament, I joined his campaign team. I spent every spare moment painting banners and putting up posters, doing clerical work, and running errands.'

'I dare say MacCallum was incredibly appreciative of your efforts.'

The hard glitter in Jack's eyes surprised Lizzie. Clearly, he disliked Mitch intensely.

'So what happened after he was elected?'

'I was given a job on his staff,' she said quietly.

'I'm sure you'd earned it.'

Jack wasn't referring to her help with the campaign, but Lizzie ignored the dig. 'We were working on really interesting and worthwhile programmes, and Mitch was invited to all kinds of receptions and charity balls. I'd never had such a busy social life.'

'And I suppose you'd moved out of the student share house by this time.'

'Yes.' Lizzie took a sip of her cooling tea as she remembered the day she and Mitch had moved into their own apartment. She'd been so thrilled. It had felt like a public announcement that she was Mitchell MacCallum's girlfriend.

Of course, she'd been desperately in love, and she'd expected that Mitch would propose to her at any moment, but there was no way she would share that dream with Jack.

She said, simply, 'I lived with him for about three months, and then—' she straightened her shoulders, determined not to let Jack see that any of this bothered her after all this time '—Mitch's party leaders decided that he needed a more settled image. They wanted him to marry.'

Jack frowned. 'So? Why didn't *you* marry him?'

'I wasn't given the opportunity.' She forced an extra-bright smile. 'Mitch married Amanda Leigh, the daughter of a former state governor. She came from one of Melbourne's most influential families, you see, so she had fabulous links to the old-school-tie network.'

'So, MacCallum showed his true colours.' Again, Jack spoke with clear distaste.

But then all the hardness fell out of his face. 'Lizzie,' he said, watching her intently. 'I can't believe you let him treat you like that.'

'It wasn't a matter of letting him. He did it on the sly. I went home to Italy to spend Christmas with my family and by the time I got back it was a *fait accompli*. My supposed boyfriend was married. He laughed it off, said we both knew there wasn't a future for us. But, of course, I'd had this silly idea—'

She bit down hard on her lip to stop herself from giving way to self-pity. 'Anyway,' she said quickly. 'I've gone off track. I was supposed to be telling you how I ended up in the senate.'

Her tea was stone cold by now, but she downed the last of it and set the mug on the coffee table. 'I resigned from Mitch's staff. I couldn't stay there—it would have been too awkward. But the party hierarchy didn't want to lose a hard worker. There was a vacancy on the senate ticket and they wanted a youthful candidate, preferably female.'

Lizzie shrugged. 'It was time to stop feeling sorry for

myself, and I could see this was a chance to do something to help others, so I said I'd give it a go. And I found myself elected.'

'And you've been there ever since.'

'It becomes a way of life.'

Jack was frowning again. 'What does that mean? Are you planning to stay there for ever?'

'The voters may not want me there for ever.' She forced a laugh. 'I certainly don't want to be an old lady senator.'

Ever since he'd started talking about the future, a worried shadow had lingered in Jack's eyes. Lizzie wondered what was bothering him. She thought about his kiss, and could still feel the tummy-tingling pleasure of his lips on her skin, the tantalising intimacy of his tongue. His thrilling mix of fire and tenderness.

It was a shock to realise that in a matter of days he'd penetrated the tough outer armour she'd spent so long building. For a brief moment, he'd exposed her softer centre. But surely he understood their kiss couldn't lead to anything serious?

She should make that clear. Now.

Before she could speak, however, Jack rose. 'You're looking pale and tired.'

Lizzie wasn't surprised. She felt emotionally drained and physically exhausted.

'You'd better get to bed.' To her surprise, Jack came towards her, bent low and kissed her cheek, just as a brother might. 'Goodnight.'

Puzzled, she watched him leave the room.

When they'd started this conversation, Jack had shown every intention of taking up where their passionate kiss had left off, but she'd achieved her goal. Her story about Mitch had been enough to make him think twice.

She knew she should be pleased and relieved. By walking away from their situation, Jack had saved her the trouble of explaining about the baby.

To Lizzie's annoyance, she couldn't feel grateful. She felt confused. And just a little sad.

She went back to her room and tried to read, but thoughts of Jack kept intruding, shattering her concentration.

The kiss loomed large, of course, and each time she struggled to fight off the memories.

She was off men. She was only here for a short time, focusing on being a mum. The last thing she'd expected or needed was a potential boyfriend in the outback.

It was all rather distressing. To centre herself once more, she leafed through her favourite book about single pregnancy, about mothers who'd met and conquered the challenges of raising their babies on their own. She lingered over the beautiful photos—even the first startling photo of an attractive blonde lawyer giving birth.

Lizzie viewed childbirth with a mixture of fascination, incredulity and awe. Right now, it was still hard to believe that it was actually going to happen to her.

She moved quickly on to other, more reassuring pictures— a mother breastfeeding her baby, another woman laughing as she bathed a chubby baby boy. There was a mother sitting cross-legged on the lounge-room floor, playing with blocks with her curly-headed toddler. Another mother pushed a pram through a park strewn with autumn leaves.

The very last photo was of a single mum with twins.

Twins. Now that was a scary thought. Lizzie always skipped quickly past this page. There were twins in her family, but she couldn't possibly imagine being the mother of twins. It would be too difficult to juggle a career and two babies without the support of a partner.

She lay awake for hours trying not to worry about that.

* * *

Jack rose at dawn and went straight to the horse paddock. Within minutes, he was mounted on Archer, a long-legged grey, and together they took off at a thundering gallop across the mist-wreathed plains.

It was good to be outdoors at this early hour. Archer was sure-footed, the autumn morning was cool and crisp, and heavy dew had dampened the earth, so the dust was at a minimum.

From as far back as he could remember Jack had loved riding, and, with any luck, this morning's long, hard gallop would knock the tension out of his muscles, and provide him with the necessary space and distance to think with a clear head.

He had to decide how he was going to handle the crazy situation he found himself in now—infatuated, after just one kiss, with a woman who couldn't be more wrong for him.

When Lizzie arrived in the kitchen for breakfast, her first surprise was a cleared table. All the mess was gone and instead there was a second surprise. A note propped against the teapot.

> *I've gone for a ride, so don't wait for me. Help*
> *yourself to breakfast. I'll catch you later.*
> *Jack.*

Her first reaction was disappointment. She'd spent far too much time last night trying to stop thinking about him. She'd come to breakfast, not sure what to expect, but determined to put last night's kiss out of her thoughts and to carry on as if it hadn't happened. Nevertheless, she'd been filled with fluttery anticipation.

It was silly, but she'd actually been wondering if he might have another job for her. She'd even practised asking super-casually...*I don't suppose you need a hand today, Jack? Sing out, if there's any odd job you need help with.*

The fact that Jack was probably avoiding her bothered her more than it should.

As she made herself a cup of tea, a boiled egg and toast she wondered if she'd totally annoyed him by responding to his kiss so eagerly and then claiming it was a mistake. It was the kind of nonsense you'd expect from a teenager. At forty, she was supposed to know better.

Problem was, when Jack was around, Lizzie felt closer to fourteen than forty.

At the edge of the plain, Jack reined Archer to a halt, and walked the grey closer to the overhang of the rugged red cliff. From there he could see the river in the gorge far below, snaking over its bed of sand.

Dismounting, he wrapped the reins around a gidgee sapling and hunkered on the red earth, watching the sunlight hit the river and turn it to silver...

He drank in the silence, let it seep into him. Then, like a dog digging up a favourite, well-gnawed bone, he let his mind tussle with his problem.

The lady senator.

Just thinking about her made his body tighten. Remembering the way she'd kissed and the way her curvy body had melted beneath his hands only made matters worse. He wanted her so badly.

And he knew she'd been turned on, too.

OK, she'd called a halt, and she'd spent half an hour telling him about that rat MacCallum who'd hurt her, but

Jack had seen the flare of disappointment in her eyes when he'd left her last night.

They were both trying to fight their chemistry. The tension was crazy. Being in a room together was a new form of torture, but what was he going to do about it?

He tried to tick off all the reasons he should stay clear of Lizzie Green. The first was obvious—she was a city-based career woman, and a federal politician, a woman with plenty of power and very big goals, and why would he get involved with someone like that when he'd finally thrown off the shadow of his pushy, overreaching father?

His next reason for avoiding Lizzie was shakier. She was quite a bit older than him, but for the life of him Jack couldn't turn that into a problem. Lizzie's age made her earthier and more womanly than any of the sweet young things he'd dated in the last few years.

It wasn't as if he were planning to marry Lizzie or anything…

Damn. He'd ridden out here to gain clarity, but the ride wasn't much help.

He'd already run out of objections…

The lady senator was worth another try.

Lizzie was finishing her breakfast when it occurred to her that Jack's absence provided a golden opportunity to phone Kate Burton. She didn't want to pry behind Jack's back, but she could ask pertinent questions about him that she should have raised before she'd left for Savannah.

To her dismay, Kate laughed at her very first question. 'You'd like to know more about Jack? Lizzie, my dear girl, that's delightful news.'

'I should think it's only common sense,' Lizzie said

defensively. 'After all, I'm living alone with him for weeks on end.'

'Of course.' Kate still sounded amused, but then she sobered. 'Jack hasn't given you any—how shall I put it?—any cause for concern, has he?'

'Oh, no, not at all. He's been a perfect gentleman—perfect *host*,' she amended quickly. 'He's rather younger than I expected.'

Kate laughed again. 'Oh, Jack's at least thirty, I'm sure.'

Ten years younger than me. Lizzie wished she didn't feel so disheartened by this news. Why was it relevant?

'You might have warned me that he would be the only other person here,' Lizzie said.

'Is he?' Kate sounded surprised. 'Where are the cook and the ringers?'

'Out on a cattle muster, apparently.'

'Oh, dear,' Kate said. 'So who's cooking?'

'Jack and I. But that's not a problem. We're taking it in turns.'

'Lovely.' Kate very quickly brightened again. 'I'm not sure about Jack's cooking ability, but at least he's good company, and he's as handsome as the devil. You must agree that's a definite plus, Lizzie.'

'Well—I—maybe.'

'Don't worry, Lizzie. Jack might look like a larrikin, but his heart's in the right place.'

'I imagine he's been quite helpful to you?'

'Absolutely. When my Arthur died, I had all sorts of trouble. People were trying to frighten me into selling Savannah for much less than it's worth. Jack stepped in and rescued me. It was just wonderful to see the way he stood up to those fellows.'

'Thank heavens he did.'

'Yes, Jack's a darling, and he's totally trustworthy. I wouldn't have sent you to Savannah if he wasn't.'

'Oh, I didn't doubt that.' The word *trustworthy* settled inside Lizzie. Given her disastrous history with men, it gave out a warm little glow. 'Thank you for reassuring me. I'm surprised Jack didn't—'

Lizzie broke off in mid-sentence, suddenly distracted by the sight, through the window, of a horse and rider galloping towards the homestead.

The rider had to be Jack, but he seemed to be approaching at a breakneck speed, heading straight for the stockyard fence, and it was a tall fence, made of solid timber rails.

Lizzie gasped. Surely the fence was too high. Jack couldn't possibly clear it.

'Lizzie, are you there?'

'Yes, Kate. I—um—just a moment.'

Another gasp broke from her as Jack and his horse thundered closer.

Why wasn't he slowing down? Lizzie was already flinching, sure there was going to be a horrible crash.

Horrified, she held her breath as Jack's figure crouched low in the saddle while the magnificent grey horse gathered its long legs beneath it.

'Lizzie!' Kate cried. 'Speak to me. What's going on there?'

In the next instant Jack's horse took off in a magnificent leap, sailing over the fence and clearing it easily, landing in the home paddock as neatly as a ballet dancer.

Lizzie let out a whoosh of breath, and realised she was shaking. 'I—I'm sorry, Kate. It's just that Jack took his horse over this terribly high fence and I didn't think he could possibly make it.'

'Not the stockyard gate?'

'Yes. How did you know?'

'Good heavens. Is he all right?'

'Yes,' Lizzie said again and she was grinning now. 'He's fine. Absolutely fine.'

Kate let out a surprising whoop of delight. 'Lizzie, that's amazing.'

'Is it?'

'Yes. Good heavens, dear, Jack's just done something quite extraordinary. Only four horsemen have jumped that gate in the last hundred years.'

'Really?'

'Their initials are carved in the gatepost.'

'Gosh. I thought it was high. That's quite a feat, then.'

'It is,' Kate agreed. 'Quite a feat. Jack's never tried it before and that's what surprises me.'

As Lizzie replaced the receiver she knew she should go straight to her room to start work. There were emails waiting for her, and hard work and efficiency had become a habit, a good habit she enjoyed.

And yet…this morning she felt a mysterious urge to abandon her desk and to wander outdoors… She wanted to breathe in the gentle autumn sunshine, to smell the roses, so to speak, although there probably weren't any roses in the neglected Savannah gardens.

She thought how soothing it would be to drink in the peaceful landscape, to admire the beautiful horses, and the never-ending plains and the wide open sky.

With the idea only half formed, Lizzie found herself on the veranda, and Cobber, Jack's elderly cattle dog, came bounding up the steps to greet her. He looked up at her with gentle, honey-brown eyes and she patted the soft fur on the top of his head.

She thought how comforting it must be to have a faithful dog as a constant companion. She'd never had a dog, but there'd always been cats and kittens in Monta Correnti and she'd spent many happy childhood hours with a warm, purring cat curled in her lap while she read, or day-dreamed.

Cobber followed her quietly as she went down the front steps and onto the grass. She caught an animal whiff from the horse paddock, but it was quite pleasant when it came mixed with the sweeter scent of hay.

A kookaburra on a fence post began to laugh and the comical, bubbling call brought a ready smile to her lips. She remembered the first time she'd ever heard a kookaburra, when she'd come to Australia at the age of eighteen. She'd been delighted. Still, all these years later, the sound never failed to make her smile.

She saw the silver threads of a spider's web hanging loosely between the branches of a neglected rose bush, and found one small, pretty pink rosebud. She was contemplating plucking it when Jack appeared around the corner of the shed.

His face broke into a smile, and a sweet pang speared her chest, spreading through her veins like a witch's potion. He looked more appealing than ever in his soft blue jeans and his faded shirt, and with a heavy, cumbersome saddle slung over his shoulder. As usual, he handled the saddle easily, as if it were as light as thistledown.

She thought—*He's like catnip for me. I can't stay away.*

But she spoke calmly as she said, 'Hello.' And her eyes wide with surprise as she tried to pretend he was the last person on the planet she expected to see.

'Good morning, Lizzie.'

'You look happy.'

'Actually, I'm feeling pretty damn good.'

'I—um—saw you take that gate. I was worried. I was sure you'd never make it. It looked too high.'

Jack nodded, smiling. 'Matter of fact, that gate is a chal-lenge I've been avoiding for a long, long time.'

'But you took it this morning.'

'I did,' he said with a beaming smile. 'Piece of cake.'

Lizzie was so used to the chest-beating of politicians that she waited for Jack to brag about being one of only five riders who'd cleared the gate. But Jack wasn't like other men she'd known. No bragging for him.

No crowds to applaud his magnificent jump. No spray-ing champagne, or kisses from pretty girls.

He simply looked pleased and quietly happy, and, look-ing into his eyes, Lizzie couldn't help feeling pleased and happy, too.

In fact, happiness was fizzing through her like soda bubbles, and on a reckless impulse she took two steps to-wards him, grabbed a handful of his shirt, and kissed him on the mouth.

CHAPTER SIX

LIZZIE smiled into Jack's surprised eyes. 'There's no champagne, but you looked so pleased with yourself for clearing that jump, and I thought you ought to be congratulated.'

'Well, thank you, Senator.'

Before she could slip away, he reached around her, gripping her low on her behind, trapping her against his denim thighs, and next moment, he was answering her kiss with a kiss of his own.

And *his* kiss wasn't a mere smack on the lips.

His kiss was mesmerising, slow and thorough—a happy kiss, perfectly in tune with Lizzie's mood and with the beauty and brightness of the morning. He tasted of the clean, crisp outdoors, wild and untamed. He hadn't shaved, and his beard grazed her jaw, but she loved the maleness of it, just as she loved the faint hint of dust and saddle leather that clung to his clothing.

The saddle slid to the ground, landing with a thump and a clink of buckles. Jack pulled her closer and deepened the kiss, and she felt her desire blossom like a flower opening to the sun, while her good sense unravelled.

'Let's go inside,' he murmured, grazing kisses down the line of her jaw until her reasoning processes ceased to function.

In a warm and fuzzy daze, Lizzie allowed him to lead her, with a strong arm around her shoulders, to the steps. She knew he was planning to take her to his room, and she was struggling to remember why it wasn't wise. Why *should* she resist Jack?

How could she?

It wasn't till they turned down the hallway leading to Jack's room that she was finally stabbed by her reluctant guilty conscience. Of course, there were solid reasons why she shouldn't let this happen, and the main reason was becoming more evident every day.

Jack's kisses might feel wonderfully, perfectly right, and perhaps her feelings for him were more than a mere, mid-trimester spike in her hormones. But was her all-consuming need sufficient excuse to sleep with him?

In the doorway to his room, Lizzie's conscience began to shout. She stopped him with a hand on his arm. She had to be strong, had to be honest with him. It would be unconscionable to make love when Jack didn't know she was pregnant.

Bravely, she said, 'Jack, I'm sorry. This isn't a good idea.'

'Nonsense. It's the best idea you've had since you got here.'

She almost protested that it hadn't been her idea, but she knew that wasn't exactly honest. After all, she hadn't gone outside looking for fresh air and scenery. She'd been looking for Jack, hadn't she? And she'd more or less thrown herself into his arms.

'I'm sorry,' she said again, and with stronger emphasis. 'There's a reason we shouldn't do this, and I really should have told you.'

His forehead furrowed in a deep frown. 'What are you saying? What reason?'

Unable to meet the ferocity of his gaze, Lizzie looked through the doorway into his room. Which wasn't much help. She saw his king-size bed piled with pillows and a thick, comfy, black and grey striped duvet, and she fought off pictures of Jack lying there. With her. Kissing her all over.

She swallowed. 'Can we talk?'

He touched a thumb to the corner of her mouth. 'Sure. As soon as we've finished here.'

Lizzie wished her legs felt stronger. 'No, Jack. Can we go to the lounge room?'

'Not another talk in the lounge room.'

'Please.'

Jack gave a disbelieving shake of his head, but finally, tight-lipped, and without another word, he turned back down the hallway.

Shooting her a puzzled glance, he said, 'I suppose you're about to tell me exactly why you've come here.'

'Yes.' Lizzie had intended to sit down, to have a civilised conversation, just as they'd had last night, but she felt too agitated to sit still. 'I probably should have told you straight away.'

'I said I didn't need to know. It's none of my business why you're hiding.' Jack's throat rippled as he swallowed. 'Of course, that was before—' He stopped, clearly hesitating. His green eyes shimmered. 'Before I became attached to the idea of taking you to bed.'

Help. His words stirred all kinds of tremors inside her.

He said quietly, 'Is that what you're going to tell me? That there's a very good reason why I shouldn't take you to bed?'

Lizzie nodded. Her baby was the most important reason in the world for holding Jack at bay. Her longing for Jack might have temporarily got in the way, but her longing for her baby was much more important and meaningful than any physical yearning.

Her baby was everything. Her future. The sole focus of her love. The very best thing in her life.

Jack stood at the end of the sofa, hands thrust deep in his pockets, and she could feel his tension reaching across the room to her.

'There's something important I should have told you before this,' she said quietly.

'Speak up, Lizzie. I can't hear you.'

She turned, forcing herself to face him, knowing that what she had to say would for ever wipe the sexy sparkle from his eyes, but she didn't want him to think she was ashamed of the dear, precious baby growing inside her.

Lifting her chin, she said proudly and clearly, 'I'm pregnant.'

Pregnant?

Jack couldn't have been more surprised if Lizzie had announced she was a vampire. He felt as if the earth had slipped from beneath him.

'But—' He tried to speak, realised that he needed air, took a breath and tried again. 'But you told me last night there's no man in your life.'

'Well, yes, that's right.'

The anxious tremor in Lizzie's voice and her nervous pacing were *not* helping Jack's concentration.

'What's happened then? Has he left you?'

'No, Jack.'

Bewildered, he lifted a hand to scratch at his head. This was *not* making sense.

Lizzie stopped pacing and stood by the window, chewing her lip as she parted the curtain and looked out across the sun-drenched landscape. Despite his shocked bafflement, he could still taste her kiss, could smell the subtle fragrance of her hair, could remember the happy burst of longing he'd felt when she'd grabbed him and kissed him. As if the floodgates had opened.

He longed to haul her back into his arms and kiss the soft, sulky tilt of her mouth. Coax a smile.

She's not available.

She's pregnant.

The thought dug into him. *Pregnant.* His brain clamoured with questions. *Who had made her pregnant? Why? When?*

Just looking at her, he couldn't tell that she was expecting, but he wondered now if the lush fullness of her breasts and hips had been enhanced by the presence of her growing baby.

A baby. For crying out loud, her body was a haven for another man's child. How could she have told him there was no man in her life?

Jack challenged her. 'There has to be a father.'

Lizzie turned from the window and gave a faint shake of her head.

'Where is he?' Jack demanded.

'I don't know.'

'For God's sake, Lizzie, *who* is he, then?'

Her chin lifted a notch higher. 'I don't know his name. All I can tell you is he's six feet three, and thirty-six years old, and he's an engineer with an interest in classical music and long-distance running.'

Jack's jaw sagged.

What the hell? How could she rattle off the guy's vital statistics, yet claim that she didn't know his name?

'He's donor number 372,' she said tightly.

Donor?

Jack blinked. 'Your baby's father is a sperm donor?'

'Yes.'

Shock ripped through Jack. He was well acquainted with artificial insemination—it was a common practice in the cattle industry—but why would a hot-blooded, attractive woman like Lizzie need a clinical insemination? It didn't make sense.

He stared at her as she stood there, her flowing curves outlined against the rectangle of blue sky. He remembered her eagerness both this morning and last night.

Why would a beautiful, passionate woman like Lizzie Green reject a living, breathing lover and choose an anonymous donation in a syringe?

'Hell, Lizzie, if you wanted a baby, all you had to do was put the word out. Blokes would have been lining up.'

I would have been there at the head of the queue.

Jack grimaced, aware that after two kisses the possessiveness he felt for her was totally unjustified.

On the far side of the room, she leaned against the wall, looking down at her hands, twisting them anxiously. 'I hope I didn't sound flippant about the donor. The decision wasn't made lightly.'

'But it doesn't make sense.' Jack's voice rang loudly in the quiet room, echoing his confusion. 'How can an anonymous donor be the best option?'

A wistful smile tilted her mouth. 'That's not easy to explain. It's why I'm here at Savannah. Avoiding that very question, because I know that whatever I say, there'll be people who won't understand. I don't want journalists hounding me, asking stupid questions, blowing my story out of proportion and whipping up the public's emotions.'

'But you can't hide here for ever. You'll have to explain eventually.'

'Yes.' Arms crossed, Lizzie drew a deep breath, let it out slowly. 'I just wanted time to get used to being pregnant, and to make sure everything's OK with the baby before I face the music. Ideally, I'd keep this quiet until the baby's safely delivered.'

'Is there much chance of that?'

Lizzie shrugged. 'Unfortunately, I can't hide for ever. But I'm sure people will react differently when there's a real live baby to show them, but right now the focus will be on the whys and hows of the pregnancy, and most people can't understand why I chose to go solo.'

And who could blame most people? Jack thought grimly. 'I can't promise to understand, but I'd like to hear your explanation,' he said.

Her smile was doubtful. 'Of course.'

At least she came back to sit on the couch.

Jack sat, too. At the opposite end.

In a perfect world, Lizzie would have kicked off her shoes and tucked her legs beneath her, settling in for a cosy, heart-to-heart chat.

No, in a perfect world she would have been in his arms, continuing where their kiss left off.

Instead, she began to trace the leafy pattern of the uphol-stery with her forefinger. 'It's hard to know where to start. It's not as if I woke up one morning and thought I'd like to have a sperm-donor baby. The idea more or less evolved.'

She lifted a hand to rub her brow as if it would help to clarify her thoughts. 'I'd been so focused on my career, you see, and on other people's problems. Throw in a couple of unlucky love affairs, and I was nearing forty before I realised I was missing out on things that were really important to *me*.'

'Like a family?'

'Yes, a family.'

'But most women start with a partner.'

Lizzie nodded. 'That was my dream once, to find a partner first, then have a baby.'

'But?' Jack gestured for her to answer.

Lizzie hesitated.

'Don't tell me you've never found another man to step into MacCallum's shoes.'

'Oh, I found one, all right. Problem was, he fitted those shoes only too well.' Her eyes glinted with the threat of tears, but she managed a shaky smile. 'An upwardly mobile corporate banker. Head of a couple of investment companies. We were together twelve months and I thought he was serious.'

Her mouth opened as if she was about to say more, then changed her mind. 'Can I ask you a question, Jack?'

'Sure.'

'Why aren't you married?'

'I— I—' An uncomfortable sensation blocked his throat. He swallowed. 'I guess I haven't looked all that hard, but—' he shrugged '—I haven't found the right woman.'

'Exactly. And I haven't found anyone I was happy to marry, but I chose a donor because I'm fussy. Not because there were no men available.'

Her mouth twisted in an embarrassed smile. 'It's really hard to talk about this to a man, especially after—'

'After we've just kissed each other into tomorrow,' Jack supplied in a grating tone. 'What was that about, Lizzie? Don't tell me you were simply happy to see me.'

The colour in her cheeks deepened. 'You jumped the gate—and I got caught up in the moment—and then we got a bit carried away.'

Blushing, she stared at a spot on the carpet. 'I said I'm sorry, Jack.'

He shrugged. There was no point in carrying on like a

whipped puppy. He had no doubt that Lizzie enjoyed a wide circle of friends and acquaintances, and it was sobering to know that she hadn't found one guy who measured up to her high standards. Damn it, how high were these standards anyway?

He was still mulling over this when she said, 'The thing is I simply wasn't prepared to marry some poor unsuspecting man just because I wanted a baby.' She met his gaze and her hazel eyes flashed. 'It's not a very honest reason to tie the knot, is it?'

What could Jack say? 'I—I guess not.'

'I gave it a lot of thought,' she added, finally kicking off her shoes, as if she could relax now that her confession was complete.

Unhappily, Jack watched as she curled into her corner of the sofa with the unconscious grace of a cat. He thought about the way he'd thundered back to the homestead this morning, confident that he should try again with her.

Arriving at that decision had felt good, *really* good, and he'd taken the stockyard gate in a burst of triumph, and then Lizzie had met him, her face glowing, full of smiles and kisses…

Now, she began to speak again, earnestly, as if she felt compelled to explain and justify every reason why their kiss had been a mistake.

'Single mothers can do a great job. My mother's a prime example. She gave my sisters and me a very happy childhood. Being raised by a good single mum has to be better than being raised in a bad marriage.'

Jack couldn't argue with that. His parents' marriage had been desperately unhappy, and his childhood had been blighted by their endless fights and arguments. He could remember lying in bed at night, head beneath the pillow, fingers jammed in his ears, trying to shut out their bitter, angry voices.

'What about your father?' he said. 'Was he happy for your mother to keep you to herself?'

'Actually, no.' Lizzie dropped her gaze. 'Not that I knew much about my father when I was a child. It was only later when I came to live with him that I realised how hurt and excluded he'd felt. That's another reason I settled on a sperm donor. Knowing how Dad felt, I knew that an affair with someone just to create a baby would cause all sorts of emotional fallout.'

No question about that, Jack thought. Lots of guys took being a father pretty seriously.

After the rough time he'd had with his old man, he'd spent a lot of time thinking about the fatherhood role. He couldn't deny that some fathers were jerks, but all his married mates were nuts about their kids, and he'd always reckoned that he would be, too, when his turn came.

'So,' Lizzie said, watching him carefully. 'That's my story. I—I hope you understand.'

Jack swallowed. He hated the thought of Lizzie facing parenthood alone. It seemed such a waste. But, clearly, it was none of his business.

'You put up a fair case,' he said.

'That's good to know.'

'But this doesn't mean you're staying clear of men for ever, does it?'

Her eyes widened with surprise. 'I—ah—haven't made any plans past my baby's delivery.'

A pulse thundered in Jack's throat. Lizzie mightn't have made plans, but he'd had plans. His plans had involved exploring every inch of her luscious skin. He'd planned to make love to her with finesse and passion.

Now his plans were toast, and this morning's notions were nothing but a bag of bulldust. Hell, there was no point in even thinking about getting closer. Lizzie was focused on her baby. She didn't need or want a man in her life. And why would he want to be there, anyway?

Why would he want to be involved with a woman who came with so much baggage—a headache career, and now a baby that wouldn't even know its own dad?

No, thank you.

Jack cleared his throat, eager to put an end to this conversation. 'If I sounded critical, I apologise. I spoke out of turn. You have every right to make your own decisions. It's your life, your baby.'

He stood quickly, forced a quick smile as he tried to ignore the tempting picture she made, curled on the sofa, tanned legs glowing, dark hair shining in a stream of sunlight. 'I'm sure you're busy.' Already, he was heading for the door. 'So I'll let you get on with your work.'

It was time to get out of here.

His previously hazy reasons for staying clear of Lizzie were multiplying madly and already he was telling himself he'd had a lucky escape. It was time to get out of there before he said or did something foolish. There was no point in turning a bad situation into a flaming disaster.

CHAPTER SEVEN

STANDING at the open doorway of her room, Lizzie looked at the sunburnt plains, while she applied herself to the extraordinarily difficult task of *not* missing Jack.

He'd headed off somewhere to work, and she'd come here to her room—to *work*—but it was proving impossible. Jack was front, back and centre of her thoughts.

No doubt he was puzzled and possibly upset after she'd rushed out to greet him with kisses, then retreated, and promptly delivered the news of her pregnancy.

How could she have been so irresponsible? She prided herself on her prudence. She'd never been reckless around men. Well…not after she'd learned two very difficult lessons. But now, to her shame, she couldn't stop thinking about Jack's kiss.

Even though she'd stopped it, and delivered a speech that ensured it would never be repeated, he'd ignited a craving in her.

Lizzie knew it was wrong. Regret was such a useless emotion.

She'd never been a thrill-seeker, had never been bothered by any kind of addiction, not even to chocolate, but now every cell in her body screamed for the return of

Jack's lips. She wanted his mouth, teasing and warm, on her skin. She longed for—

Enough.

Angry at her weakness, she whirled away from the doorway, sat down at her desk and clicked on her Internet connection. Listening to the internal whirring of her laptop, she watched a raft of emails download. Her heart leapt when she saw a different name sitting in the middle of the familiar addresses of work colleagues.

Isabella Casali. Her cousin. At last, a message from Monta Correnti.

Lizzie smiled with relief as she opened the message. She'd been worried.

The message was in English. Isabella was proud of her language skills and loved to use English whenever she could.

Dearest Lizzie,

I'm sorry I haven't answered your emails before now. Papa's not at all well, so I'm in charge of 'Rosa', and we've been really busy. I've been run off my feet.

I hope you and your baby are fine, and keeping well. Are you still holed up in that place in the outback? It must be fascinating. A totally different world.

Now, let me tell you about Max. Forgive me, Lizzie, while I have a small rave. Max is wonderful. I'm so happy. I can't believe how sweet he is to me. His love still feels like a miracle.

A miracle. Lizzie sensed a wealth of happiness in Isabella's word choice and she was really pleased for her cousin, but she also felt an inexplicable stab of jealousy.

I'm afraid I haven't seen your mother. I've been too busy.

And too upset with my mother, Lizzie thought. Fair enough, too.

So far, there has been no news of the twins. As you know, I really wanted to go to New York to find them, but Papa can't spare me. Actually, this message will have to be brief as I have so much to do, and there's a problem in the kitchen.

I'll try harder to keep in touch.

Ciao,

Isabella.

Lizzie let out a sigh of relief, pleased to finally have contact from someone at home. After all these years in Australia, she still thought of Monta Correnti as her home.

If only her family could be more harmonious.

She thought of her mother—stunningly beautiful, fiercely independent, still harbouring deep resentment towards her half-brother, Luca.

It was such a pity. Why was she still so angry, after all this time? Why couldn't she let go?

On an impulse, Lizzie dialled her mother's number, but she only got her answering machine. She left a brief message. 'Thinking of you, Mama. Love you. I'm well. Please get in touch when you're free. *Ciao*.'

Over the next few days, Lizzie saw very little of Jack. He seemed to be extra busy with station work and she kept busy, too, working at her desk, and taking short morning walks and even shorter afternoon rests. She told herself that she was pleased at last to be able to give her full attention to the books she'd brought.

Jack's busyness was a good thing. This distancing from

each other was highly desirable. It was exactly what she needed. Now she could focus on her work and her baby, the two things that mattered.

Everything else, including Jack, was a distraction. She only wished she didn't have to tell herself this so many times. Every day.

She saw Jack at mealtimes, of course, and they continued to share the cooking. But while they talked easily about their different worlds, and she felt they both enjoyed getting to know more and more about each other, Jack was careful to keep any inference of flirtation out of their conversation. There were no stolen kisses. No sparkling glances. No touching.

It was a shock to learn that, despite the endless lectures she'd given herself, she missed the sizzle that had simmered between them. It was hard, *really* hard to let it go. To her dismay, she still found Jack incredibly attractive.

Too often, way too often, she had wicked fantasies.

One afternoon, she was busy answering an email from Canberra when she heard Jack's footsteps on the veranda, and she froze, fingers poised above the keyboard, listening with her full attention.

He went past her room, and turned into his room, and she heard his shower taps turn on. She tried—honestly, she *did* try—to stop herself from imagining him standing there, naked. She tried not to picture the soap bubbles sliding over his shiny bronzed shoulders, slipping down his muscly chest. Then lower.

Heat flared like tiny bushfires inside her. The picture of Jack sprang into painfully clear focus. She could see the gleaming slickness of his wet skin stretched over bands of muscles. She thought how blissfully liberating it would be to run her hands over his bare back, then over his front.

It wasn't till the sound of the water stopped abruptly that her common sense slammed a door on her thoughts.

For heaven's sake, how could she have forgotten so much, so quickly? Why was it so hard to remember she was a forty-year-old, pregnant woman, who'd chosen, yes, *chosen* to be a single mother?

Three evenings later, after another carefully polite and un-satisfactory dinner conversation, she ran into Jack. Literally.

It happened in the hallway, when she was coming back from the bathroom, after a long and supposedly calming soak in the tub. She'd wrapped a towel around her wet hair and she was wearing her white towelling bathrobe— nothing else—and her skin was warm and flushed and smelling of rose and lavender bath oil.

She'd used up almost all of Kate's collection of bath oils, and she'd made a note to try to buy some more.

She'd been reading in the bath till her toes were frilly, and she was carrying the thick paperback novel back to her room, intending to continue reading in bed. She had her head down, checking that she'd marked her place, when she banged into Jack.

The book fell to the floor.

'Sorry!' they both cried at once, and simultaneously they both stooped to retrieve the book.

What happened then was quite strange, like something out of a movie. Lizzie was bending down, conscious that her bath robe was gaping, revealing quite a bit of her cleavage, pink and perfumed from her bath, but instead of feeling em-barrassed, or coy, instead of modestly adjusting the robe, she was frozen, as still as a statue, mesmerised by Jack.

He was kneeling inches from her, and they were both holding her book, staring at each other, breathing unevenly as if they'd run a hard race.

She could feel his heat, enveloping her like a mysterious fog, and they rose in slow motion, still holding the book. In unison, Jack took a step towards her and she took a step back, and it was like dancing a slow waltz.

Lizzie found herself against the cool paintwork of the hallway, holding her book. Trapped by Jack. His hands were now on the wall, on either side of her head, and she had stopped breathing.

Stopped thinking, had become nothing but a mass of wanting.

He was close. So close. Touching close. Kissing close. She could see each individual pinprick of his beard, and the surprising softness of his lips.

Her body was hot and tight with wanting.

Through the open neck of her bathrobe, Jack's fingers traced her skin, burning a trail from her throat to between her breasts, making her gasp.

'Lizzie,' he whispered and he smiled directly into her eyes. 'You know you only have to ask.' His mouth brushed a nerve-tingling, fiery sweep over her lips.

Then he stepped away, turned down the hallway, and disappeared into the darkness.

Somehow, Lizzie made her way back to her room, where she fell in a trembling mess onto her bed. She was shocked by the strength of her desire for Jack, by the force of her aching, physical longing.

You only have to ask...

She wasn't going to ask. She couldn't possibly ask, could she? She was so much older than he was, and pregnant. How could he find her desirable?

You only have to ask...

His words wouldn't leave her alone. They danced in her

head like haunting, beautiful music. Like tendrils of enchanted smoke, they curled around her heart.

Only have to ask...

The idea was so alluring. Jack was so disturbingly attractive, and she'd been alone for so long.

But it was a mistake for all kinds of reasons. It was, wasn't it?

Wasn't it?

With one touch, Jack had destroyed her certainty.

Jack couldn't quite believe he'd said that to Lizzie.

You only have to ask.

Fool. He needed his head read.

Except...he hadn't been thinking with his head.

Lizzie had been there, practically naked, fresh from the bath and smelling of every temptation known to man, her skin so soft and pink and warm, her mouth trembling in anticipation of his kiss.

Thank God he'd managed to resist.

There was now a long list of ways she was wrong for him. After a childhood locked in a rigid career pattern, he was finally happy with his life. Why spoil it by getting involved with Lizzie and the complications of her high profile career, her ambition, her lifestyle, her pregnancy with another man's baby?

Problem was, he knew all that, but he still wanted her like crazy.

You only have to ask.

As if she would ask. He might be a fool, but Lizzie had her head screwed on.

And yet...

He'd seen the flash of disappointment in her eyes

when he'd backed away. If he were a gambling man, he'd bet that he still had a chance.

That evening there was an email from Isabella. Lizzie clicked on it eagerly, keen for more news of her family and relieved to be distracted from her latest dilemmas over Jack.

Hi Lizzie,

I have such good news and I'm so excited. I've managed to track down Alessandro and Angelo's contact details, and I'm going to send emails introducing myself as their sister.

Actually, there's some other news, but I'm not sure that I should tell you.

Lizzie's heart gave a sickening thud when she read this sentence. She closed her eyes, not wanting to read the rest of Isabella's message. In her everyday life, she never avoided bad news, but this was different, this was family, and she felt a flicker of fear like the darting of a snake's tongue.

She opened her eyes and kept reading.

My father told me something today, something very disturbing. I'm sorry, Lizzie. I'm afraid it concerns Lisa.

I guess you're bound to hear some time, so I wanted to warn you, but I think it would be better if you heard it from your mother.

I hope I'm not scaring you, Lizzie. It's not an emergency. Your mother isn't sick. But I think you should ask her to explain her behaviour when my father went to her for help. I'm sorry if that sounds terribly cryptic, but that's all I want to say at the moment.

Love,

Isabella.

Appalled, Lizzie read the message again, trying to make sense of it. *Ask her to explain her behaviour when my father went to her for help.*

What could her mother have done?

Acid rose, filling Lizzie's throat.

As a child, she'd idolised her mother. Lisa Firenzi was regally beautiful, strongly independent, and the successful owner of Monta Correnti's most sophisticated restaurant. Lizzie's ideal woman.

Even after Lizzie had come to Australia to be close to her father, she'd modelled herself on Lisa. Her mother's example of self-sufficiency and feminine triumph was the one thing that had saved Lizzie when Mitch MacCallum had so heartlessly thrown her aside. It had helped again years later when Toby the banker had caused so much grief.

There'd been many times during her political career when Lizzie had used Lisa's strength as inspiration.

Without her mother as a role model, she might never have embarked on this pregnancy…

But what have you done, Mama?

It was a question she hardly dared to ask, but, unhappily, she knew she had no choice. Lizzie knew she must ask it, even though she was positive she wouldn't like the answer.

Her hands were shaking as she picked up her phone and began to press the buttons.

CHAPTER EIGHT

JACK stopped outside Lizzie's bedroom door.

He thought he'd heard crying, but that was impossible. Lizzie was so strong. He'd seen that with his own eyes, and he'd been reading on the Internet about her reputation for being a particularly tough senator.

Apparently, Lizzie had rarely let the opposition break her down, and he couldn't imagine her collapsing into a fit of weeping, but when he leaned closer to the door there could be no mistake. Lizzie was definitely crying. No, it was worse than that. She was sobbing uncontrollably, as if her heart would break.

Alarmed, Jack tapped on her door, but she was crying so loudly she couldn't hear him. He gave the door a gentle push, and it swung forward to reveal Lizzie sprawled on her bed, abandoned in misery, her face red, tear-stained, twisted with despair, her body shaking.

The sight sliced into Jack. At first he was too shocked to think, but then he raced through possibilities.

Was there a problem with the baby? A miscarriage?

He felt a slug of fear, but almost immediately reasoned that if there were pregnancy complications Lizzie would have come to him for help. She was too smart to suffer in silence. She would have asked him to take her to a doctor.

No, this had to be something else. Worse? Jack couldn't bear to see her like this. His impulse was to sweep her into his arms, to hold her close, to soothe her, as if she were a child. But he was uncomfortably aware that she wouldn't welcome such intimacy from him.

Uncertain and anxious, he hovered near the end of her bed. His eyes hunted her room for clues. It was all very tidy. Nothing appeared to be amiss. Her laptop had been turned off, but there was a mobile phone lying on the bed beside her. He wondered if she'd heard bad news.

Abruptly, as if she'd sensed his presence, she lifted her head and saw him, and then she sat up quickly, her hands flying to swipe at her tears.

'I'm sorry to disturb you,' Jack said. 'But I couldn't help hearing how upset you were and I was worried. I was hoping I might be able to help somehow.'

She swiped again at her tear-streaked face. 'That's kind, but no. It's just—' Her face crumpled and she gestured frantically towards her desk in the corner. 'Could you pass me that box of tissues?'

Jack did so quickly, and she pulled out a great wad of tissues and mopped at her face and blew her nose. When she'd finished, she dumped the damp clump on the bedside table, and tried, unsuccessfully, to smile.

'I must look a fright.'

'I don't scare easily.' He was relieved. Things couldn't be too disastrous if Lizzie was worried about her appearance. 'Anyway, a red nose looks good on you.'

This time she did manage a faint, shaky smile.

'Are you sure there's nothing I can do, Lizzie?'

She shook her head. 'It's just—' Her hands flapped in a gesture of helplessness. 'My crazy family in Italy. Sometimes I just want to—'

She stopped, and sat there looking lost, and Jack's heart went out to her. Everything about her sent a message of huge need—the deep emotion in her eyes, the vulnerable droop of her shoulders, the lingering tremor of her soft lips, her hands now twisting a tissue to shreds.

When she looked up directly into his eyes, he read a silent entreaty to take her in his arms, to kiss away her tears, to sweep her away from whatever was troubling her.

Or was he getting carried away?

Prudently, he remained still. It would be all too easy to take advantage of Lizzie's vulnerability—but right now he simply wanted to help her.

He cleared his throat. 'Can I get you something? A cup of tea?'

Inside, he winced. He sounded like a doddering aunt who believed all the world's problems could be solved by a cup of tea.

Lizzie looked surprised, too. She blinked at him. 'Tea would be lovely. Thank you, Jack.'

'Hang in there,' he said gently. 'I'll be back in two shakes.'

She gave him a bleak smile. 'I'll go wash my face.'

Lizzie hurried to the bathroom, filled the basin with warm water, and washed her face with liberal splashes.

Normally, she hated to cry, but tonight after her phone call to her mother, she'd felt so alone, she'd more or less collapsed. Now, with her face washed and patted dry, she was already better. Cleansed. Calmer.

She took a cautious glimpse in the mirror, saw that her eyes and nose were still red and swollen.

At least she felt more composed. Actually, she'd begun to calm down when she'd discovered Jack standing at the end of her bed. He'd looked wonderful standing there, so tall and handsome and reliable in his old blue jeans and a faded brown countryman's shirt. A steadying anchor.

She was very grateful that he'd braved her closed door and come in. His strong, companionable presence had made her feel suddenly safe and she'd wanted to fall into his arms, to dry her tears on his shirtfront, to bury her face against his shoulder.

It would have been perfect. With Jack's arms about her, she would have felt comforted, safe again, rescued from that awful feeling that she'd lost her bearings.

But Jack had kept his distance. He'd been friendly and kind and concerned—and distant—and shame on her for expecting anything else. This was what she'd demanded of him—to be a friend, not her lover. She knew she should be grateful. She *was* enormously grateful.

Now she stared hard at her reflection. *Come on, Lizzie. Shoulders back. You're strong, remember.*

She still didn't feel particularly strong as she went back to her room, where Jack very soon joined her with two mugs of tea.

'You should make yourself comfy,' he told her, in a kindly tone.

So she sat on Kate Burton's comfortable bed, with the pillows plumped up, and her legs, in slim cream Capri pants, stretched out in front of her. Jack swung the chair out from her desk and sat there, on the far side of the room, with an ankle propped on a knee.

'That chair looks too small for you, Jack.'

He sent a cursory glance to her bed, the only other place in the room, apart from the floor, where he could sit. 'This chair's fine, thanks.'

Lizzie dropped her gaze, and took a sip of her tea. It was very hot and strong and sweet, exactly what she needed.

'You're looking better,' he said. 'Not so pale.'

'I'm feeling much better, thank you.' She drank more tea, then smiled at him. 'You're a really nice man. You know that, don't you?'

'I hear it from the stockmen every day.'

They shared a grin and as they sat there, drinking tea in the quiet house, Lizzie found herself wanting to tell him about her family and why she'd been so upset.

'Do you mind if I talk? Get it off my chest?'

'Of course not.'

'I suppose it's a female thing—needing to offload emotional baggage.'

'As long as you don't think of me as a girlfriend.'

'Fat chance.'

Settling against the pillows, she began to tell him about her family, about the two rivalling family restaurants, Rosa and Sorella, and the tensions that seemed to have existed for ever, and about her uncle Luca and the twins, and how Isabella had always worked so very hard.

'But tonight, it got so much worse,' she said. 'There was an email from Isabella, telling me to ring my mother. So I did.'

Tears threatened, and Lizzie took a deep breath. 'It seems Luca's first wife, Cindy, went back to America, leaving him with their twins. He was struggling financially, so he asked my mother for help, for money.'

She closed her eyes, remembering the coldness in her mother's voice as soon as Luca's name was mentioned. All the usual warmth had vanished. It was like turning off a switch.

'My mother refused to help him.' Lizzie's voice broke on a sob, and she reached for the tissues and blew her nose.

'Maybe she had good reasons for refusing,' Jack suggested gently.

Lizzie shook her head. 'Luca's her brother, Jack. What kind of sister would refuse to help her own brother? I know the two of them have always fought like cats and dogs, but this was inexcusable. She's always had plenty of money, and Luca was struggling. How could she turn him away empty-handed? He had two little mouths to feed. But my mother, their aunt, wouldn't help and—'

Tears chased each other down Lizzie's cheeks. 'He had to send Alessandro and Angelo away to America because he couldn't afford to feed them.' Her voice rose on a note of horror. 'And it was my mother's fault.'

She could still picture those bright, eager little boys with their shiny eyes and cheeky smiles. It would have broken Luca's heart to give them up, to willingly separate himself from his sons. And now they'd been gone for so long.

Her mother's lack of compassion shocked Lizzie to the core. She felt betrayed by the person she loved most.

Twice in her life she'd loved and admired someone so much that she'd allowed that person to shape her life. Those two people had been Mitch MacCallum and Lisa Firenzi.

First Mitch had let her down badly, and tonight Lizzie felt as if her mother had pulled her very foundations from beneath her feet.

Such a big part of her decision to have a sperm-donor pregnancy stemmed from her certainty that her mother would approve and applaud her. Now she wondered why Lisa's opinion had seemed so damned important.

Nothing made sense any more.

Setting aside her mug, Lizzie sent Jack a shaky smile. She felt drained by her confession. 'You probably think I'm making a mountain out of a molehill.'

'Not at all,' he said. 'It's never easy to accept flaws in someone you love.'

Jack understood. He really understood. She'd momentarily forgotten his problems with his father, but, of course, he probably understood a great deal. Knowing that, and sitting here with him now, in her bedroom, wrapped by the silent outback night, she felt astonishingly close to him.

They talked on, sharing stories about their childhood, about their parents, and the difficulties of accepting that idols too often had feet of clay. They even talked, eventually, about the possibility of forgiveness, and Lizzie found the idea extremely comforting.

She would have liked to go on talking for ages, but when she yawned Jack stood and collected their mugs.

'Thanks so much for the tea and the talk,' she said, hoping she didn't sound too disappointed.

He looked down at her, an ambiguous expression in his gorgeous green eyes. 'You'd better get some sleep.'

He was leaving and she felt suddenly, desperately lonely. Truly lonely. It made no sense. To be alone was what she wanted—to be single and solitary and strong.

Like her mother.

Oh, help.

Jack's voice whispered in her head. *You only have to ask.*

On impulse, she reached for his free hand. 'Do you have to go?'

He went very still. 'Are you asking me to stay?'

'Yes, I think I am.' She held her breath. She couldn't believe she was doing this. Jack had said that she only had to ask, but how could she be sure he really wanted her? He was so hunky and fit and ten years younger. She was pregnant.

Embarrassment flamed her cheeks as she remembered the recent changes in her body. She'd always been full-breasted, but now her breasts were bigger than ever, and heavy. Her baby bulge was becoming noticeable, too.

Silently, Jack set the mugs down on the small bedside table, then sat on the edge of her bed. Her heart thudded as the mattress dipped beneath his weight. She caught the faint drift of soap on his skin, saw that his green eyes were clouded with a smoky mix of wariness and desire.

His throat rippled as he swallowed, and the air in the room seemed to tremble.

Nervous flutters danced in Lizzie's stomach. After the way she'd turned Jack away in the past, she couldn't really blame him if he got to his feet again and walked out the door.

'If I stay, I'll want to make love to you, Lizzie.'

Her throat was so full she couldn't speak, could only nod.

The caution in his eyes gave way to his trademark sparkle. He hadn't shaved and her fingertips touched the masculine roughness of his beard.

She smiled. 'You're so lovely and whiskery.'

His hand captured hers, and he kissed her fingers. 'You're so lovely and silky.' Leaning in, he kissed her lips. 'And you're so soft.' He kissed her again, gently at first, and then with open-mouthed thoroughness. 'Lizzie... I love the way you taste.'

'How do I taste?'

'Like moonlight. Perfect.'

'You taste of sunlight. Perfect too.'

He smiled. 'Night and day.'

Their kiss deepened and he gathered her in to him, nipping, tasting, delving. Happiness flowed through her. For too long she'd lived in a vacuum of touch, but now Jack's hands were making dreamy circles on her arms, on her back, over her throat, her shoulders, and his mouth was awakening a thousand forgotten pleasures.

When he began to undo the buttons on her blouse she

was no longer nervous, but rosy and warm, edgy with excited anticipation.

Her blouse fell open, and the night air was cool on her skin, and she closed her eyes as he kissed a sweet line from her throat down her chest.

But when he removed her bra her eyes snapped open, and she felt compelled to explain. 'My breasts have changed. Because of the baby. I hope you don't mind.'

Gently, almost reverently, he tested their weight in his hands. 'You're beautiful, Lizzie. Amazing. More perfection.' He lowered his head, bestowing the softest of kisses. 'But I don't want to hurt you.'

'You won't.' Already, desire was sweeping her coyness aside. 'Don't worry. I'm fine and so is the baby.'

'More than fine.' Jack's voice was thick and choked, and when he kissed her again any lingering shreds of doubt were exploded by her gathering desire and excited certainty.

She needed this. Every touch, every kiss was vitally, crucially important, and so very right for her.

Jack was right for her, so good to her, and she needed his loving. So much. Too much.

Morning. Jack watched the gentle sunlight filter through the curtains as he lay beside Lizzie, and his heart seemed to spin with happiness. What a lovely sight she was, with her cheeks warm with sleep and her dark hair a messed-up tumble on the pillow.

He still found it hard to believe that last night had happened. He'd known at the outset that Lizzie was primarily seeking comfort, but to his surprise she'd responded with stunning sweetness and passion, and it had seemed to him that she'd given so much more than she'd taken. This morning he was floating.

Unable to resist, he dropped a kiss onto her soft, sexy lips. She opened her eyes and smiled.

'Hey there,' she said softly.

'Hey to you.'

She yawned and stretched and smiled again. 'Wow. I'm remembering last night. It was amazing, wasn't it?'

'It was,' he agreed, and he kissed her bare shoulder. 'So are you and your baby OK?' He had to ask. He felt incredibly protective now.

'We're fabulous, Jack.' Lizzie met his gaze shyly. 'Thank you.'

Smiling, she slid her hand down her body, her marvellous, lush body, and let it rest on the gentle swell of her abdomen and the secret miracle inside her. 'I dreamed about her last night.'

'About the baby?'

'Yes. I dreamed I could see right inside, and she was curled up like a sweet little fern frond. She had dark eyes and tiny, perfect arms and legs, and tiny fingers and toes, just like the pictures in the medical books.'

'Wow.'

'It was so reassuring.'

'A good dream, then.'

'The best.'

'Do you already know you're having a girl?'

The lips he'd kissed so thoroughly last night pouted. 'Actually, no I don't know the baby's sex yet, but in the dream she was definitely a girl and I was so pleased. I called her Madeline, and now I feel certain that I'm going to have a girl.'

'I can picture you with a daughter.'

'So can I.' Lizzie grinned. 'It feels right. I grew up with sisters and no brothers, so I think I'll feel much more comfortable with a little girl.'

To Jack's dismay he found that he was jealous of this little girl who was not and never would be his daughter. He pushed the thought aside. 'Madeline's a pretty name.'

'It's a very feminine name, isn't it?'

'I guess.' To cover his feeling of exclusion, he resorted to teasing. 'But I thought you'd consider names like Cleopatra, or Boadicea.'

'Why would I want to call my poor baby—?' Lizzie stopped and watched him closely, then laughed. 'Oh, right. Sure. I should follow my mother's example and name my daughter after a strong woman.'

'Italians like to follow family traditions, don't they?'

'Not this Italian.' She gave his arm a playful punch. 'Anyway, I'm half Australian.'

'So you are.' Possessively, Jack traced her silky smooth hip. 'I wonder which half of you is Italian and which half is Australian.'

When she began to laugh, he stopped her with a kiss. 'I'd be willing to bet that your lips are Italian.'

She groaned softly. 'Jack, no. Please don't start seducing me now.'

'Why not?'

'I can't spend all morning in bed.'

'Of course you can.'

'I can't. I have a mountain of work to get through today, and I can't undo the good habits of a lifetime in a single day.'

'Why not?' he asked again, and he began to kiss her. All over.

'Because—'

He touched her with his tongue and she let out a soft whimper.

'You're right,' she said in a breathless whisper. 'Why not?'

* * *

If she concentrated, Lizzie could get on with her work. Except ...every so often she simply had to stop...to remember how happy she was...and how truly perfect Jack's loving had been.

She'd felt perfectly safe entrusting her body to him, and he'd taken her with just the right balance of tenderness and passion, so that she'd felt totally free and relaxed and uninhibited, and everything had been—in a word—

Blissful.

That evening the Savannah paddocks were bathed in a soft purple twilight that matched the gathering silence as, one by one, the bird calls stopped, and the sun slowly sank, bleeding streaks of crimson into the western sky.

In the kitchen, Lizzie was running late. Having worked too long after her late-morning start, she'd almost forgotten it was her turn to cook, and now she was busy throwing together a last-minute scratch meal. Curried chickpeas, a staple from her university days, was something she still served in rare emergencies. It involved little more than a diced onion and garlic thrown into a pan with a handful of spices, a can of chickpeas and another of tomatoes.

Normally, Lizzie served it with naan bread, but the Savannah pantry didn't run to packets of reheatable naan, so she steamed rice instead, and hoped Jack wouldn't mind a vegetarian meal.

She was listening to jazz on the radio, something she hadn't done for years. A blues tune, slow and moody with a saxophone crooning and a double bass deeply plucking the beat. The music soothed her, as did the aromatic fragrance of the spices, and she thought with a sense of wonder that she couldn't remember the last time she'd felt so calm and deeply happy.

'Something smells delicious.'

At the sound of Jack's voice she turned from the stove.

It was the first time she'd seen him since he'd left her bed and she felt a sweet pang, exactly as if an arrow had speared her heart. She also felt just a little bit coy, but Jack was, as always, completely at ease, and he flipped her a friendly grin.

'You say the food smells delicious every night I cook.'

'Because you always cook something delicious.'

'Or because you're always ravenous.'

'That too.' After a beat, he said, 'Cool music. That's Fox Bones, isn't it?'

'Who?'

'Fox Bones, on the sax.'

'Oh? I'm not sure.' She shot him a curious smile. 'Do you like jazz?'

'Sure. It's my favourite kind of music.'

'I had you pegged as a country and western fan.'

'I thought you'd be an opera buff. All those Italians. Pavarotti.'

Lizzie shrugged. 'He's good, but I prefer Fox Bones.'

They exchanged happy grins.

Jack came closer, shooting a curious glance at the contents of her frying pan. 'That's not Italian, is it?'

'I've pretty much exhausted my Italian repertoire.' She felt compelled to warn him. 'Tonight it's chickpeas.'

He nodded. 'Chickpeas and—?'

'And rice.'

'And what kind of meat?'

'No meat, Jack.'

He stared at her.

'It doesn't hurt to have an occasional meatless meal,' she said defensively.

'Says who?'

'The health experts.' Lizzie was about to expand on the theme of a balanced diet when she caught the cheeky gleam in Jack's eyes.

Was he teasing her again?

Apparently, yes. When she served the meal, he tucked into it with enthusiasm.

She thought, *I'm getting too used to this companionship sharing leisurely meals without being interrupted by a phone call or having to rush off to a meeting...having someone to talk to about everyday things that have nothing to do with work...looking forward to seeing him at the end of each day...*

As if he could read her thoughts, Jack said suddenly, 'I was wondering about your plans, Lizzie.'

'My plans?'

He smiled cautiously. 'You know—how long you'll be staying here, and what you're going to do when you leave.'

To her dismay she was suddenly flustered and stammering. 'I—I—well, you see—I have to be back in Canberra next month.'

'What happens then?'

'Senate will be in session. That's what I'm preparing for now. There's so much reading to get through, and all sorts of preliminary discussions by email.'

'But after the session?'

'After?'

'Yes,' he said with quiet insistence.

'I have a decision to make.'

Jack's eyes widened.

She knew she should explain. 'I won't be able to keep the

pregnancy a secret, so I'll have to decide whether I'll carry on with my current responsibilities and face the barrage of questions from the press, or resign and slip quietly away to have my baby out of the limelight. In Italy perhaps.'

'If I were you, I'd be taking the second option.'

Lizzie fiddled with her water glass. 'That would certainly be the easy way out. But as a politician, I feel almost duty-bound to stay in the senate, to be a sort of advocate, I guess, for single women's rights.'

'They don't need you. It's too much to take on. Too much pressure can't be good for you when you're pregnant.'

'That's true.' Before she could say anything more, the phone rang in Jack's study, down the hall.

He let out a huff of irritation. 'I suppose I'd better go and answer that.' Already, he was on his feet. 'Excuse me.'

After he'd gone, Lizzie stared at his almost-empty plate thinking about the way his face had sobered as she'd talked about the future. She couldn't expect him to understand that her career had to come first.

She was proud of her fierce commitment to her electorate, and she couldn't let one night of blissful lovemaking cloud the truth. Nothing had changed. She and Jack had very little in common. They were as different as espresso coffee and beer. Heavens, if she'd been in Jack's shoes she wouldn't have dreamed of staying back at the homestead to play host to a stranger when she could have been taking charge of the cattle muster.

When it came to the big things in life, they would always make different choices, but man, oh, man, it was hard to remember that when Jack was kissing her.

There'd actually been dangerous moments last night when she'd almost wished she'd never started her pregnancy quest. But she couldn't think like that. It was wrong, and she had to stay strong. She knew she'd made her decision carefully and for all the right reasons.

Jack wasn't on the phone for long. Lizzie was putting the kettle on, and when he came back into the kitchen the look on his face was rather puzzling. Lizzie couldn't tell if he was pleased or upset.

'That was Bill,' he said.

'Bill? The cook?'

'Yes.' With a wry smile, he came and stood beside her.

Lizzie caught a whiff of his aftershave and she had to fight an urge to lean in to him, to inhale the scent of the smooth, tanned skin above his shirt collar.

'So,' he said, standing so close that they were almost rubbing shoulders. 'Do you want the good news or the bad news?'

Bad news? Startled, she said, 'The good news, I guess.'

'You don't have to do any more cooking. Bill's coming back.'

She almost blurted out that she didn't mind cooking. She'd really been enjoying their meals, with just the two of them alone.

'Well,' she said, letting out a huff of surprise. 'I guess that'll give us both more time for our work.' Cautiously, she asked, 'So, what's the bad news?'

'I don't suppose it's actually bad news,' Jack said with an awkward smile. 'The men have finished the muster, and the team's coming back.'

'Back here?'

'Yes.'

'I see.' Lizzie was shocked by the slug of disappointment that hit her as she pictured Savannah teeming with cattlemen.

She'd become so used to being alone with Jack. Coming to Savannah had been like being shipwrecked on a desert island with a gorgeous man. Wasn't that every woman's fantasy? And wasn't it typical that she was only realising now how very much she'd enjoyed this time with him?

'The place will be swarming with people tomorrow,' Jack said, and he shot her a sharp glance. 'You know what this means, don't you?'

'I certainly wouldn't want to give any impression that we've been—um—close, Jack. I can't afford to have tongues wagging.'

He nodded and pulled a face. 'I thought you'd say that.'

'But you agree, don't you?' She felt a riff of panic. 'We don't want a scandal.'

Jack's mouth twisted as he grimaced. 'I'd hate to compromise you. Gossip spreads like wildfire in the bush. It's going to be bad enough when the men simply set eyes on you. They'll give me a ribbing, for sure, but, of course, I'll tell the Savannah ringers to pull their heads in.'

He let out an impatient sigh. 'Some of the team are contract workers. They'll be moving on from here, and who knows what they'll say? So, yeah, I agree we'll have to be careful.'

'Exactly,' Lizzie said sharply, but she was shocked to discover how miserable she was. Unreasonably so.

Jack reached for her hand, interlacing his fingers with hers, and, to her dismay, the simple contact made her feel warm and glowing, as if her insides were lit by something far deeper than lust.

'At least we have tonight,' he said in that easy, warmly persuasive way of his.

Oh, heavens. Was that wise? Minutes ago they'd been talking about her plans for the future. Jack wouldn't be a part of that future, but another night together would make their eventual break-up harder.

Perhaps the return of the ringers was a blessing in disguise. A wake-up call.

She looked down at Jack's hand, linked with hers. It was very workmanlike, broad and brown, and there was a pale, crescent-shaped, almost-healed scar on the knuckle of his thumb. This morning, this very hand had traced the letters of her name on the inside of her thighs.

The memory drugged Lizzie, making her hot and hollow, urging her to curl into Jack, to beg him to touch her again, there and everywhere, to cover her with kisses.

His thumb rubbed slowly along hers, silently seductive. When she looked up she could see the quiet certainty in his face, the barely contained desire.

When it came to longing, it seemed they were on the same page.

He slipped his arms around her shoulders, surrounding her with his strength, and the heat of his desire. Gently, he nuzzled her chin. 'We can't waste this one last night, Lizzie.'

With his arms around her and his lips roaming her throat, anything he said sounded perfectly reasonable.

The tide of longing rolled over her and she thought she might drown if she refused him. How could she spend this last night alone? What harm could there be in one more night with Jack?

One last, heavenly night, before her life went back to normal.

CHAPTER NINE

MIDNIGHT, and the moon shone so brightly it seemed to come right into bed with them. They were in Jack's bed, a symphony in grey, black and silver, and Lizzie lay on her side, so she could see him in the moonlight, amazed that she felt utterly at peace with herself and with the world.

Jack was a perfect lover and the loveliest man, and she didn't want to analyse this moment, or to try to justify in her head exactly why she was lying here with him. She just wanted to drink in the memory, to save it for the future…this feeling of perfect happiness and safety, of being in the right place, with the right man…at the right time…

Except…in the silver moonlight Jack's eyes were too shiny.

'Are you OK?' she whispered.

'Yes, of course.'

'You look sad.'

'Not sad, just thinking.'

'What about?'

He made a small sound of impatience, rolled onto his side, facing her, and lifted her fingers to his lips. He kissed them gently one by one. 'It's nothing,' he said. 'A bad memory. It's gone.'

Lizzie leaned closer, rubbed her lips over his jaw, loving the scratchiness of his beard 'I hope you're feeling OK, because I'm feeling very OK. I might even be feeling a little bit smug.'

Jack smiled, and she was relieved to see that he looked more like his old self. 'So, I'm fine, and you're fine. How about Madeline?'

She laughed. 'Madeline's fine, too.' She settled her hand over the bump of her baby, which seemed to be growing incredibly fast. Almost immediately, to her utter astonishment, she felt a tiny flutter—a bumping motion under her hand.

'Jack!'

'What is it?'

Instantly he was up on one elbow, leaning over her, blocking the moonlight, so she couldn't see his face, but she thought she heard fear in his voice.

'It's OK. It's just the baby. I can feel her moving. She's kicking.'

'Yeah?' There was a shake in his voice, as if he was excited now. Or scared.

The little flutters inside her went on, making her think of the times she'd caught a moth in her hand and had felt its wings flapping against her palm.

'Here, you feel it.' Grabbing his hand, she pressed it against her. 'Can you feel that?'

'No,' he said. 'I can only feel you.' He let his hand slide over her skin. 'And you feel as silky and sexy as—'

He stopped, and then suddenly, ever so softly, 'Oh-h-h…'

'Can you feel it now?'

'Yes, I can…wow.'

'Isn't it the most amazing sensation?'

'She's certainly a cute little kicker. Better sign her up for the Moulin Rouge. Has she done this before?'

'I've never felt her before.'

'She's punching *and* kicking now,' Jack said.

'Is she? Let me have another feel.' Lizzie pushed her hand under Jack's and gasped when she felt two sets of tiny, bumping movements. 'She can't decide whether she wants to be a boxer or a soccer player,' she said.

'I wonder who she'll play for. Italy or Australia?'

Lizzie grinned happily into the moon-streaked darkness.

'I guess it depends on where you decide to live,' he said.

'Yes,' she agreed, aware that a sober note had crept into his voice.

After a bit, the baby quietened and Lizzie yawned and snuggled against him, not wanting to worry about the future.

It was lovely to lie here with Jack, just the two of them in the silent homestead, surrounded by the quiet outback night. Then she spoiled the peace by picturing Jack in the future, long after she was gone from here, sleeping in this house, in this bed perhaps, with his young, country bride.

'Oh, God, I wish—'

She cut off the words, horrified that she'd almost spoken her thoughts aloud.

'What?' Jack said. 'What do you wish?'

That I was ten years younger.

Lizzie shook her head, pressed her lips together to make sure the words couldn't escape.

'Come on, Lizzie. You tell me your wish, and I'll tell you mine.'

So he wished for something, too.

Lizzie remembered the shiny glitter in his eyes. Had they been tears?

This conversation was getting risky.

Sexual attraction was one thing. Sharing intimate wishes and dreams was another matter entirely. When physical intimacy included emotional intimacy, a casual affair became...

What?

What was the next step? Love?

Lizzie sat up abruptly, clutching the sheet over her breasts. 'The men might get back early. I should go back to my room now.'

'Don't. There's no need to go yet. They won't break camp until daybreak, and it'll take them half a day to travel back here.' Gently, Jack pulled her down beside him. 'Sleep here, Lizzie,' he said. 'No more talking. Just curl up and sleep.'

She was actually too tired to argue. Besides, sleeping was safe enough, and, when she considered the inviting curve of Jack's shoulder, Lizzie knew there was no nicer place to sleep.

Jack lay awake in the darkness with Lizzie's curves nestled against him. He could smell her hair, feel the gentle rise and fall of her breathing, and he wished this night might never end. When Lizzie was in his bed she was soft and womanly, and vulnerable and sweet. She was wild. She was his, and his alone.

In the morning she would retreat. Before the mustering team returned, she would tie her lovely hair into a tight knot and pull on her armour, like a crab shrinking back into its shell.

If he'd had his way, and if Lizzie had been any other woman, he would have spoken up tonight. He would have told her how he felt, how very much he wanted her, that he was pretty damn sure that he was falling in love with her. Then he would have told her. No, he would have *insisted* that there was no need to hide their feelings from outsiders.

Why should they give a damn what anyone else said or thought?

All very well for him, of course. He wasn't a federal senator. He'd never faced the press crying scandal because word of a liaison had leaked out. The only newspaper he'd been featured in was the Gidgee Springs freebie. Lizzie had come here in the first place to escape the press, so she had every right to call the tune.

No point in trying to change her mind…it would only ruin a perfect night.

Lizzie woke to the sound of a teacup rattling against a saucer. She opened her eyes to see Jack setting a cuppa on the table beside her.

'Good morning,' he said with a smile.

'Is that tea? How lovely. What time is it?'

'Half past seven.'

'Goodness, are the men here?'

'No, don't panic. I told you they won't be here for ages.'

She looked up at Jack shyly. He was already showered and dressed. 'Have you been up long?'

He shook his head.

'I slept very well.'

'I know.' Jack smiled and sat on the edge of the bed. 'I could hear you, all night long, snoring away.'

Lizzie stared at him, appalled. 'I don't snore.' Quickly she added, 'Do I?'

'Like a buzz saw.' Jack's right eyebrow hiked skywards. 'Hasn't anyone told you?'

'No.' Her voice was shrill with horror. 'It—it's been a while since I—' She bit her lip. 'Maybe it's the pregnancy.'

It was only then that she saw the mirth twinkling in his eyes.

'Hey,' she cried. 'You're pulling my leg again.'

'Only because you're so easy to tease.' He grinned as his hand fastened around her ankle through the bedclothes.

Lizzie rolled her eyes. Prim-mouthed, she reached for her cup of tea. 'Thanks for making this,' she said super-politely.

'Thank *you*, for last night,' Jack answered with soft emphasis.

'It was—' Lizzie discarded words like wonderful, and fabulous. She had to back off now. With the return of the stockmen, it was time to widen the emotional distance between them. She left the sentence dangling, and perhaps it was just as well, because suddenly her throat was choked with emotion.

Backing off and widening emotional gaps were all very well in theory, but they weren't very easy to put into practice. She liked Jack so much. Too much, and for all the right reasons.

Just sitting here, drinking a morning cuppa with him, felt like the nicest possible way to start the day.

I'm going to have to give him up, cold turkey, she thought, unhappily—*before I become hopelessly addicted*.

Jack broke into her thoughts. 'I should warn you—there'll be a slap-up dinner tonight for everyone. It's a tradition on Savannah. At the end of every big muster, we always put on a big dinner at the homestead for the whole team.'

'That's nice. Would it be best if I ate in my room?'

He looked surprised. 'No way. You're part of the household. You should be there. The guys will want to meet you.'

She managed a broken smile. It was the end of paradise. Setting down her teacup, she began to tidy her hair.

It was early afternoon when Jack heard the distant growl of a motor signalling that the mustering team was almost home. He went out onto the veranda, with Cobber at his heels. The dog's tail wagged and his nose twitched at the first scent of dust stirring on the horizon.

Together, man and dog watched the familiar cavalcade emerge out of the dust. First came the large mob of horses, then the truck with the gooseneck trailer carrying the stores and the kitchen. These were followed by the tray-back ute and a second trailer loaded with a trio of quad bikes.

This was the first time in years that Jack hadn't been part of the muster. For him, the big muster at the end of the wet season was one of the best things about his job. He always enjoyed being out there with the team, on the back of a sure-footed horse, dodging saplings and melon holes as he chased stragglers and cleanskins out of the thick scrub.

He loved camping out, too, yarning around the campfire at night with the men, sleeping under the stunning canopy of stars. This year, he'd fiercely resented Kate's request that he stay back at the homestead to play host to the lady senator.

It just showed that a man never knew the strange twists and turns his life might take. Now the appeal of the cattle muster was nothing compared with the hold Lizzie Green had on him.

Admittedly, Jack had never been one of those men, like many of his friends, who were totally wedded to the outback life. He knew guys who'd swear that there was no place on earth as good as this wide brown land, but those fellows had never really considered doing anything else. They'd gone away to boarding school for six years or so, and then they'd headed straight back to the bush.

More than once Jack had thought that he might have been happier, if he'd been like them. Knowing exactly where you belonged in this crazy world had to be a huge bonus. But he'd had his heart set on the Air Force and, once he'd known it was out of his reach, he'd returned to the outback as a second-best option.

Now he was setting his sights on another goal that was beyond his reach. Was he mad to feel so far gone over a high-flying woman from a different world? He knew deep down that he had little chance of a future with Lizzie, but the crazy thing was—he no longer seemed to have a choice.

She'd struck fire in his veins, and his life would never be the same again.

More than that—Jack knew now that it wasn't only his own happiness at stake. Deep in his bones, he was pretty damn sure he could make Lizzie happy, too. And her baby. Those two mightn't know it yet, but they needed him, no doubt about it.

He just had to find the best way to prove it.

'What do you want?' barked a voice in response to Lizzie's knock on the kitchen door.

'I was wondering if you'd like a hand.'

The man at the sink whirled around, and when he saw Lizzie his eyebrows rose high above his spectacles, his jaw dropped, and for a moment he seemed unable to speak.

She took a step into the kitchen and smiled. 'You must be Bill,' she said.

He nodded, shoved his glasses up his nose with a hand covered in soapsuds, and gave her a shaky smile.

'I'm Lizzie Green. I'm staying here, and Jack said you were putting on a big dinner tonight. I know he's busy, helping the men with the horses and everything. But I thought, after all the travelling and unpacking you've had to do, that you could probably use a spare pair of hands in here.'

'Well, that's mighty kind of you, miss—er—ma'am.'

'Lizzie,' she corrected, noting the remnants of his English accent.

Bill smiled shyly, showing a flash of gold in his front tooth, and he cast an anxious glance at the kitchen table, which was now almost sagging beneath the weight of unloaded camping supplies—half-used sacks of flour and sugar, bags of potatoes, tins of golden syrup, and bottles of sauce.

'So, what can I do?' Lizzie asked. 'What are you planning for dinner? I'm a dab hand at peeling potatoes.'

The cook swallowed his surprise and beamed at her, and she could tell she'd made a new friend.

The dinner was roast beef with Yorkshire pudding and roast vegetables and it was eaten in the big dining room that was hardly ever used.

Lizzie found a large white damask tablecloth and napkins in the linen press. They hadn't been ironed so she attended to that, and she found the good china and cutlery in the sideboard and had fun setting the table. She even went outside into the garden and found a few straggling daisies that made rather a nice centrepiece when combined with sprigs of purple bougainvillea.

At half past six, the men turned up on the veranda for pre-dinner drinks. They had showered and changed into clean clothes. Their riding boots were polished, and their hair was damp and carefully slicked back. They were all lean, wiry, sunburnt fellows, used to hard, physical work and unpractised in small talk.

Even so, while at first glance they seemed shy, when Jack introduced Lizzie they weren't fazed by the fact that she was a senator, and it wasn't difficult in the least to put them at their ease.

If she hadn't been pregnant, she would have had a beer with them. Instead, she accepted a glass of tonic water, and leaned back against a veranda post, asking only a few questions, happy to let the ringers talk about the weather and cattle, and the muster.

She rather liked the quiet, laconic manner of these men of the bush, and she thought how pleased she was to be gaining this insight into another aspect of Australian life.

Of course, she couldn't help noticing how disturbingly attractive Jack was by comparison. In a dark blue, long-sleeved shirt and cream chinos, he was the handsomest man in the group by a country mile. Across the veranda, she caught his eye, and for one heartbeat their gazes held, and she felt her skin grow hot.

Quickly, she looked down, hoping no one else had noticed her reaction. But she was sure she'd read approval in Jack's quiet smile, and she felt inordinately happy.

Jack would never have said as much, but he'd been uncertain about the likely success of the dinner party. The reserved outback men were bound to be a little star-struck about having a lady senator in their midst, and he wasn't sure if Lizzie would fit in.

He quickly realised that he shouldn't have worried. Lizzie put the men at ease straight away. Her clothes were right to start with—slim blue jeans and a dark red sweater with a simple V-neck that showed off the tiny gold cross— and she seemed to know exactly the right questions to ask, showing an interest in the men without being nosy.

Bill's enthusiasm for her was an unexpected bonus. The cook told everyone about Lizzie's help in the kitchen— another surprise for Jack. It seemed that, not only had she taken care of all the vegetables, but she'd helped stow away the provisions from the muster, *and* she'd got the dining room ready.

As the wine flowed so did the compliments from the men, corny or otherwise.

'Best peeled spuds I've ever tasted.'

'Better watch out, Cookie. You might lose your job.'

Fortunately, the men were sensitive enough to leave Lizzie's politics out of the conversation, so all in all the meal was relaxing and enjoyable for everyone.

It was all smooth sailing until one of the travelling contract musterers, a guy nicknamed Goat, dropped a clanger, out of the blue.

'I've seen a story about you,' he said to Lizzie. 'Saw it in a magazine down at the ringers' barracks.'

'Really?' Lizzie sounded cool enough, but Jack detected a nervous tilt to her smile. 'Which story was that?'

'Something in an old *Blokes Only*. I thought it was you and I checked it out before dinner.'

Jack stiffened, sensing trouble, then he saw the colour drain from Lizzie's face.

He forced himself to sound casual. 'Anything in that old mag is bound to be a lie.'

'Nice photo though,' Goat said, grinning stupidly. 'Would you like me to go and get it?'

'No!' Lizzie looked as if she might cry. 'I can't believe there are still copies of that around. It was years ago.'

'That's the bush for you,' chimed in Bill, clearly unaware of the undercurrents. 'People out here hang onto magazines for years, especially *Blokes Only*.'

'Anyway, it was all good,' said Goat. 'That old boyfriend of yours was full of praise. Said you were twelve on a scale of ten. In the sack, that is.'

'Goat!' Even Jack was surprised by the steely command

in his voice. Too bad. He was furious with the idiot. 'Pull your head in.'

Every head at the table turned to Jack. No one spoke.

His hands were tight fists, ready to slam the next mouth that let rip with a stupid comment. 'Show more respect to our guest,' he said coldly.

The men looked sheepish. Goat mumbled apologies.

Lizzie managed a brave smile. 'Has Jack told you that he jumped the stockyard gate?'

Jack's ears burned as attention turned to him, but he had to admire the skilful way Lizzie had deflected everyone's interest.

'What's this, Jack? You didn't take the round yard gate, did you?'

'With miles to spare,' Lizzie announced.

This was greeted by exclamations and cheers and thumping on the table.

Old Archie, the ringer who'd served the longest on Savannah, was grinning from ear to ear. 'Jeez, mate, you're a dark horse. When were you going to tell us?'

It took a while for the excitement to die down, but then Lizzie excused herself, saying she had to make an international phone call.

The men didn't talk about her again, at least, not in Jack's hearing, but he was pretty damn sure they'd be gawking at her in *Blokes Only* just as soon as they got back to their quarters. He couldn't believe how angry the thought made him.

Much later, when the men had gone and the house was in darkness, there was still a light showing under Lizzie's door.

Jack tapped lightly.

'Who is it?' she called.

'Me,' he said simply.

She came and opened the door just a chink. Her hair was loose to her shoulders and she was wearing a deep rose dressing gown, buttoned to the throat. Blocking the doorway, she stood with her arms crossed, eyes narrowed warily. 'How can I help you, Jack?'

'I just wanted to apologise for the way that fool carried on at dinner.'

'Thanks, but why should you apologise? It was hardly your fault.' She looked tired, with smudges of shadow beneath her eyes.

'I feel responsible,' Jack said. 'I knew how upset you were.'

She gave an exaggerated shrug. 'I'm OK. I'm used to it. The Iron Maiden Senator, remember?' With a glance down the darkened hallway, she said, 'Have they all gone?'

'Yes.'

She looked as if she planned to close her door. Jack said, quickly, 'Who spilled that story? It wasn't Mitch, was it?'

'No.' Lizzie closed her eyes, leaned back against the doorjamb. 'Even Mitch was above that. This time it was Toby.'

'Another boyfriend?'

She sighed wearily, slowly opened her eyes. 'Yes, the one I dated after Mitch. The successful banker I thought was serious. We'd been going together for twelve months, and we were unofficially engaged. I'd even started planning our family.'

A steel band tightened around Jack's chest. He wished he hadn't asked. He couldn't believe how much he hated hearing this, hated to think of Lizzie loving other guys, hated to see the bleak resignation in her eyes. But now she'd started, it seemed she needed to tell him the whole story.

'There'd been warnings,' she said. 'Photos of Toby in the

press with his arms around lovely models. He laughed it off. Said he'd been set up by the media and, like a fool, I believed him. Then I hardly heard from him for a month. He wasn't answering my calls. Suddenly the article in *Blokes Only* turned up. "Behind Closed doors with Senator Green".'

'How could you bear it?'

She tried to smile but her mouth wobbled. 'Not very well, especially when Toby admitted later that he'd done it partly because he knew I'd drop him. He hadn't been brave enough to tell me he wanted to break up.'

A groan broke from Jack.

'I toughed it out as usual,' she said, 'but it didn't do my career any good. I was about to chair a senate committee for family services. The story put an end to that.'

This time, her mouth turned square, and she really looked in danger of crying. She took a deep breath. 'So that's the story of Toby the toad. I'm going to bed. Goodnight, Jack.'

'Lizzie, I'm so sorry.'

He was talking to her closed door.

The next few days were particularly depressing for Lizzie. Not only because the whole business of Toby had been painful to relive, but because the recollections had made her see how very foolish she'd been to become romantically involved with Jack.

She'd sworn off men. She knew they always let her down, and yet once again she'd fallen.

But she wasn't only worried about her feelings; she was concerned about Jack too. When she remembered the genuine affection he'd shown to her, she felt a pang of guilt. She found herself thinking about her mother and father's affair.

Goodness, how could she have forgotten that salutary lesson?

Lisa Firenzi had enjoyed a holiday fling with Heath Green, a handsome, young Australian, and then she'd moved happily on without a backward glance. Not once had she stopped to consider that Heath might have been hurt by her love-him-and-leave-him attitude.

It wasn't until Lizzie had come to Australia many years later that she'd realised how deeply the affair had affected her father. He'd loved Lisa and he'd taken ages to get over losing her, and as a result he hadn't married until his late forties.

He was now very happily married to the widow of one of his best friends, and he was a very proud stepfather to her two sons…but he'd travelled through some very dark years.

Remembering again her father's pain, Lizzie left her desk and went to the doorway to look out at the long stretch of pale golden paddocks.

The more she thought about it, the more she knew she couldn't afford any more reckless moments with Jack. A casual affair rarely stayed casual, especially when the couple in question were living together, but there was no way she could expect her relationship with Jack to last beyond her stay at Savannah. It couldn't possibly work.

Jack belonged out here in the outback. How could she expect him to adapt to her lifestyle ruled by endless phone calls and meetings, interference from the media, cancelled holidays and interrupted meals? He would be much happier here, and he would make an amazingly fabulous husband for some lucky, *young* countrywoman.

He had all the right husbandly credentials. He might not be rolling in money, but he'd be a steady provider, good with children, caring and calm in an emergency. Throw in his good looks and his masterly bedding techniques and the man was a rare prize.

It couldn't be long at all before some smart girl snapped him up. And Jack would live happily ever after.

This, Lizzie told herself, was a very important reason why she must not mess up his life.

For heaven's sake, she'd chosen to have a sperm-donor baby so she could avoid awkward emotional entanglements. But from the moment she'd stepped from the plane on Savannah soil she'd been slipping under Jack's spell. The red outback dust had barely settled before the change had started.

But had she been terribly selfish?

CHAPTER TEN

Two mornings later, Jack gave up trying to stay away from Lizzie. He stuck his head through her doorway and found her sitting at her desk, concentrating as usual on her laptop screen, so he knocked.

Her eyes lit up with pleasure when she saw him, and his heart skipped like a day-old colt.

'How busy are you?' he asked.

'Why? Is something happening?'

'I thought you might like to get out of the office for a bit. We could go for a drive and I could show you the gorge.'

Her eyes widened. 'What gorge?'

'Porcupine Gorge. It's quite spectacular, and part of it runs through Savannah land.'

Frowning, she looked from him to her computer, then back to him again. The frown faded and colour rose in her cheeks. 'I must say this work on the Senate Appropriations Bill is very tedious. I'm very tempted to take a break.'

'Great,' Jack said, not giving her room for second thoughts. 'How long do you need to be ready?'

'Five minutes?'

He grinned, and Lizzie smiled back at him, her eyes

flashing with the glee of a schoolgirl released from a boring detention.

They set off, driving across the plains, and Jack was pleased that Lizzie seemed at ease and happy. She sat with the window down, not minding at all that her hair was being blown about.

He wished he felt as relaxed. He'd hated the silence between them and the subterfuge of this past week. He'd hated having to deny to every man and his dog that he was mad about Lizzie.

Pretending indifference was torture. Lizzie was in his thoughts first thing in the morning and last thing at night and most of the times in between. This whole charade was driving him insane.

And the men knew it, damn it.

Jack had sent Goat packing after one too many risqué suggestions, and he'd given the other men fleas in their ears over their nudge-nudge, wink-wink innuendoes.

But now he'd had enough of living the lie, which was why he needed to talk to Lizzie today. He'd always been a straight shooter, the kind of man who laid his cards on the table, then dealt with the consequences.

Today, however, the consequences were potentially huge. His relationship with Lizzie was at stake and he was sick with nerves.

Beside him, Lizzie had settled her hand on her belly, as if she was feeling the baby kick, and he had to ask, 'How's Madeline?'

She smiled shyly. 'She's turning into quite a gymnast. I'm amazed how active she is. I hate to think what she'll be like in a few months' time.'

He pictured Lizzie in the months ahead, wonderfully

ripe with pregnancy. She would be lovelier than ever, a beautiful, Madonna-like mother-to-be.

'I suppose all babies are active, whether they're girls or boys,' he said.

'I'm sure they must be.' Lizzie turned to him and frowned. 'Jack, you're not suggesting that Madeline might be a boy, are you?'

He grinned. 'I wouldn't dare.'

The frown lingered as she brooded over this. Eventually, she said, 'I can find out next week, if I want to.'

'What happens next week?'

'I have to go into Gidgee Springs for a check-up. There's a doctor who comes from Charters Towers once a month and he brings a portable ultrasound machine.'

'That's handy. I was wondering what you'd do about doctors.'

Lizzie patted her tummy. 'By next week, the baby should be big enough for the scan to pick up its sex, and I'll have to choose whether I want to know, or not.'

'Haven't you decided?'

She shook her head. 'I'm hopeless. One day, I'm absolutely positive I have to know straight away. The next, I don't want to know till it's born. I want to keep it as a surprise, the way it's always been for women all down the ages.'

'And for men,' Jack couldn't help adding.

Lizzie sent him a careful glance, as if she was trying to gauge his mood. 'I guess I'll make up my mind on the day of the ultrasound.'

'What day's that? I'll make sure I'm free to drive you into town.'

'Don't worry. I can just borrow a vehicle.'

'No, you won't, Lizzie. I'm not letting you drive all that way on your own.'

'Well...thank you,' she said quietly. 'My appointment's next Wednesday.'

As they continued on across the grassy plains, the sun climbed higher and the autumn mists melted, leaving the air as crisp and sparkling as champagne. Lizzie watched a pretty flock of galahs take off in front of them, filling the sky with a fluttering mass of soft grey wings and rosy pink breasts.

She thought how familiar the landscape seemed now after only a short time on Savannah. She doubted it could ever feel like home for her, but she was beginning to understand why people like Kate Burton and Jack could live here quite happily for most of their lives.

Jack parked the ute in the sparse shade of a gum tree, but Lizzie, peering through the windscreen, saw nothing but plains ahead.

'Where's the gorge?'

'We need to walk the last little bit.'

With Cobber following, tail wagging madly, they left the vehicle and strolled across red earth dotted with occasional trees and pale, biscuit-coloured clumps of grass. The ground gradually became stonier and eventually turned to rock.

And then, in front of them, the ground disappeared completely, dropping away into a deep, wide ravine.

Lizzie took a cautious step forward. 'Oh, dear.' A wave of dizziness washed over her, and she swayed precariously.

'Whoa.' Instantly, Jack pulled her back into the safety of his arms. 'Careful.'

'I'm afraid I don't have a very good head for heights.'

'Come away from the edge, then.' He drew her further back, keeping an arm about her.

'It's OK now. I want to see it, and I'm starting to feel better.' Especially now that Jack's arms were around her.

She allowed herself to sink back against the solid wall

of his chest, and she closed her eyes, savouring the wonderful sense of sanctuary he gave her.

Jack, lovely Jack.

Carefully, she opened her eyes again, and discovered that she could look down at the sheer fall of the red cliffs and the narrow ribbon of the river way down below without feeling faint. 'You're right,' she said. 'It's spectacular.'

As his strong arms encircled her he pressed a kiss to the side of her neck, and she could smell the special spiciness of his aftershave.

The warm pressure of his lips was unbearably sweet on her skin, and she very nearly made the mistake of leaning her head to one side, in an open invitation for Jack to kiss her neck and her throat.

Just in time she remembered that this shouldn't be happening.

Oh, good grief. Oh, help.

Damn. She'd promised herself she would be strong.

'Jack.'

His arms tightened around her and he murmured something dreamily incomprehensible against her neck.

'Jack, you mustn't…we shouldn't…'

'Of course we should.' His lips continued their mesmerising journey over her skin, and she loved it.

Oh, heavens, she adored it. But she'd spent a week telling herself that she mustn't let this happen. She was older than Jack and supposedly wiser. It was up to her to call a halt. She had to; she must.

'Jack, no!'

It came out too loudly, so loudly that he couldn't mistake her command. He let his hands drop and he stepped away.

Crossing her arms over her front, Lizzie felt cold shivers chase each other over her skin. She'd wanted to be in his arms, wanted his kisses…wanted his touch…wanted everything…

But to let things continue could only be selfish. She took several deep breaths as she struggled to think calmly and clearly.

Jack was standing with his legs spread, hands hanging loosely at his sides, jaw clenched, green eyes unhappy. Wary.

Lizzie tried to smile and failed. Their morning was already spoiled and it was her fault. 'I'm sorry, Jack.'

After the longest time, he said, quietly, *too* quietly, 'I've brought picnic things. Why don't you sit on this log, while I fetch them?'

She was startled by the change in him. She'd expected sparks and anger laced with charm, not this quiet, contained politeness. Sinking onto the broad, silvery log of a fallen river gum, she watched Jack go without another word back to the ute, with Cobber following.

He brought a woven cane picnic basket, a tartan rug and a blackened billycan, which he set on one end of the log, before he scouted around for dried leaves, twigs and branches for a fire.

'Can't have a picnic in the bush without boiling a billy of tea,' he said, without smiling.

'No, I guess not.' She couldn't help admiring the picture Jack made, crouched beside the fire, feeding in sticks, then lighting the match and holding it for a moment between his cupped hands, letting the flame burn steadily before carefully setting it to the dry leaves.

She was trying very hard to push aside memories of those same strong, capable hands making love to her. She concentrated very hard on the first wisps of smoke, then the red flames appearing, flickering and crackling. She caught the unique eucalyptus scent of scorched gum leaves and very soon the kindling blackened, then turned to ash, while the larger wood burned.

Jack set the billy in the middle of the fire, and she was relieved to see that he was almost back to normal. He'd always been so very good-humoured; it was disconcerting to see him upset.

Just the same, they had to talk. They couldn't go on without settling things. It was important that they both agreed their romance didn't have a future. Friendship was a much saner option.

When the tea was ready, Jack spread the rug on shaded grass with a fabulous and less scary view of the gorge. Sprawled comfortably in the dappled shade of an ironbark, they drank from tin mugs and ate biscuits.

Lizzie broke a biscuit in half. 'Is Cobber allowed one?'

Jack shrugged. 'Sure.'

She tossed it, and Cobber caught it in mid-air, downing it in one blissful, doggy gulp. She laughed, then quickly sobered. She mustn't put this off any longer.

'Jack, I'm sorry about…what happened before. I overreacted.'

He looked away, fixing his attention on a windblown tree that clung precariously to the edge of the opposite cliff. 'I guess it was bad timing.'

'I'm afraid it's not as simple as timing.'

His gaze snapped back to her. 'What do you mean?'

When he looked at her with those beautiful, challenging green eyes, Lizzie wanted to give in, to admit that resistance was beyond her.

Heavens, she had to be stronger than this. 'I'm sure you understand that we can't continue…the way we were…'

A muscle in his jaw jerked hard, and he sat up, abruptly. 'We could if we were prepared to be honest. It's crazy to try to hide how we feel.' He shot her a sharp glance. 'The men have guessed anyhow.'

'But if we're honest, what exactly can we tell them, Jack? That we've had a fling?'

'*Had* a fling?' He stared at her for long, painful seconds. 'You're talking in the past tense.'

'I know. Because—' Lizzie swallowed painfully '—I don't see how it can be anything else.'

More silence, longer and more painful than the last. Jack's unhappy eyes searched her face. 'What are you going to tell me next, Lizzie? That we both knew our relationship was going nowhere?'

Yes, this was exactly what she needed to tell Jack, but they were the very words Mitch had used all those years ago. Had Jack remembered?

Pinching the bridge of her nose, she tried to hold back the tears that threatened, tried to think sensibly. 'You know we can't have a long-term relationship, Jack.'

'I don't know that at all. Why can't we? I'd be happy to go back to Canberra with you.'

'No.'

'Why not?'

'You'd hate it. I know you would. You don't understand what my life's like. All the meetings. The pressure. Living out here is a holiday by comparison.' Despairing, Lizzie shook her head. 'Jack, we have to get this into perspective.'

She blinked, took a breath. 'We're a man and a woman, who suddenly found each other, and we were totally alone, with complete privacy, and there was…an attraction.'

'There's still an attraction.'

'Well, yes,' she admitted. At least she owed him that much honesty. 'But we both knew from the start that we couldn't have a future together.'

'We both knew?' he repeated coldly.

'Yes! For heaven's sake, Jack. You're a thirty-year-old man. You knew that I'm ten years older than you. You knew that I'm pregnant with a child that's not yours. You knew about my career and that I'm only here for a short stay.'

Jack merely smiled into the distance. 'Is that list supposed to scare me off?'

'I would have thought so, yes.'

Slowly he brought his gaze back to her, and it was so hard, so unlike the Jack she knew, she began to tremble.

'What if I told you that not one of those things bothers me, Lizzie? I don't give a fig about your age. You're you.' His eyes shimmered, turning her skin to goose bumps. 'You're a beautiful and gutsy woman. I could give you a list of qualities that's as long as your arm. Your age doesn't come into it.'

Oh, Jack. Any minute now she was going to spoil everything by bursting into tears. 'Jack—'

He silenced her with a glare. 'No matter what you say, I'm damn sure that baby of yours could benefit from having a father around. As for going back to the city to continue your work—' His shoulders lifted in a sudden shrug. 'I'm not tied to the bush.'

'But you've lived here all your life.'

'So what? This place doesn't define me.' With a wave of his hand he dismissed the gorge, the grassy plains, the bright blue sky. 'I'm here by default. My plan, when I was growing up, was to join the RAAF, as a fighter pilot.'

'A fighter pilot?' She couldn't hide her astonishment.

'It was all I ever wanted. I had no plans to stay in the outback. I worked my butt off to escape, to get away from here, and I made sure I had all the qualifications, the skills.'

Shocked, she tried to picture this alternative version of Jack. 'What happened?'

His mouth twisted in a bitter smile. 'I failed the psych test. Didn't have the vital mix of aggression and cockiness. I'd seen too much of that in my old man, and I couldn't pump my ego to the level they needed.'

This made perfect sense to Lizzie. Of course, Jack didn't have a killer instinct. Even so, she could feel the pain of his youthful disappointment, and her heart ached for him.

'But if you went to the city now, what would you do?'

'I have a few ideas. Business plans.'

Lizzie found herself entranced by this idea. 'Bill told me you've a great head for business. He said you do amazing calculations in your head, and you have a nose for the stock market.'

Jack frowned. 'When were you talking to Bill?'

'While we were working together in the kitchen.'

He shrugged. 'I've looked after my finances and I've made some successful investments. I don't want to make the same mistakes my old man made.'

She almost allowed herself to be swept away by the thought of Jack in the city, by her side, running his own business, and helping her to bring up her child. It seemed perfect. Too good to be true.

It *was* too good to be true.

Too soon the bubble burst, and Lizzie could see the real picture—the inevitable journalists swarming around them. The headlines about Jack, the photos, the questions.

Are you the reason Senator Green went into hiding? How do you feel about her sperm-donor baby? How old are you, Jack? Who do you vote for? Why aren't you the baby's father? Are you sterile?

Oh, heavens. She couldn't put him through that. It would be horrendous. He'd hate it. It couldn't work. She couldn't believe he would be happy.

And how could she take such a risk with *her* own happiness?

Twice before she'd fallen deeply in love—and she'd promised herself that she wouldn't line up for an agonising third bout of heartache. Not now, not with her baby coming.

She had to break up with Jack. Now. Cleanly and quickly. Not like the cowards, Mitch and Toby, who'd been too scared to face her. Their spinelessness had hurt her even more than losing them.

Straightening her shoulders, Lizzie turned to Jack, and her heart hurt as if it held splinters of glass. 'You know it can't work for us, Jack. I've told you why I settled on a sperm-donor baby, why I plan to live as a single mother.'

A muscle twitched in his jaw. 'Because you won't risk getting involved again.'

'Yes, that's part of my reason.' If only he didn't look so unhappy. 'But this isn't just about me. I'm trying to think about your happiness, too. You're a fabulous catch for any woman—any *young* woman, that is—and there must be oodles of girls, closer to your age, who'd snap you up in a heartbeat.'

Her brave admission was greeted by silence and she was left to stare, through a blur of tears, at the long, never-ending stretch of flat plains and the cloudless blue dome of the sky overhead. She knew the age difference was a poor excuse. Jack had a natural maturity that set him head and shoulders above men much older than him.

Hoping Jack couldn't see, she lifted her hand to dash the tears away. Then she heard his voice.

'Just think about one thing, Lizzie. Ask yourself if you were making love.' He spoke quietly and coldly, so unlike himself. 'Or were you just having meaningless sex?'

Without waiting for her response, he stood and began to stamp out the embers of their fire.

As they drove back to the homestead their chilled silence filled the ute's cabin. Lizzie wished she could think of something helpful to say. She wondered if she should offer to leave Savannah immediately, and she was shocked by how wretched that possibility made her feel.

When at last they drove through Savannah's gates she turned to Jack. 'Thanks for showing me the gorge.'

'My pleasure,' he said in his driest tone.

'About next week, Jack, when I go to the doctor, I'd be happy to drive into—'

Her words were cut off as he slammed on the brakes.

'You're not going to drive into Gidgee Springs. I won't allow it.'

'But it's a sealed road.'

'Lizzie, for crying out loud.' His hand thumped the steering wheel. 'It's over a hundred kilometres of bush, and there are no shops, no garages. No nice policeman to come to your rescue if you have a flat tyre. You'll be stranded.'

She knew that his anger was fuelled as much by their break-up as his concern for her driving safety. It was scary to know she'd pushed easy-going, sanguine Jack to the limits of his self-control.

'I'll take you in,' he said stiffly.

'Thank you,' she said, suitably chastened. 'That's very kind.'

Outwardly as calm as the quiet, copper-tinted afternoon, Jack stood at the horse-paddock fence, elbows on the weathered timber rail, while he inwardly wrestled with Lizzie's low blow.

He'd been through the gamut of emotions today. First he'd been angry at the way he'd stuffed up, rushing everything—the kiss, the conversation, the whole catastrophe. Hell, Lizzie had gone to the gorge expecting a pleasant diversion from her work. Instead, he'd put the hard word on her.

He hadn't told her nearly enough of the things he'd meant to say, about how important she was to him, how she made him feel, how special she was, the hundred reasons he was mad about her.

He'd returned, sunk in disappointment and despair. But now, at last, he was beginning to feel calmer, and he knew he wasn't going to throw in the towel. Not yet. There was no point in simply giving up, the way he had when he was a kid after he'd lost his career dreams.

No doubt Lizzie was expecting him to take her rejection sweetly on the chin and walk away without a fight. Laid-back Jack, easy to like, easy to let go.

Not so, sweetheart.

The woman had no idea how much he wanted her. Or why.

Truth to tell, Jack had asked himself that question many times this afternoon, running again through the list of negatives Lizzie had rattled off.

Why her? Why a politician? Why a forty-year-old? Why a woman who was pregnant with another man's child?

The more he thought about it, the more he was certain of his answers. To start with, he knew for sure that the overwhelming feelings he had for Lizzie weren't merely about her superb good looks. Lizzie was different, unique. Special. If she were eighteen or fifty, she would still be the woman he wanted.

Little things made him wild about her. The way she could turn to look at him and smile, tilting the left-hand side of her mouth more than the right. And then there was the gliding way she walked, and the way she carried herself like a proud princess, with her head high, shoulders back.

Lizzie had presence. She was smart. He totally understood why her political party had grabbed her. She was one classy woman.

But the biggest thing, damn it, the overwhelming reason Jack couldn't let Lizzie go was the dazzling chemistry between them. He'd sooner lose an arm than let *that* die.

Not that he had a clue how to win her back.

Only one thing was certain. It wasn't going to happen until she realised that she needed him. She did need him. Jack was sure of that—and Lizzie was too clever to overlook the truth—but it meant he had no choice but to be patient.

Sadly, patience was not his strongest virtue.

Over the next few days, Lizzie found Jack to be polite and friendly and distant, a perfect gentleman who treated her like a visiting lady senator. He respected her privacy, he ensured she had every creature comfort, and, in response to her questions, he courteously provided any amount of general information about the running of a cattle property.

She hated every minute of it.

She wanted the old Jack, the cheeky, cheerful Jack. Most of all, she wanted to see that intriguing, devilish sparkle in his eyes.

It was very alarming to discover that she was utterly two-faced. She'd told Jack flatly that their affair was over, and then, immediately, she was dying for it to resume. Her integrity seemed to have deserted her.

The worst of it was that, instead of feeling calm and relieved, she was more distracted than ever, unable to concentrate on her work, or her reading. Most nights, she reached for her book about single mothers and their babies, in the hope that it might clear her mind of Jack.

By the light of her reading lamp, she looked again at the photographs of women who'd become single mothers by choice. Giving birth, bathing babies, breastfeeding, cheering their babies on as they learned to crawl, or to place one block precariously on top of another.

Each charming photo was glowing evidence that a mother and her baby could be perfectly happy and a complete unit. Alone. Just the two of them, the way she'd planned when she'd first embarked on her pregnancy project.

The photos were supposed to help, but each night when Lizzie turned out the light and tried to sleep the only picture in her head was Jack.

She was beginning to think she had no choice but to leave Savannah sooner than planned—thank Kate kindly, but admit that the experiment hadn't worked—then return south, to face the music.

Alone.

On the morning of the doctor's appointment, Lizzie woke up feeling quite butterflies-in-her-stomach nervous.

Jack was taking her to town in Savannah's best vehicle, an air-conditioned four-wheel drive, and he had it waiting at the bottom of the front steps, promptly as she'd requested, just before nine o'clock.

When she came down the steps he strode around the front of the car, opened the passenger door, and greeted her with a frown. 'First time I've seen you in a dress.'

'I thought I'd better make an effort seeing as I'm going to town.'

'Gidgee Springs is not exactly Queen Street.'

'I'm not overdressed, am I?'

The look in Jack's eyes brought a lump to her throat. 'You're perfect.'

They drove out along the track that wound across the paddocks, stopping to open and close gates—Lizzie was now an expert—then onto a long, flat blue ribbon of bitumen.

'By the way, I've decided I want to find out,' she said.

His eyebrows rose. 'Whether Madeline's a boy or a girl?'

'Yes. After all, I'm having a very twenty-first-century pregnancy, and it makes sense to take advantage of all available information.'

He nodded. 'It's a red-letter day, then.'

'Yes, I'm pretty excited.' *And nervous.* She wouldn't tell him that. 'What will you do while I'm at the doctor's?'

'Oh—' He shrugged elaborately. 'I'll be busy. There's always plenty of business to see to when I'm in town.' He shot her a sharp glance. 'Unless you'd like someone there. For support.'

Her heart did a weird little jig at the thought of Jack sharing such a momentous experience, but she couldn't use him like that. For days she'd been feeling ashamed that she'd been the one to initiate their lovemaking. Jack was right to have asked about her motives. Looking back, it seemed terribly selfish. She couldn't lean on him any more.

'Thanks,' she said. 'That's a very kind offer, but I'll be all right.'

The visiting doctor from Charters Towers smiled at Lizzie. 'Now, if you'll just hop up onto this table, we'll check your baby's progress with the ultrasound.'

So this was it. The moment of truth. As Lizzie tried to make herself comfortable on the hard narrow bench she felt flutters of panic, and she wished that Jack were there beside her.

He'd been doggedly cheerful and perfunctory when he'd dropped her off at the doctor's surgery, saying that he'd be back in half an hour. While she was here, having her scan, he would be dashing around Gidgee Springs on business—calling at the saddler's, at the hardware store, at the bank, and the stock and station agency.

Once Lizzie was finished with the doctor, she was to join Jack at the Currawong café to try their famous hamburgers before they headed back to Savannah.

Their plan had all sounded exceedingly straightforward and sensible. Until now.

Now, on the very brink of discovering her baby's sex, the moment felt suddenly too big to experience on her own. Which was pretty silly considering there'd been no one besides the doctor when she'd been artificially inseminated, or when she'd been told she was pregnant.

She tried to cheer herself up by imagining Jack's reaction when she told him about the baby at lunchtime.

'All set?' the doctor enquired.

Lizzie nodded, and concentrated on slow, calming breaths as he applied cold gel to her abdomen. She'd never liked medical procedures, and she could never make sense of the black and white shapes on the ultrasound screen, so she closed her eyes, letting the doctor do his job, while she tried to relax.

Think yoga. You're drifting on a cloud…

She felt the probe sliding over her skin, and she remembered the dream she'd had about her baby—a perfect tiny girl curled inside her. The dream had been so very reassuring. All was well. She clung to the memory now.

The probe moved on, stopping every so often while the machine made clicks and beeping sounds.

'Well, well,' said the doctor suddenly.

Lizzie's eyes flashed open. She saw the surprise in the doctor's eyes and her relaxation evaporated. 'What is it? Is something wrong?'

CHAPTER ELEVEN

JACK chose a booth near the window in the Currawong café, so that he had a clear view across the street to the doctor's surgery. He couldn't believe how nervous he was, how much he cared about Lizzie and this baby of hers.

When the surgery door opened and Lizzie appeared, his heart gave a painful thud.

She looked beautiful, dressed for town in a sleeveless, aqua-blue dress, bare-legged and wearing sandals of woven brown and gold leather. His eyes feasted on her as she crossed the street, hips swaying seductively. She'd left her hair down for once, and it flowed about her shoulders as she moved, shining in the sunlight, dark as a raven's wing.

She reached the footpath and looked towards the café, and that was when Jack saw that her face was too pale and her eyes were glazed with shock.

Instantly, he was on his feet, his chair scraping the tiles, his heart knocking against the wall of his chest.

The doctor had given her bad news. There could be no other explanation. A rock the size of a tennis ball lodged in his throat. His fists curled tightly as he steeled himself to be strong. For Lizzie's sake.

He loved her.

As he watched her come through the café doorway he could no longer avoid the truth. If Lizzie had bad news, it was his bad news. He would do anything for her, would go anywhere in the world, work at whatever he could find, take on whatever role she wanted.

To his eternal shame, he also felt a glimmer of hope. Surely now she must know that she needed him.

Lizzie's mind was still reeling as she entered the café. She saw Jack standing at the table by the window, saw him wave and smile, and he looked so handsome and familiar and dear she could have kissed him.

She might have kissed him if the group of countrywomen at a nearby table hadn't all stopped talking and turned to stare at her. Lizzie gave them a nod and a scant smile, and she could feel their eyes following her as she made her way to Jack.

'You look as if you need to sit down,' he said, solicitously pulling out a chair for her.

'Thank you.'

Her shoulder brushed his arm as she sat, and she caught a comforting whiff of his familiar scent and his laundered shirt. He resumed his seat and looked at her with a complicated expression of tenderness and concern.

Tears threatened. Lizzie took a deep breath and willed them away.

Jack had ordered a pot of tea but it sat, untouched, between them along with the requisite cups and saucers, small milk jug, sugar bowl and tea strainer.

'How did it go?' he asked. 'Are you OK?'

Was she? She felt strangely numb. It was the shock, she supposed. 'It didn't go quite as I expected.'

Jack swallowed. 'Is there something wrong?' He repeated his first question. 'Are you OK?'

'Yes. I'm fine. Fit as a healthy horse.'

Lizzie sent a hasty glance over her shoulder and caught several women at the other table watching her from behind their teacups.

Leaning across the table to Jack, she lowered her voice. 'But I'm afraid there's not going to be any Madeline.'

'What's happened?' he whispered, and he looked understandably worried. 'You're still pregnant, aren't you?'

'Oh, yes. I'm most definitely pregnant.' It was hard to talk about this in whispers.

After a puzzled moment, Jack said, 'Does that mean you're having a boy?'

Lizzie nodded. 'But not just one boy.'

For a moment he simply stared at her, and then his brow cleared and his face broke into an incredulous grin. 'Twins?'

A nervous laugh escaped her. 'Twin boys. Can you believe it?'

The café fell silent. Too silent, Lizzie realised. Had she raised her voice?

'That's fabulous, Lizzie.' Reaching across the table, Jack gripped her hand. 'But I think we should find somewhere else to have this conversation, don't you?'

'Yes, please.'

'I've ordered our hamburgers. I'll tell them we want to take them away and we can find somewhere for a picnic.'

'Good idea.'

Avoiding the curious glances of the other customers, Lizzie went to the counter with Jack, where he paid for their tea and burgers and bought two bottles of lemon mineral water. Then they left quickly, escaping into the dusty, almost empty main street of Gidgee Springs.

Outside, Jack turned to her, grinning madly, clearly excited. 'Twin boys. Wow! That's amazing. Congratulations.' He gave her a one-armed hug. 'Aren't you pleased?'

'I don't know.' It was all Lizzie could honestly say. She still couldn't quite believe she was having twin boys. Two big, bouncing boys, the doctor had said. She knew she should be pleased. In time she was sure she'd be pleased, but she'd had her heart set on one manageable little girl.

Balancing her career with one baby, whether it was a boy or a girl, had always seemed doable. But twins? Twin boys? Even with a nanny, how on earth would she cope with raising two boys on her own?

'Here's our car,' Jack was saying, and Lizzie dragged her mind back to the present. 'I suggest we drive to Emu Crossing.'

'Is it far?'

'Five kilometres. There's a nice spot on the creek bank for a picnic.' Jack smiled. 'You can get over your shock without half the town watching.'

'I'd appreciate that. Thank you.'

As they drove out of town Lizzie watched the passing scenery in a kind of daze. Dimly, she was aware that everything about her seemed normal—vivid blue skies, ochre-red earth, white-trunked gum trees and grass the colour of pale champagne—but her head was buzzing with the idea of twins. Twin boys.

Double the trouble.

What on earth did she know about boys?

She had friends with sons, of course. From what she'd observed, little boys played endless soccer and cricket, and one or two of them had kept frogs in their pockets. Others had spent hours in the backyard—*heavens, my apartment doesn't even have a backyard*—playing with their dogs until they were covered in mud and came inside smelling like puppies.

Their mothers adored them, of course, so Lizzie was sure she would adore her boys, too.

Just the same, the idea of having two of them was overwhelming. Two rowdy and messy boys instead of one tidy and quiet girl. Perhaps it was some kind of cosmic joke?

Out of the blue, a new question arrived. Would the boys look like their father?

For the first time, she wished she knew more about donor number 372. What would it be like for boys to grow up without knowing him?

Then she remembered, with a bigger shock, that history was repeating itself. Her family would have another set of twin boys to follow on from Alessandro and Angelo. Another generation.

It was a sobering thought on all kinds of levels, and now, thinking again about the whole sorry business between her mother and Luca, Lizzie made an instant decision. She wouldn't let her little boys down. Whether she stayed in politics or found another job, she would do everything in her power to give her sons the very best start in life.

Encouraged by this resolution, she sent Jack a smile. 'I think I'm slowly starting to adjust to the news.'

'Good for you.'

'I just have to wrap my head around the idea that I'll be bringing up two boys.'

'It'll be interesting.'

Jack slowed down, then turned off the main road, disrupting a flock of grazing budgerigars that took off in a wild fluttering of bright green and yellow.

Ahead of them now lay a perfect picnic spot—a grassy bank overlooking a creek lined with majestic paperbarks that leant out over the wide, still water, as if they were admiring their reflections. Close to sandy shallows a lone white heron waded silently, patiently.

Jack threw down the tartan rug, and when Lizzie was comfortable he handed her a hamburger. 'Better tuck into these before they get soggy.'

Fortunately, the burgers weren't the least bit soggy. Lizzie licked her lips. 'This is so good. I hadn't realised I was hungry.'

'You're eating for three,' Jack said, smiling, and then he raised his drink bottle. 'Anyway, here's to your news.'

'It is good news, isn't it?'

'Of course it is. The best.' Slowly his grin faded and his expression grew serious. 'Do you think two boys will bring the father into the equation?'

Lizzie felt her cheeks grow hot. 'How do you mean?'

Jack shrugged. 'I know it's a long way off, but I was thinking that your boys will eventually want to know who their father is.'

'Oh.' Her stomach churned uncomfortably. 'I suppose it's more than likely that they'll want to make contact with him when they're older. They can do that now, when they're eighteen.'

'So your six-feet-three engineer could be a busy man.'

'Why?'

'He could have fifty or more kids trying to track him down.'

Lizzie winced. 'I—I suppose that's possible.' She hadn't allowed herself to think too much about the other babies her donor might have fathered.

'Eighteen years is a long time, Lizzie. Your sons will be adults by then, and in the meantime they won't have a male role model.'

'I'm aware of that,' she said tightly. 'But I grew up without a father, and I wasn't harmed.'

'But as soon as you were old enough, you came to Australia to be with your dad. And I imagine he welcomed you with open arms.'

Too true. Would her boys be so lucky? A sudden, painful ache burned in Lizzie's throat. Her eyes stung, and her appetite was ruined.

She dropped the last of her hamburger back into the paper bag, and leaned forward, hugging her knees, remembering her tempestuous teens, and her growing need to come to Australia to get to know her father. She could still remember exactly how she'd felt when she'd hurried from the plane at Sydney airport.

She would never forget that spine-tingling moment when she'd seen her dad, and the way his eyes had glittered with tears, and how he'd hugged her, so tightly she couldn't breathe.

He'd taken her to his flat near Sydney Harbour and they'd sat on the balcony overlooking the water, arms linked, talking and talking for hours and hours and hours.

The next day he'd taken her sailing, teaching her the ropes with gentle patience, and she'd felt as if she'd truly come home.

The memories brought goose bumps out on her arms, which only grew worse when she projected forward, and imagined her boys in their teens. Teenage boys were always a worry. More often than not they were angry about something, no matter how carefully they were raised. How would her boys feel about the unusual circumstances of their birth?

Had she made a terrible mistake, trying to do this alone? For so long she'd put her career first, but then she'd wanted a baby so much, and she'd planned to be both mother and father, but it wasn't possible, was it?

She stole a glance at Jack. He was, of course, perfect father material—warm and loving and full of fun, manly and athletic, tough without being rough. Her little boys would adore him.

She would adore him.

A hot tear fell onto her hand. Aghast, she tried to dash it away without Jack noticing.

Jack noticed.

He saw the way Lizzie's hands tightened around her knees, and he watched her chin tremble. Then, oh, God, a silver tear slid down her cheek.

It was too much. He couldn't stay away a second longer.

'Hey.' Leaning forward, he drew her gently into his arms. 'Hey, Lizzie… Lizzie.'

He couldn't bear to see her crying, but, if she needed to cry, this was how it had to happen. On his shoulder. In his arms. She might not have worked it out yet, but this was where she belonged. He loved her, and she needed him. The certainty of that was not fading.

'I'm sorry,' she sobbed, pressing her hot face against his neck.

'It's OK.' Jack stroked her silky, fragrant hair. 'You've been under too much pressure.'

For sweet seconds, she clung to him with a kind of desperation, but then, abruptly, she lifted her head, and took several deep breaths. 'I don't want to cry. I'm not really sad.'

'Just stressed,' he suggested.

'Yes.' Offering a watery smile, she touched her fingertips to his jaw. 'Thank you.'

He captured her hand in his. 'Lizzie, you've got to let me help you.'

'You have helped me, Jack. You've been…perfect. I'm really grateful.'

'I want to go on helping you.' His heart began a fretful pounding. 'If you give me a chance, Lizzie, I won't let you down.'

'It's too much to ask of you. I'm leaving here, Jack. And I'm forty, and I'm about to get huge and give birth to two babies and—'

'And I don't care. Honestly, Lizzie, none of those things bother me. Can't you believe that?'

Lizzie shook her head, as Jack knew she would, but he could no more remain silent than fly to the moon. 'I love you, Lizzie, and I want the whole package. To be a part of your life. I mean it. I love you.'

Her hazel eyes filled with tears and Jack felt his heart drop from a great height.

'Don't say that,' she whispered. 'You mustn't.'

'But it's the truth. I've been falling in love with you from the moment you stepped down from that plane. I'm mad about you, Lizzie. There's so much I want to do for you. Your life is so hard and it's going to get harder and you're trying to do it all on your own. I know you need me. And your boys are going to need me.'

'Oh, Jack.' Her face twisted miserably as she pulled her hands from his. She scrambled to her feet. Jack followed.

'Can't you understand?' she cried. 'I can't turn to you now, simply because my life's getting difficult. I've already worried myself sick because it looks as if I've simply used you. I don't want to make it worse by asking you to help me now, because I'm expecting twin boys. I'd really feel I was exploiting you.'

'Exploiting me? Are you crazy? You're the best thing that's ever happened to me.'

With a frantic shake of her head, she looked away, down the creek. 'I've been thinking for days now that I've imposed on you for too long. I know you feel sorry for me now, but it's time I left Savannah. I want you to get your life back to normal.'

'Back to normal. Hell, Lizzie!' He gave a wild laugh. 'Back to normal would be taking you back to my bed.'

Her response was a soft, sad little cry, half groan, half sob, and she seemed to sway on her feet as she closed her eyes.

Jack stared at her lowered lashes, at her quivering mouth, so lush and sexy, even though it was distorted by her effort not to cry. Without the slightest hesitation he stepped forward, wrapped her in his arms and kissed her.

And he delivered a message Lizzie couldn't miss.

Oh, heavens. Lizzie was full of great intentions. From the first, she tried to resist Jack's kiss. She stiffened the moment his lips touched hers, but then his arms tightened around her, and she was enveloped by the smell of sunlight on his skin…and then his tongue touched hers, and she was clinging to him, and she couldn't remember how to resist. Or why it was necessary.

Her protests were swept away by whispers in her head that Jack loved her, loved her, loved her…and by blissful sensations…and soaring happiness…

Until he finally released her.

Only then did she hear the ripple of wind on the water and in the trees. She felt its coolness on her skin, and she came, panting and breathless, to her senses.

Quickly, she regathered her wits, and her armour. 'That kiss wasn't very helpful, Jack.'

His eyes glittered with a knowing green light. 'Now that's where you're wrong, Lizzie.'

'Why? What do you think you've proved?'

'That you do want me.'

Unfortunately, it was true. Lizzie only had to hear Jack say the words—*you want me*—and coils of longing tightened inside her again.

She straightened her shoulders. 'We've been through all the reasons why we can't have a future. Why are you trying to make it hard for me to leave?'

'Because you're being stubborn. You won't admit how you feel.'

She couldn't meet his gaze. If she looked into Jack's eyes again, she'd weaken. 'I have to go, Jack.'

For his sake, she had to be strong. Why couldn't he see he should be with some pretty-eyed, horse-riding country girl? 'This should have been a straightforward holiday romance, and I'm sorry if I let it get out of hand.'

For the longest time Jack didn't speak.

Then Lizzie heard the snap of a twig. Her head jerked up and she saw him toss broken sticks into the water.

The pain in his face made her want to weep.

He wouldn't look at her.

'I have to do this on my own, Jack.' Oh, God. She felt as if she'd volunteered to have surgery without anaesthetic, but she forced the tremors out of her voice. 'I have responsibilities, but they're my responsibilities. Not yours.'

The journey back to Savannah was strained and silent.

'Unless you change your mind, I'd rather you didn't talk,' Jack ordered through tight lips, and he stared straight ahead, knuckles white as he gripped the steering wheel, never once looking Lizzie's way.

The tension was awful—suffocating—and Lizzie sat in an agony of despair. Over and over, she reassured herself that she was doing the right thing. Leaving Savannah was her only option, and she had to make her departure as quick and clean as possible.

It might have been different if she was sure she could make Jack happy, but how could she? He was such an easy-going, and likeable and genuinely warm guy, and if she transplanted him into her world, if he became her life partner, dealing with the pressures of her job, her babies, and her family, he would be forced to change.

How could he be happy then?

Her only solution could be to give up politics, but should she give it up for a man, when she'd stopped trusting men years ago? Where men were concerned she'd totally lost faith in her own judgement, and now, when she'd just had a shock, was the worst possible moment to ditch the wisdom she'd garnered over so many years.

Loving Jack might feel wonderful and right, but with her track record she couldn't trust something as intangible as feelings. Her only sensible option was to stick with her original plan, which meant she had to leave.

Each day she stayed here only messed up Jack's life more, and she cared about him too much to go on hurting him.

By ten o'clock that evening, Lizzie's matching pale green leather suitcases sat, packed and ready, on the floor beside the wardrobe. Her reading material was packed into the green leather holdall, her laptop was stowed away, and she'd organised her charter flight for first thing the next morning.

She had no idea where Jack was. She hadn't seen him at dinner.

Bill told her he'd joined the ringers for a meal and to discuss a problem they had with one of the bores, so she'd eaten alone, and she'd had to leave a note for Jack, explaining her arrangements. Now she was alone again in her room, miserably searching her soul for the five thousandth time.

The problem with soul-searching was that it dug up answers she didn't want to find. Like her feelings for Jack...the way her heart lifted whenever he walked into a room...the way being with him made the simplest things special...the way his skin was warm and smooth beneath her fingers...

She tried to force the thoughts out of her head and to concentrate on the amazing fact that in a little over five months she would have two babies. Two cuddly, snugly, warm and cosy baby boys.

They would be everything Lizzie needed, the perfect, sweet companions. They had to be. Lizzie was pinning her faith on it.

No maternal pressure or anything.

Oh, gosh. Jack had said that on the day she'd arrived at Savannah, when he'd learned that she'd been named after Queen Elizabeth. Now she pressed a hand to her mouth as painful questions clamoured.

Was she asking too much of her little boys? Before the poor darlings had even been born, was she expecting them to fill the Jack-sized gaps in her life?

CHAPTER TWELVE

THE small plane was due to arrive at nine-fifteen.

Jack rose early, skipping breakfast to clear the horses and flatten the anthills on the airstrip. Then he returned to the homestead to find Lizzie's luggage at the bottom of the steps, waiting to be packed into the back of the ute.

He'd been trying to stay numb ever since he'd read her note, and he loaded the suitcases like an automaton. It was the only way he would get through this.

Lizzie had been in the kitchen saying goodbye to Bill, but now she appeared, dressed in Jack's favourite soft blue jeans and the pale green top with the ruffles down the front.

Last week, she'd joked that she wouldn't be able to wear these clothes much longer, and they'd talked about ordering maternity clothes over the Internet. Now she was leaving, and Jack was stunned that it was all happening so fast.

He'd failed. Again.

If he'd been smarter, he would have found a sure-fire way to convince Lizzie that he loved her, that she belonged with him, and he with her. Maybe he should have told her earlier, later, with flowers, on bended knee. Anyway he looked at it, he'd stuffed up.

And Lizzie had morphed back into Senator Green, organising her return to the city and the plane that would fetch her with one efficient touch of a button on her mobile phone.

Now it was too late.

In the skies above Savannah, the plane was already circling like a silver toy, glinting in the sunlight. Even Cobber knew what that meant, and the dog leapt lightly into the back of the ute.

It was time to go.

Apart from a polite hello and a nodded thank-you when Jack opened the door for Lizzie, neither of them could find anything to say on the way to the airstrip. They reached it at the same time the plane landed, amidst its usual cloud of red dust.

Lizzie was pale as she got out of the ute.

Jack had to ask. 'Should you be flying? You don't look well.'

'I'm OK. I didn't sleep much, that's all.' She looked across to the plane. 'Jack, I really do want to thank you for—for everything.'

He was dying inside, but he forced himself to speak. 'Look at me, Lizzie.'

She gave the tiniest shake of her head.

'Lizzie.'

Slowly, she turned, and he saw the sheen of her tears. Her chin trembled.

'I love you,' Jack said, and to his horror his eyes filled with tears, too. 'I love you so much. I'd do anything.'

'Jack, please.' Her tears spilled onto her cheeks. 'Don't make it worse.'

'It can't be any worse.' In despair, he said, 'You know you're going to take a long time to get over this, don't you?'

Her face crumpled, but abruptly she turned and, stumbling a little, she began to walk towards the plane.

Jack didn't follow her. He couldn't bring himself to meekly step forward, carrying her suitcases, when all he wanted to do was to throw her over his shoulder, and stop this insanity.

How could he let her go?

He thought of wild schemes to stop the plane—ripping its propeller out, tearing off its wings.

Already, Lizzie was halfway across the stretch of red dirt that took her to the plane's metal steps.

It was happening. Heaven help him, she was determined to walk out of his life, but it was like watching a loved one die, or walk the green mile. How could she do this to herself?

How would he live without her?

Ahead of him, Lizzie stopped and looked back at him as he stood there with a suitcase in each hand.

She looked at the plane, then to Jack again.

She was clearly hesitating and Jack stood his ground and his heart began to hammer. Blood pounded in his ears.

Only a few more steps.

Eyes wide in a bid to stem the tears, Lizzie stared at the little plane as if, somehow, staring could help. But all she could see was a figure, ridiculously dressed in white, stepping down from that cabin, and seeing Jack for the first time. That had been the beginning…

She looked back at Jack again. He hadn't moved.

Was he going to make her go back to fetch her own bags?

He was standing there, and she knew from the set in his shoulders and the stiff way he held himself that he was hurting. So much.

What am I doing?
Going back to face my responsibilities.
Why?
Good question.

For so long she'd put her career first. Even now, she was turning away from Jack because he wouldn't fit in with her career.

Like someone drowning, Lizzie saw her life at Savannah flash before her—saw the morning she'd worked on the truck's brakes with Jack. Saw herself driving the truck to feed the weaner calves. The over-the-top ossobucco meal. Jack jumping the stockyard gate. Tearing outside to kiss him. Making love. Talking with him long into the night about families.

Families.

Oh, help.

Jack wanted to join her and her boys to create a little family. He loved her. He wanted to love her sons, yet here she was, walking away from him, just as Angelo and Alessandro's mother had walked away from her uncle Luca. Just as her mother had walked from her father…

What-am-I-doing-what-am-I-doing-what-am-I-doing?

How could she do this? To herself? To her boys? Most of all how could she do it to Jack?

How could she pretend that Jack would be happier without her? How many times did he have to tell her that he loved her before she believed him?

As her heart began to break Lizzie turned.

She began to run.

Jack saw Lizzie running.

Tears were streaming down her cheeks, but she was smiling. Laughing.

The bags fell from his hands, tumbling to the ground, and Lizzie, smiling through her tears, ran into his arms.

'I couldn't do it,' she sobbed. 'I love you.'

'Of course you do.'

'I thought I could leave you, but I can't. I couldn't take another step. I was leaving for all the wrong reasons. I wanted you to be happy, but it's not going to work, is it? If I leave we'll both be unhappy for the rest of our lives.'

'Darling girl.'

'This is not a plea for help with the babies, Jack.' She touched her fingers to his lips. 'This is just about you, and how I feel about you.'

He kissed her fingers, her nose, her eyelids.

'We can make it work. I can leave politics.'

'Not on my account, Senator. Only if you want to.'

'I've done enough. I want to leave. I want you, Jack. I want us to be a family. I promise I'll make you happy.'

'You've already made me happy.' He would have swung her around and around, if he weren't worried about making her dizzy. Instead, he kissed her again, on the chin, on the ear, then said, 'There's only one thing that could make me any happier.'

'I'll do anything. I love you. What is it?'

'Marry me.'

A sudden voice called from behind them, 'Is everything all right, Senator Green?'

The pilot, clearly puzzled, had climbed down from the cockpit.

'Everything's fine,' Lizzie called back to him. 'Jack's asked me to marry him and I'm about to give him my answer.'

Turning her back on the plane, she looked joyously

into Jack's eyes. 'And the answer's yes. A thousand times yes. I promise we're going to have the happiest marriage of all time.'

Although the Italian summer was just around the corner, it was cool on Sorella's terrace when Lizzie took Jack outside to show him her favourite Monta Correnti view.

'Come here,' he said, noticing that she'd shivered, and putting his arms around her. 'Let me keep you warm.'

Lizzie laughed. 'Any time.'

Snuggling against him, she looked out over the sea of pale terracotta rooftops to the sloping green rows of the vineyards and the neat olive groves, and further on across the valley to the distant purple hills. 'What do you think of my home town?'

'Amazing. It's so beautiful here. I don't know how you ever left.'

'Beautiful landscapes can only go so far,' she said. 'They can't actually make you happy.'

Jack kissed her cheek. 'I won't argue with that.'

Turning in his arms, Lizzie smiled at him and held out her left hand to admire, yet again, her beautiful green sapphire engagement ring. 'These last few days have been the happiest days of my life.'

'And the busiest.'

'Yes.' She remembered all the meetings, the press conferences…especially the one with Jack at her side helping to explain about her pregnancy and her choices for the future. It was all behind them now. 'I'm so glad I've resigned. Such bliss. I still haven't got used to the freedom.'

'I don't think you'll regret it.'

'I won't, Jack. I know I won't. I promise. I just love

knowing that we're both free to make whatever plans we want for our marriage, and our own little family.'

She was rewarded by a warm hug and another kiss, on the lips this time.

When they drew apart, she said, 'What do you think of my mother's offer to hold our wedding reception in Romano's palazzo?'

'It's a very generous offer.'

'She's trying to make up for all the trouble she's caused.'

'A palazzo sounds very grand.'

'It is rather grand.'

'Would you like a reception there?'

'I have to admit it's a fairy-tale setting. On Lake Adrina.' Lizzie slipped her arms around Jack. 'Don't be alarmed, but I'm thinking it would be wonderful if we had a really big wedding and invited everyone in the family—even my long-lost cousins from New York.'

Jack grinned. 'I'll go along with anything as long as we tie the knot.'

'And I'll invite my sisters, of course.' Lizzie was pensive for a moment. 'There's been a silly problem between Scarlett and my cousin Isabella ever since they were children. Actually, Scarlett doesn't get on too well with Jackie either, for that matter. Our wedding can be the perfect excuse to bring the family back together.'

'Then there's no question,' Jack said. 'Let's invite the lot.'

'I'll ring everyone tonight to warn them to start making plans.' With a tender smile, Lizzie traced the line of his jaw. 'Have you noticed, my darling, that you've been a huge hit with every member of my family that you've met so far?'

'They've been very kind to me.'

'Kind?' Lizzie laughed. 'They're smitten. They adore you,

Jack. You've charmed them to pieces. Especially my mother. Even Isabella, and she's madly in love with her Max.'

Isabella, however, wasn't quite so charmed when Lizzie rang her later that evening to tell her the latest wedding plans.

'Romano's palazzo?' Isabella was clearly agitated. 'Why would you want a reception there?'

'Why not? It's a gorgeous setting on Lake Adrina. I thought it would be perfect.'

'Yes, it's beautiful, but—'

'But *what*, Isabella?' It was hard not to sound annoyed. 'You're as bad as Scarlett.'

There was a distinct gasp on the other end of the line. 'Have you been talking to Scarlett?'

'Of course. She's my sister, after all.'

'Well, yes.' Isabella's voice was thin and decidedly anxious. 'What did Scarlett say when you told her about the palazzo?'

'Her reaction was almost the same as yours. She wasn't happy, but when I pressed her she couldn't give me any proper reason. It didn't make sense.'

'I suppose it is silly to be worked up about a venue.' Isabella sounded distinctly calmer now.

'It is if neither of you can give me a solid reason why I shouldn't have the reception there.'

Later, in bed in the best guest room in Lisa's villa, complete with marble floors and views through arched windows to the diamond-studded sky, Lizzie confided in Jack. 'I'm beginning to think this wedding of ours will either make or break my family.'

'You worry too much. It'll work out fine.'

'How can you be sure?'

He nuzzled her neck, drawing her in. 'We're so in love it's going to rub off on the others.'

Lizzie wrapped her arms around him. 'Wouldn't it be wonderful if you were right?'

'I am.' Jack's lips met hers, the first kiss of the night. 'You wait and see.'

* * * * *

MIRACLE FOR
THE GIRL NEXT DOOR

BY
REBECCA WINTERS

Rebecca Winters, whose family of four children has now swelled to include five beautiful grandchildren, lives in Salt Lake City, Utah, in the land of the Rocky Mountains. With canyons and high alpine meadows full of wildflowers, she never runs out of places to explore. They, plus her favorite vacation spots in Europe, often end up as backgrounds for her Mills & Boon® Cherish™ novels, because writing is her passion, along with her family and church.

Rebecca loves to hear from her readers. If you wish to e-mail her, please visit her website at www.cleanromances.com.

To my one and only darling daughter,
Dominique Jessop,
who recently signed her first contract with
Mills & Boon. Her study experience abroad in
Siena, Italy, has caused her to become a lover of all
things Italian, just like her mother. With her input on
Limoncello, my novel has been enriched.

CHAPTER ONE

CLARA ROSSETTI had started to descend the steep, narrow steps between the ancient buildings of the hillside town when she heard a deep male voice behind her say, "Hey, Bella—how many men have told you you're a remarkably beautiful woman?"

His seductive delivery had been spoken in the local Italian dialect and had a slightly familiar ring. But Clara assumed he had to be talking to some other female making her way down to the Piazza Gaspare below.

Picking up her pace, she moved across the busy square to the bus stop where she would catch her bus. It would be the last one of the day. Timing was everything when she felt this tired. Once back at the farm she would eat a light dinner and go to bed. Tomorrow she'd feel better.

Footsteps were gaining on her. "Clarissima—surely you haven't forgotten!"

A quiet gasp escaped her throat followed by a burst of joy. *Tino.*

After nine years' absence her best friend from childhood was back? Valentino Casali was the only person in the world who'd ever called her Clarissima—a combination of Clara and *bellissima*. Clara had often thought it a joke since from adolescence she had been a chubby girl who'd grown into a heavy young woman. That was the curse of all the Rossettis.

She turned around to stare into the flashing dark brown eyes of Europe's most eligible playboy, but to Clara he represented her exclusive partner in all the craziness of their years growing up. When they'd both turned eighteen and he'd left Monta Correnti, his departure had left a void no one else had ever filled.

Since then he'd become Italy's poster boy, a wealthy, world-renowned adventurer and playboy whose photos appeared in the tabloids on a regular basis. He was constantly on the cover of Italy's hottest celebrity gossip magazine.

"No, I haven't forgotten," she said in a husky voice. Clara had seen him through every stage of his youth, from incorrigible rascal to outrageously handsome teen. His intelligence and daring had distinguished him from all the other guys in the region, leaving an indelible mark. To her he'd always been the picture of precious life itself. Her heart groaned in response to that undeniable reality. "How are you, Valentino?"

Her question seemed to bring him up short, as if he were expecting something else from her while he stared into her eyes. "Better now that I've caught up with my oldest friend."

Delight filled her system to hear him acknowledge it. He might belong to the world now, but those early years she could claim for herself.

After he had kissed her on both cheeks, his narrowed gaze traveled over her classic features as if trying to reconcile the changes that had taken place since she'd grown up and become the slender, five-foot-four woman who'd shed the excess weight she had carried when younger.

"Friend, you say?" she teased. "Whatever happened to the postcards and gifts from the four corners of the world you were going to send me? I don't recall your carrying out any of those periodic visits you once promised to make."

He gave an elegant shrug of his broad shoulders clothed in an expensive-looking open-necked cream sport shirt and jeans. His index finger trailed across her lips, a gesture that appeared as automatic to him as breathing, but he'd never touched her like that in their lives. A shock wave traveled through her body.

"I meant to do it all. You know that," he whispered, always the charmer. The man oozed a sensuality that would be lethal for the many women clamoring for his exclusive attention.

She flashed him a wan smile, struggling to recover from her reaction to his touch. "I *do* know. Your good intentions could pave the road to heaven." Their history went back too far for there to be misunderstandings. In truth Clara could never be angry with the Valentino she remembered—the one who'd always been kind and caring despite his devil-may-care attitude.

From an early age on, the local *ragazzi* had made their typical remarks about her and her younger sister Bianca for being fat, but Valentino had never joined the chorus. That was probably because he'd never looked at her in the man/woman way. They might have been joined at the hip, but he'd had far more important things on his mind than Clara Rossetti.

Having been born in this quiet little mountain village between Rome and Naples, he'd put Monta Correnti on the map. His fame had brought the tourists, as well as a few celebrities from various parts of the world who'd chosen to live here, but there was no question that the heartthrob Formula 1 race-car driver who made his home in Monaco was the most famous celebrity of all.

Valentino cocked his attractive head. She noted he needed a shave, yet it only added to his virility. In the last nine years, he'd become a man in every sense of the word and so gorgeous she could hardly breathe.

"Are you aware you bear a superficial resemblance to Catherine Zeta-Jones? Only younger, of course."

Clara preferred not to look like anyone else, but since film stars made up part of his world she had to assume he'd just bestowed a serious compliment on her. "No. I had no idea. Have you met her?"

He gave a slight nod. "You're much more beautiful." His white smile faded and he stared at her with increasing intensity. "What happened to your long hair?"

The hair she'd foolishly hoped would hide the rest of her?

Surprised he'd noticed, let alone changed the subject so fast, she said, "This April has been warmer than usual. Besides, I was due for a change." Her silky hair, more black than brown, had become too difficult to deal with recently so she'd had it cut in a jaw-length style that fell straight from a center part.

"I liked it long, not that I don't like it the way you're wearing it now, of course."

"Of course," she teased, wishing she felt better, stronger. "I notice you're wearing your hair shorter these days." His midnight-brown hair was now wavy rather than curly. "Remember when you let it grow out to your shoulders? Signor Cavallo thought you'd be perfect for the role of Prince Valiant in the school play."

A rumble of laughter came out of him. "Are you talking about the time you denuded me?"

"That was *your* fault. You're the one who made me cut your hair off so you wouldn't have to be in *King Arthur*. Can I help it if I made a mess of it? Those poultry shears from your father's restaurant kitchen weren't supposed to be used on humans. I thought Signor Cavallo was going to strangle you when you walked in class the next day."

His grin broadened. "With your help, I got out of the part. What would I have done without you always helping me squeeze out of trouble?"

"Aminta almost strangled me when you told her I was the

culprit. She had the most terrible crush on you. Even back then you could have your choice of every maiden in the land."

"Tonight I choose you," he said in a voice of deep velvet. "For old times' sake, come to the restaurant with me and we'll celebrate my return."

"To sneak some *bruschetta* when the chef isn't looking?" She kept up the banter. There was no one more exciting in this world than Valentino. "Those were the days, but we can't get them back."

"No, but there's something we *can* do. Tonight's your lucky night. For a change we'll walk through the front door and I'll *buy* you dinner. Everything up front and aboveboard."

His invitation sounded heavenly, but she was growing weaker by the minute. "That would be a change all right, but, much as I'd love to, I can't. Thank you anyway. It's been wonderful to see you, Valentino."

Over his shoulder she saw the bus pull to a stop. She was thankful it had come to her rescue. Seeing Valentino after all these years had brought back the past and drained her of any reserves she had left. Several people started to board the bus and she moved to get in line behind them.

He put a hand on her arm to detain her. "Wait—where are you going?" She discovered a strange tension coming from him she'd never experienced before. Something was troubling him to produce that slight grimace, but she had to admit the years had been kind to him. Despite the lines of experience in a sun-bronzed face—or perhaps because of them—he was more dashing than ever. No other man came close.

"Home. The family's waiting for me."

"But I just got into town. We have years to catch up on. Is this evening an important occasion? I know it's not your birthday."

He might have forgotten *her* for nine years, but his razor-sharp memory had an amazing capacity for trivia. Valentino would keep it up until she capitulated. He never did know when to quit, but this was one time Clara couldn't stay around while he managed to talk her into it. She was embarrassed to admit he'd always been able to get her to do what he wanted.

"Mamma has planned a special dinner for my grandmother. I promised to be on time to help."

Again he looked mystified. "Then let me drive you. It will only take me five minutes to go for my Ferrari."

That was too far away. Clara needed to sit down on that bus or she was going to faint from exhaustion. "Thanks for the offer, but my ride is here now. If you're going to be in town for a few days, maybe I'll see you whizzing around and we'll grab a bite together. What color is your car?"

"Black," he muttered.

"You once wanted a red one."

"I did buy one, fire-engine red, but discovered I was somewhat a target for the police."

"Well, you *will* insist on driving too fast. As I recall, you had the police chasing us on your scooter on a weekly basis at least! Sorry, but I have to run now. *Ciao*, Valentino."

She eased away from him and climbed on board, grateful he'd finally let her go without saying anything else. Knowing him, he'd be gone from Monta Correnti by morning to make his next car rally here in Italy or England, probably accompanied by his latest girlfriend.

Clara had seen a clip of him and the newest young French starlet Giselle Artois on the ten o'clock news last month. The journalist had asked him if it was true about the rumors they were planning to marry and settle down in a small palace along one of the fashionable *faubourgs* of Paris.

He had made a noncommittal remark with his breathtaking half-smile, but Clara had noticed the French *vedette* wore a mysterious smile on her face. They looked good together.

Maybe this was the woman who'd finally snagged Valentino. Up until now he seemed to try new adventures and change girl-friends with the seasons, but whatever had caused him to run from himself all these years, it was nothing to do with Clara.

Taking a fortifying breath, she worked her way to the back of the bus. Every seat was taken and she finally squeezed in the last row between a stout man and a nun in her habit.

Out of the window on the right she watched Valentino watching her beneath his dark, furrowed brows, his expression devoid of all animation. After the bus pulled away, his brooding image remained. His lean, six-foot body had made millions for the companies that produced posters of him doing a solo trip across the Indian Ocean in a one-man catamaran, or flying around the track in Dubai testing out his latest Formula 1 car.

From childhood he'd been a fascinating adventurer who'd had an obsession with speed and breaking records. Though the Casali family had lived on the shores of Lake Clarissa, fifty ki-lometers from Monta Correnti, he'd actually spent most of his time in town after school working on his motor scooter.

One of his friends, Luigi, had let him tinker with it in the back of his dad's garage. To hear Valentino speak, none of the existing models were fast enough. Clara had spent many hours in that garage listening to him talk about his dreams of building one that would outperform all existing models.

After he'd left for Monaco to break into the racing world, he'd taken his innovative motor-scooter design with him and it had become the prototype for future scooters. By his twenty-first birthday he'd formed Violetta Rapidita, the Italian scooter company that had catapulted him to international fi-nancial success.

Long ago Clara had thought of him as a Renaissance man, pitting himself against the clock, against nature, against anything that would give him a thrill. By listening to him she'd experienced vicarious thrills herself, but there were times when she wondered if his fast living served as camouflage for unexplained demons driving him.

Though she didn't know what they were, she suspected their roots originated from within the complicated Casali family and that they still continued to haunt him. It was interesting that his elder brother Cristiano didn't come home to Monta Correnti very often either.

Only their sister Isabella had been the constant, spending most of her time at Rosa's helping her father run the restaurant. How different was Valentino's family from the huge, hard-working Rossetti clan who always rallied around each other!

She had countless aunts, uncles, cousins and second cousins who helped run the farm, so many in fact you couldn't count them all. Though they lived hand to mouth, even her own four married siblings showed no signs of leaving the farm that had been the hub of the Rossettis' existence for generations.

Clara was no different. As hard as life had been lately, she loved Monta Correnti and couldn't imagine living anywhere else. But fate had been cruel to have allowed her to lay eyes on Valentino today.

Until he'd called out to her, she'd been holding her own, dealing with her challenges on a day-to-day basis, determined not to let them defeat her. But he was like this overpowering force field, a super-bright constellation in the heavens whose magnetic pull drew the world to him.

His appearance had managed to shatter the fragile shell of her existence. She rested her head against the back of the seat and closed her eyes, tortured by her own inner demons that seemed to have magnified a hundredfold by running into him without warning.

* * *

The second the bus rounded the corner and was out of sight, a troubled Valentino moved swiftly toward the hub of the village where his father's restaurant was located. Right next to it—in fact adjoining it by a back terrace—sat his aunt's restaurant. The courtyard in front of both opened up into the bustling center square.

Sorella, a restaurant started by Valentino's grandmother Rosa, was now owned by his aunt Lisa Firenzi who'd turned it into a chic, contemporary place serving an international cuisine. His father, Luca Casali, had fallen out with his sister and had broken away from the family business, starting his own Italian traditional family restaurant he'd named Rosa. Isabella was the day manager.

Valentino had kept in touch with her and their father through e-mails, but in the last nine years he'd only come home fleetingly. The most recent had been just last month on the occasion of his father's birthday. Much to his sister's chagrin he'd only stayed the evening.

Just remembering that fateful evening and the fireworks that had ensued caused him to shudder. He always experienced an unpleasant sensation in his gut at the thought that two warring factions of the same family would want to be anywhere near each other. Valentino abhorred confrontation and was continually mystified that two intelligent people like his father and his aunt Lisa, who'd had a jealous rivalry going for years, still maintained businesses side by side.

It was a sick kind of symbiosis. They were like organisms surviving in close approximation, not able to live with or without the other.

As he reached the courtyard he was reminded of the ugly confrontation that had gone on out here during the party. Tempers had flared. Uncaring of who might overhear them, his aunt had lost control. In her rage she'd blurted out a sensitive secret about Luca that had rocked the entire family.

Pain had gutted Valentino. Unable to deal with all the ramifications, not the least of which was his bitter disappointment in his father, he'd left Monta Correnti after having barely arrived not knowing when he'd ever be back. If it weren't for his father's declining health and Isabella's plea for help with him, Valentino wouldn't have canceled his next two races to be here now.

However, his overriding concern tonight had nothing to do with his father. After leaving the furnished villa he'd just rented at the upper end of the village, he'd been making his way down to the restaurant on foot, never dreaming he would run into Clara Rossetti within hours of arriving back in town.

Their chance meeting had saved him the trouble of looking her up at the farm. The knowledge that he could reconnect with her while he was in Monta Correnti had been the only thing he'd been looking forward to on his return.

Clara had been his saving grace, had always accepted him with his flaws and imperfections. After the party he'd needed desperately to talk to her about what he'd learned, but he'd been in such bad shape at the time he hadn't been willing to inflict himself on her.

He wasn't doing much better now, but seeing her again made him realize how much he wanted to talk to her. There was no one as insightful or as easy to be with as Clara. No one understood him the way she did, but at first glance he hadn't recognized her except for her eyes.

Those incredible irises studded with luminous, diamond-like green dust hadn't changed though everything else about her had. Gone was the overweight teenager with the pretty face who'd been his abiding friend since they'd first attended school as children. In her place stood a gorgeous woman, albeit a little too thin, no longer hidden beneath a cascading veil of glossy dark hair. Just looking at her amazing coloring and figure stopped him in his tracks.

But more startling was the fact that, beyond the drastic alteration in her physical appearance, she didn't radiate that joie de vivre he'd thought inherent in her nature.

Instead of crying out 'Tino', the name she used to call him, she'd proffered the more formal greeting of his name, treating him as she might a former acquaintance. In reality they'd been partners in crime, doing everything together, getting in and out of trouble on a regular basis.

The old fun-loving Clara, always ready for a new adventure, wouldn't have gotten on that bus.

Maybe she was telling the truth and did have to get home, but something had been missing. She'd said all the right words, yet the warm, compassionate girl he'd turned to in his youth— the one person who'd always listened to him and had never scoffed at his bold ideas—had put him off.

That had come as a shock.

He'd been arrogant enough to believe in some corner of his mind that, of all the people who'd come and gone in his life, she'd placed their friendship on a higher par—or at least on a unique plane that meant it was something special, even if he hadn't written letters or sent her pictures. It seemed she didn't want to spend time with him now.

With the Rossettis' farm of lemon, orange and olive groves located several miles south of town, the formerly vivacious Clara wouldn't have turned him down for a ride home. He'd never known a woman who didn't want to take a jaunt with him in his Ferrari. Valentino supposed his ego was hurt that she wasn't impressed, let alone that her memories of him had made no lasting mark on her psyche.

Her dark-fringed eyes might have flared with interest when she'd first seen him, but as they had talked it had felt as if she were staring through him, making him feel at a loss. That spark of life he'd always associated with her had been missing, delivering a one-two punch to the gut he hadn't expected. In truth, he had to reach back to being five years old again to remember that same sensation, leaving him feeling devastated.

He quickened his pace and hurried inside the restaurant where the staff was setting up for dinner. They called out greetings he acknowledged, but he was in too big a hurry to get engaged in conversation. Without hesitation he headed toward the kitchen where his recently engaged sister was probably doing ten tasks at once to keep things running smoothly.

After taking possession of the villa where he planned to live for the next few months, he'd come here with every intention of eating his evening meal, but, after the strange experience with Clara in the piazza, he was now put off the thought of food.

Rosa, named after his grandmother, delivered traditional, home-cooked Italian food in surroundings of frescoed walls and terracotta floors. The rustic restaurant represented his father's dream of owning his own place. He'd wanted it to be evocative of his mother's warm, family-oriented spirit.

In that regard, he hadn't failed. Aside from Clara, who'd made up the best part of the background fabric of his life, Valentino's few good memories included the experience of walking in here to encounter the distinctive aroma of the tomato sauce, Rosa's house specialty, wafting past his nostrils.

William Valentine, his English grandfather, had passed his secret sauce recipe to his sweetheart Rosa who had later passed it on to her son Luca, Valentino's father. Luca had then improved on the recipe, which was the reason for the restaurant's popularity, even if at this point in time he was heavily in debt.

Valentino had the finances to help him out. At Isabella's repeated urgings, he'd come back home for a while to do just that, but the latest revelation about his father made it damn near impossible to want to approach him.

Being back home brought all the painful memories of the past flooding to the surface, one of them still unbearable if he allowed himself to think about it too much. To make matters worse, he had to maneuver carefully because of his father's declining health and fierce pride.

For two cents he'd leave for Monaco tonight and make arrangements to race in the next Grand Prix. But he couldn't do that and disappoint Isabella again. He'd made her a promise to spend time at the restaurant. Tonight he'd talk to her about some ideas he had to promote the business. With a quick fix he could be out of here a lot sooner!

His sister saw him enter the kitchen. A glance from her expressive blue eyes told him she wanted to talk to him. She took her leave of the chef and signaled with her head that Valentino should follow her out the back door to the nearby stream that ran through the town. In recent years it had been cemented into a channel with bridges where they could lean against the railings and talk in private.

"I was hoping you'd get back in time for dinner," she began without preamble. "Are you going to take the villa? It's been empty for ages. Max hoped you might be interested in it."

Valentino nodded. "I told Max I would rent it on a month to-month basis. It's roomy and the view is great. It's an ideal solution for my temporary situation."

She looked chagrined. "I thought you said the whole summer."

He'd thought so too until his own pride had suffered a debilitating blow from Clara, the one person he would never have imagined could inflict hurt of any kind, not even unconsciously. It surprised him how much he cared. He was a fool to let it bother him, yet it was eating at him like a corrosive acid and he didn't like the feeling.

"You know me. I have an aversion to being pinned down." Isabella didn't like hearing those words, but she had played mother to him and Cristiano for so many years, she couldn't help but try to manage everything, even now.

Once he'd committed to coming home for a while, she'd insisted he stay at the vacant Casali home on Lake Clarissa now used for vacations. It was only a half-hour's drive from town. When she'd first mentioned it, he'd told her it was too far away to be convenient. In truth, he didn't know if he could ever step inside that building again. What had happened there so many years ago would haunt him to the grave.

"I'm sorry you didn't choose to stay in the apartment with Papa. He was hoping you might move in with him."

Isabella was out of her mind to say something like that. He swore his sister lived in denial. Her constant desire to make everything right between everybody and get along drove him around the bend. He was still furious with her for insisting they get to know their two older half-brothers, Alessandro and Angelo. Until little more than a month ago, no one in the family had known of their existence. Unbelievable!

Yet thanks to his trouble-making aunt, Luca's guilty secret had been exposed and now Isabella was determined to make them a part of their dysfunctional lives. No, thank you.

"I'm afraid I've been on my own too many years, Izzy. Besides, let's be honest. You're always looking in on Papa and don't need a second person being underfoot, even if I am your brother. Please don't take that the wrong way."

She kissed his cheek. "I didn't."

"I admire you for taking care of him." That part was the truth. In her own right she was a terrific person. With her long, wavy black hair and olive skin, he considered her the quintessential Italian woman. "Papa couldn't have made it this long without you." She'd been the glue holding the family together.

"Thank you," she said in a quiet voice.

"I should have said something long before now." When he saw the work she did without complaint day after day, it made him feel all the more uncomfortable that already today he'd been entertaining thoughts of bolting before morning.

Her eyes searched his. "You're in a strange mood. You burst into the kitchen like you were being pursued, and now you're being uncharacteristically reflective. What happened to you after you talked to Max about the villa?"

Like a mother with eyes in the back of her head, his sister saw more than he wanted her to see. He'd run into Clara Rossetti on the way here, but their unexpected encounter hadn't turned out as he'd anticipated, leaving him strangely unsettled.

"I've had an idea on how to expand the business. Unfortunately Papa is such a traditionalist, I don't know if he'll hear me out. I'm the last person he wants advice from."

"How can you say that?" she cried. "You're an international success in business. You could double your fortune showing others how to make it big."

"That doesn't impress a bona fide restaurateur like Papa."

"Of course it does!"

He shook his head. "Let's not play games, Izzy. *You* know why." They stared at each other. "I'm not his biological son. I'm a reminder that I was Mamma's love child from another man."

"Papa raised you as his own with me and Cristiano."

"Yes, and every time he sees me on television or hears about me on the news, he has to wonder about the stranger who was half responsible for my existence. I gave up caring a long time ago when I realized my birth father didn't want anything to do with me either."

Her soulful eyes looked up at him helplessly.

"If he had, he would have made arrangements with Mamma for visitation. Papa had to take me when he took Mamma back.

After she died, he was stuck with me. Considering he didn't want his first two sons, let's just say the bastard child comes in last on all counts."

"No, Valentino!" She threw her arms around him. "That's not true. You simply can't believe those things."

"Let's not talk about it anymore, Izzy. It's water under the bridge." He didn't want to get into the subject of their father. The shocking revelation that his first marriage had produced two sons living somewhere else on the planet had done too much damage to Valentino. He felt emotionally wiped out. Erased.

Isabella wiped her eyes. "Then tell me about your idea."

"I don't know if it will work, but I think it's worth a try. This establishment has been Papa's dream. None of us wants to see it go under." In Luca's own way he'd been a good father to Valentino. It was payback time.

"We can't let that happen."

"Agreed. What would you think if we did some advertising with various tour-group operators from Rome and Naples to bring in more people? I'll do the groundwork, of course. If it's a go, I'll contact other operators in Florence and Milan."

"That's pure genius!" she cried excitedly.

He shook his head. "Papa will probably hate it. Secondly I'd like to set up an Internet Web site for us. Anyone seeing our name on a restaurant list can contact us to make advance reservations. Once we're set up on the best search engines, we ought to see an increase in traffic."

"Those are both fabulous ideas. Once people discover us, they always come back for repeat business."

"The trick is to get them here. We just need to spread the word. When do you think would be the best time to approach Papa?"

"Mornings, after he's up and dressed for breakfast."

"I'll come tomorrow. Depending on how he's feeling, I'll broach the subject."

"I'm so glad you're here."

Wishing he could say the same, he hugged her instead. Unfortunately being back meant having to face his old ghosts. The fact that Cristiano was in Australia only reminded Valentino how far the Casali family had grown apart emotionally. Which reminded him of something else unpleasant.

"Did I tell you I happened to see Clara Rossetti in the piazza this afternoon?"

"Oh, yes? You two were inseparable growing up. Sometimes I think she was the only person you ever truly cared about after Mamma died. I used to be jealous of her."

He blinked, not only shocked by her admission, but by the fact that his attachment to Clara had been so obvious, his own sister had been affected by it. "I had no idea."

"Of course you wouldn't. I saw her at church recently. She's grown up to be a real beauty."

"I noticed." Maybe it was the weight loss that had affected her behavior and made her seem less than her herself. The way she'd brushed him off had stung.

"Bianca, too. You remember her sister."

"Very well." She was a year younger than Clara and almost as sweet. Too bad he couldn't say the same about Clara's twin brother, Silvio. The Casalis and the Rossettis had attended the same schools, but from the beginning Silvio had taken a distinct dislike to Valentino.

By high school he'd become Clara's self-appointed guardian, doing his best to keep her away from Valentino, always reminding her she was needed back at the farm. Though it had never come to an actual fight, they'd exchanged heated words on occasion when Valentino had stood up for Clara.

"Rumour has it that Clara has been seeing one of the Romaggio brothers from the valley."

So *that* was the reason she'd seemed changed. "Which one?"

"I think it's Leandro, the really good-looking one who has his own vegetable farm now. Apparently Clara is the envy of all the girls around here."

Izzy had to be kidding—Leandro was the one with more brawn than brains. Valentino had known the Romaggios in school. Clara had an intellect that could run circles around any of the guys. He wasn't her type at all!

For some reason the news made Valentino restless. "Thanks for backing me up in my ideas. Now I've got to go. I left Monaco early this morning and fatigue has caught up with me."

"That doesn't surprise me. I need to go back inside, too. The staff will be wondering where I am."

"I'll see you tomorrow." He kissed her cheek before wheeling around to make his own way through the ancient town and up the hillside to the villa.

Valentino hadn't been completely honest with Isabella. After being up since five that morning to drive to Italy, he would normally be tired and wanting his bed. But the old saying that you couldn't go home again seemed to be in operation here. Meeting up with a changed Clara had disturbed him and he found himself wide awake.

Once he reached his destination, he let himself in the villa originally built in the 1800s by a member of Prince Maximilliano Di Rossi's family for a summer getaway. Because of his love for Izzy, Max had made the villa available to Valentino, who had insisted on paying him rent. He didn't like owing anyone for favors. With no strings attached, he could move about freely in his world.

The villa was much smaller but no different in style from Valentino's home in Monaco. Both had been built around the same period of time and contained similar furnishings. The only real difference besides size was the view. It looked out on the picturesque countryside rather than the Mediterranean.

At the sound of his footsteps echoing throughout the interior, Valentino realized that without warm bodies inhabiting this domicile it was nothing more than an empty tomb. Valentino wasn't used to the peace and quiet. He didn't know if he could stand being here for even a month. Already he was climbing the walls.

He had thought about asking his latest companion, Yvette, to come and bring her friends, and knew she would be here in an instant. But he couldn't do that because then she would read more into his invitation than he meant. Like the other women he'd been with over the years, her hints about settling down weren't so subtle and the last thing Valentino could imagine doing was giving up his freedom.

His thoughts jumped to his father, who'd been married twice. Though divorced from his first wife, he would probably still be with Valentino's mother if she were alive. Valentino wasn't like him. He enjoyed taking risks, but not when it came to women.

Though he knew nothing about his birthfather, he suspected that, since he hadn't shown a fathering instinct where Valentino had been concerned, he'd probably never married either.

At a totally loose end, Valentino headed to the kitchen for a beer. He phoned Roger, his longtime friend at the track. They talked shop for half an hour, then he checked in with Claude, the manager of his bike company in Monaco. Following that, he took a hot shower and got ready for bed.

To his irritation, his scattered thoughts returned to Clara. Throughout his years growing up in Monta Correnti, she'd been the only female constant besides his sister. He couldn't help but wonder how close she was to settling down. For the hell of it, maybe he'd take the time to find out tomorrow.

CHAPTER TWO

WHILE Clara was getting dressed in jeans and a pink cotton top with three-quarter sleeves, Bianca, who was barely pregnant again, walked in the bedroom carrying her six-month-old boy. "Mamma wants to know how you're feeling this morning."

"I'm fine," Clara murmured as she slipped into her sandals. "How's my little Paolito today?" The little boy was old enough now that when she gave him kisses on his tummy, he laughed out loud. "Do you have any idea how much I love you?" She kissed his tender neck.

"He loves his *zia* more."

Together they walked down the hall of the small stone farmhouse to the kitchen where the family ate all their meals. It used to bulge at the seams, but these days it was home to Clara, her parents and grandmother on her mother's side who lived on the main floor. Because of a stroke, the ninety-one-year-old woman was in a wheelchair. Bianca and Silvio lived upstairs with their spouses and children.

The other married siblings and extended family lived in homes on the outskirts of Monta Correnti. Now when they gathered for meals three times a day, there were only twelve at their noisy table.

Her father cast her an anxious glance. "Ah, good. You're up."

Clara kissed him on top of his balding head. "I'm up and hungry." She turned to her mother, who waited on everyone. "I'll get my own breakfast. Sit down, Mamma. You work too hard."

"No, no. You must preserve your strength."

"I have plenty of strength this morning."

"That's good to hear. Now you sit and eat!"

"Yes, *Mamacita*." She took her place across from Silvio, smiling secretly at his three children aged seven, five and three who giggled to hear their *nonna* get mad at her.

Silvio's pregnant wife, Maria, darted her a friendly glance. "You look better this morning."

"I feel good enough to run the stand today." She drank the freshly squeezed orange juice waiting for her.

"Absolutely not!" Silvio barked, so overprotective of her these days she felt smothered.

"Do you think you should?" her anxious mother questioned as she put the hot omelet in front of her. Her devoted mother who did the work of a dozen people went out of her way to make certain she was well fed.

"Of course I do. Thank you, Mamma."

"Are you telling us the truth?"

"If I weren't, I would stay in bed." Clara was getting desperate and wanted to scream, but only because everyone was so good to her and worried about her continually. More than anything she hated being a burden, yet within the last three months that was what she'd become to her hard-working family.

"So you really feel up to it?" Her father stared hard at her.

"*Sì*, Papa," she answered in a controlled voice. "Some days I wake up feeling worse than others. Right now I feel good and want to do my part around here on the days when I can."

His eyes grew suspiciously bright before he nodded. "Then it's settled."

Grazie, she murmured inwardly, but Silvio set his mug of

coffee down too hard, telling everyone his opinion. He was the sibling who stifled her most with his concern. As a result, he was the most difficult member of the family to be around.

The hot liquid splashed on the table. Maria told seven-year-old Pasquale to run and get a cloth for his father. While the mess was getting cleaned up, Bianca's husband, Tomaso, walked in the back door in his overalls. He'd been out early setting up the fruit stand for Clara before doing his own work.

His gaze shot straight to Clara. "You've got a visitor." By his awestruck countenance, it told her this was no ordinary person.

"Who is it?" She struggled to keep herself calm, already anticipating the answer with far too much excitement.

"Valentino Casali. He's driving the latest Ferrari 599."

Amidst the audible gasps, Silvio jumped to his feet, letting go with a few colorful expletives their household hadn't heard in a long time.

"*Basta*!" their father admonished him.

"Clara hasn't had anything to do with him in years, Papa. He's no good and he's not welcome on our farm. I don't want him here!" Silvio muttered angrily.

Aghast at her brother's venom, Clara felt a sudden feeling of weakness attack her body, but she fought not to show any vulnerability. She'd thought of course Valentino had only come to Monta Correnti for a few days and might even have left Italy as early as this morning.

In all the years growing up, he'd never once come to the farmhouse to see her for any reason. Every time he'd given her a ride home on the scooter on his way to the lake, she'd insisted on getting off once they reached the road leading into the farm.

"I'll go outside and see what he wants." Out of necessity she'd brushed him off too abruptly at the bus stop yesterday. Since then she'd been suffering guilt...and also regret for missing out on spending more time with him. There was no one like him! Because she'd teased him about not visiting her once in the last nine years, he'd probably decided to stop and say goodbye on his way out of town.

While everyone was reeling from the shock of their hometown celebrity showing up here, she rose from the table and walked out the back door. After rounding the corner of the house she spied the black super-car parked further down the drive.

Valentino levered himself from the front seat and strolled toward her, wearing bone-colored chinos and a black, open-necked sport shirt. He looked so fantastic she could hardly swallow. His sensuous mouth curved into a half-smile. "*Buon giorno*, Clarissima! Forgive me for coming by this early?"

Her assumption had been right. He *was* on the verge of leaving.

His eyes lingered on her soft curves before scrutinizing her from her sandaled feet to the roots of her hair. It didn't surprise her. Three years ago she and Bianca had finally taken off the weight that had plagued them most of their lives.

The diet plan she'd chosen had been part of an article by a film star featured in a celebrity magazine with a photograph of her and Valentino on the front cover. A section had been dedicated to the woman who had claimed to stay thin on the prescribed regimen and swore by it. Naturally there were no pictures of fat girls inside the pages of that magazine or any others.

For some reason seeing Valentino smiling at the slender beauty who'd kept her weight off had annoyed Clara. Out of anger she had started dieting and Bianca had joined her. Once they began to see results, they became local wonders for a while, but now everyone was used to the way they looked, except for Valentino, of course.

"There's nothing to forgive. You know we're a farming family, up with the sun."

His expression sobered. "I could have called your house, but thought I might have more luck talking to you if I came in person."

She was so glad he did. No doubt he was remembering how Silvio used to run interference and decided not to take the chance of her brother answering the phone. It was a good thing. Silvio's jealousy of Valentino had been over the top then. If he should see him now...

"Your car gave Tomaso a big thrill."

"But not you?" He sounded intense again, as he had yesterday.

"Of course it does!"

"It's the only transportation I have at the moment," he murmured in a voice deeper than she remembered. The eighteen-year-old Tino had become an incredibly attractive male. "Come for a drive with me. I need to talk to you."

With that silken tone, Valentino had a way of getting under her skin, but the last thing she wanted was for him to know about what was going on in her life. To spend any time with him when he was no doubt leaving town again would be like standing too near a white-hot conflagration. No more pain...

She shook her head. "I'm afraid I don't have the time. When you drove in, you saw Tomaso opening up the stand for business. I'm running it today."

"Give me five minutes."

Clara got this suffocating feeling in her chest. "Can't we talk right here?"

His striking features darkened with lines. "What are you afraid of?"

The blood hammered in her ears. She backed away from him. "Nothing! I just can't imagine what's so important you would come all this way. It's been years."

"Nine, to be exact. That's too many between old friends. I'm here to atone for my sins." His lips smiled, but for a brief moment his dark eyes looked haunted. "Surely you wouldn't refuse me as easily as you did yesterday when I offered to drive you home—"

"The bus was there. I saw no reason to put you out, but I meant no offense," she added to appease him.

"None was taken." He cocked his head. "Since you're busy now, I'll come by later in the day when you're ready to close up the stand."

Later in the day? "Please don't—" she cried, working up to a panic. After a full day's work, she would need to rest and he'd know something was wrong.

His dark brows lifted. "Have you already made plans for this evening? With a boyfriend, perhaps?"

"Yes." She leaped at the excuse he'd just given her.

Since her weight loss she'd been besieged by different guys from the valley wanting to go out with her. She'd had a lot of dates. One of the guys, Leandro, had been fairly relentless trying to get her to go out with him. When she did, she realized she had no interest in him. But Valentino didn't know any of her dating history and she wanted to keep it that way.

"What time will he be picking you up?"

"When he gets off work," she improvised.

"So when will you close the stand?"

"I—I don't know," she stammered.

"You don't know?" he enquired smoothly. "Four o'clock? Five?"

"Why are you asking me all these questions?" she blurted before realizing she'd displayed her anger. Since Valentino had never witnessed this side of her nature, he stared at her as if she'd turned into a complete stranger. In a way she *had*. Right now her heart was thudding so hard she felt ill.

"I was hoping you'd find a few minutes in your busy schedule for me." To his credit he held onto his temper.

She averted her eyes. "I'm afraid I don't have any time today," she said in a subdued tone.

"I can hear Silvio in your voice," his voice grated. "Forgive me for coming here and disturbing you. That's the last thing I wanted to do." He turned away and headed for his car.

After he'd mentioned her brother's name, she couldn't allow him to think what he was thinking. "How long are you going to be in Monta Correnti?"

He opened the car door. "For as long as it takes."

"What do you mean?"

"My father's not well."

She swallowed hard. "I'm sorry. Is it serious?"

"I hope not." He started to get in the car.

"Wait—" she called out before she realized how anxious she sounded.

His dark head reared back. "Yes?"

"I'm going into town in the morning to do some errands. If you want, I'll meet you at the Pasticceria Bonelli in the Piazza Gaspare where I caught the bus. We could have a cup of coffee or something beforehand."

"What time?"

"Shall we say ten o'clock?"

"I'll be there. *Grazie, piccola.*"

At eight the next morning Valentino dressed in a polo shirt and jeans before leaving the villa to walk to the restaurant. He entered through the back door into the kitchen with the key Isabella had given him. His plan was to eat breakfast with his father so they could talk business.

Valentino didn't hold out much hope of getting anywhere with him. His father knew the restaurant business inside and out. You couldn't tell him how to run it. Valentino could only try to make a suggestion, but even then his parent would probably resent it.

At first he didn't think anyone was about, but as he passed by the storage area that served as a pantry of sorts he glimpsed someone through the door that stood ajar. On closer inspection he realized it was his father up on a small stepladder with a clipboard. Valentino noticed his cane resting against the leg of the ladder.

Not wanting to startle him by calling out, he moved over slowly to where his father stood, but when the older man saw him, he still jumped and almost fell off the ladder. Valentino rushed to steady him. He was thinner than the last time he'd seen him just a month ago, but he still had a full head of brown hair though it was streaked with silver.

"Why did you sneak up on me like that?"

What a great beginning! Valentino had to tamp down his temper. "I was afraid if I announced myself in the doorway, you'd turn suddenly and fall. I can see you're doing the inventory. Don't you think—?"

"Not you, too—" his father barked, interrupting him. "Go on—say it! Everyone else does. Your aunt Lisa yelled at me the other day that I'm too old and crippled to run my own restaurant. That's the only reason you came back to Monta Correnti, isn't it? Isabella probably sent you in here to stop me!"

Valentino winced. His father didn't want him here. What else was new? "I haven't seen Isabella today. Isn't she at market?"

"Who knows?"

That was a lie, of course. His father knew everything. "Actually I came early so I could help you do whatever needed doing. Inventory is the only thing I'm good at when it comes to running the restaurant."

Valentino had thought he could broach his ideas for promoting Rosa while they worked together, but that was what he got for thinking. Clearly it was too soon to offer Luca anything, let alone money. His father had way too much pride for that and would throw it all back in his face.

Coming home had been a big mistake. Valentino was the last person his father wanted anything to do with. "Why don't you take a break and have breakfast with me?"

"I can't stop now."

That was clear enough. "Is there anything I can do for you today?"

"No, no. You run along and have a good time."

With those words Valentino felt about five years old. All that was missing was a pat on the head. "Then I'll see you later."

As he reached the doorway his father said, "How long will you be in town?"

The temptation to tell him he was leaving right now and wouldn't be back got stuck in his throat. "Long enough to help you. *Ciao*, Papa."

Though Valentino had been a grown man for quite some time, Luca had the power to make him feel small and unnecessary. He left the restaurant and headed through town to the piazza to wait for Clara. He wanted to be here ahead of her, in case she came early.

During their conversation he'd purposely brought up Silvio's name, knowing she'd always defended Valentino to her brother in the past. His gambit had worked enough for her to feel guilty and agree to meet him.

After ordering a cup of coffee in the pastry shop, he took it to one of the tables outside and drank it while he watched for her. At twenty to ten, Clara got off the bus.

He took a second to study her womanly figure encased in hip-hugging denim capris. She wore a three-quarter-sleeve blouse in a yellow and orange print that buttoned down the front and tied at her waist. The knockout picture she made caused male heads to turn in her direction.

Without doing anything, she elicited wolf whistles and remarks from the drivers in the heavy morning traffic circulating around the piazza, but she appeared oblivious to the attention.

He put the mug down on the table and started toward her. "Looking for someone, *signorina*?" he asked in a quiet voice.

She heard him and turned her head in his direction. Obviously she hadn't been expecting him yet.

A tiny cry escaped her throat. "Tino—" Her green eyes played over him.

Good. In that unguarded moment she hadn't forgotten after all. His lips twitched. "Do I dare confess you look good enough to eat this morning?" His comment caused color to seep into her pale cheeks. "Come inside with me. There's a *torta setteveli* with our names on it." She could do with gaining a few more pounds.

"Oh, no, not mine," she said with the infectious laugh he remembered. It made him want to provoke that response from her as often as possible. "Those days are over."

Valentino hoped not. She'd always been so happy before, but he decided not to push it. After they walked in, the woman at the counter smiled at them. "What can I get for you?"

"A large slice of that." He pointed to the *torta*. "Put it on a plate with two forks, and we'd like two cappuccinos, *per favore*."

They always used to drink it together. When she didn't demur, he assumed she still liked it.

"*Bene, signore*."

After pulling some Euros out his wallet to pay the check, he cupped Clara's elbow and steered her toward a table for two in the corner away from the window. "We'll hide over here."

"From the paparazzi, you mean?"

"From Leandro Romaggio actually. Is he the jealous type?" She looked stunned. "How did you hear about him?"

"Restaurant gossip. You can't avoid it. Would he mind?"

Once they were seated across from each other she said, "If he knew I were here with you, he'd ask me to get your autograph. You're so famous you've become a household word in Italy."

For some reason her comment irritated him. "Does my supposed fame impress you?"

"Of course. It makes me a little sad for you, too."

His brows met. "Why do you say that?"

"Because you were always such a private person. It's quite ironic what's happened to you when I know how much you hate to be recognized everywhere you go. I honestly don't know how you've dealt with it for this long."

Her comment pleased him in ways she couldn't imagine. "Perhaps now you understand why I wanted to see you again. While the rest of the world makes the wrong assumptions about me, you alone know the real truth."

She flashed him a wistful, yet beguiling smile. "You used to complain on a regular basis that you always minded your own business, so why didn't everyone else mind theirs instead of yours!"

A chuckle came out of him. "That doesn't sound so good. I must have been pretty impossible to be around."

"Not at all. You were your own person who spoke the truth. I liked that as much as I enjoyed watching the genius at work."

"Genius—" he scoffed as the woman placed their order on the table.

"Don't be modest, Tino," she said after they were alone again. "All those drawings and experiments you did on that scooter made your fortune. A lot of the guys were jealous of you, my brother among them." She paused. "He was the reason you never stepped on our farm, wasn't he? Mamma always wondered why you stayed away."

"I didn't want him to get upset with you because of me."

"Papa told him to watch over Bianca and me. I'm afraid he took his job a little too seriously."

He took a deep breath. "That's all in the past. I'm sure Silvio does very well for himself these days."

"I'll admit he's a great help to Papa. Out of my three brothers *he* will be the one to take over the farm one day."

"Unlike me," he muttered. "I just came from being with my

father. When I offered to do the inventory with him, he told me to run along. I'm a no-account in his eyes."

"You've been away a long time. He's probably so thrilled to see you, he's terrified you'll leave again if he says something you don't like."

Her observation surprised him. "You think?"

"I know."

She said it with such authority he almost believed her. "In his eyes I'm not the dependable type, not like Silvio."

"You've already proven you can be whatever you make up your mind to be." She studied him thoughtfully. "If you're here to help your father, just give it a little time and he'll start to believe it."

Maybe she spoke the truth, but right now Valentino didn't want to talk about his father or her brother, who'd given them both grief growing up. He pushed the *torta* toward her. "The cake of the seven veils. Why don't you eat the top layer, I'll start at the bottom and we'll meet somewhere in the middle." He handed her a fork.

With a mysterious smile, she took it from him. "Maybe one bite."

While she toyed with a couple of mouthfuls, he didn't waste any time making inroads. After swallowing some of the hot liquid he said, "So that's the secret behind your weight loss."

A little chocolate remained at the corner of her pliant mouth, tempting him to taste both. The errant thought took him by surprise. Before he could blink she wiped it away with her napkin.

"The Rossettis have always been a hefty bunch. Three years ago I saw a diet plan in a magazine and decided to try it. Bianca had just gotten married and she went on it with me."

"Does she have an hourglass figure, too?"

Again he watched the blush fill her cheeks. "She looks good. Now she's pregnant again."

"Bianca has a baby?"

"Yes. Little Paolito. He's so sweet. I wish he were mine."

The throb in her voice didn't escape him. "How old is he?"

"Six months."

So much had gone on while he'd been pursuing his dreams. "So tell me what you got up to after I left Monta Correnti."

"You mean besides running the fruit stand?"

"Anything you want to divulge."

She studied him for a minute. "Do you remember Lia?"

"Of course. She was your favorite cousin who had a little white fox terrier named Horatio."

"Yes. I'm afraid he finally died of old age. Anyway, she met a man from Naples who has his own construction company. They got married five years ago and live there with their two children. Last year she begged me to come and stay with them.

"I accepted her invitation thinking I'd only be gone from the farm two weeks. Instead I got a job in his office and started business classes at college."

His dark brows lifted in surprise. "Business? What aspect of business were you thinking of going into? You told me you would never leave the farm." He'd thought he knew all of her dreams.

"The inspiration didn't come into my mind until after you left for Monaco."

"Which meant I stunted your growth."

"Don't be silly." Though she broke into gentle laughter of denial, Valentino realized he really didn't know all there was to know about her at all. That bothered him. In the past he'd taken everything about her for granted. For the first time it hit him what a shallow man he'd been. That bothered him even more.

"You've got me intrigued." Mystified was more like it.

"As you know, I spent my life in our lemon groves. One day I got this idea for doing something with lemons besides selling them."

"But not lemon furniture polish since it had already been invented, right?"

More laughter rumbled out of Clara. "Actually I came up with my own recipe for limoncello."

"Limoncello—?" In his opinion her mother was the best cook on the planet, so he probably shouldn't have been surprised. Again it showed him he'd been so consumed by his own thoughts and interests back then, he hadn't taken the time to explore hers. "Is it good?"

"My business teacher thought it was the best aperitif he'd ever tasted. He urged me to work up a model for its manufacture and distribution to present in class."

Valentino felt a sudden onset of adrenalin. "I'm jealous he got to sample it first. When am I going to taste it?"

"There's some left at Lia's, I think. I'll phone her and ask her to bring it when she comes for a relative's party tomorrow. You're welcome to try it."

"I'm going to hold you to that offer. So tell me how your project went?"

"I'm afraid I can't," she said, glancing at her watch. "I'm behind schedule now and have to go."

He stifled a protest of exasperation. Just when he was enjoying this conversation more than anything else he'd done in years, Clara was running off again. Her announcement was unacceptable to him. "Where are you going?"

"Shopping." She took one more bite of *torta*, then drank the last of her coffee.

"I'll come with you. I need to pick up a few things myself."

She laughed and shook her head. "I'm afraid this is an expedition for women only. You stay and finish the *torta*." She stood up. "It's been wonderful talking to you again, reminiscing. Thank you for the treat."

Valentino couldn't believe she was ready to leave so fast.

Why don't we meet up later and I'll drive you back to the farm?" He got to his feet.

"That's a very generous offer, but I've made other arrangements. Now I really do have to run."

To Leandro?

He walked her to the entrance, knowing better than to try to detain her. "Thank you for meeting me, Clara. It meant a lot. I'll be in touch."

She darted him a breezy smile. "That would be lovely."

His body tautened. That would be *lovely*? Clara, Clara. What's going on with you? "*Ciao, piccola.*"

"*Ciao!*"

Frustrated by her hurried departure, he watched her progress. She had an enticing little walk that fascinated him before she disappeared around the corner. Once she was out of sight he took off in the other direction for the villa.

His father had dismissed him, and the too brief interlude with Clara had knocked him off balance. He needed to get out of Monta Correnti in the Ferrari. Opening it up always cleared his head. Why not strike out for Naples?

He could look up some old sailing buddies and visit a few tour operators to drum up business for his father. Some entrepreneur he was when he *knew* better than to approach Luca before he had something concrete to present.

The change in Clara since their first meeting must have affected him more than he'd realized, or else he was losing his edge. *Diavolo!*

CHAPTER THREE

BEFORE breakfast was over Bianca had asked Clara if she wanted help at the stand, but Clara had turned her down. Her sister suffered from bad morning sickness and helped with their grandmother and took care of Paolito while their mother did the cooking and the dishes. Her sister-in-law Maria did the house-cleaning. Everyone had their chores. Clara liked running the stand.

Their farm did big business with outlets all over the region. Trucks came and went from as far as Naples and Rome. As for the fruit stand, it existed for locals and the occasional tourist wanting a small amount of the spillover fruits or olives they could take with them in a bag. The daily intake of money from the sold produce bought the family's groceries.

After dressing in jeans and a filmy light orange blouse with a ruffled neckline and three-quarter sleeves, Clara went to the kitchen. On the days she worked at the fruit stand, her mother always packed her a lunch.

Once she'd grabbed it and a bottle of water from the fridge, she headed out of the farmhouse. There were only a few wispy clouds above. The air was soft, just the right temperature so she wouldn't overheat while she waited on customers.

Clara felt brighter than usual today. She could attribute her energized condition to Valentino, who'd made yesterday morn-

...magical for her. He would hate it if she told him he'd been like Cinderella's fairy godmother, transforming her life for that hour they'd spent together. It had been liberating to be treated like a normal person.

With her thoughts so full of him, she didn't realize it was Silvio, not Tomaso, who'd done the setting up with the produce from his truck and was waiting for her at the stand.

That was why he'd left the breakfast table early. Now that they were alone, she braced herself for what she sensed was coming. The knowledge cast a shadow on the beauty of the morning.

His dark eyes squinted at her. "I heard you were at the *pasticceria* with Valentino yesterday morning. Signora Bonelli's son was in the back working and saw you."

"So?"

After a sustained pause, "You shouldn't be letting that scum hang around you."

She took a deep breath. "Don't talk that way about Valentino to me. You know nothing about him. Furthermore, you don't have the right."

His scowl grew more pronounced. "You spent your whole life being his shadow. When he went away, he never gave you another thought. Now that he's back and has seen how beautiful you are, he's decided to make you his next conquest before he leaves town again."

Clara rubbed her temples with her fingers, feeling the beginnings of a headache coming on. If she put herself in her brother's place, she could understand where he was coming from except for one reason. "We're friends, Silvio. He doesn't feel that way about me, nor I him." Valentino doesn't try to protect me.

Silvio's face looked like thunder. "A man like him is capable of using a woman whether he has feelings for her or not. It infuriates me that he has suddenly shown up and taken over like he used to do."

"What do you mean take over? We were close friends all the years we were growing up. Is it so terrible that he wants to see me and catch up while he's in town?"

"What about Leandro?"

"What about him? I wasn't interested in him after our first date."

His features grew hard. "No one wants you to find love more than I do, but we're talking about Valentino Casali, who isn't capable of it, Clara. You realize it's all over the media that he's been living with that French actress."

"I know, but while he's here to see his father, he has decided to take time to renew some old friendships. We met on the staircase near the Piazza Gaspare by accident the other day. You make this sound so sinister when it's nothing like that."

Her brother wasn't listening. "You're risking your happiness to be with him again. Are you out of your mind to let him come around you?"

"If I am, it's *my* business."

"Clara—" he cried, and put his hands on her shoulders, suddenly contrite. "I didn't mean that the way it sounded."

"I know you didn't." Silvio's heart was in the right place, but he'd forgotten she wasn't a child he could order around anymore.

"Don't you know I'd do anything for you? I love you. That's why I don't want to see Valentino take you for a ride and then dump you like he's done all the other women in his life."

She eased away from him. Valentino had never shown her anything but friendship. But the implication that her brother had only ever thought of her as someone to be exploited by him, rather than be considered a lover, carried its own cruel sting.

To her relief a car pulled up the to the covered stand, preventing further conversation. It was a former customer who got into a lively conversation with her. By the time the man drove away again, Silvio had already taken off in his truck for another part

Much as she loved her brother, she was glad he'd
ed to get back to work.

the next five hours business was fairly brisk. Clara sat
at the small wooden table with the cash box and ate lunch
while she waited for more customers. She'd brought a mystery book to read, but the conversation with Silvio had shaken
her and she realized her mind was too focused on Valentino
to get into it.

Around two-thirty she saw an old blue half-ton pickup truck
coming closer. It lumbered up to the stand. The gears ground
before it pulled to a stop. She got to her feet.

"*Buon giorno, signore!*" she called to the man in the straw
hat and sunglasses climbing out of the cab. With his burgundy
T-shirt and jeans covering his well-honed physique, she thought
he looked familiar.

"It *is* a good afternoon now that I've arrived and see you
standing there."

That voice—like running velvet over gravel. "*Tino*—"

"I guess my disguise isn't so bad."

She laughed so hard she almost cried. He threw his head
back and laughed with her. Only Valentino would come up
with something so completely outrageous. Beneath the brim,
his sensual mouth had broken into a heart-stopping smile she
couldn't help but reciprocate.

Everyone else wrapped her in cotton wool, but not Valentino.
He was such an original and so charismatic, her heart took flight
around him. Right now it was racing too fast and made her
slightly dizzy. "Until you got out, the old truck and the kind of
hat my grandfather used to wear had me completely fooled."

"Then it's possible I've eluded the usual horde of paparazzi."

Before she could countenance it, he went around to open the
truck's tailgate. The next thing she knew he'd produced about
twenty new bushel-sized baskets that he stacked near the table.

"Is this all that's left of today's produce?" He motioned to the few remaining baskets of fruits and olives.

"Yes."

Without saying anything else he loaded them in the back of his truck and shut the tailgate. Then he pulled out his wallet and put some bills in the cash box. They represented double the amount she would have received if she'd sold everything by the end of the day.

"Don't worry," he said, reading the question in her eyes. "The produce I've purchased won't go to waste."

She shook her head in amusement. "What are you up to?" The sunglasses hid a lot from view.

"What do you think? I intend to spend the rest of the day with you. Now that you've been bought out, you're free to take the time off and enjoy yourself. *Vieni com me*! I'll drive you up to the house so you can take the money inside, then we'll go." He opened the passenger door.

He'd put her in a position where she could hardly refuse. In truth she didn't want to no matter how tired she was already, no matter how loudly Silvio's warnings rang in her ears. "Will the truck make it that far?" she baited him.

His dark brows lifted. Under that hat he looked devastatingly handsome. "Shall we find out?" He helped her inside, then handed her the box after he'd climbed behind the wheel.

"Where did you get this truck?"

"From Giorgio, the sous chef at the restaurant. He has agreed to let me borrow it for a while. I've given him the use of my Ferrari whenever he wants."

"That's a trade he'll never forget, but he'll probably be terrified to drive it."

"You don't know Giorgio. Before the day is out we'll probably see him whizzing around the countryside racking up speeding tickets."

She laughed. "No doubt with the press hounds in hot pursuit."

"Exactly." He drove them up to the farmhouse, then handed her the metal box after she got out.

"I'll take this inside, then I'll be back."

"There's no hurry. I'm planning to feed you after we get to our destination."

"That sounds exciting, but I hope it's not too far. This evening I have plans I can't break." It was the truth. After a day's work she was too tired to do anything but rest. "I'll need to be home by five-thirty at the latest."

"Message received," he muttered.

She jumped down from the cab with the money box and hurried inside the farmhouse to freshen up. Luckily her mother wasn't in the kitchen at that moment. After the run-in with Silvio, she couldn't take defending her actions to anyone else, least of all her parents, who killed themselves trying to remove the stumbling blocks from her path.

While Valentino waited for Clara, his jaw hardened in frustration because she continually kept him on a short leash. Yet the minute she emerged from the farmhouse the sight of those translucent green eyes lighting up as she smiled at him broke through his borderline anger to mesmerize him.

When she climbed in the cab, he turned his head toward her. "You're meeting Leandro later?"

She averted her eyes. "I haven't seen him for a while. For your information I'm going to watch the children while the rest of the family attends my great-uncle's birthday. It's the party Lia's coming to. None of them gets a break very often. My family wants to go early so they can get home early." She flashed him an impish smile. "Both Bianca and Maria get morning sickness at night."

It was on the tip of his tongue to suggest that, since he had nothing else to do with his evening, he'd be more than happy to help her with the children. However, he thought the better of it when he remembered that, besides Paolito, the other three were Silvio's offspring. Clara's brother would probably explode in a fine fury to discover Valentino in the house. That in turn would place Clara in hot water.

"I had something else in mind for us, but under the circumstances I'll drive us to the Trattoria Alberto. They're supposed to give quick service."

"That's the place where a lot of tour buses stop. It's not too far from here. I haven't been there in years." She sounded so relieved he wondered what in blazes was going on with her.

He started up the truck and they left the farm. "How would you like to play spy?"

A chuckle escaped her throat reminding him of the old Clara. "At the trattoria?"

"Yes. One of the reasons I'm in Monta Correnti for the summer is to see what I can do to help improve business at Rosa."

"You're here for the whole summer?" The shock in her voice wasn't feigned.

"Your comment yesterday decided me."

"What comment?"

"That it will take time to get anywhere with my father." He could also see that he was going to need that much time to get back in Clara's good graces. Nine years away without checking in had done its fair share of damage.

"But what about your bike business and your racing?"

He shrugged his shoulders. "I can run it with my laptop and phone calls. Missing a few races is of little consequence right now. Papa is heavily in debt. Something needs to be done before he plunges any further. Isabella's doing her best. I need to do my part."

A hand went to her throat. "I had no idea."

"Yesterday I met with some tour operators who gave me their itineraries. They all stop at the Trattoria Alberto when they pass through Monta Correnti. I'd like to find out why they think it's a better place than Rosa. While we're eating, let's make a list of what's good and bad about the place and the food. We'll check prices and the number of menu items."

Her face lit up. "This is going to be fun."

Valentino laughed in pure delight to see her act excited. "I thought it might appeal to you."

It didn't take long before they reached the outskirts of town and pulled into the parking area at the side of the trattoria. He showed her inside and they took a seat that gave them visual access to all areas of the dining room. Without a tour-bus crowd, there were quite a few empty tables because it was still early.

Clara chose chicken and he opted for the veal, the two dishes most tourists ordered. They tested two house wines and ordered the most popular desserts. "Your father will be impressed you went to this much trouble in the name of research."

Valentino let out a caustic laugh before swallowing the last spoonful of his gelato. "To tell you the truth, his opinion of me is so low, I doubt he'll give me the time of day to present my findings, but I have to try. He raised me, after all."

She looked at him in seeming consternation. "Why do you say that? What father wouldn't be the proudest man in the world to have a son who has accomplished so much?"

"You'd be surprised." He studied her through shuttered lids. "You're very sweet, Clara."

He had half a mind to unload his secrets on her, but she seemed to have run out of steam. Her eyelids fluttered like someone who was exhausted. When he saw her glance at her watch, he knew the drill. Defeated for the moment, he laid some money on the table and ushered her outside to the truck.

On the way back to the farm she tried to keep up her end of

the conversation; but the spark she'd shown earlier had fled. After he turned onto the road leading up to the farmhouse he said, "Will you have coffee with me at Bonelli's in the morning and we'll compare notes before I head to the restaurant to see my father? I'll pick you up."

"No—I mean y-you don't need to do that," she stammered before opening the door. "I'll come on the bus, but it will have to be early, say nine o'clock. I have a dentist appointment at ten."

That was a lie. He felt it in his bones, but he couldn't prove it. "Understood. Thank you for doing this. I'm anxious for your input."

"After the delicious meal you bought me, it's my pleasure. *Domani*, Tino."

He waited until she'd entered the farmhouse. She couldn't seem to get inside fast enough. By the time he took off for Rosa, he was convinced Clara had been playing some kind of game with him from the beginning. He didn't like it. She flitted in and out of his life like a hummingbird, driving him mad.

Evidently she and Leandro weren't an item. If she were still afraid of Silvio's opinion, why risk more grief by being with Valentino at all? Her behavior raised more questions than it answered because he knew she enjoyed their time together. So did he.

All the subterfuge and time limits had to end. When he asked himself why he cared so much, the answer hit him smack in the gut. Every time you're with her, it's harder to say goodbye.

It came as a shock to discover that when we was with Clara, the thought of chucking it all in and whizzing back to Monaco held less and less appeal. This had never happened to him before.

Valentino drove in the alley at the side of the restaurant and pulled up to the back door behind the Ferrari. He got out of the

50   MIRACLE FOR THE GIRL NEXT DOOR

truck and undid the tailgate to carry the baskets of produce into
the kitchen. When he unlocked the door, Giorgio smiled at him
and came out to help him bring everything inside.

"The Ferrari is sweet," he said in a low voice, kissing his
fingers. "The paparazzi chased me everywhere."

"Better your picture than mine showing up in the newspaper. Many thanks for the use of your truck, Giorgio."

"My pleasure."

"I wasn't harassed once and would like to use it again
sometime soon."

"No problem at all. We can make a permanent trade any time
you want," he teased. "Look at the size of this!" He picked up
one of the lemons. "The olives are big, too. Where did all this
wonderful-looking fruit come from?"

"The Rossetti farm."

"Ah. I've heard of it. Did you sign a contract with them?"

Valentino had a hunch the type Giorgio was talking about
would have to be done over Silvio's dead body. "That's up to
my father. Has he been downstairs tonight?"

"No. I haven't seen him."

"What about Isabella?"

"She's out in front setting up for dinner."

"Then I won't disturb her. I'm going back to the villa. When
you see her, tell her I'll be over tomorrow."

"*Bene*, Valentino."

They traded keys before he left Rosa and rocked up the
mountainside in the Ferrari full of his plans for tomorrow. Clara
posed an intriguing challenge, but no one loved meeting one
more than Valentino.

When Clara entered the kitchen, her mother had already started
cooking breakfast. She looked over at her. "Up so soon? Do you
feel sick?"

"No." Just weak. She rubbed her palms against her hips in a nervous gesture.

"That's good. Your papa will be happy to hear it. He worries on these days."

"I know."

"Sit down and I'll serve you now."

"Not today, Mamma."

"But you have to eat!"

"I know. I'm having breakfast in town early."

"Are you getting together with Gina?"

"No." She hadn't talked to her friend in several weeks. "Valentino asked me to meet him at Bonelli's. He's trying to help expand his father's restaurant business."

"Why would he want to do that? It's been doing well, hasn't it?"

"Between us, his father is in debt." Her mother made a tsking sound in her throat. "We had dinner at a competitor's yesterday. This morning we're going to discuss what worked and what didn't. If he can find a way to increase tourist traffic, it will be good for his family...and him."

Clara had seen suffering in his eyes yesterday. She hadn't realized he'd had serious problems with his father. Evidently the breach between them went back years. The pain in his voice had haunted her all night.

A worried look crossed over her mother's expressive features. "Do you think it's a good idea to get this involved with Valentino?"

"We're old friends, Mamma."

"That may be true for him because you're the best friend any person could ever have and he knows it! But the difference is, you've *loved* him since the first time you met him at grade school."

"Yes, I loved him and I always will. You're confusing it with being *in love*."

"That's good you recognize the difference. You're almost twenty-eight, too old to still be nursing a dream that could never become a reality."

Clara lowered her head.

"Forgive me if that hurts you, but you see the news on television," her mother continued talking. "Valentino's been involved with that French actress lately. Last year it was a German model. Before that, an American Olympic skier." With every word that poured forth, her mother drove the nail a little deeper. "How long is he going to be in town?"

"For the summer. His father's not well."

Her mother looked shaken by the news. "Even if he stays that long, which I doubt, his home and his business are in Monaco. Eventually he'll have to go back. In the meantime you can be sure the women in his life have followed him here and won't leave him alone. Don't forget he can be with them whenever and wherever he chooses because he has the means."

"I know." *I know*.

Her mother sniffed. "If he's sandwiching you in between them for a diversion, it's only natural for him, but you're a Rossetti and Rossettis aren't content to be the crumbs off anyone else's table!"

"I agree, Mamma."

"That's good because I don't want my sweet *bambina* getting hurt in the process."

"Silvio gave me the same lecture earlier."

"Your brother feels more fiercely than the others because you grew up together. What affects you, affects him. That's how it is with twins."

Clara knew that, too. Tears streamed down her cheeks. She took a ragged breath. "When I'm with him, he treats me like we were young again, you know?" She didn't dare say she felt like an invalid around the family or it would hurt her mother.

"You think I should just tell Valentino it's time for us to let the friendship go?"

"It's not what I think—it's what you *feel* that matters!" She threw her hands in the air. "I'm just afraid you're too vulnerable right now. He wasn't voted the world's most irresistible playboy for nothing!"

She blinked. "How did you know that?"

"I happened to see it in a magazine Bianca was reading. I'm afraid your sister used to have a terrible crush on him. Do you understand what I'm trying to say? If my words sound cruel, I'm sorry because you know I love you to death."

"I love you, too," she whispered in turmoil.

"I would never say such a thing in front of the men in our family, but I say it to you. And now that I have, it is your decision what happens from here on out."

Her mother's words stayed with her while she washed the tears from her face. "I'll see you later today, Mamma." On the way out the door she grabbed an apple from the bowl to eat on the bus.

By the time she joined Valentino a half-hour later, she'd made up her mind to enjoy this morning's get-together. Maybe by the end of this day she would have gained some wisdom and would know how to tell him she couldn't see him anymore.

The problem was, he was sensitive deep down; Clara knew that and she would never want to hurt his feelings. No one would believe an insecure man lived beneath his famous persona. It stemmed from the troubled relationship with his father. He'd let her see inside him just enough for her to feel a little of his torment. *Oh, Tino.*

Valentino stood at the bus stop waiting for Clara. Through his sunglasses he watched the activity in the piazza. So far his navy headscarf and striped sailor shirt with the long sleeves had disguised him enough to keep the paparazzi away.

His outfit must have done a better job than he realized because when she got off the bus at ten to nine, she walked past him in her blue print blouse and denim skirt without realizing it. He followed her into Bonelli's.

There were half a dozen people drinking coffee at individual bistro tables while they read the newspaper. He'd already staked out their table in the same corner as before.

"I'm over here, Clarissima."

She wheeled around in surprise. A slow smile broke out on her stunning face. "I would never have guessed it was you! You look like a French seaman on leave from Marseille or some such port."

"That's the way I'd like to keep it."

"I know," she said in a quiet voice. "I won't give you away."

He held her chair, then sat down opposite her. "Help yourself." He'd already taken their cappuccinos and ham-filled croissants to the table.

"Thank you. After all the food we ate last evening, can you believe I'm hungry again?" She bit into her breakfast.

Valentino smiled as he devoured his. "How did the babysitting go?"

"None of them wanted to go to bed. We ended up having our own party."

He'd wanted to be there. The night had been endless for him. "Is that why you seem a little tired this morning?"

"Yes," she murmured, but she didn't look at him as she said it.

"Did Lia bring the limoncello with her?"

Her lips curved upward. "She did."

"Good. I'm already salivating for it." Color seeped into her cheeks. "Have you given serious thought to the plus side of the trattoria?"

Clara sipped her cappuccino. "Yes. The placement of the tables was conducive to private conversation. The service was good. The chicken was tender, the gelato excellent." He liked watching her mouth as she spoke. Even when she had been a girl it had a passionate flare.

"What about the negatives?"

"The *bruschetta* was mediocre, the wine so-so, the pasta seemed too greasy and the bathroom needed attention."

He chuckled. "My sentiments exactly, *piccola*. Bravo. I was going to add that the prices were too high."

"Yes, but they obviously lower them for the tour-bus crowds. Oh—something else. The decor wasn't that unique. Not anything like your father's restaurant."

"Well, it's possible Papa will be interested in our findings and can point out the differences to the tour directors when I invite them to Rosa for a meal."

"Rosa's sauce is to die for, Tino."

"My father will be delighted to hear that Signora Rossetti's daughter has given her seal of approval. What Papa really needs is your mother in his kitchen. I ate most of your lunches at school, if you remember."

"I haven't forgotten anything," she admitted in an odd tone before suddenly getting to her feet. "Thank you for breakfast. Now I need to get going to my appointment."

For once Valentino was ready for that and stood up. "I appreciate your taking the time to meet me first." He walked her outside. "After I've met with Papa, I'll call you and tell you what he said."

As she gazed at him her eyes clouded over. "I hope he shows you how thrilled he is that his wonderful son is trying to help him." Her earnestness resonated to his insides. He couldn't hold back any longer.

"I'm not his wonderful anything, Clara. He's not my biological father. You might as well know I'm the product of an extramarital affair."

He heard her long gasp. "Your mother was unfaithful?"

"Yes. She and Luca hit a bad patch in their marriage, but they made up."

She looked devastated for him. "Do you know your birthfather?"

"No, and when I learned about it, I didn't want to know him. Neither did Luca apparently, so I was raised as a Casali."

"Then he must have loved your mother and you very much."

Valentino studied her upturned features. "You come from a very loving, close-knit family. You see only the good. It's a remarkable trait. Don't ever lose it."

She bit her lip. "You've never told anyone?"

"Isabella and Cristiano know. Our parents told all of us before Mamma died so there'd be no secrets, but it's not common knowledge."

"I'll never say anything," she whispered.

"You think I don't know that?"

"Tino—" She sounded distressed. "I—I'd like to stay longer and talk to you, but I have to go or I'll be late. Forgive me."

"Of course. I'll be in touch."

She nodded before hurrying away across the piazza. Once she disappeared he rushed after her, realizing she'd taken the set of stairs where she'd come down that first day.

When he reached it and mounted the narrow staircase to the next level of the town, she was nowhere in sight. There were more residences than shops in this area. He looked all around, noticing the local clinic on his left. He'd never known a dental office to be in there, but maybe things had changed.

Give her a few more minutes before you burst in looking for her, Casali.

If he did find her inside, he'd be risking her anger because it smacked of invading her privacy. She might never speak to him again.

After the conversation they'd had the other day on the

subject of maintaining one's privacy, there was a certain irony to this kind of thinking—and danger. But that was what he thrived on. At this late date he couldn't change his character if he tried and determined to take his chances.

He watched the locals go in and come out the doors of the clinic. He waited another minute, then walked inside. Just as he'd thought, the wall plaque didn't indicate any dentists in the building. Beyond the foyer was a waiting room full of patients. He couldn't see Clara among them. She might not be here at all, but he had to check.

Chagrined that he hadn't followed her more closely, Valentino had no choice but to approach the receptionist at the desk. When she got off the phone he said, "Could you tell me if Clara Rossetti has already gone in for her appointment?"

"I'm sorry. Even if she were a patient here, I can't give you that information unless you're the police or her next of kin."

For no good reason the hairs lifted on the back of his neck. The receptionist had given nothing away, yet for the first time since coming back to Monta Correnti a little frisson of alarm darted through him. It was that same feeling he got on the race-track when he sensed something wasn't right and braced himself for what was coming around the next curve.

"I'm her fiancé," he lied without compunction. "I've been at sea for a long time, but got shore leave specifically to see her. Her sister Bianca told me I'd find her here for her ten o'clock appointment." If lightning struck him, he didn't care.

"In that case, go back to the foyer and down the hall to the dialysis clinic."

Dialysis—

A shudder rocked his body. That meant kidney failure. People *died* from it.

No. Not Clara. He'd just come from being with her. Though she'd looked tired, she'd seemed healthy to him.

He shook his head, trying to make sense of it.

She couldn't be dying. That was preposterous! Valentino didn't believe it. He must have misunderstood the receptionist.

Bile rose in his throat. He couldn't seem to swallow.

"*Signore*? Are you all right?" The woman at the desk stared up at him anxiously.

"Yes," he whispered.

"You didn't know?"

A groan escaped his throat. Her question made it all too real. It meant that the first day he'd seen her on the staircase between the buildings, she'd just come from the clinic.

And the other morning when she'd said she had shopping to do, she'd been on her way here...

He half staggered out to the foyer where he saw the sign for directions to the dialysis clinic.

CHAPTER FOUR

AFTER having to tear herself away from Valentino, Clara had been plunged into a new low of despair. This time it was for him.

Luca Casali wasn't his birthfather?

Though Valentino might have been living with that knowledge since childhood, a boy would still yearn to know his own flesh and blood father, or at least have *some* information about him. While Cristiano and Isabella had lived with the security of enjoying both parents' love, Valentino couldn't claim the same thing.

If Clara's life didn't depend on this treatment, she wouldn't have left him standing there in front of Bonelli's looking tortured.

Like a slot machine that went chink chink chink, little pieces of memory started fitting together in a mosaic that explained to some extent why he'd been drawn to Clara more than his own siblings during those early years. When he'd lost his mother, he'd needed a friend, no doubt because he didn't feel as if he belonged to the Casali household in quite the same way as the other two.

No one at school had had any comprehension of his struggles, including Clara. While she lay there, she wept for the boy inside the incredible man he'd become.

It was impossible to settle down and concentrate on anything else right now. Normally after she was hooked up to the large hemodialysis machine and the clinician had left the room, she could absorb herself in a good mystery novel. She'd put a new one in her purse, but hadn't opened it yet. She couldn't.

As weak as she'd felt after getting off the bus earlier today, the sight of Valentino wearing jeans that molded his powerful thighs had set off a burst of adrenalin, giving her an extra boost of energy.

He was an impossibly handsome man. In that headscarf and sailor shirt revealing his well-defined physique, he looked like a cross between a dashing pirate and a Gypsy. It couldn't be easy being so famous he had to go to such lengths to avoid the constant crush of the media.

It took a remarkable man to rise above his pain. Valentino made every moment of life exciting. That was one of his many gifts. Who else would have ordered a decadent chocolate dessert they could share and make the moment seem like a fabulous party he'd created just for her?

If Silvio knew the true Valentino the way she did, he wouldn't have grilled her so mercilessly the other morning while she'd been running the fruit stand. He'd fired questions at her she couldn't answer and wouldn't anyway.

When Valentino had come by the farm in the latest model Ferrari, it had reminded her brother of the differences between them, but that wasn't the underlying reason for his bitterness. To her dismay, the girl her brother had been infatuated with in high school had wanted nothing to do with him because she'd been so crazy about Valentino and he had gone through girls like water.

Even though Silvio had moved on to other women and had eventually married Maria, her brother's pride had never got over the rejection. As Valentino's fame grew, so did Silvio's envy for the women—the money—everything that seemed to come to him with what looked like no effort at all. In truth he couldn't forgive Valentino and didn't want Clara to have anything to do with him. In this area, he'd become irrational.

If he knew how hard it had been for Valentino growing up, even if Luca had been good to him, her brother would have a different perspective. Silvio basked in the love of both parents. All of the Rossettis did. How lucky they were!

Depleted physically and emotionally by the distressing revelation, she let out a deep sigh and closed her eyes, aching for Valentino's pain and wishing the treatments didn't take so long. But she couldn't complain, not when they were keeping her alive.

While she lay there on top of the cot fully dressed, she heard the door open. The clinician checked on her every little while. With her eyes still closed she said, "I'm doing fine, Serena."

"That's music to my ears," sounded a deep, familiar male voice.

Her eyelids flew open at the same time her heart clapped inside her chest. She discovered Valentino bigger than life, standing at the side of her bed opposite the machine. He removed his sunglasses and scarf, revealing disheveled dark brown hair. It only added to his potent male appeal.

"You *followed* me!" she cried in a combination of anger and exasperation.

"Guilty as charged."

No one had ever looked less penitent. "How did you get in here?"

"They weren't going to let me in, but I found your clinician. When I told her I was your fiancé she took pity on me."

Of course she did. Serena was a female. No woman was immune to Valentino's charm.

Clara should have been furious he'd found out her secret, but it was so like Valentino to go where angels feared to tread when he wanted answers to questions, she started to laugh and couldn't stop. Maybe it was contagious because he laughed, too. Soon the tears actually trickled from the corners of both their eyes.

They were still laughing when a smiling Serena poked her head inside the door. "I've never heard you laugh before.

There's nothing like a fiancé showing up to turn your world around, eh, Clara? I didn't know you had such a gorgeous one. You're a dark horse, you know that?"

After giving Valentino another once-over, she grinned and shut the door again. It wouldn't be long before Serena connected his looks with the legend that preceded him and would know it was all a lie. But right now Clara didn't care.

Those intelligent dark eyes of his searched hers for endless seconds. His expression grew solemn. "How long have you been undergoing these treatments, *piccola*?" he whispered in a shaky voice.

"Three weeks."

He pulled up a chair and sat down next to her with his tanned hands clasped between strong legs. She saw him looking at the graft below the place where she'd rolled up her sleeve. The loop had been surgically inserted in her right arm where her blood was drained and bathed in solution to separate the impurities before returning to her bloodstream.

She heard his sharp intake of breath. "Is this the reason you've lost so much weight?"

"No. I was perfectly healthy until two months ago when I cut my leg on one of the thorny twigs of a lemon tree at the farm. It developed into a blood infection that led to hemolytic uremic syndrome. That caused an acute failure of my kidneys."

A pulse throbbed at the corner of his hard, male mouth. "They don't function at all?"

Clara shook her head. "I have what's known as ESRD."

A bleak look entered his eyes. After a long pause, "Does this mean a kidney transplant is the only cure?" She felt his solemn tone in every sick atom of her body.

"Yes, provided it's the right match. My parents and siblings have tried to donate theirs, but because of weight problems or high blood pressure or pregnancy, they've been turned down."

He rubbed a hand over his face. "Tell me you're on a waiting list—"

"Of course."

"What kind of time are you talking here?" He fired comments and questions at her so fast she was dizzy. In fact she'd never known him to be this intense. The businessman in him had come out.

"I don't know. Waiting for a suitable match is a complicated process. You think there's one available, but then, for one reason or another, it can't or doesn't happen."

"You have a big extended family. Surely there's someone."

"Two of my relatives would be matches, but they have diabetes so that rules them out. One of my aunts was prepared to go through tests, but she has had cancer in the past and the risk is too high for her. My best chance is to receive a kidney from an altruistic donor, but they're hard to come by when thousands of people ahead of me are waiting for one."

"Tell me what you mean by altruistic."

"A non-related person who wants to give a kidney to a loved one, but it's not a match, so they still donate a kidney to someone who is. There are chains of groups of people who do this, but it's a case of finding them and linking up so their serum can be tested against my PRA."

He frowned. "PRA?"

"It means my serum has been mixed with a panel of sixty random donors to see the reaction to the antibodies. Mine is fairly low which is a plus. Kidney allocations are based on a mathematical formula. It awards points for factors that affect a successful transplant."

"What are the other factors?"

"Age and good health. I have all those things going for me."

He reached out to grasp her free hand. "How often do you come here?"

"Three times a week."

"That's virtually every other day—" He sounded aghast.

"It's not so bad when you consider there's no other way for my blood to get filtered."

"Why isn't someone in your family driving you here and picking you up?"

"I don't want to be a burden to them."

He seemed to have trouble sitting there. "You've never been a burden to anyone in your whole life."

Unbidden tears filled her eyes. "I am now. Everyone works so hard at the farm. It's bad enough that I can only do my part on the farm three days a week. There's Nonna who needs taking care of now that she's in a wheelchair and learning to talk again. Bianca has a baby and another one on the way, and Maria's expecting for the fourth time."

Valentino squeezed her fingers gently. "I've upset you when I didn't mean to. Every time we've been together, you've always had to leave. It has been so unlike the Clara I used to know, I've been at a loss. Because you didn't explain your condition to me, I had to find out the truth for myself. Forgive me for bursting in on you like this?"

His pained eyes were so imploring, she didn't want him to feel bad. After the painful experience he'd had with his father the other morning, she didn't want to add to it. "There's nothing to forgive. I didn't say anything because I've loved spending time with someone who didn't know about my condition and treated me like a normal, healthy person. If anything, I'm the one who needs to ask your forgiveness."

"*Clara…*"

She smiled at him. "You wouldn't be Tino if you hadn't made up your mind to do something no one else would think of doing to get inside this room."

"How did all this start?"

"You don't want to hear all this."

"Let me be the judge of that."

She moved her head back and forth. "Are you sure?"

Lines hardened his features. "You know me well enough to realize I never do anything I don't want to do."

Perhaps that was true once. She had no way of knowing what he was like now, but, since he showed no signs of leaving her bedside, she decided to humor him.

"After I got sick, I had to leave Lia's to come home. The doctor sent me to a specialist, who diagnosed my condition. One thing led to another and I was forced to drop out of school."

A shadow crossed over his handsome features before he found her hand again and kissed the fingertips one by one. His touch melted her like a serving of gelato left in the hot sun. "I'm going to let you rest. Before I leave, is there anything I can do for you?"

She knew it. Now that he'd learned about her condition, he was going to start treating her like all the others. In a matter of seconds she'd gone from being his fun-loving friend to invalid. He'd never held her hand and kissed it before. She couldn't bear it now. Not from him.

"Yes," she said brightly, removing it. "Will you open my purse and bring me the book I brought to read? It's on that table."

Within seconds the task was accomplished. He glanced at the title. "I've heard this is good."

"I hope so." She took it from his hand. "Thank you."

Before he left, taking all the excitement with him, he put on his sunglasses and tied the scarf around his head. "Think I'll still fool the paparazzi?" He flashed her a dazzling white smile, reminding her of the French fictional character Marius who went to sea in the story from Pagnol's *Fanny*.

At the time, she could see that Valentino totally related to the young man who dreamed of seeing the world. Clara, on the other hand, could totally relate to Fanny, who loved him, but knew she had to let him go in order for him to be happy. It was one of their favorite books in lit class. "But of course! *Au revoir*, Marius!"

Marius?

Valentino forced a grin, not having thought about that story or their involved discussions of the characters in a long time. Her humor in spite of her condition humbled him, but inside he was dying.

She looked so damned beautiful and helpless lying there, he couldn't take his eyes off her. The urge to do many things for her was so great, he needed to get out of the room in order to hold onto his sanity.

"*A presto*," he whispered, kissing her forehead.

Once he left her room, he saw Serena and headed in her direction. "Can we talk for a moment?"

"By all means."

"I lied to you before."

She smiled. "I know. If I hadn't recognized you as Valentino Casali, you would never have made it in to see Clara. The way you two were laughing in there, I knew I'd done the right thing. It's the best medicine for her."

He nodded. "Thank you for allowing me in. Would you do me one more favor and give me the name and number of her specialist?"

"Come over to the desk and I'll write it down. Dr. Arno's office is in Rome, but he's overseeing Clara's case."

Once Valentino had it in hand, he thanked her again. After leaving the clinic, he quickly found the secret alleyways through the upper region of the town, not stopping until he reached the villa.

When he checked his watch, he realized Dr. Arno would be

in his office for hours yet, that was if it were a normal day for him. No matter what, Valentino needed to talk to him.

The receptionist at his office in Rome answered. When Valentino explained the nature of his emergency, she said the doctor was on vacation and wouldn't be returning for a few more days. But she'd make certain he got back to Valentino ASAP.

Wild with pain, he needed a lot of information pronto! After hanging up, he put in a call to Dr. Rimbaud, his own doctor in Monaco, asking him to phone him back. While he waited for the call, he showered and changed into chinos and a sport shirt. He was drinking some coffee when his phone rang. Valentino grabbed for it.

"Dr. Rimbaud—thanks for getting back to me so fast."

"I thought I'd better in case you've been in another crash," he kidded him.

"Not this time."

"You sound serious, not like yourself. What's wrong?"

"Will you tell me what you can about kidney failure?"

"Uh oh. Anyone I know?"

"No. It's a close friend of mine."

"I'm sorry to hear that. Give me a few particulars."

Once Valentino had unloaded about Clara, the doctor told him what he could. "Those treatments take between four and five hours. Afterward she'll be weak and need rest. Sometimes the patient suffers a sudden loss in blood pressure or gets muscle cramps. One or all of those reasons was why she'd been in a hurry to get on the bus the other day."

"Of course." Valentino had read all the signs wrong. She'd run from him because she wasn't well, and because she had her pride. The Rossettis possessed that in abundance. Clara wouldn't even let her family drive her to the clinic and back.

"Depending on her individual health, she probably needs to eat more animal protein. If necessary she might have to cut milk, cheese, salt and soft drinks. She'll do better on the day after each dialysis treatment. That explains her ability to work at her family's fruit stand."

"How long can she go on like this?"

"Most patients live longer on dialysis these days, but her End Stage Renal Disorder might be more severe. Perhaps she's been diagnosed with anemia. There could be other problems, too, like bone disease, nerve damage or high blood pressure. These are complications you'll have to discuss with her specialist. Naturally the most desired thing would be to find a compatible donor for a transplant as soon as possible."

He closed his eyes tightly. Dr. Arno couldn't call him back fast enough. In the meantime, Valentino intended to be there for her in every conceivable way.

"Thank you, Dr. Rimbaud. What you've told me helps a lot."

"Call me anytime."

As soon as he hung up, he phoned for a taxi to take him to the local market. Once there he did some shopping, satisfied that the paparazzi would be looking in vain for his Ferrari. Until further notice it would stay in the garage. He would wait outside the doors to the clinic in the taxi until she emerged, then offer her a ride home.

"*Signore*?" the chauffeur called to him. "We've arrived."

"So we have."

He instructed him to wait in the loading zone. His pulse picked up speed when he finally saw Clara start out the clinic doors. She looked good, not as pale as she'd been last evening. He stepped out of the taxi into her path so she had to stop.

"How come you keep following me?" he baited her gently.

She lifted her beautiful head so he could see the green flecks in her eyes.

"Tino—"she cried in shock, but her eyes lit up. This was a bonus he hadn't expected after barging in on her treatment.

"Come on. I've brought cold fruit juice and a chicken sandwich for you. You can eat it on the way back to the farm."

He could tell she wanted to argue with him, but she didn't have the kind of strength she needed for that. "Where's the Ferrari?" she asked as he helped her into the backseat.

After he gave the driver directions, he handed her a sandwich and a drink before sitting back to answer her question. "It's out of sight for a variety of reasons."

"That will drive the paparazzi crazy." She took several bites of her sandwich. "I have to admit this tastes delicious. You're spoiling me with good food again."

He'd bought himself a fruit drink and drained most of it. "I wonder how many hundreds of times you shared your lunch with me at school because I was too busy doing some project to stop and eat. Your mother made the best lunches in Monta Correnti."

A trace of a smile hovered on her lips as she continued to eat. "Our family carried around the excess pounds to prove it."

He flashed her a sweeping glance. "Not any longer."

She avoided his gaze and drank more juice.

"Does your mother know she kept me alive with her cooking?"

"I didn't dare tell her."

Valentino chuckled. "You're lucky you've had her in your life all these years. Do you want to know a secret?"

Clara's head turned in his direction. She'd finished the last of her sandwich. He was thankful she'd had an appetite. "What is it?"

"I was jealous you had a mother who fussed over you every day. You and Bianca always seemed so happy. You didn't know it, but having two parents who were alive and loved you gave you a confidence I would have given anything to feel."

Her expression sobered. "I understand that now, but you did have Luca."

"Yes, and he indulged me without limits."

"That was only natural. After your mother died, he would have tried to play both roles. He loved you, Tino. I know he did. Otherwise his marriage to your mother wouldn't have worked out."

"I guess he wanted her badly enough to include her excess baggage."

In a surprise gesture she covered his hand with her own and squeezed it gently. "I'm so sorry you've carried this pain with you all these years. I often sensed something was wrong, but you never opened up about it."

"I couldn't."

Her head was bowed. "None of us is exempt from problems, but somehow we deal with them because we have no choice, right?"

He marveled at her courage. "*Sì*."

She let go of his hand. "We're almost to the farm."

Valentino told the driver to turn onto the private road where you could see the sign advertising produce at the Rossetti farm. He told him to follow it all the way in to the farmhouse and pull to a stop.

The minute the taxi slowed down, Clara had the door open. He knew better than to ask her to stay with him and talk. She was probably craving her bed.

"Thank you for the food and the ride, Tino. You saved my life today."

Would that were possible.

"I always enjoy being with you."

She couldn't meet his gaze. "Where are you going now?"

"Home to work on the Web site."

"What did your father say about your ideas?"

"I've decided to wait until I have all the facts at hand, then present them in one go and see how he reacts."

"I think you'll be surprised how accepting he is of your ideas."

"We'll see. Your optimism gives me hope."

"That's good," came her fervent reply.

He leaned toward her. "I'm going to come by for you in the truck after you're off work tomorrow."

Clara felt her pulse race. "What did you have in mind?"

"I thought we'd drive to Gaeta—we went there once, remember? We'll enjoy a meal on the coast. It's not too far. We'll take it in stages. If you feel like sleeping on the way, you can."

He still wanted to be with her?

"I'd love it!" she broke in. To go to the sea with him sounded divine.

His mouth broke into a satisfied smile. "I'm happy to hear it. Get a good sleep. I'll be by about three."

"All right. *Ciao.*"

Clara entered the kitchen feeling more light-hearted than she'd been in days. Who else but Valentino would have pretended to be her fiancé so he could gain access to the treatment room? She'd noticed that none of the workers at the clinic were immune to his compelling personality and looks. He'd been the talk of the place. Serena had been totally won over.

As for the taxi waiting for her, it might as well have been a golden coach whisking her away from the castle with her dashing prince while he fed her on the way. Because of his kindness, her body didn't get a chance to feel depleted as it did when she had to walk down to the piazza and then wait for the bus.

She'd been utterly shocked to see him outside the doors. And grateful... He could have no idea how wonderful it was to just get in the car and be waited on as if she were a princess.

Though he'd told her earlier that he had no interest in knowing the identity of the man who'd had an affair with his mother, Clara couldn't help but think his birthfather must have been an extraordinary person with exceptional looks and drive. Otherwise Valentino wouldn't have turned out to be such a brilliant entrepreneur and heartthrob.

"What's the great Valentino Casali doing bringing you home in a taxi?" Silvio had just walked in the kitchen. He wasn't usually home this early.

"He was thoughtful enough to give me a lift from town."

Her brother grimaced. "Did he think that by not bringing you in the Ferrari, the family wouldn't notice?"

"Why would he be concerned about that?" she asked, attempting to control her temper without much success. "If he didn't choose to drive it, it was probably because he was tired of the paparazzi following him every second of his life."

"Why do you let him do it?" he demanded. "Don't you get it?"

"You can stop worrying. It hardly smacks of the kind of attention you're talking about. I'm a dying woman."

"Don't ever say that again!" he cried.

"But I *am* dying, Silvio. You have to face it. We're all going to die some time. I just happen to know that without a new kidney, it will happen to me sooner than later."

"How can you talk that way?"

"How can I not? You've got to stop being angry about it. As things get worse, Mamma and Papa are going to need your strength, not your rage."

His eyes grew moist. "You've been so brave. If the almighty Casali had any idea what you're dealing with now—"

"Actually he does. In fact he sat with me in the clinic today while I was getting my treatment."

"I don't believe it," his voice shook. "You *told* him you have ESRD?"

"No. We met in town before my appointment. After I said goodbye to him, he followed me to the clinic and pretended to be…a relative." She caught herself in time. "He did that so he could get in to see me. At the end of the treatment he brought me home so I wouldn't have to take the bus. He even brought food and drinks because he knew I needed it after dialysis."

Silvio looked dumbfounded.

"Please let's not argue over him. He's been nothing but kind to me and now I'm tired." She felt his eyes on her as she left the kitchen to go upstairs. All she wanted to do was go to bed and dream about tomorrow when he came for her.

One more outing, then she'd tell him that, as much as she enjoyed his company, her illness was slowly draining her to the point that any social life had to end. She was hurtling through space toward a black void from which there could be no return. Where she was going, he couldn't go.

She knew Valentino well enough to know his compassion for her condition would prompt him to continue making himself available to her. She also knew herself well enough to know she would cling more and more to him because he *was* life to her.

Clara couldn't think of a worse scenario for a man whose freedom meant everything to him.

On the way back to town, Valentino had to admit it was getting more difficult to drive away after they'd been together. When he thought about it, he'd never liked parting company with Clara. Until he heard from the doctor, he was going to be on tenterhooks.

In the meantime he needed to keep so busy he wouldn't be able to think. But he soon discovered that work was no panacea for his heartache. Nothing could take it away. It went so deep, he couldn't find solace.

Every time he thought about her pain and what she was facing, he was pierced to the quick. His agony drove him to get in his car. He started driving through the countryside with no destination in mind. While he was en route, the wildflowers seemed to flaunt their fragrance in the night air as if to impress upon him the delights Clara might not be able to enjoy much longer.

Crazed by the thought that a life as sweet and innocent as

hers could be coming to an end, he found himself headed for the church. Eventually he pulled up in front of the rectory. It was after nine p.m. when he levered himself from the car and was made instantly aware of the sound of crickets chirping. Tonight all his senses had come alive to nature, sending bitter-sweet pains through his body.

He took the steep steps two at a time to gain the porch, not hesitating to tug on the bell pull. In a few minutes, a much younger priest he didn't recognize opened the door.

"Yes?"

"I'm here on an emergency to see Father Orsini. Is he still awake?"

"I believe so."

"Will you tell him it's Valentino Casali? If he can see me, tell him I'll be out here waiting for him."

The other man studied him for a brief moment. "*Bene*," he said before shutting the door.

Unable to remain still, Valentino walked to the wrought-iron railing and looked out over Monta Correnti. The lights of the town with its red-tiled roofs and centuries-old palazzos spilled over the undulating hills, creating a fairyland illusion. In the distance, the Rossetti farm made up part of the magical landscape.

Would that what he'd learned at the clinic today were just a bad dream from which he'd awaken at any moment.

"Valentino?" came a familiar voice. "Don't tell me you're here to confess ten years' worth of sins?" He'd asked the question in a joking manner, but the ring of hope lingered in the night air.

Consumed by a guilt so deep he'd never been able to talk about it, he turned to face the gray-haired priest who'd grown much more frail over the last decade. "Not tonight, Father. Otherwise you would never get to bed," he teased. Their easy relationship stretched back to Valentino's childhood.

Father Orsini chuckled. The years hadn't deprived him of a sense of humor, for which Valentino was thankful. "It's good to see you."

"Then you'll understand how pleased I was when Father Bruno told me Monta Correnti's most legendary figure was outside waiting for me."

"Let's not play games, Father. A legendary figure should at least connote someone worthy." He shifted his weight. "Forgive me for calling on you so late, but this couldn't wait."

"Evidently not. Let me put it another way. What's troubling Luca Casali's most famous son?"

"Famous for what?" Valentino muttered in self-abnegation. "Certainly nothing that matters." When the priest blinked in astonishment, Valentino added, "Did Luca or my mother ever take the opportunity to tell you I'm not his birth son?"

"*What is this?*" Father Orsini cried out aghast.

"I don't blame you for being bewildered. Forget I asked."

"My son—"

"It's all right, Father. If you *did* know, you couldn't reveal it anyway. He and Mamma told me the truth years ago. It was a good idea at the time considering I don't look or behave anything like Isabella or Cristiano."

"Do your siblings know?"

"You mean that my infamous qualities can be laid at my biological father's feet?" he mocked. "Yes, but that's not why I'm here. What I'm hoping is that you'll be able to help me over another matter. It's of life and death importance."

The priest cleared his throat. "If I can, but that places a great burden on me."

Valentino squinted at him. "I knew you'd say that, but I have nowhere else to turn." He stared at the priest. "What do you know about Clara Rossetti?"

In the quiet that followed, a sadness entered Father Orsini's eyes and he pursed his lips, giving Valentino the answer. Fresh pain arced through him as surely as if he'd crashed on the track and the paramedics couldn't separate his body from the wreckage.

The compassionate priest put a hand on Valentino's shoulder. "She doesn't want to die and is fighting this with everything she has in her."

Valentino's body trembled. "I know. I've been with her every day since I came home. She's so courageous, I'm in awe of her."

"You two were very close growing up."

A sob got trapped in his throat. "Very. I don't want her to die, Father."

"Of course you don't. After being away such a long time, this news must have come as a great shock."

Shock hardly covered it. Shame for his narcissistic lifestyle had seeped into his soul. Up to now Valentino had lived only for his own pleasures. He'd avoided marriage and children in order to pursue new adventures without suffering any more guilt than he already dragged around.

In the process he'd pretty well abandoned his family, not to mention Clara. Valentino wasn't only selfish, he was a coward unwilling to face certain unpalatable truths. After his aunt Lisa had leaked the latest family secret, his first instinct had been to run away and stay in denial. That had been his pattern over the years.

That was the mortifying part. After spending time with him during their growing-up years, Clara had become so well acquainted with his self-focused obsessions, she'd written him off when he'd left in his late teens. And why not?

What had he ever done for her?

His hands curled into fists.

Nothing! Not a damn thing!

It strained his credulity that she'd given him the time of day since he'd been back. While he'd been off in his superficial world, angry at life while he tried to break barriers and set new bars, she had been battling for her life!

Somewhere in his psyche Valentino had known there'd be a price to pay for always running away, for always taking without giving anything back. He just hadn't expected it to come now, in this particular form. Clara, more than any other human being, had shown him unqualified friendship, but he hadn't realized or understood until it was too late.

"I can see you're in pain, my son."

"I want to help her, but I don't know where to begin."

"She could use a good friend."

Something he hadn't been.

"Is there anything else you'd like to discuss with me?"

Valentino shook his head. "No, *grazie*." He had quite enough on his plate and had said more than he should already. Calling on the priest this late at night constituted a special act of selfishness all its own, the kind for which Valentino was famous.

Luca's "famous" son who really wasn't his son. The negative connotation fit.

"I've intruded on your time long enough. Thank you for seeing me, Father. *Buona notte*." He started down the stairs.

"Don't be such a stranger!" the old priest called after him.

Valentino deserved that particular distinction, too. A stranger was one who was neither a friend nor an acquaintance. Those who knew his name would say that pretty well summed up his existence.

He waved to the priest from the lowered window of the car before he headed back to the villa. His black thoughts drove him to the kitchen where he made a pot of strong coffee. On an empty stomach the caffeine was guaranteed to keep him wired for the rest of the night. He did his best thinking when he prowled around in the dark.

The priest's words wouldn't leave him alone. *She could use a good friend.*

That meant making a commitment you didn't break.

For the rest of the night Valentino searched his soul. By the time morning came eight hours later, he'd determined Clara Rossetti would discover how good a friend he could be, even if she didn't believe it right now.

CHAPTER FIVE

"VALENTINO has come for me, Mamma. We're driving to Gaeta. Just so you know, I've come to a decision. After today, I won't be seeing him anymore. He knows I'm dying, and he'll respect my wishes."

Her mother let out a heavy sigh and stopped stirring the sauce she was cooking. "I'm glad to hear it, for his sake as well as yours. And I'll tell you something else. You're not going to die if *I* can help it! The doctor has assured me they're doing everything to find the right donor for you. God hears me beg for your life every minute of the day and night."

Clara lowered her head, humbled by her mother's love. The doctor had told them they needed a miracle, but she knew that even if a kidney became available from a non-relative, there was always the possibility her body would reject it.

"See you later, Mamma." She hugged her mother, then hurried outside to the old truck. Valentino got out of the cab wearing the same straw hat. When she drew closer, he flashed her a broad smile.

"*Buon giorno, piccola.*" He was hiding something behind his back.

"What have you got there?"

"You need a disguise, too," he said before putting a matching hat on her head. "You look very fetching with it perched at that angle. From a distance we'll look like an old farming couple taking a break after a busy morning."

She loved it! They left the farm and headed in the direction of the coast. The truck made for slow going, but she felt very much at home in it. The Rossettis didn't drive anything but trucks.

They ate some plums he brought and made desultory conversation while they drove through the enchanting countryside. Clara felt so carefree and relaxed that in time she found her eyelids drooping and fought to stay awake.

Nestling against the door, she closed her eyes, telling herself it would only be for a moment. The next time she became aware of her surroundings, she was cognizant of two things: the tangy smell of the Mediterranean and the feel of Valentino's hard-muscled arm against her cheek and shoulder. He'd always smelled so good. It had to be from the soap he used in the shower.

"Oh—I'm sorry—" She sat up horribly embarrassed that she'd been asleep for an hour with her arm against him. Her hat was askew. How was it she'd ended up pressed to the side of his fit body instead of the door? Looking straight ahead, she glimpsed the Gulf of Gaeta spread out before her like a sparkling blue jewel in the sunlight.

Valentino had removed his sunglasses and cast her a sideward glance. "Why apologize? You needed your sleep. I'm hungry and presume you are, too."

"I am." Food had never sounded so good to her before.

"After we eat, we'll take a walk on the beach if it's warm enough for you and you're up to it."

Mentally she was up for everything he suggested, but her body had other ideas. Still she wouldn't think negative thoughts right now, not when this would be her last outing with him. Certainly not when they were passing through hills of rich green vegetation where she spied a fabulous pink hotel surrounded by palm trees and a fabulous garden. "I remember that place from before! Didn't you tell me it was once a monastery?"

"You have an excellent memory. It's the Villa Irlanda. I thought we'd eat by the pool where there's a view of the coast. I was in too big a hurry to stop here last time. It's an oversight I intend to correct now. When I look back on my life, I think I was always in a hurry, but no longer."

Valentino waited in the hotel lounge for Clara, who went into the ladies' room. When she came out again a few minutes later, he escorted her to the pool where they settled on loungers to soak up some sun. They had the place to themselves. He signaled one of the waiters, who came right over.

After greeting them, he named half a dozen entrees on the menu. "But may I suggest that the oven-roasted *abbacchio* with rosemary, white wine and peppers would be a superb choice. You couldn't go wrong with a side dish of *carciofi alla romana*."

"What do you think, Clara?" In the late afternoon sun her eyes glowed an impossibly iridescent green. Fringed by her long black lashes, their color mesmerized him.

"I love lamb. As for artichokes, I've never had them stuffed with mint. It all sounds delicious."

"I think so, too." He placed their order, asking that it be served with his favorite pinot noir. When the waiter walked away, Valentino turned to her. She was a totally feminine creature, one of the few who could wear a blouse with a ruffle like that. "Can you drink wine?"

"In moderation. I have to stay away from sodas."

Valentino thought she looked a little pale. No doubt her work at the fruit stand had drained her. "How are you feeling right now?"

"Good."

"Still, I can tell something's wrong. You don't have to hide anything from me."

She let out a small laugh. "Apparently I'm not able to hide anything from you. To be honest, the air's not as warm here as it was at the farm."

"If you're chilly, that's an easy fix." Valentino was relieved the temperature had turned out to be the culprit for the moment. "Come with me." He helped her to her feet and they walked back inside the hotel to the front desk.

When he told the concierge he wanted a room with a view of the sea, he could see Clara shake her head no, but he pretended not to notice. After making arrangements for dinner to be brought to their room, he escorted her upstairs to a suite with a sweeping vista of the grounds and coastline. It was definitely warmer inside.

"Tino—" She laughed as he moved the table and chairs in the corner of the room to the center of the window.

"I want a view while we eat," he declared. "In the meantime, you can lie down until our dinner comes."

"Have you forgotten I slept in the truck?" Ignoring the suggestion, she sat down on one of the chairs. "Why didn't we just eat in the restaurant?"

He could tell something was bothering her. "Because I wanted you to feel totally comfortable."

"That's very considerate, but are you sure you weren't afraid the paparazzi would sneak in and take pictures of us that will make tonight's ten o'clock news?"

He took a fortifying breath while he tried to understand her sudden burst of heated emotion. "For once the thought hadn't even crossed my mind."

"I don't think Giselle Artois would be happy about it."

Ah. Giselle… Valentino frowned. "She's engaged to her long-time British lover."

Her eyes widened. "But on the news it sa—"

"Forget the news," he cut her off. "They say and print whatever they feel like, but it has nothing to do with the truth. In all honesty there's something I have to say to you and I wanted it to be in private. The restaurant wouldn't have afforded us a moment to ourselves."

To his dismay she paled a little more. It wasn't his imagination that she was all tensed up.

"Tino? Can I speak frankly?"

"Always."

"You said you need to talk me, but there's no point in going to these elaborate lengths in order for us to be alone." More of that hidden temper of hers was showing.

"What are you getting at, *piccola*?"

She plucked at her napkin. "Since you came back to Monta Correnti, don't think I haven't appreciated everything you've done for me, but now it has to stop."

He put his hands on his hips. "Where's all this coming from?"

Before he knew it, she'd jumped to her feet. "Over the last few days you've more than made up for the nine years of silence, and I'll never forget your kindness. But we're going in different directions and I'm not unaware you have personal commitments and a business to run. Entertaining me wasn't your plan when you came here."

A knock on the door interrupted them. He'd never seen her this wound up in his life. Normally unflappable Clara had just delivered the longest impassioned speech she'd ever made, revealing another unexpected side to her nature.

"I'll get it."

One of the staff from the kitchen wheeled in a tea cart with their meal. Valentino gave him a tip, then shut the door and pushed it across the room to the table. With her beautiful body still taut, she held onto the back of one of the chairs while she stared out the window.

Intrigued by her behavior, he put everything on the table and invited her to sit down. "We need to eat our food while it's hot. I wanted this to be special for you. Earlier you admitted you were hungry."

The reminder eventually forced her to comply. Gratified to see her food start to disappear, he poured them some wine and picked up his glass. "I'd like to propose a toast."

Her fingers tightened around the stem of her wine glass as if she were barely holding onto her control and would like to crush it. After a minute she lifted the glass. "Let me go first."

"By all means," he murmured.

"To our old friendship."

He'd seen that one coming. After he touched her glass, they both drank.

"Now it's my turn." Trapping her gaze, he said, "To our new one."

The second the words were out, she looked down without drinking. He swallowed the rest of his wine while he waited for her to absorb what he'd just told her.

She pushed her glass away. "We can't have a new one. I'd like to go home now, Tino."

"Not until you've heard me out."

Her head reared back. Green sparks flew from her eyes. "I'm not trying to be intentionally rude, but I don't want to listen to anything else."

"Not even if this is vitally important to both of us?" When she didn't immediately shut him down he said, "Last night I went to see Father Orsini, but there was one thing I couldn't bring myself to confess to him."

He saw the shiver that ran through her body. "If you're thinking of telling me what you couldn't tell him because I'm dying, please don't. I'm not a priest."

His chuckle permeated to her insides. "No, you're not,

grazie a Dio. But you *are* the woman I want to marry as soon as possible."

After a long silence, he heard hurtful laughter come out of her. "Me—marry you—" she mocked in a brittle tone.

"Yes."

"It sounds like you've come to the rock bottom of your many excellent adventures. I thought you were the one person who wasn't like everyone else, but I was wrong."

Like the lash of a whip, he felt her salvo. "That's the first unkind remark you've ever made to me."

"Maybe it's because even a dying farm girl doesn't relish the idea of being the object of Valentino Casali's pity."

She got up from the table hot-faced and made a dignified exit from the room. He hurried down to the front desk to pay the bill, then raced after her. When he crossed the parking south of the hotel he found her waiting for him in the cab of the truck with her hat on.

They started back to Monta Correnti. He noticed she stayed close to the door so neither their arms or legs would brush by accident. "Pity comes in many forms, *piccola*," he began. "It depends on the point of view. I'm counting on yours to save me from myself."

Clara didn't want to listen. Valentino had a way of twisting words and meanings until he threw her into a state of confusion. Maybe she was having some strange, distorted dream where the impossible was happening and everything was out of her control.

"Before you consign me to my rightful place, which is a great deal lower than the angels, you need to know I called my doctor in Monaco. Among the things we talked about, he said I can be trained to help you do dialysis at home so you don't have to go to the clinic. They have these new machines so you can even travel with them and carry on your activities."

She couldn't imagine anything more wonderful, but not at Valentino's expense.

"Your mother can show me what kind of meals to make for you. I'm a good cook. I've had to be. The villa has a view of the town and valley from every window. Your family can visit all the time. You can visit them and still run the fruit stand if you want.

"While we're waiting for a kidney, we'll do everything together like we did when we were at school. We'll have fun. When was the last time you had fun? I know I haven't had any. I have to reach back to those years with you to remember what it was like to enjoy a carefree day. Marry me and make me respectable. I need you so much more than you need me."

Oh, Tino. The issues with his father had robbed him of so much confidence. She'd never dreamed they were this serious.

"Allow me to take care of you, *piccola*. Now that I've come home, I can't be around my family, my aunt and cousins, without your help. Since you talked to me about my father yesterday, you've made me realize I have to try harder."

She couldn't believe what she was hearing. "What about the woman in your life? I'm not talking about Giselle now."

"What woman?"

"Don't tease about this, Tino. It's too important."

"I agree. I guess it's confession time. There have been other women, but not as many as you have imagined. Even the few I had a relationship with didn't inspire me to get married. I suppose I didn't feel I could count on them for the long haul. If I'd wanted to make a lifelong commitment with one of them, I wouldn't be here now."

"Even so—"

"Even so nothing! What about the men in your life? Don't tell me there haven't been any because I wouldn't believe you."

"No. I won't tell you that, but my illness has changed everything."

"Then there's no problem."

She sucked in her breath, trying to keep her wits about her. "Of course there is! You can't just give up your racing and let your team down."

"You haven't been listening to me. Though I haven't officially announced it yet, it's over."

"Since when?"

"It's been over in my mind for quite a while. Isabella has been after me to come home, but it wasn't until I knew I wanted to marry you that the issue was finally settled for me. Our marriage needs to take place right away so we don't lose any more time. Something quiet and private that won't wear you out."

What he was saying had shaken her to the foundations.

"When we get back to the farm, I want to tell your family so we can make plans right away. The one thing they won't be able to say is that we haven't known each other long enough. From the age of seven to eighteen, I probably saw or spent time with you every day of your life, whether at school or church."

Clara stirred restlessly on the seat, trying to get her bearings. "That's true, but they're going to ask about all the years since then."

A smile hovered around his male mouth. "Surely your parents read about mine or watched it on TV. My last nine years have been lived in a fish bowl. The public seems to know more about my life than I do, but the one thing no one knows except you is my pain. It's time for the pain to end for both of us. Don't you agree?"

She knew what he was asking, but she couldn't answer him. Bands constricted her breathing. They made the rest of the trip home in silence. When he drove them straight up to the farmhouse and turned off the ignition, she started to panic.

"I need an answer, Clara." He turned to her, his eyes blazing. "If it's no, I'll still go on doing everything in my power to help you, but I'm telling you right now it won't be enough for me."

While she sat there trembling from the reasons he wanted this marriage, he got out of the truck and came around to help her down. He'd given her a choice. They could go on being friends as they used to be, always parting company at the end of the day. Or, they could be friends around the clock so he had the support he claimed he needed to be around his family and in return she would get the support she needed through her illness.

If it was an elaborate lie he'd concocted to make her feel better, she couldn't bear it. Finally she turned to him. "I'm afraid the answer has to be no, but I'll never forget your generous gesture. *Arrivederci*, Tino."

While Luca was having a bad morning and stayed upstairs, Valentino got to work and finished the inventory. It had taken him until four in the afternoon.

He found Isabella in the kitchen talking to Giorgio. "The deed is done, Izzy." He put the clipboard in her hands.

She stared at him in shock. "You're a speed demon."

"It's what happens when you're focused." He'd kept up a frantic pace so he wouldn't go crazy waiting for Clara's dialysis to be over for the day. "I would tell Papa myself, but I'll be late picking up Clara." His glance swerved to Giorgio. "Thanks for the use of the truck again."

"Anytime. You know that."

He kissed his sister's cheek and hurried out the back entrance where he'd left the Ferrari.

En route to the clinic he checked with Serena to be certain Clara hadn't left yet. To his relief she wouldn't be out for fifteen more minutes. That gave him time to pick up some food and drinks for them.

After he'd made his purchases, he parked in the loading zone and got out to watch people as they exited the clinic. Eventually he saw her emerge dressed in a yellow top and white skirt. She looked fabulous in anything, but her features were drawn and pale. To know she was so ill squeezed his heart to a pulp.

"Clara?" he called to her.

She glanced at him, then picked up her pace in order to get away from him. In a few swift strides he caught up to her and spun her around gently.

Her eyes looked tormented. "You shouldn't have come."

"I told you I'd be here for you no matter what."

Clara shook her head. "This has to stop, Tino."

"Let's argue about it in the truck. Come on. I brought food. I know you're starving and so am I after putting in a full day of work at the restaurant. You'll be pleased to know I got the inventory done for my father."

"I'm sure that made him happy."

"We'll see." He helped her into the cab, then walked around and got behind the wheel. "I thought we'd eat at the park by our old school before I take you home. It's on the way."

As they drove off she stared out the passenger window not saying anything. "Was it a bad day, *piccola*?"

"I'd rather not talk about it."

"Then we won't."

Before long they wound around to a grassy section of the park. He slowed to a stop beneath some shade trees. "I think you're too tired to get out, so we'll eat right here." He handed her a sandwich and drink from the bag sitting between them.

Her hunger won out and she ate. After they'd both finished their food he turned to her. "I didn't get to say all I needed to say to you last night."

"You said enough and I told you no."

"Five more minutes is all I ask. If your answer is still no, I won't bring it up again."

She lowered her head. "What is it?"

"I want to tell you the secret I couldn't tell Father Orsini."

"Tino—"

"It's about the details of my mother's death."

Here came his tentacle hooks, grabbing hold of Clara so she was a captive audience, but she kept telling herself she was going to wake up at any second and find herself at home in bed, or at the clinic.

"Did I ever tell you Mamma was a diabetic?"

"No." She hadn't heard that.

"She suffered from dizzy spells, a lot, and was battling a severe one the day she slipped on one of my toys and fell down the stairs. We were alone in the house. I was only five at the time and tried to get her to breathe again, but she wouldn't wake up."

Stop talking, Tino.

"I can still remember my terror because I didn't know what to do. I didn't know how to use the phone and there weren't any neighbors close by. A helplessness went through me the likes of which I'd never known. I loved her so much and remember lying down next to her, sobbing. Cristiano was supposed to be home. I prayed for him to come."

You're breaking my heart.

"The second I heard him come in the house, I ran screaming to him and told him what had happened. He took one look at Mamma and called for the ambulance, but when it came, it was too late. The look he gave me made me want to shrivel up and die."

A moan escaped Clara's throat.

"Her death has plagued me all my life. I always felt the family blamed me, especially since I wasn't Papa's real son."

Her head flew back. "But you *were* his son in all the other ways that counted."

He shook his head. She still couldn't reach him on that point.

"From then on I stayed away from the house as much as

possible. You were always kind to me. You were so good and pure and you accepted me for the way I was. I found myself clinging to you."

"Oh, Tino—" Clara had had no idea of the depth of pain he'd suffered.

"I figured that one day when I was older, I would go away so no one would have to be reminded of what a terrible person I was."

"But you didn't do anything wrong!" she cried, shaking her head in despair.

"When I grew to adulthood, I gained an intellectual understanding of what had happened, but emotionally…? To make matters worse, my long absences from home did a lot of damage to the rest of the family. My aunt Lisa took great satisfaction in letting me know I'd let everyone down."

She held her head in her hands. "All this was going on inside you and you never said a word."

"I couldn't. I felt too frozen inside. Isabella kept begging me to come back and help with Papa, but I was too torn apart by my fears to do what she asked. I know Cristiano hasn't come back because deep down he still blames me and would rather not be around to be reminded of what happened."

"That couldn't possibly be true!"

"She was our mother, Clara. He adored her, too. I should have done something—I should have been able to find a way to get help—"

She couldn't stand to hear him go on like this. The torment in his voice was too much. His features were etched in the kind of pain and deep-seated sorrow she wished she could take away.

"Let me ask you a question, Tino. If it had been Cristiano instead of you who was home that day, would you still be blaming him?"

He took a fortifying breath. "You already know the answer to that. He was older and could have prevented her death."

"How do you know she didn't die on impact? If that's the case, then no one could have saved her. Did you ever see the coroner's report?"

Valentino stared at her as if he'd never seen her before. "No," he whispered.

"Then I suggest you ask to see it before you go on crucifying yourself."

Before she could countenance it, he grasped the hand closest to him. "You see how much I need you? How good you are?" He squeezed her hand tighter. "There's only one reason I told you about Mamma's accident. When I saw you lying there getting a treatment the other day, that same feeling of helplessness and despair swept over me. Do you know why?"

She shook her head.

"Because *you* are part of that part of my life, Clara."

"I—I don't understand." Her voice faltered.

"In my mind I can't separate you and our memories from those early years. Since we met again in town and I felt you push me away, a sense of panic took hold of me until I could get to the bottom of your behavior. I swear it was like the angels had shoved me away from heaven's door."

"I'm sorry." Clara bowed her head, her emotions in utter chaos.

"Maybe what you've said is true and no one could have helped my mother stay alive. It's all in the past now anyway, but if I'm your husband, I can help *you* stay alive. I can be there night and day for you to do things no one else can do to ease your burden."

What Valentino was saying went through her like a thunderbolt.

She wasn't prepared for him to pull her into his arms. He buried his face in her hair. "Let me do for you what I couldn't do for my mother," he begged with tears in his voice. "I need to do this, Clara."

His entreaty reached down into her soul. Given the option of being with him all the time, there was no other choice for her, not now that he'd opened up all of his soul to her. He was tortured by his mother's death and the guilt that went with it, but then her soul was tortured, too.

She stayed in his arms for a long time. Last night she'd been so tormented, she hadn't been able to sleep. Though she'd been tempted to accept his proposal, she'd kept remembering her mother's comments about being Valentino's crumbs.

But just a little while ago she'd felt the terrible guilt he carried over *his* mother's death. It went so deep she couldn't ignore his plea.

"While your father's alive, you need to make peace with him, Tino. Otherwise you'll always be unhappy."

"I know," came the surprising admission. "Because of you, I've already begun."

Eventually she lifted her head. Pulling out of his arms, she moved herself next to the door. There was something else he had to understand before things went any further. "You do realize that if we were to get married, you could be a widower within the next six months."

The blood left his face. "That's how long Dr. Arno has given you if you don't get a new kidney?"

"Yes."

His features hardened. "I need you in my life, Clara, so that means we're going to have to find you a new one fast!" Valentino's declaration exploded with a ferocity she didn't know he was capable of. He was a fighter; she'd give him that. To have him on her side was like being handed a precious gift. She felt the blood pounding in her ears.

The next thing she knew he started up the truck and they headed for the road leading out of town. He didn't speak again. They eventually turned into the farm and he pulled up to the house.

"Forgive me for keeping you from your bed. I know you're exhausted." He got out of the truck and went around to help her down. "I'll call you tomorrow."

As he started back to the driver's side of the truck she cried, "Don't go yet—"

There was a sharp intake of breath before he wheeled around. She saw a flare of light in the recesses of those dark brown eyes. His reaction astounded her. "I take it that's a yes."

He *knew* it was.

"Shall we go inside together, or do you want to alert your parents first that they're about to have company?"

Her family would be gathered around the table for the evening meal. She couldn't believe this was really happening and moistened her lips nervously. "I'll tell them you're outside waiting to talk to them."

"I swear you won't regret this." Before she could think, he cupped her face between his hands and pressed a warm kiss to her mouth, the first one he'd ever given her. It brought heat to her cheeks she could feel as she broke away from him and hurried inside.

Everyone greeted her as she walked in the kitchen filled with noisy conversation. Her mother eyed her with an anxious expression, probably noticing her heightened color. "You were gone so long, we got worried you missed the bus."

Silvio cast her a questioning glance. Her father patted the empty chair next to him. "Come and eat."

"I've already had dinner, Papa." Her heart thundered in her chest. "Valentino is outside and wants to speak to you and Mamma. Is it all right if he comes in?"

She watched her parents share a surprised look before they nodded.

On less than sturdy legs, she hurried back out to the hall and opened the door. "Tino?"

He came inside and followed her through to the kitchen. After all these years the moment was unreal to see him enter her parents' home at last. Her father stood up. Silvio and Tomaso followed suit.

"Please sit down," Valentino urged them. "Good evening," he said to all of them. "Excuse us for this interruption, but Clara and I decided our news couldn't wait." He moved closer and put his arm around her waist. "Today she agreed to become my wife."

Immediately she heard gasps from everyone, her mother's the loudest.

"There's nothing I want more than to take care of her. With my help, I'm hoping we can find her a matching kidney donor as soon as possible."

She saw her father cross himself.

"You have a right to know my plans. I've given up racing. From now on I'll be helping my father at the restaurant and doing consulting work for my business. For the time being we'll be living at the villa here in Monta Correnti. That way Clara can remain close to all of you."

Silvio paled while her father looked knocked off balance.

"I've already asked Father Orsini to marry us."

At that news Clara almost fainted from shock. He held her tighter.

"Because of her condition, he'll waive the normal waiting period and perform the private ceremony at four o'clock on Saturday at the church. He'll make it short so it won't be hard on her."

She saw her mother start to weep.

"The only people we want in attendance will be your immediate family and mine, provided my father is well enough. If everyone will agree to keep this a secret, there won't be any paparazzi around to ruin it. Do we have your blessing?"

Clara saw her parents stare at each other in amazement before her father turned to them. "Is this what you want, *figlia mia*?"

She took a deep breath. This was truth time. *It's what you feel that matters*! her mother had counseled her earlier.

"*Sì.*"

Her father's dark moist eyes swerved to Valentino. "Since my daughter says yes, then I say welcome to the family." He walked around to embrace him and kiss him on both cheeks. Clara's mother joined them.

Valentino kissed her on both cheeks. "Earlier today I told Clara that when I was a boy, I envied her belonging to a happy family like yours. Sometimes she let me eat the delicious food you made for her lunches."

"That's true," Bianca chimed in with a smile on her face. "I watched it disappear, Mamma. Clara made me promise never to tell."

"You're the best cook in Monta Correnti, Signora Rossetti, but I've never told my father that. I let him think the food at Rosa is superior. Secretly I have to tell you I like the idea of belonging to your family."

Clara knew he meant what he was saying. The loss of his mother and the tragic circumstances surrounding her death had blighted his life. She could also see his natural charm was lethal. Already he'd seduced everyone in the kitchen except Silvio, who eyed both of them with a hostile expression.

Valentino turned to her. His gaze played over her with relentless scrutiny. "You look tired. I'm going to leave so you can get to bed. I'll let myself out."

After kissing her cheek, he left the kitchen. She didn't want him to go, but, with the family clamoring to talk to her, it was the only thing to do.

"So," her mother said with a new sparkle in her eyes, "we will have to buy you a wedding dress. I always hoped you would wear mine, but look at you—you're so thin it would fall off you and lie in a puddle on the floor."

Everyone laughed including Clara, who needed to be satisfied with the reason Valentino was marrying her and allow her family to be happy for her. Until a few minutes ago they couldn't have imagined another wedding taking place in the Rossetti family. Neither could she.

"Doesn't it bother you that he didn't propose until you lost all your weight?" Silvio's question stunned everyone.

"No," she answered in complete honesty. "If all he'd wanted was a thin wife, then how come he never married one of the film stars or top models he's been seen with over the years? He's had ample opportunity." He could have married the girl *you* wanted, Silvio—but of course Clara would never have said anything that hurtful to her brother.

His face screwed up in pain. "Just tell me one thing—"

She knew what he was going to ask and took him aside out of earshot. They weren't twins for nothing. Forestalling him, she said, "He needs me, Silvio." Until she'd heard him talking to her mother, she hadn't realized just how much.

Her brother didn't say anything after that, but she knew what was on his mind.

Is he in love with you, Clara? Did he say those words to you? Because if he didn't...

CHAPTER SIX

VALENTINO drove to the restaurant and parked the truck behind the Ferrari. When he stepped inside, he walked over to Giorgio. "The truck's outside filled with gas."

"You didn't have to do that."

"I wanted to. I'm grateful for your help. Do you know where Isabella is?"

"Out in front tabulating the receipts."

"Good. I need to talk to her. See you later. Thanks again for everything." They traded keys.

"*Ciao*, Valentino."

With a nod to the others still cleaning up, he walked through the door into the restaurant.

"There you are," his sister said as soon as she saw him. "Papa is anxious to talk to you."

"Did he find mistakes in the inventory?"

"No. He sounded sorry you ran off so fast."

"That would be a first."

"I told him you had to leave to meet up with Clara."

"Clara's the reason I'm here now. There's something I have to tell you."

"I'm all yours." She finished the last of the receipts and closed up the register. "What's going on?"

He eyed her directly. "Maybe you should sit down. This is important."

A look of alarm crossed over her face and she did his bidding. For the next few minutes he told her about Clara's kidney failure. As he explained the gravity of her condition tears rolled down Isabella's cheeks. "Oh, Valentino. That poor, dear girl."

"I have more news." He sucked in his breath. "Father Orsini is going to marry us in a four o'clock ceremony on Saturday afternoon at the church."

Isabella looked thunderstruck. His stunning revelation actually caused her to drop the money bag she'd been holding. He picked it up for her and put it on the counter.

"I'm not going to let her die if I can help it," he vowed. "Until a kidney is available, she needs help around the clock. The only way to give her the kind of attention she requires is to be with her twenty-four hours a day, so I am going to become her husband."

His sister stared at him in shock. "I don't doubt your sincerity, but what about your racing?"

"Those days are over."

"Just like that?" came her incredulous question.

"I've been considering it for quite a while now."

"Will you live in Monaco?"

"No. At the villa here."

"You're serious—"

"Clara needs her family around. You and Papa need my help at the restaurant."

The blue eyes studying him swam in liquid. "I take back the ugly things I shouted at you the night of Papa's birthday party while you were driving away." So saying, she threw her arms around him and gave him a surprisingly strong hug.

"Don't get ahead of yourself. I'm everything you called me and more, but that girl doesn't have a selfish atom in her entire body. What's happening to her isn't fair."

"It's awful."

"I'm going to find her a kidney if it ends up taking all my money to do it." That was what he intended to tell Dr. Arno when they talked. Clara's doctor still hadn't called him, which meant he hadn't returned from his vacation yet. "Her chances of a long life will be vastly increased if one is found soon."

"Then you *have* to make it happen! You're known for doing the impossible."

"Is that right?"

She smiled. "You know it's true."

"Let's hope this time it is," he ground out. "I'm going to ask the clinician to start training me how to do her dialysis so she can have it at home when we are married. Right now I'm going upstairs to tell Papa I'm getting married."

"He's always wanted you back home. Your news is going to make him happier than you know."

"Happy enough to attend the ceremony with you?" Valentino knew otherwise, but that wasn't important right now. He'd promised Clara he would try to get along with his father. "I'm not sure he's well enough."

"Papa wouldn't miss it. Do you want me to phone Cristiano?"

In the past he'd always let Isabella do everything, but no longer. This was something Valentino had to do himself, though he dreaded it.

"I'll call him," he murmured. "Except for Clara's immediate family, no one else is invited. I don't want Aunt Lisa or our cousins to get wind of it. This has to be kept so quiet the media won't have any idea of it until long after the fact. I'll do anything to prevent the press from intruding on Clara's private agony."

"I understand."

He breathed in deeply. "Once we've said our vows, we'll drive straight to the villa. Fortunately with the church so close, it'll be a quick trip for her."

She put a hand on his arm. "No celebration?"

"Only if Clara is up to it after we're home. I'm leaving that decision to Signora Rossetti."

"You can count on me for any help."

"I know that." His dark brows furrowed. "Too bad you were let down in the younger brother department. From now on I'll try to do better, Izzy."

As he gave her a hug his father entered the empty dining room with his walker.

"What's going on?"

Valentino intercepted Isabella's glance before they moved toward him. "I was just on my way upstairs to talk to you."

"Giorgio told me you were in here. I decided I'd better find you before you ran out again."

"Let's sit down, Papa."

Isabella patted their father's arm. "I'll be right back."

"I don't need to sit. You did an excellent job on the inventory, by the way."

Incredible. "You're the one who taught me."

They eyed each other cautiously. For the first time in his life Valentino got the impression his father seemed nervous of him. He thought back to what Clara had told him about Luca being terrified Valentino would leave town at the first sign of trouble.

His father squinted at him. "You said you had something to tell me?"

"Wouldn't you rather sit? This could take a few minutes."

"All right." He moved the walker to the nearest table and planted himself on a chair. Valentino sat opposite him.

"I've been doing some research to help bring in more business. It's just an idea, but it might be worth investigating."

"I'm listening."

Valentino presented his ideas about the Web site and attracting the tour-bus crowd. When he'd finished his explanation his father pursed his lips. "That's what you and Isabella were hugging about?"

The question wasn't the response Valentino sought. He couldn't tell what his father was thinking, but at least he hadn't rejected the suggestions out of hand. "No. I was saving my other news until last."

"Go on."

"I've been seeing Clara Rossetti since I've been home. She has agreed to be my wife. We're getting married on Saturday at the church and we'll be living here in Monta Correnti. I would like it very much if you could be there." Despite all grievances, he discovered it was true. "However, I know you're not well," he added to give him an out.

His father stared at him for a long time. "She's a fine girl."

"I agree," Valentino said in a husky voice. I'm in love with her. He'd always been in love with her, but he hadn't known until he'd seen her lying there in the clinic and realized she could be taken from him.

"What do you think?" Clara came out of the dressing room wearing a simple white A-line silk gown with a scooped neck and long lace sleeves that covered her graft.

Her mother, bedecked in the pale blue dress she wore to Mass, let out a sound of approval. The tears were never far away. "We bought the right one. You look like a princess."

For once in her life Clara felt like one. It didn't seem possible when just last week she hadn't thought she'd live long enough to see this day. And certainly not with Valentino! How many times in her secret fantasies had she imagined him coming home to Monta Correnti because deep inside he'd always loved her and wanted her for his bride?

When she'd lost all her weight, she'd done it with him in mind. More than anything in the world Clara had wanted to be the beautiful woman on the cover of the magazine standing next to him.

That first day on the stairs when he'd called her Clarissima and told her she was a remarkably beautiful woman, she'd known he'd meant it. She'd seen it in his eyes, in the tone of his voice. It was the look she'd always hoped to see. Today Clara knew a joy so powerful it was already draining her.

Her family had insisted she stay in bed this morning. For once she didn't fight them. They brought her breakfast and lunch. While Bianca did Clara's nails, her mother washed and combed her hair. They wouldn't let her get up until it was time to drive to one of the local bridal shops in Monta Correnti.

Bianca, also in her Sunday best, carried the shoulder-length, matching lace mantilla Clara would put on right before the ceremony. She kissed her cheek. "The gown is perfect on you. I wish all the relatives could come to the church to see you."

"So do I," her mother said with a sigh, "but we'll just have to take pictures for them to see later. Valentino was right about doing everything possible to keep the paparazzi away. So far no one knows anything."

"Except the saleswoman," Clara reminded her.

"Ah—but she has no idea who's going to be your husband."

"And he's going to be upset if we don't get her to the church right now!" Bianca put her arm through Clara's good one. "We need to hurry out to the truck. Papa is waiting."

The three of them made their way to the outside of the shop. Their mother got in the truck first with a bag holding Clara's regular clothes. Bianca helped Clara in next, taking care with her wedding dress, then she got in Tomaso's truck with the children. Silvio had muttered something about meeting them at the church.

Clara's father drove the truck through the town and they followed the winding road up the hillside to the lovely seventeenth-century baroque church of San Giovanni where their family had been attending for generations.

The air was warmer than the day Valentino had driven her to Gaeta. She couldn't have asked for a more beautiful wedding day. While the others were brimming over with excitement— Silvio being the exception—a calm had descended over Clara.

This was a surreal moment for her. Within the hour she would be Signora Casali, a role many women had coveted. She wasn't naïve. Clara understood exactly the unique place she held in Valentino's psyche. She knew what marriage to him meant, and what it didn't mean.

No one wanted to live a long life more than she did. If it wasn't her destiny, then Valentino would be given his freedom soon, but it would be with the knowledge that he'd done everything in his power to keep her alive. She'd witnessed that desire yesterday when Serena had spent the four hours teaching him how to administer Clara's dialysis.

His intelligence allowed him to absorb directions quickly. Valentino was at his best when faced with a challenge. Over the last few days she'd watched him take on this new job of health-care giver with a seriousness and dedication that touched her heart.

That plus his assurance that he was working on his relationship with his father meant more to her than he would ever know. For Luca and him to find peace would guarantee they had a happier marriage. She wanted that with every fiber of her being!

When the end came for her, she had every confidence there'd be no demons to torture him the way they had after his mother had died. In the meantime she planned to devote the time she had left to supporting him around his family and making him as happy as her sickness would allow.

Already she was tired, but that was because this was a day like no other. With so many emotions running rampant inside her, she felt more drained than usual and prayed she'd make it through the ceremony before she wilted.

Her father drove them around the back of the church and pulled to a stop in front of a door used only by the clergy. Tomaso followed in his truck. After the women and children got out, Bianca draped the mantilla over Clara's head. The oohs and ah-h-hs coming from everyone made her smile.

By now her other married brothers, Dante and Cesare, and their families had arrived, bringing her grandmother. She was thankful Tomaso was taking pictures so this day would be preserved.

Father Bruno opened the door and ushered them inside. The younger priest had a serious nature so different from Father Orsini's. Clara got the feeling he didn't approve of this clandestine marriage about to be performed behind doors locked to the public for the next half-hour.

"There you are," Valentino murmured, suddenly appearing in the hallway behind the chapel. He mesmerized everyone as he moved swiftly toward her.

A white rose had been tucked into the lapel of his formal dove-gray suit. Beneath the jacket he wore a darker gray vest. The clothes fit his powerful frame like a glove. In the dazzling white shirt and silk jacquard tie of silver and gray, he could easily have been taken for some important Italian prince. He looked so handsome, her legs almost buckled.

"I can't find the words for how lovely you are," he whispered as his dark, searching eyes played over her face and figure. With that compliment she almost sank to the floor in a puddle, bringing to mind her mother's comment about her wedding dress being too big for Clara.

Valentino seemed to have invisible radar because he put his arm around her waist for support and led her the rest of the way into the chapel. His dark-haired sister Isabella stood nearby.

"Clara? You look beautiful," Isabella said softly and handed her a bouquet of white roses.

"Thank you for coming and for these. The flowers are gorgeous." She buried her face in the petals to hide her emotions while she inhaled their sweet scent.

Next to her sat an imposing Luca Casali with his cane. He'd dressed in a midnight-blue suit for the occasion and looked very distinguished. Valentino helped his father to his feet. The older man patted his son's arm before turning to Clara.

"Welcome to the family," he said in a voice of surprising emotion and gave her a kiss on both cheeks.

"I'm so glad you were well enough to make it," she whispered.

"I wouldn't have missed it and couldn't be more pleased with my son's choice. You were always the best influence on him," he confided sotto voce.

"That's very kind of you to say." He'd sounded as if he meant it. Just then her gaze met Valentino's. Her husband-to-be looked happier than she'd seen him in days. Thank you for coming, Luca. You have no idea what it means to your son and to me.

She wished she could say the same for her twin brother, who sat a few feet away with Maria and the children, unable to pretend something he didn't feel.

While both families greeted each other, Silvio stayed put and only stood up when Father Orsini entered the chapel from a side door. The priest nodded to everyone. "If you will all be seated, I'll ask Valentino and Clara to come and stand in front of me."

Valentino clasped her left hand and drew her toward the priest who'd been their spiritual mentor for the whole of their lives, but the broad smile he'd always had for them was missing. In its place he wore a solemn expression, as if he no longer saw them as children. His wise black eyes seemed to say it was time to put childish things aside for the real test of life.

Father Orsini knew this wasn't a normal marriage between

two young lovers desperate to belong to each other. He was a realist who, though he hoped and prayed for the very best for them, had to consider there would probably be dark days ahead in the near future.

"Clara and Valentino? Normally we would celebrate Mass first, but, considering the unique circumstances, I'm going to marry you now. This will in no way make your marriage less sacred."

She could have kissed the priest for his understanding, but she realized it was Valentino who'd prevailed on Father Orsini to keep the ceremony brief.

The older man cleared his throat. "I have one piece of advice for both of you. Strive to lose yourselves in making the other one happy, then you cannot fail."

Since Clara had already determined to do her part no matter what, it wouldn't be hard to take his advice.

"I see Valentino has already taken you by the hand, Clara. If you'll repeat after me."

Within a few minutes they'd both pledged to love, honor and sacrifice for each other, in sickness and in health. Maybe Valentino didn't realize it—or maybe because he did—his fingers tightened hard around hers when the priest said, 'As long as you both shall live.'

"You wish to exchange rings?"

"Sì, Father."

Clara couldn't repress a slight gasp as he produced a gold ring with a brilliant light green stone. He slid it onto the ring finger of her left hand. It fit perfectly.

She in turn waited for Bianca to hand her their grandfather's ring so she could slip it on Valentino's finger. Yesterday morning her grandmother had insisted she take it to give to her intended. It was one of those precious moments in life Clara would always treasure.

Father Orsini nodded. "I now pronounce you, Clara Rossetti, and you, Valentino Casali, husband and wife. In the name of the Father, the Son and the Holy Spirit, Amen."

"Amen." Valentino's deep male voice resonated throughout the chapel. Before she could think, he slid his hands to her shoulders and his mouth descended on hers, sending a river of heat through her already weakened body. It wasn't like the warm kiss he'd given her in front of the farmhouse the other night. With this one she felt unmistakable desire arc through her.

Until now she'd had the impression she was in a strange and beautiful dream, but no longer. All of a sudden this man who'd just become her husband felt so alive and real, she was shaken by powerful new sensations. She broke off their kiss and eased away from him in confusion.

"Are you all right, *piccola*?" She could hear the concern in his voice.

"I'm fine."

"No, you're not. The ceremony has exhausted you. Go with your parents. We'll meet at the villa in a few minutes as planned." They'd agreed it would be better if they weren't seen together leaving the church. Soon enough the world would learn Valentino Casali, the world's most exciting, desirable bachelor, had married a little nobody from a town few had ever heard of.

Clara gave a slight nod. Without looking at him she started for the door where they'd come in a little while ago. She was the first down the passageway and out the back of the church, clutching her bouquet in her hand. Everyone hurried after her and rushed to the trucks parked a few feet away.

Once they were in the cab, her mother cried in alarm, "You look like you're going to faint."

"I'm all right, Mamma."

"We're almost to the villa," her father muttered. "Then you will lie down and have a good rest."

Wrong. Valentino had brought her senses alive. For once in her life, rest wouldn't cure what was wrong with her.

His home was a small, ochre-colored palazzo perched on a summit of vegetation in flower. All the Di Rossi family's royal properties had been built in the prime locations of the region. Any local could point them out, but you couldn't get inside the grounds without passing through the gate.

Valentino had already given her father a remote and directions to the private road leading up to it. Clara's family was still in awe that she would be living in this one with him. For her the only important thing was that she would be an intimate part of his life from now on. The setting was immaterial but lovely as they pulled up to the front with its profusion of flowers and ornamental trees.

Somehow her brand-new husband had beaten them here. He came out the tall paneled doors and pulled her from the truck into his arms.

"Tino—what are you doing?"

He flashed her that devilish smile she remembered from so long ago. "Isn't it obvious?" he murmured against her tender neck.

Once he'd swept her over the threshold, she glanced around her in astonishment. "I've never seen anything so beautiful."

From the elegant foyer to the salon, fresh flowers in every shade possible had been arranged around the period furniture. Flowers reflected in the gilt mirrors, creating the illusion of a wonderful garden.

"You love nature so much, I wanted to bring it inside for our special day."

She was overcome. "I don't know what to say."

"You don't have to say anything. Do you need to go to bed, *piccola*?"

"Not until later." Not after everything you've done to make me happy. "Please put me down."

"Where?"

"How about the love seat over by those tall windows? The view has to be glorious from up here."

Once he'd set her on the small couch and had helped arrange her dress for more pictures, Valentino showed her family through the house. Before long food appeared from the kitchen. He brought her a plate of her mother's cooking. While he sat next to her so they could eat together, Tomaso started taking pictures of the family.

Clara could almost believe she was a normal bride with the normal expectation of a long life with her loving husband and the children who would be born to them.

When she'd eaten all she could, Valentino took her plate. Holding her gaze, he said, "We got away with it, *piccola*. No paparazzi."

"No, thank heaven."

Her father raised his wine glass in salute. "To *all* my married children." He winked at Clara. "I've wanted to say that for many years."

"Papa…" She smiled at him. "Sorry it took so long."

It prompted Valentino to make his own toast. He got to his feet with his powerful legs slightly apart. His gaze fell on Clara. "All good things come to him who waits. To my precious bride."

A blush started at her toes and swept up to warm the crown of her head. With a toast like that coming from such a magnetic personality, there was no question he'd won her family over. But she didn't have to look across the room to feel Silvio's icy glitter.

She'd always been able to read her brother's thoughts…

Valentino's not in love with you, Clara. Personally I can't stand to watch the show he's putting on for the family, let alone that Mamma and Papa are buying into it. Let's not pretend about what's going on here. If you weren't seriously ill, he wouldn't be making a martyr of himself in order to gain the world's attention in a brand-new way.

A new terror seized her heart. Was Silvio right?

Valentino had asked the florist to put flowers in their bedroom. Not as many as in the front of the house, but enough to create atmosphere. While Clara was in the en-suite bathroom taking a shower, he lit the white scented tea-light candles he'd placed around, then he turned out the lights and headed for the guest bathroom at the other end of the hall.

Ten minutes later he returned wearing his navy sweats and discovered her lying under the covers in the middle of the king-sized bed. Her green eyes glowed like jewels above the blue and gold quilt.

"Good evening, Signora Casali."

A smile lit the corners of her mouth. "Good evening, Signor Casali."

"Alone at last."

"My family didn't want to leave."

He sat down on the side of the bed. "It was my idea of the perfect wedding. Short and to the point. The groom gets to whisk away the bride. No endless throngs to navigate. No flash-bulbs going off. Fabulous food, compliments of my new mother in law. Of course that's the selfish part of me talking. I'm sorry you couldn't have your best friends and the whole town turn out after the banns were posted."

"I had the part that mattered." She smoothed her hand against the sheet, letting him know she had a lot more on her mind. "Why didn't Isabella and your father come to the house after?"

"Papa told me he felt light-headed after the ceremony. I believed him. He rarely goes anywhere, so Isabella drove him home, but she wanted to come."

Clara eyed him soulfully. "He was very sweet to me."

"How could he not be?"

"I think he was so moved to see you get married, it affected him physically."

"Tonight I'm in the mood to think only the best thoughts, so I'll go along with your take on it."

"Good."

Valentino held up his left hand. "This ring came as a big surprise." He had to wear it on his littlest finger.

"My grandfather had smaller hands than you. Nonna wanted me to give it to you. It's her way of letting you know she approves."

"I'm honored. Now I need to know if *you* do."

"That question was answered the first day we met at school years ago. You made me laugh so hard, the teacher got mad at me instead of you."

"Sorry about that."

"No, you're not," she responded with a quick grin. "You don't need to fish for compliments, but I'll tell you one thing if it will make you feel better. You have exquisite taste."

Looking at her right now, he agreed. She was sitting up in bed and rested against the headboard, allowing him a glimpse of the soft pink robe she'd put on. The color added a tint to her creamy complexion, drawing his attention until he couldn't look anywhere else.

"I love my ring." Her hand moved so the facets caught the light from the candles, but he found himself mesmerized by the glints in her dark, silky hair. She'd been blessed with perfectly shaped eyebrows the same color. His gaze fell to the alluring contour of her mouth. The desire to kiss her grew so intense, he was shaken by his feelings and got to his feet.

"I hoped you would like it. Is there anything you want from the kitchen before I put out the candles?"

"Nothing, thank you."

In the next minute he'd blown them out. "Are you tired, *piccola*?" he asked in the darkness.

"I'm happy."

He should have known better than to ask his valiant bride, whose exhaustion had probably reached its peak before their guests left the palazzo. "I want to get to know all your habits so I can be of the most help. When you go to bed at night, what do you normally do?"

"Just what I've done tonight. Take a shower and climb in bed. Usually I'm asleep as soon as my head touches the pillow. What about you?"

"The same, but I usually toss and turn for a while first. When my restlessness is bad, I turn on television. The noise usually puts me out."

"Isn't it strange we've known each other since we were children, yet we don't know all those little things about our everyday lives."

"This is a new adventure for both of us, one I'm already enjoying more than you can imagine. If you'll take the right side of the bed, then I won't worry about rolling onto your arm in the night."

He heard the bedding rustle, then he climbed in and stretched out before pulling the covers over them. Her fragrance was so intoxicating, he feared he'd be walking the floors within the hour.

He turned on his side so he was facing her, but he didn't dare touch her tonight. His fear that she'd push him away was very real. He was still raw from her rejection after he'd taken her to Gaeta. How could he bear it if she accused him of making love to her out of pity? What he needed to do was seduce her slowly; a kiss here, a caress there, until the moment when he knew she wanted all of him.

"Now that I'm your husband, everything has changed. We're going to build a new life together."

He leaned over to kiss her lips. "*Buona notte, mia sposa.*"

CHAPTER SEVEN

WHEN Sunday morning came, Clara was awake before Valentino, whose well-honed body took up most of the bed. In truth, after he'd given her that brief kiss, she'd spent the rest of the night in agony because he hadn't reached for her.

Valentino afraid to make love to her because she was ill? Tears smarted her eyes. She'd give anything to go back to a few days ago when he didn't know about her condition. In the natural progression of things she felt sure he would have started kissing her until neither of them could hold back.

While he slept she was able to study her husband's striking features without his being aware of it. To know she would be waking up next to such an exciting man from now on filled her with intense pleasure, but if he never possessed her, she didn't know how she'd be able to stand it.

Already she loved their new life together so much, the thought of it coming to a quick end because of her illness too unbearable to contemplate. Before she gave in to her emotions and kissed him awake, she slid out of bed and hurried into the bathroom to freshen up and brush her teeth.

With her robe still on, she padded down the hall to the kitchen to fix them a meal. The key was to stay busy. For days now Valentino had been doing everything for her. It was time for him to be the recipient.

Her mother had stocked the fridge with food. All Clara had to do was warm things up and they'd have a feast for breakfast. After making cappuccino, she was ready to go get him when she heard him call out her name.

"I'm in the kitchen!"

He emerged from the hallway in his sweats looking disheveled from sleep and sounding the slightest bit out of breath. The shadow covering his firm jaw made him even more disreputably gorgeous. "Why didn't you wake me?"

"Because you were in a deep sleep and needed it."

She could tell he wasn't in a playful mood. "This wasn't supposed to happen!"

"What? That your wife got up to make breakfast?"

"You know what I mean." That hint of anxiety was in his eyes.

"Tino—when I'm feeling good, I intend to do what comes naturally. If I need help, you'll know about it. Unfortunately you haven't always seen me in top form and it has made you think I'm a twenty-four-hour invalid. Come and sit down."

He was clearly out of sorts and raked a hand through his dark hair before doing her bidding.

"Mamma left us a veritable banquet," she chatted. "I don't know about you, but I'm starving this morning. At our house we always put a little chocolate in the cappuccino. If you don't like it, I'll make you regular coffee."

To her delight he drank a whole mug before lifting his head. At last she saw a smile. "I'll never drink anything else again." On that note he popped two sausage-filled rolls in his mouth. "After we eat, I'm taking us for a scooter ride."

The situation was improving. "On your latest model?"

"I think so."

"I can't wait!"

When he looked at her, she could tell he wanted to ask her if she was sure she was feeling well enough, but he refrained.

She'd never seen his brown eyes so alive. "Neither can I. Even though the temperature's supposed to climb today, we'll dress you warmly."

She finished munching on a roll. "Where are we going to go?"

"Here and there."

Just as they used to do after school. "I'll hurry and get ready."

Valentino devoured two more rolls. "While you do that, I'll shave."

"No, don't—"

His eyebrows lifted.

"I—I mean, you don't have to do it," she stammered.

An unexpected gleam entered his eyes. "You don't mind my scruffy look?"

"It suits you," she mumbled before clearing the table.

"Leave the dishes, Clara. While we're gone the housekeeper will be in to clean up and unpack the bags your parents brought over in the truck. All you need to do is get ready."

By tacit agreement they left the kitchen and walked back to the bedroom. Valentino disappeared in the walk-in closet and brought out some packages he put on the bed. A ghost of a smile hovered around his mouth. "After you're dressed, put all this gear on. We'll see if I bought the right sizes for you."

The second he walked out the door, she pulled underwear, jeans and a cotton sweater from one of her suitcases and was dressed in a flash. In the first bag she found socks and black boots. The next bag contained a woman's stylish leather jacket in white with green side stripes and a mandarin collar. Another bag held matching gloves. In the last large sack she found a woman's helmet.

"Everything fits!" she cried when he came walking in their bedroom a few minutes later carrying his black helmet. He wore black boots and a black leather jacket with blue side stripes. His powerful body looked even bigger in his riding gear. She felt his dark eyes roam over her in male appreciation.

"You have a stunning figure, *piccola*. In an outfit like this, it's dynamite. You'll have to hold me tight around the waist so some dude doesn't pluck you off the back while we're tearing around."

"Tino—" His absurd remark made her laugh.

"You think I'm kidding—" The sudden seriousness of his tone caused her pulse to race. "Have you looked in a mirror lately? Maybe taking you out in public is going to be too dangerous."

"That's what I've thought about you for years." She spoke her mind before she realized what she'd said. In a quick move she dropped the helmet's shield so he couldn't see how red she'd turned. "Shall we go?"

He led her down the hall to the back of the villa. They stepped outside into a small courtyard where she could see the garage. With the remote on his key chain he opened the door. Next to the Ferrari sat a gleaming cobalt blue and gold motor scooter.

Valentino put on his helmet before walking it out into the courtyard. "They brought over the deluxe Tourister. See this pillioned seat?" She nodded. "It lets you ride higher behind me. When I designed this, I had you in mind because you always used to tell me you wished you could see better when we rode around together."

He shouldn't have told her that. It meant too much to her. "The Violetta Rapidita is a beautiful machine, Tino." Her voice caught.

"Wait until you ride on it. You'll be totally comfortable. Climb on behind me."

His excitement infected her. After she got settled and wrapped her arms around his torso she said, "Your mother would have been thrilled to know you named it after her."

When her words computed, he squeezed her mid-thigh. She felt the sensation like a dart of flame. "Outside of my family, no one knows its origin. Nothing escapes you, does it? Are you ready?"

"Yes."

He lifted his hands to put on his leather gloves, then they were off. She felt his imprint long after they'd passed through the gate and were zigzagging down the hillside past the patchwork of charming villas partially hidden by lush foliage.

With one of the world's greatest drivers at the controls, Clara gave no thought to anything but the joy of being alive to share this incredible day with Valentino. Sitting on the scooter put you right next to the earth where you could feel and smell nature, hear all the sounds, yet the higher seat allowed her the full sight of her surroundings.

This was so different than riding in a car or a truck or bus. It took her back to her early teens when he offered her rides home after school or church. Sometimes he'd drive haphazardly on purpose, sending her into peals of laughter while the locals shook their fingers at him. Of course they were much younger then and didn't wear the safety equipment they wore now.

In those days the two of them felt invincible. Was he remembering those matchless moments, too? Half the time his old scooter had let him down and he'd had to walk it or push it. Though she would offer to take a turn so he wouldn't have to do all the work, Valentino always refused. Even then there'd been a chivalrous streak in his nature.

Sometimes they ended up walking all the way to the road leading into the farm. When he waved goodbye and kept walking, she always felt a wrench. In truth she'd been so crazy about Valentino, if he'd asked her to go on a walk around the world with him, she would have gone.

Clara had dreamed her dreams, but she could never have imagined that over a decade later she would end up being his wife, riding pillion on this streamlined version of comfort and perfection he'd invented. She nestled tighter against him, resting her chin on his shoulder to feel his body and prove to herself he was flesh and blood, not a fantasy conjured in her imagination.

"Are you all right?" he called to her, turning his head to the side.

"I'm wonderful!" she shouted back. "This is heaven!"

At her comment he twisted the throttle, accelerating them around the next curve where the countryside opened to their gaze. Euphoric, they whizzed past manicured fields and vineyards. Without a cough their scooter ate up the kilometers of rolling hills.

Before long they veered onto a farming road rarely used by tourists. It eventually circled around the furthest end of her family's lemon groves. There was no sight like the straight rows of twenty-foot trees thriving in the sun. Delectable yellow fruit peeked out from the dark green foliage.

It was at the top of one of the trees she could see in the distance where she'd cut her leg, but she didn't want to think about that right now. Please no shadows. Not today.

Valentino didn't slow down. He kept heading south past other farms and cypress trees. This whole area burgeoned with nature and represented paradise to her. She couldn't get enough of it. Eventually they came to the shimmering blue water of Lake Clarissa. Valentino had grown up along this shoreline.

She'd driven past his home many times out driving in her family's truck with Bianca, but that had been when Valentino was winning races in other parts of Europe or the States. Clara had yet to see the inside of his home; knowing it held one of the most painful memories for him, she could understand why he didn't want to stay there now.

He drove them around the west end. When they came to a lay-by, he pulled into it and shut off the motor. They both removed their helmets to take in the lake's beauty. There was a path leading through a meadow-like patch to the water.

Anxious to follow it down, she swung her leg over and climbed off the scooter.

"I think we'll rest here and enjoy a snack." He fastened their helmets to the bars, then opened the trunk. To her surprise he'd packed a light blanket. Beneath it she discovered bottled water, apples and a carton of chocolate biscotti. He must have made preparations after she'd fallen asleep last night.

"You remembered—" she cried in awe before reaching for it. "I haven't eaten these since the last time you got sick after splurging on three packs at once."

He tossed back his dark head and laughed. It was a man's deep belly kind of laughter. She felt it rumble through her nervous system with a sense of wonder.

"If you noticed, I only bought one this time. I can't risk becoming indisposed when I'm driving such precious cargo around."

"Indisposed hardly describes your former condition," she quipped to cover her emotions, which were jumping all over the place. Gathering the other items, she started toward the path.

A chuckling Valentino followed her. Several feet from the shore of the lake he spread the blanket over the wild grass and they both sank down. She whipped off her gloves so she could open her water and drink. "Um. That tastes good."

"It does," he agreed after swallowing half of his in one go.

Clara fell back against the blanket and stared up at the sky, where she could see clouds building. "There's going to be a storm later today."

He lay down next to her and opened the carton. "Then it's good we came out here early."

Suddenly he rolled on his side, bringing him breathtakingly close. Without saying anything, he put a cookie to her lips. There was a mirthful glimmer in his eyes. She took a bite. He finished it off and fed her another one.

After three bites she couldn't keep up with him. "No more."

"No? Then how about a different treat?"

"I think I'll save the apple for later."

"I wasn't thinking of fruit." The amusement she'd seen had faded. In its place she glimpsed something else that made her mouth go dry and sent pleasure pains to her palms. "In the past you and I did just about everything together, but we never played six minutes in *paradiso* or spin the *bottiglia da vino*."

A smile turned up the corners of her mouth. "That's because you were too busy playing those games with every other girl in our class. It made the boys furious. As I recall Aminta, Bettina and Crocetta were all enamored of you at the same time."

He traced the line of her mouth with his finger. "I've grown up since then and have developed an appetite for a new treat. Be kind to me, *piccola*."

Valentino didn't give her time to think before he covered her mouth with his own. For once she didn't want to think. His playful mood had infected her, making her want to give in to the sensuous side of her nature. She had one, but had never allowed herself permission to enjoy what other girls took for granted.

Now that there was a time bomb ticking away inside her, she didn't want to leave this world never having known this pleasure with Valentino. "If it's kindness to kiss you back, then I can't think of anything I'd like to do more."

His jacket was open. She slid her hands up his chest and wrapped them around his neck to get closer. In a slow, sweet rhythm she began responding to the urgency of his demands. The pressure of his mouth invading hers melted her insides, sending a languorous warmth through her body.

This was what she'd been waiting for last night. It was ecstasy. She knew what the word meant and had an intellectual knowledge of it, but now that she was experiencing it she didn't want to do anything else. The freedom to do whatever she desired had taken hold of her.

He was such a beautiful man she needed to kiss every centimeter of his face. The best way to do that was to slide on top of him in order to find those favorite spots. She wished they weren't wearing their leather jackets, but she was too enraptured to take the time to remove hers.

"When did you get this scar?" she asked some time later, having discovered it while she was kissing his eyelids.

"I don't remember," he answered in a husky voice. "At sea, I think."

He reversed their position so he was half lying on top of her. "There's not a mark on your skin anywhere. It's like a baby's. Absolutely like velvet and flawless. Everything about you is flawless."

Clara raised her head to kiss the end of his nose. Unused to his compliments, she said, "Except on the inside." But the second the words were out, she regretted them.

With that slip, the enchantment of the moment was gone—not for her, but for him. She knew it by the way he checked himself before moving away from her and lying back on the blanket.

She couldn't bear for this to end and leaned over him. "Don't you want to play anymore?"

Valentino *had* been playing with his wife. He'd never enjoyed anything so much in his life. But if this was just a game to her to make *him* happy, then it changed the rules.

He hated games.

Clara wasn't like other girls who'd passed through his life. She'd been the different one. *His rock*. You didn't trifle with her kind.

When he dug deep down, he realized he didn't want her trifling with him. Anyone else, but not his *piccola*.

Not unless she meant it.

With this new weight troubling him, he felt confused and restless. He raised his hand to smooth some of the hair away from her flushed cheek. "I could play with you all day, but the sky's getting darker and the temperature has dropped. We can't afford to get caught in a storm. The last thing you need is to come down with a cold."

Valentino saw the glint of pain in her eyes before she moved away and got to her feet. Her kidney disease was a fact of life. Since leaving the villa he'd been the one to live in denial. Yet not even the game he'd started—the game he knew she'd enjoyed and would still enjoy if they continued— could make either of them forget. That would be asking the impossible.

Ten minutes after they'd arrived back at the villa, the rain started. While Clara disappeared into the shower to get warmed up, Valentino heated the chicken and pasta her mother had brought.

As soon as lunch was over they were expecting an important visitor. His wife would be surprised, but he knew it would be a good one. "Clara? Lunch is ready," he called to her.

"I'm coming." Within seconds she appeared in the kitchen dressed in a thin light blue cotton wrapper like the one she'd worn last night. It had long sleeves and fell to her knees, barely hinting at the lovely mold of her body beneath. Evidently it was a style and weight she found comfortable for her treatments. "This looks delicious, Tino. Thank you."

"We have your mother to thank for a few more days, then the real test will come when you have to survive on my cooking."

One graceful eyebrow lifted. "You mean *our* cooking. We'll be sharing the work around here."

He let her comment pass and poured them coffee before sitting down at the table with her. Their morning jaunt had depleted her strength. She would never admit it unless she had to, but he'd been around her long enough to tell when she was getting tired. Her eyelids fluttered a little and she lost some color.

As they were finishing the last of their food, he heard the sound of a vehicle pulling up in the rear courtyard. Clara heard it, too, and looked at him in surprise since no one could enter the grounds without authorization. "Are you expecting someone?"

He nodded. "I set the master switch to open the gate. Sit still and I'll get the door."

Once outside, he greeted Serena and the two other clinicians who'd come with her. After telling her she'd find Clara in the kitchen, he helped the men unload the mobile dialysis machine and wheel it into the villa.

They were good people to come on a Sunday. Even though he was paying them a great deal extra for this service, he was grateful Clara would be able to get a treatment today and wanted them to know it.

He could hear the two women talking and took advantage of the time to show the men to the bedroom where they could set up the machine. Valentino's work with Serena had been instructive.

If Clara could do a longer, slower dialysis every night while she slept, not only would it free up her days and give her more energy, it wouldn't be as hard on her body. She wouldn't get as many cramps and she'd suffer less nausea. Except for a new kidney, he couldn't ask for more than that during this interim.

Serena was scheduled to work with Valentino this afternoon, then the men would each come for two nights to continue training him. By then he'd be able to take care of Clara himself. Provided God was in his heaven, she wouldn't need dialysis once a kidney had been found.

"Hi," his wife said softly as she came in the bedroom with Serena, her gaze finding Valentino's. "This was an amazing surprise considering it's a Sunday. Thank you. All of you," she added the last. Her moist green eyes reflected her gratitude. It brought a boulder to his throat.

"Shall we get started?" Serena asked. "Since you'll be getting a longer treatment tonight, we'll do a shorter session now. Clara? While you get comfortable on the bed and roll up your sleeve, I'll ask Valentino to wash his hands, then put on rubber gloves. We'll leave a box of them in the bathroom."

Three hours later everyone left with the proviso that Carlo would be back at eleven p.m.

Valentino saw them out, then went back to the bedroom with some juice and a roll for Clara. She was sitting up against the pillows. Her color was somewhat improved. He put her food on the bedside table next to her. "How do you feel?"

"I was just going to ask *you* the same question."

"If you want to know the truth, I'm relieved we've gotten this far."

"You've taken on a huge responsibility." Her voice throbbed.

"It's what I wanted."

She eyed him soulfully. "I believe you, but that doesn't make it any easier on you."

"The job itself isn't difficult."

Her brows formed a delicate frown. "Tell me what's troubling you the most."

"It's something Serena said."

"What was that?"

"She said that humans might have invented a dialysis machine to filter out the impurities that our kidneys can't, yet it can only do fifteen percent of the job done by a four-ounce kidney God created. We're going to find you a kidney, Clara," he whispered almost savagely. "I won't rest until then."

She patted the bed. "I'm the luckiest woman in the world to be married to you. Come and lie down by me. You look tired. Don't deny it."

He flashed her a wry grin. "I won't."

While she ate and drank, he stretched out next to her and closed his eyes. A few minutes later he felt her fingers furrow through his hair. Her touch electrified him. "Did I tell you I had the most wonderful day of my life today?"

Valentino grasped her hand. "Would you believe me if I told you I felt the same way?"

"They say you can't go back, but we did."

His lids opened. "Now I'm anxious to move forward with you. While we were riding on the back roads, I saw that the old Brunello place was for sale."

"I noticed it, too. It used to be a beautiful little farmhouse, but now it's run down. The small lemon grove has been sadly neglected." After she eased her hand from his, she looped her arms around her raised knees covered by the quilt. "Can you imagine any family being willing to give up their land?"

"Maybe there was no one to inherit."

She made a funny sound in her throat. "In the Rossetti family, that would be unheard of."

"In the Casali family, too, believe me." They both smiled. "If you're feeling good tomorrow, how would you like to drive back there and walk around to get a feel for it?"

A curious look crept into her eyes. "Are you thinking of buying it for an investment?"

"I'd like to buy it for us so we can live there."

Clara looked shaken. "I don't understand. What about this villa?"

"It belongs to the Di Rossi family. When Isabella begged me to come home, she talked to her fiancé, Max, about letting me rent it. I was saved the trouble of having to find a furnished place."

"I didn't realize you hadn't bought it."

"There are many things we still don't know about each other. Little did I expect that as soon as I got here, I'd become a married man so fast. Now I want a home of my own to put down roots and build a life with you."

She scrambled out of bed. "But you own a fabulous villa in Monaco. I've seen pictures of it in *Hello* magazine."

"When I made enough money from the motor-scooter sales, I bought it for an investment, but I rarely live there. Maybe this weekend we can drive there and stay over one night before I sell it. Though the economy is poor, I'm still pestered by a few interested parties who are anxious to take it off my hands. I'll put the money to good use on our own plot of ground."

"But, Tino," she cried, "you're not a farmer!"

"Maybe not, but I'm married to a farmer's daughter and Monta Correnti is home to me, too. Does the idea have any appeal, *piccola*?"

Clara's eyes slid away from his. When shadows darkened her features, he felt as if a giant hand had just cut off his oxygen supply. "Of course it does," came a small voice, "but I'm afraid you're getting ahead of yourself."

Her comment coincided with the ringing of his cell phone. Her crushing reply, guaranteed to stifle all hope of a long life together, turned his mood dark. He finally got off the bed and pulled it out of his pocket.

"It's your family," he said after glancing at the caller ID. "Your phone must be turned off. While you talk to them, I'll make certain the house is closed up for the night." He tossed the phone on the bed before striding out of the bedroom.

She sank down on the side and reached for it. "Hello?"

"Clara? Are you all right? Valentino told us he'd arranged for you to start your dialysis at home today."

"He did, Mamma. Serena just left. I—I couldn't be better." Physically it was true. Getting another treatment this afternoon instead of having to wait until tomorrow had already made a difference in how she felt.

Because of Valentino she wouldn't have to go to the clinic anymore. From now on she'd sleep through her treatments and start to live life during the day like a normal person. But the situation with him was unraveling fast. Twice today she'd said something to ruin the moment. Father Orsini had counseled her to make her husband happy.

"You're doing a great job, Clara."

"What did you say?" her mother asked.

"Sorry. I was thinking out loud. Thank you for all the wonderful food. Valentino sings your praises."

"He's a wonderful man." *I know.* "Even your father says so."

Her parents would be overjoyed if they knew about his plans to purchase some farming property. She was in awe of his unselfishness, not just because money wasn't his raison d'être, but because he gave of himself.

Tonight he would have to stay up and work with Carlo till four in the morning while he was trained to perform this service for her. Tears sprang to her eyes and wouldn't stop running down her cheeks.

"Clara? Are you crying?"

"Yes."

"Because he makes you so happy, *sì*? He does everything for you."

"Yes." Her husband did his duty better than any husband alive. It was time she did something for him in return.

"Both Gina and Lia phoned. I hope it's all right that I told them you got married."

"Of course. I'll call them tomorrow."

"By now your father has told everyone else in the family."

Clara smiled. "Pretty soon the word will get out and it will be all over the news. Don't be surprised if the paparazzi come by the farm for an interview and pictures."

Her mother laughed. "Come visit us soon."

"We will, Mamma, and we'll have you come to the villa for dinner. Tell Papa and Bianca I love them, and tell Nonna that Valentino loves his ring."

"That will make her happy."

She bit her lip. "How's Silvio?"

"Grumpy. He misses you."

"I lived in Naples for a long time. He didn't miss me then."

"Oh, yes, he did, but this is different, and *you know why*," she whispered.

Just then her brother's nemesis walked in the bedroom. She needed to talk to him. "Kiss little Paolito for me. *Buona notte*, Mamma."

Wiping the moisture off her face, she hung up. "My parents send their love."

A mask had descended over his arresting features. He took the phone from her. "No doubt they're worried about you."

"Actually they think I'm in the best of hands, which I am." Her voice trembled. "Talking with Mamma brought your father to mind. Could we go visit him tomorrow after we've been out to the Brunello farm?"

He placed his phone and wallet on top of the dresser. "I think we'd better put both those ideas on hold for the time being."

"I don't want to," she said with a pounding heart. He darted her a quizzical glance. "You'll have to forgive me for speaking so impulsively earlier. Ever since I was diagnosed, I'm afraid I stopped planning for a future and have been trying to be content by living day-to-day."

His mouth thinned. "In your shoes I would probably do the same thing."

"But we're husband and wife now, and I'm not the only person in this marriage. Naturally you're not going to be content renting a place when you could have your own home in the countryside we both love. It was shortsighted of me. Please let's drive out there tomorrow and look at the house."

To her relief Valentino rubbed the back of his neck, a sign that he was thinking, listening. "I'll phone the realtor in the morning and we'll go from there."

"Good!" She was pleased he'd agreed to that much. "Do you think your father's too sick for company?"

"No."

When he didn't say anything else she said, "You're tired. I'm going to go in the study and watch television while you get some sleep. The bed in this room is bigger than the one in the guest bedroom. Eleven o'clock will be here before you know it."

She started to leave, but he called her back. "Now I'm the one who's sorry. Forgive me for being abrupt with you." His eyes narrowed on her face. "We'll go over to the restaurant tomorrow only if you're up to it."

"You don't have to apologize for anything."

"Of course I do. You made a perfectly normal suggestion to drop in on my father, but there are things you still don't know."

There was more?

"It meant a lot to me that he came to our wedding, but I still struggle. Bear with me."

"You know I will. Tell me the rest."

He nodded. "Papa and Lisa have never gotten along. Being business rivals, you don't know what it's like when they're together. They have this way of going for the jugular."

"That's horrible."

"Before long their squabbling grows into a major conflict

that makes everyone so uncomfortable you want to run for your life. I ran to you a lot during those times. Isabella reminded me I preferred your company to anyone else's."

The revelation took Clara by surprise. She didn't know what to say.

"Growing up I had the sense that something ugly had occurred for them to be at each other's throats all the time. Sure enough it all exploded the night of my father's birthday party. Isabella and I heard angry voices coming from the courtyard. You'd think the party would have given them a reason to try to get along for one night."

He sprang from the bed, unable to sit still. "We got up to investigate. I could hear my aunt announcing to anyone listening that not all my father's children had shown up for the party. She was baiting him relentlessly.

"Isabella and I thought she meant Cristiano, but then she said, 'It's time the secret was out, Luca!' Papa tried to shush her up, but she just kept talking. 'Your children don't know you have two older sons! Don't you think it's time they found out?'"

"What?" Now Clara was on her feet and moved closer to him.

His body tensed. "It seems my father had twins with his first wife, Cindy. She was an American and after their divorce went back to live in the States. Father kept the twins with him for a while, but then, for some reason, he sent them to live with their mother in America and he never bothered to tell any of us about the boys. Of course Aunt Lisa knew all about it and took great delight in exposing his secret. She'd seen the one named Angelo in the newspaper back in New York. The other one is called Alessandro."

Twins. "How old are they?"

"Thirty-eight. Papa gave them up at the time of the divorce. When he married my mother and the three of us came along, he never breathed a word about them."

"No one else ever mentioned them?"

He shook his head. "I found out our cousin Lizzie knew, but she was little at the time and Aunt Lisa told her to keep quiet about it. My aunt has a cruel side. So does my father apparently. I'm not saying he wasn't good to me, but I'm having a hard time dealing with the fact that he has two other children he's never acknowledged."

Luca Casali was an enigma to Clara. There had to be an explanation for a man who could accept Violetta's love child as his own and raise him, yet abandon his oldest flesh and blood sons and pretend they didn't exist.

Clara was desperate to ease her husband's pain. Knowing he wasn't Luca's blood son had made Valentino insecure his whole life. Now to learn about two older brothers had raised all those old issues of jealousy and feeling inadequate.

Maybe one day when emotions weren't running as high, she'd be able to talk to him about it, but right now Valentino was in no state to hear anything. All she could do was listen.

"Would you believe my sister wants to get to know them?"

Yes. As long as Clara had known her, Isabella had been a do-gooder. She'd been raised as Luca's biological daughter, so she didn't have the same emotional struggles as Valentino. But again Clara had to keep those thoughts to herself.

She put a hand on his arm. "Under the circumstances, do you have any idea how much I admire you for coming back home to help your family? For trying to make peace with your father? You had every right to stay away and refuse to deal with the problems. You could have excluded your father from our wedding. But you didn't do any of those things. That's because you're a real man, Tino."

Rising on tiptoe, she kissed his hard jaw and headed for the study.

CHAPTER EIGHT

WHILE Clara was fixing their breakfast the next morning, the long-awaited call from Dr. Arno came through. Valentino took it in the bedroom where he could talk to him in private.

"Thank you for phoning me, Doctor."

"You're very welcome. I'm sorry you had to wait so long. It isn't often I get someone as famous as Valentino Casali asking me to call him back. I'm a keen fan of yours."

"Thank you very much."

"My receptionist told me you're an old friend of one of my patients."

"Yes. In fact Clara and I were just married."

"*Married*?"

"Yes. We did it quickly so I could be with her around the clock to help her."

"Well, congratulations. She's a courageous young woman. A lovely one, too. You're a lucky man."

"I couldn't agree more. If you have time now, I'd like to hear anything you have to tell me about her condition that Serena might not have shared. Most of all I want to know how I can help find Clara a donor sooner."

"I understand your impatience, Signor Casali, but be assured our department is doing everything humanly possible for her.

Since her family hasn't been able to produce one, I'm hopeful we'll find her an altruistic donor."

A tight band constricted Valentino's breathing. "I've thought everything over and would like to be one *if* it's possible."

"She has Type O blood. What's yours?"

Valentino's heart did a kick. "The same. I'm in perfect health. No weight problem, no high blood pressure, no history of diseases, no steroid use, no tobacco, no drugs, recreational or otherwise. Dr. Rimbaud in Monaco will send you all my medical records."

"You sound too good to be true."

"Except that I'm not related to her."

"That isn't necessarily a problem. Over the last several years, immunosuppressive medications have improved to the extent that our transplant center often considers poor tissue matches between donors and recipients. Certainly a kidney matched at four, five or six antigens from a family member may do better in the long term than others, but, as I said, the new medications are proving highly effective."

He gripped his phone tighter. "In that case, let's move ahead immediately."

"Can you come to the hospital in Rome for tests tomorrow?"

"I'll be there in the morning." He would tell Clara he had business. Maybe she could spend the time with her family.

"That's wonderful. I'll set everything up for you and we'll get started on your blood work."

"How long before the transplant can actually take place?"

"If all looks good, I'd say seven to ten days."

"How involved is the surgery?"

"Obviously not as much for you as for Clara, but there are always those normal risks. We have a new technique that takes around three hours and is not as invasive. You'll both be in the hospital four to five days to recover.

"During the transplant operation, you'll both be under a general anesthesia and administered antibiotics to prevent possible infection. Once the new kidney is attached, I may or may not remove her diseased ones. It all depends on the circumstances surrounding her kidney failure. Barring complications, you'll both leave the hospital to face a normal life."

A normal life.

Relief swamped him that they might be able to have a normal life and everything that went with it. "I don't want Clara to know anything about this yet. We can tell her when the time comes, not before."

"That's a very wise decision for both your sakes. If it turns out you're not a good candidate for some reason we don't know about yet, then there's no point in getting either of your hopes up. Before she knows anything, I'd like us to be absolutely certain of optimum results. But I can tell you this much—your being a live donor will give her twice the chance of recovery since your kidney will be healthy and fresh."

Just hearing that made him want to get the surgery done as soon as possible. He thanked the doctor, eager to follow through with his plans.

Clara waved to the realtor as she and Valentino left the Brunello farm on the scooter under more overcast skies. "The man is besotted by you, *piccola*. In that cherry-red cotton sweater you're wearing, I can't say I blame him."

"Don't be silly." She wished her body didn't react every time he made a personal remark. Clara thought it was only redheads whose emotions were too close to the surface. "He's old enough to be my grandfather."

"Didn't you know they have the worst fantasies?"

She chuckled, aware she was feeling different this morning. Better. For the first time in weeks she'd awakened without a hint of nausea. Two treatments since yesterday when she normally wouldn't have had one until today proved the effectiveness of nighttime dialysis. Only Valentino could have made this possible.

He had to be exhausted after his five-hour vigil last night, but he hadn't shown it while they'd inspected the farmhouse. What a disappointment it had turned out to be. The whole place reeked of neglect and was in much worse shape than she'd thought. They'd left without giving the realtor any indication of their true feelings. Naturally Valentino wanted to keep looking.

While she was deep in thought, he said, "On our way back to town, I'd like to stop at your parents' long enough to get that sample of limoncello you told me about. We're almost there now."

"How did you even remember?" Clara had thought he was going to suggest they find a newspaper and see what else was for sale in the Monta Correnti area.

"I've been salivating for a taste of it ever since you mentioned it."

A dissenting sound escaped her lips. "You made that up to make me feel good."

"I'm glad if it did, but, to tell you the truth, the few times I've been served it, I haven't been impressed."

"Now I'm afraid."

"Not you—you're the most courageous person I've ever known. You *are*, you know, so humor me," he said in his deep voice. "It's possible the daughter of Signora Rossetti, who cooks the best food I've ever tasted, has inherited her mamma's special gift."

"You're so full of it, it's no wonder my mother is crazy about you. She'll be thrilled to see us."

A few minutes later they pulled up to the farmhouse. Valentino waited for her to alight. After they took off their helmets, they went inside. Maria was in the kitchen feeding lunch to her youngest and to Paolito, who was in the high chair.

Clara gave them kisses, then hugged her sister-in-law. "Where's Mamma?"

"Giving Nonna a bath because Bianca is too sick."

"Is it her nausea?"

"That and her pain. Tomaso took her to the clinic. It sounds like a bladder infection."

"I know about those." Clara's voice shook.

Valentino slid his arm around her shoulders and pulled her close. "I'm sure she'll be all right, *piccola*."

"Of course she will," Maria assured her.

"If you and Mamma need help, Valentino and I can stay."

"No, no. Everything's fine."

"If you're sure."

Maria smiled. "You two are still on your honeymoon." But it wasn't the kind Clara's sister-in-law was talking about. "I'll tell Mamma and Bianca you came by."

She nodded, still uncertain.

"Where's the limoncello? I'll get it," Valentino whispered.

"Oh—I forgot. It's right over here." She moved out of his hold and found the corked bottle in the cupboard by the door. She found a sack to put it in. After handing it to him she hurried over to give the children another kiss. "I'll call Bianca later to see how she is."

"She'll probably be home in another hour."

"*Ciao*, Maria," Valentino called out from the doorway.

"*Ciao*, Valentino."

Clara followed her husband out to the scooter. He gave her a kiss on the neck while she was putting her helmet back on. "Do you want me to drive to the clinic in case she's still there?"

"No, Tino, but thank you for offering. She'd think I was crazy. It's just that they've all been wonderful to me, especially Bianca."

They headed down the drive for the main road. "You two were always close. I'm afraid I can't relate where Cristiano is concerned."

"I'm so sorry." She'd give anything to help him.

"Don't be. I shouldn't have brought him up."

"I'm glad you did," Clara said, emotion clear in her voice. "You need to talk about it."

"Now you're spoiling *me*," he bantered.

"It's about time. What you need is a long nap after being up all night."

"Only if we do it together."

Clara couldn't wait until lunch was over. Sleeping or waking, she craved every second being with her husband.

The next afternoon, Valentino returned from his visit with Dr. Arno in Rome and walked in the kitchen to find Clara just getting off the phone with her friend Gina. He wore an expectant look on his handsome face. "How good do you feel?"

It wasn't an idle question. "Happy now that you're back from Rome. Did your business go well?"

"Better than expected. I think Papa is going to be surprised when I tell him several more tour operators are considering his restaurant very seriously."

"That's wonderful!"

He smiled. "Feel like getting out?"

"I've got lots of energy if that's what you're asking."

"Then I'm going to let you do the honors." He put the Ferrari keys in her hand.

She blinked. "I wouldn't dare drive your car."

"*Our* car," he corrected her. With his hands spanning her waist, he held her a few inches above the ground. "Say it."

"Tino—put me down."

"Say it!"

"All right. *Our* car."

"That wasn't so hard, was it?" He pressed a surprisingly hungry kiss to her mouth before walking her outside to the driver's side of the Ferrari. After he opened the door for her, she was so dizzy with reaction she almost fell into the black leather seat.

He joined her in a minute. She stared helplessly at him.

"Get into the harness first."

After she managed to do that, he fastened the lap belt, then kissed her lips again. He was no stranger to intimacy, but this was new to Clara. He needed to stop doing that or she wouldn't be able to concentrate.

"Tino—I don't know what to do—"

"Sure you do. You've driven a truck before. You can drive this. Feel down the side of the seat and press the button forward until you're close enough."

Going on faith, she reached down. To her surprise it worked just the way he'd said.

"Bravo. Now put the key in the ignition and turn on the power." As soon as she did it, the car came alive like a beautifully tuned instrument. "It's automatic. Just put it in drive. No clutch to worry about."

Pressing her lips together, she did his bidding. The car crept forward. She turned right at the end of the alley and joined in the mainstream traffic. At first she was terrified, but after a few minutes of navigating through the center of town she started to feel braver.

"You're doing fine, *piccola*. There's the sign for Lake Adrina. Let's head that way. If you get too tired, I'll take over."

Tired? What was that? This was so thrilling, she felt that any second now they were going to take flight.

Little by little they left the traffic behind until she couldn't see any cars, then she pressed on the accelerator. The car took off like a rocket, causing her to cry out in sheer delight. Valentino's face had broken into a broad smile. For the moment he looked so carefree, it filled her with joy.

"Oh—I can't believe it! This is the most fun I've ever had in my life!" The car hugged the curves. Her confidence grew as she passed slower cars and trucks. Clara could see the needle on the speedometer climbing, but she didn't care. In no time at all the lake appeared in the distance. They'd already come fifty kilometers!

Valentino leaned closer to her. "Do you want to stop for a drink?"

"No!"

More laughter poured out of him.

She could have gone around the lake, but the drive back to town would allow her to go a lot faster, so she turned and headed back toward Monta Correnti. "I never understood your love of speed, but I do now!" Already she was addicted.

Halfway back she heard sirens, but didn't associate them with her driving until two police cars pulled alongside her. "Uh oh. Tino—" The officer in front motioned to her that she should pull off the road. "How can I stop when the road is this narrow?"

"Do it anyway," he answered in a calm voice. "It's their problem, not yours. After you've stopped, put the window down and start looking for your driver's license."

Valentino had obviously been through this experience before. Hot and flustered, she pulled to the right as far as she dared, then slowed to a stop. Immediately four officers got out. Two waved the traffic past them, while the other two approached the car.

"Do you have any idea how fast you were going, *signorina*?" the older one with the moustache demanded, but the second he saw Valentino a look of shock altered his fierce expression. He

turned to the other officers. Soon everyone knew the famous
Valentino Casali was in the car.

"*Mi dispiace tanto*, Signor Casali. We didn't realize it was you."

By this time Valentino had put down his window. "That's all
right. My *squisita* bride has been dying to drive my car. Today
she took it into her head to take off with it when I wasn't
looking. I had to run to catch up with her."

That brought a roar from the men.

"It's a good thing you stopped her when you did because I
was starting to get nervous. I was never this nervous at the track."

"Tino!" His comment had the officers reeling with laughter.

They each took turns going around to his side to talk to him
about his last race. One of them got a camera from his police
car and started taking pictures. She could tell they were ecstatic
to have met their favorite hero. Finally the same officer tore
himself away long enough to talk to her.

"I'll only give you a warning this time, Signora Casali," he
said with a smile.

"Did you hear that, *bellissima*?" He'd undone his harness
and leaned over to give her a lingering kiss on the lips. "You're
very fortunate they are being so kind to you. Thank them nicely,
per favore."

While she muttered something indistinct, they took pictures
of her, of them, of the Ferrari. If the officers didn't have a job
to do, they'd have probably hung around Valentino all afternoon
and evening. No doubt they'd never pulled over a celebrity as
famous as her husband.

When all the *arrivederci*s had been said and they'd driven
off, she finally found herself alone with Valentino. "They did
us a great favor today. I saw the way that officer was looking
at you. It's a good thing I married such a beauty or your punishment could have been a great deal worse."

Too many emotions were fighting for expression. She

squinted at him and could tell his shoulders were shaking. "I'm glad you think this is so funny."

"Don't you? I knew you were brave, but I never dreamed I had such a little daredevil on my hands."

"Neither did I," she admitted before she found herself laughing, too. "It's the car's fault."

"That's as good an excuse as I've ever heard." Their shared laughter filled the empty spaces in her heart.

She started the car and they took off again, but she forced herself to stay within the speed limit. When they reached the town she had the feeling they were being followed.

"Tino?"

"I've already seen them. It's the paparazzi. They no doubt listened in on the police band. We've been found out. Keep driving to the villa. They won't be able to follow us past the gate."

He was so used to being followed and harassed, she could tell he took it in his stride, but this was a new experience for her. "I wish I were in a tank, then I'd mow them down until they resembled a sheet of aluminum foil."

"Putting you behind the wheel has brought out the spitfire in you. I would never have believed it." Valentino was still chuckling after they'd parked the car and gone inside the house.

Once inside he fastened his dark brown eyes on her. "I'm starving and imagine you are, too."

"I have to admit our adventure has given me an appetite."

"Good," he said, getting down two small liqueur glasses. "This is the perfect time to try out your homemade aperitif. A good appetizer should improve our meal." He pulled the cork from the bottle sitting on the counter and inhaled the aroma. "I can smell your family's lemon grove."

Her pulse sped up. "It's the taste that's important. I hope it won't put you off your food."

He poured a little of the yellow liquid into each glass, then took a drink and savored it for a moment before swallowing all of it. She watched him nervously before he poured himself another glass.

Like déjà vu he lifted it. "I'd like to propose a toast." His penetrating gaze sought hers. The way he was looking at her made it difficult to breathe. "To the success of my brilliant wife."

"At least you didn't choke on it." She clinked her glass with his and they both drank. "You're a terrific sport."

His expression sobered. "I don't think you understand. This liqueur is going to put your name on the map."

She smiled. "I don't want it to be on the map, but you're very sweet to say so."

Lines marred his features. "I'm not sweet at all. You've got a recipe here someone would kill for. Does your teacher at the college have a copy of it?"

His question surprised her. "No."

"Do any of the students?"

"No."

"Where is it?"

"In my school notebook at the farm."

"We'll pick it up tomorrow." He put the cork back in the bottle. "This needs to be kept in a safe place."

While he put it in one of the cupboards, she started getting a meal ready. Soon they were able to sit down and eat. She kept looking at him while he devoured his food.

"You're acting preoccupied just like you used to when you were working on your scooter designs. What's going on?"

"This and that," he murmured evasively.

He wouldn't tell her about his trip to Rome until he was ready. "You sound tired. Why don't you take a nap, while I phone Bianca? You're going to be up again most of the night."

Valentino shot her a glance. "We'll take a rest together." They'd done the same thing yesterday. It had been heaven. "No matter how well you've felt today, you need some downtime, too."

"I confess that sounds good."

They left the kitchen and headed into the bedroom where both of them took off their shoes and stretched out across the top of the quilt. "Here. Use my phone."

"Thank you." She took it from him and called her family's home number. Her mother answered.

"Clara? I heard you came by yesterday."

"We were sorry to miss you, Mamma. How's Bianca?"

"She's resting right now, but she's going to be fine."

"The poor thing. She needs to get a lot of sleep."

"We'll see to it. Don't you worry about anything."

She glanced at her husband, whose eyes were closed. "Tino won't let me. He keeps me too busy to think."

"That's good."

"Guess what I did today?" For the next five minutes she related the experience driving his car.

Her mother gasped several times. "You could have gotten both of you killed!"

Ever since the police had pulled her over, Clara had been regretting her impulsive behavior. If anything had happened to Valentino because of her...

"I won't ever speed again, Mamma."

With those words Valentino's arm caught her around the hips. "Promise me," he whispered.

She'd thought he'd fallen asleep. "I promise."

"What did you say, Clara?"

"I'm sorry, Mamma. I was just answering Tino."

"I can tell you've had a good day."

"A wonderful day."

"That makes me happy."

"Me, too."

"I'll talk to you soon."

"*Ciao*, Mamma."

The minute she hung up, Valentino pulled her closer. "Let me hold you like this for a while."

She made a little moan of consent and nestled against him with her head lying on his shoulder. If they both slept now, she would read her mystery tonight. They used to read to each other when they had literature assignments. Maybe he'd like her to read aloud to him. They could hash over the plot. She'd lived for their lively discussions. He had the most fascinating mind...

No one knew how much she'd missed him over the years. To have him back in her life like this constituted some kind of miracle. As her eyes closed her hand slid to his chest without conscious thought.

She had no idea how long she slept, but when she was once again cognizant of her surroundings it surprised her that she and Valentino had changed positions. While she lay on her side, he was now turned toward her with his head buried in her neck. His hand roved over her back in ever tightening circles, wringing tiny sounds of pleasure from her throat.

When his mouth found hers, it seemed natural to indulge in a giving and taking that grew more sensual with each breath. "I love the taste of you. Your body feels made for mine." He drew in a deep breath. "I want to make love to you, Clara. Is it selfish of me to want you so badly?"

Her breath caught. He wanted her. "How could it be selfish? I don't understand what you mean?"

"Would it make you feel worse?"

Worse— "I've never felt better, but if you're asking me for health reasons, I couldn't honestly tell you how it would affect me," she whispered against his lips, unable to get enough of them. "My body seems to dissolve a little more with every kiss." She didn't want to talk right now.

"Have you ever been intimate with a man before?"

"Not like this," she murmured, thrilling to each caress.

Maybe it was her imagination but she thought she heard him groan. "Has your doctor given you any guidelines?"

"No. The subject never came up. Does it matter?" She tried to get closer to him. "I don't want you to stop kissing me."

His hands stilled on her arms. "That's my fear—that I won't be able to stop." His breathing sounded shallow.

"Would that be so terrible?" she asked, kissing him more passionately.

"Considering your condition, it would be unconscionable if I got you pregnant, *piccola*. Even the best protection isn't completely safe."

While she was digesting the long-term ramifications, he untangled his legs from hers and rolled out of reach. When he stood up, she couldn't bear it. All her joy evaporated. "Please come back to bed. We'll just hold each other for the rest of the night."

He shook his dark head, taking another step away from her. "I'm afraid not. Carlo will be pulling up in the drive any moment."

Carlo. She'd forgotten all about his coming again. Valentino had taken her to another world. If the clinician were to walk in right now, he'd find her a throbbing mass of needs her husband had aroused. She couldn't imagine getting to sleep. If he refused to touch her from now on, it would be like a second death.

CHAPTER NINE

WHEN Clara awakened early Saturday morning and opened her eyes, she saw that Valentino was already up and dressed in a pullover and jeans. Normally he slept in until ten to catch up on his sleep. During those hours she would get out of bed and leave him alone while she followed through with her own routine. Deprivation was one sure form of self-preservation.

However this morning there was an air of expectancy about him. When he was up to something, he couldn't hide it from her. She loved that quality about him. In truth she loved all his qualities, which were too numerous to count.

Valentino took amazing care of her. What little she did for him by being a listening ear when he chose to divulge his inner thoughts could never make up for the hours he watched over her while administering her treatments. During those hours while she slept, he balanced his time between helping her and running his business from the laptop.

After six consecutive nights of dialysis she felt so normal, she had a hard time believing there was anything wrong with her.

His dark eyes swept over her face and hair. "If you feel as good as you look, I've arranged a surprise for you."

She got excited because his surprises weren't like anyone else's. Every day they went out on the scooter to explore neighboring villages and enjoy picnics. They traveled to all their old haunts and sought new ones, finding delight in everything they did.

But with each passing hour, her physical attraction to him was growing more intense. The only time she could legitimately touch him without worrying what he might think was when she clung to him on the back of his scooter.

He represented the epitome of male sensuality and could have no idea that each time he squeezed or kissed her coming and going he added to the fire raging inside her. If he thought they could go on this way indefinitely, then he truly didn't know how deeply her desire burned for him.

Despite the fact that she was ill, the nature of their relationship would have led to intimacy by now *if* they were in a normal marriage. But they weren't! Valentino needed her as a friend. Though he was a flesh and blood male with the normal urges, he'd been careful not to let things go too far.

She, on the other hand, had to fight not to reveal that a little friendly loving was slowly destroying her.

Feeling his gaze on her, she said, "Judging by the way you're dressed, we're doing some kind of activity outside. Shall I wear my leather jacket?"

"I think you'll prefer a parka, but bring your gloves. I'll meet you out in the kitchen in a few minutes."

Within twenty they'd eaten breakfast and had stolen away from the villa in the Ferrari. Dawn still lay over Monta Correnti. Clara had always considered it a magical time of day when there was a crispness in the air and all was quiet. Valentino must have been enchanted, too, because he didn't talk. They wound their way past the church where the road made a descent and disappeared into the picture-book countryside.

She didn't understand when he eventually turned off onto a

dirt road bordered by well-tended farms. Maybe he'd found another property for sale he wanted to show her.

Ahead of them she saw a van pulled to the side. A couple of men were walking around carrying items. "Uh oh. They must have had car trouble."

"Let's find out," Valentino murmured. He pulled to a stop behind them and got out of the car.

Clara craned her neck to find out what was going on and got the shock of her life to see them unraveling a huge balloon over the ground. A thrill of excitement tinged with alarm shot through her. Valentino had arranged to take them for a balloon ride?

Once she'd extricated herself from the seat harness, she joined him. The men, a father and son, greeted her with broad smiles. Evidently they were good friends of Valentino's. He introduced everyone.

"*Buon giorno*, *signora*. You have chosen the perfect morning to go up."

Valentino's gaze flicked to hers. She saw a definite look of concern in those dark brown depths. "What do you think, *piccola*? Do you want to try it?" He didn't ask how she was feeling, but she knew he was worried.

Clara had never been on a plane, let alone anything that had ever left the ground. But this was Valentino Casali who'd established a record for the longest solo balloon flight over the Caribbean. She didn't want to let him down and would show him and his friends that daredevil side he'd accused her of having when she'd driven his Ferrari for the first time.

"I'm dying to find out what it's like!"

Her unintentional slip of the tongue washed over the men, who got busy inflating the balloon, but she saw Valentino's lips tighten for a moment before he moved behind her and slid his hands to her shoulders.

He kneaded them with increasing pressure. "As I've told you several times, you're a woman of great courage, but this is one time when you have to be completely honest with me, or we won't step foot inside the basket."

She took a fortifying breath. "Physically I feel fine, but I'll admit to being scared."

He kissed the side of her neck, sending rivulets of yearning through her body. "That's natural. At first it will feel like you're in a lift that doesn't stop. Then you'll float over a world only the eagle sees. You'll be so full of wonder, you'll never want to come down. I'll have hold of you every second."

Whatever happened, if she could remain in his arms like this, nothing else mattered.

The multicolored balloon straightened as the men filled it with hot air. Valentino knew when the moment was right and helped her into the basket. "While his father is in charge, Agostino will follow our progress in the van. When we descend, he'll drive us back here."

She nodded and clung to him.

In a few minutes he whispered, "Clara?" There was a sense of urgency in his tone that caused her to lift her head. Maybe it was a trick of light, but she thought she glimpsed the heat of desire in his eyes before his mouth covered hers. The moment he deepened their kiss, she forgot where she was or what was happening around them.

Not even she could mistake the force he was unleashing as anything less than a husband's kiss. She'd been needing this for so long, her hunger for him took over and her passion flared. It would have been impossible to hold back even if she'd wanted to for propriety's sake. She had so much to tell him, show him. At this point nothing but a total merging of their bodies would satisfy her.

In the throes of rapture she cried his name with longing.

He drew one more molten kiss from her mouth before he said, "We're up now. Take a look."

She could hardly make sense of what he was saying until she opened her eyes. Then a gasp flew out of her. "Tino—"

They were airborne!

Clara had missed the ascent because she'd been devouring her husband in front of his friend with an eagerness that made her blush scarlet just thinking about it.

Valentino kept her clamped at his side while she marveled at the vista unfolding several thousand feet below. She'd never seen such a sight, let alone experienced a sensation like it.

"I feel like we're fruit blossoms being carried along by the breeze."

He folded her right up against him and kissed her hard. "You feel a little more substantial to me than that. I wish there weren't so many clothes separating us."

The unexpected admission rang of need rather than playfulness, robbing her of breath. This was the passionate side of Valentino he'd revealed before he'd had the presence of mind to end what was rapidly burning out of control.

In a moment of truth she confessed, "I had the same thought." For the next half-hour she kept her hot face buried in his neck. They passed over the fantastic tapestry best seen from this altitude, but Valentino had just unlocked a door to her own private fantasies.

At the height of her euphoria, sharp searing pain, bitter and real, attacked without warning. Please, God. I don't want to die.

He kissed her hair, increasing her agony. "What did you say, *piccola*?"

"Th-that I wish this day could go on forever," she dissembled in a tremulous voice.

"Why can't it? When we get back, how would you like to drive to Monaco? We'll stay for a few days. I'll take you to the track where we practice. I want to show off my gorgeous wife to the team. I love this new life with you, Clara."

I love it, too, her soul cried out in fresh anguish. Maybe it was wishful thinking on her part, but Valentino *did* seem happier lately, more relaxed. It couldn't all be an act, could it? Not after they'd come close to making love—unless he was carrying his husbandly duty to the extreme.

She'd lived with him long enough to know he was capable of doing anything to make life more enjoyable for her. Knowing her days were numbered, would he go that far? To add to her torment, Silvio's silent questions kept flashing through her mind.

Is he in love with you, Clara? Did he say those words to you? Because if he didn't...

They landed without incident in the middle of another country road. The van was waiting there to take them back to their car. She shook the men's hands. "*Grazie, signori.* It was *stupendo.*"

On the return trip to the villa Valentino said, "While you pack, I'll go by the restaurant and talk to Papa and Isabella so they know our plans."

Clara nodded. "Would you like me to put some things in a suitcase for you?"

He kissed the end of her nose. "I'd like that very much. So far there's nothing about our marriage that doesn't make me happy. I can't think why I waited so long. Do you have any complaints?"

"Except for the fact that you fish for compliments when you don't need to, you know I don't. Thank you for another wonderful experience I'll never forget." On that note she leaned over to peck his jaw, then got out of the car and hurried inside the villa to get ready for their trip.

Unless something unforeseen happened, she wasn't going to die today, tomorrow, or even next week. That meant she should make the most of living on the borrowed time dialysis was granting her.

When they reached Monaco, she would forget her illness and love Valentino in all the ways he would allow her. If they both used protection, there would be no worry about her getting pregnant.

Clara had loved him her whole life, but today she realized she was a woman *in love*. She couldn't go back to their platonic relationship. Not now. It wasn't possible.

On the way to the restaurant Valentino's thoughts were on Clara and the way she'd clung to him during their balloon ride. She wanted him as much as he wanted her. For purely selfish reasons this countdown needed to come to an end.

He reached for his phone to let his sister know he was coming, but realized he'd left it on the dresser back at the villa. It didn't matter. When he parked out back and joined Isabella upstairs, he found her still in the apartment making breakfast for their father. The timing was perfect. Valentino could eat with him while she went to market.

As he entered the kitchen it struck him how warm and colorful she'd made the apartment. The place looked lived in and comfortable, the antithesis of his villa in Monaco as well as the one he was living in now. He discovered he couldn't wait to move into his own farmhouse with Clara.

On top of the upright piano in the corner his sister had put photographs of their mother and the family. He wandered over to it and studied the likeness of her he remembered best. Because of a certain conversation with Clara, his stomach didn't clench as it usually did. His wife had changed him so much already, he didn't know himself.

"Izzy?" He headed into the dining room where she'd set the table. "I'm taking Clara to Monaco with me for a couple of days. I have to meet with my sponsor. He knows I've quit racing, but I'd like to tell him in person."

"Is she well enough to travel?"

"The nightly dialysis has made a new woman of her."

Her eyes watered. "I'm so glad, but waiting for a kidney must be so hard on both of you."

"We've been doing our best not to think about it." Valentino didn't tell her that he was waiting for a phone call from Dr. Arno with the results of his own tests.

"Trust me to bring it up."

He gave her a hug. "Thank you for caring so much. I didn't want to leave town without telling you and let you think I was deserting you again."

She shook her head. "I wouldn't think that, but I'm glad you're here. Papa's been asking about you. I'll get him."

"Let me do it," he interjected. "You go. I'll take care of him until you get back."

"Thanks. I realize you're anxious to get going so I won't be more than a half-hour."

"Perfect."

Once she was out the door, he walked down the hall and knocked on his father's bedroom door. "Papa?"

"Is that you, Valentino?"

He always said that, even though he knew who it was on the other side. "Who else? I came to eat breakfast with you."

"Ah—I'm coming."

"Don't forget your cane."

"No one will let me forget it!" he grumbled as he emerged in his tan trousers and matching sport shirt. His eyes stared at Valentino. "How is your Clara?"

"Good, all things considered."

His father's progress was slow. They finally reached the dining room and sat down at the table where Isabella had left warm rolls, fruit and cappuccino. Valentino helped adjust the chair for him and rested his cane against the table leg.

"She's a brave woman. Noble, too."

"That's an interesting choice of words, Papa." Valentino had thought the same thing about her, but didn't expect to hear his father express it.

"Well, isn't she? The way she carries on with that sunny disposition makes me ashamed of the way I've been complaining." He cleared his throat. "While we're alone, I want to tell you how proud I am of you for taking such good care of her."

Valentino sensed his father's sincerity. Another surprise. "Aunt Lisa asked me if I had lost my mind."

"When did she dare talk to you?"

"She phoned me the other night while I was giving Clara a treatment."

His father munched on his roll for a minute. "My sister is a born troublemaker. I happen to know you had a special feeling for the Rossetti girl from the time your poor mamma died. Listen to me, my son, because you *are* my son, even if you aren't my blood."

Valentino lifted his head to stare at this man he thought he knew.

"I can see what a terrible mistake I made by not adopting you years ago, but I was afraid."

"Of what?" Valentino whispered in shock. He couldn't believe they were having this conversation.

To his surprise, Luca's eyes watered. "I was such a failure as a father to my first two sons, I didn't feel I had the right to claim you for my own. Violetta didn't dare talk to me about it. With hindsight I can see she felt so guilty for the affair, she was afraid to ask me. But I was to blame for much of the trouble during that period. Earning a living was always a struggle. It caused difficulties in both my marriages."

In the silence that followed, his father wept quietly. "I didn't feel worthy of the honor to be your father officially."

Valentino lowered his head, unable to talk. Emotion had closed up his throat.

"I don't expect you to understand how it was for me as a

young man. I fell for the twins' mother, but she wasn't happy here in Italy. She was an exciting, glamorous American woman who had a high-powered and glamorous job to match. But she didn't feel accepted here and when our twins were born, her partying had to come to an end.

"I was struggling to keep my roadside stall running. Things just didn't work out. When the children turned two, she left them with me and went back to Boston where she divorced me."

"What?" Valentino was incredulous. "From the way Aunt Lisa made it sound, you abandoned them."

"That didn't come until later." Sorrow twisted his features. "My business didn't make any money. By the time the children turned three, I was in desperate financial trouble and asked Lisa for a loan just to buy the boys some food until the situation improved. Sorella was doing well and I promised I would pay her back with interest if she would just help me out for a while."

Valentino could already see the writing on the wall. "She didn't lend you any money, did she?"

"No. Not that she had to, but I had no one else to turn to. She told me I ought to send the boys to their mother in Boston since she had a lot more money and could take care of them properly."

It was always the money with Valentino's aunt, yet she'd never told anyone she'd turned down his father's request for a loan.

His father took a shuddering breath. "I was in dire straits, Valentino. I loved my boys more than you can imagine, but I was unable to provide for them at the time. In the end I had no choice but to send them to their mother. It was the hardest thing I ever had to do, especially when I never knew my own father."

The similarity of Luca's and Valentino's beginnings wasn't wasted on him.

"Don't get me wrong. I'm not making excuses. I'm only trying to give you an explanation for the reason I never told you children about the twins. I was too ashamed over my inability to provide for them. It took me years to start earning enough money to be a family man."

More tears trickled down. "I don't expect forgiveness from anyone. I called the boys on their eighteenth birthdays. They didn't want anything to do with me. Who could blame them?" He put up his hand. "But before you leave here today, I want you to know something.

"When you were born, I named you Valentino in honor of my father, William Valentine. Besides my love, it was the most precious thing I could give you. Your mamma wanted that name for you, too."

The revelations just kept coming.

"How she loved her Tino. The diabetes she suffered from was a terrible disease. With every blackout I feared it was the end and you children would lose your mother."

Valentino's breath caught. "*Every* blackout? You mean it happened more than once?"

"Yes, but we didn't tell you so you wouldn't get alarmed. The doctor said she was dead before she fell down the stairs. Cristiano was just old enough to feel guilty that he hadn't gotten home sooner that day."

"I felt guilty, too, and thought I was to blame because I couldn't revive her."

A heavy sigh escaped. "How sad that both my sons took on that extra burden when you were already suffering."

Clara had been right.

While his mind grappled with information that cleared up the distorted picture he'd carried around for years, they heard Isabella enter the apartment. "I'm back, in case anyone wants to know!"

"Come and join us!" their father called out.

"In a moment."

Valentino eyed him through new eyes. "Papa?"

"Yes?"

"I don't want you to worry about finances anymore. If you don't like my ideas for increasing the business, I'd like to make you a loan to help pay off any debts you have owing because I know you'll pay it back when you can."

His father resisted.

"Let me do this for you. If you hadn't given me a good life, I wouldn't be in the position I am now. Think about it and we'll talk again after Clara and I get back from Monaco in a couple of days."

He patted his arm. "I'm overwhelmed, but you need to keep it for your family now."

"There's enough to do both." Valentino got to his feet, eager to get back to his wife. He had so much to tell her, it would take the whole drive to Monaco. Only a few more days! Surely Dr. Arno would call any day with the results of Valentino's tests and Clara's transplant could go ahead. Then their lives would truly begin…

Clara had just hung up from talking to her mother to tell her their plans when she heard Valentino's cell phone ring. He'd obviously gone off without it. She lifted it from the dresser to glance at the caller ID, assuming it was someone from his company.

To her surprise it was coming from the Immaculata Teaching Hospital in Rome. Her body shook in reaction. She wondered what it could mean. Dr. Arno's office was there.

She clicked on. "*Pronto?*"

"Signor Casali, *per favore.*"

"He's not here, but this is his wife Signora Casali. May I take a message for him?"

No sooner had she said it than her husband walked in their bedroom, his dark eyes searching out her gaze.

"This is the lab calling from Immaculata Hospital in Rome. Your husband asked that he be notified the minute his test results were done. Please tell him they've been sent to Dr. Arno's office."

The person on the other end gave out a phone number before the line went dead, but Clara's mind was reeling.

She stared at Valentino. "That was the hospital in Rome letting you know Dr. Arno had the results of your tests. They must have you mixed up with me, but before I could question it, they hung up. You'd better call them back."

As she handed it to him her cell phone rang. It was still lying on the bed. She reached for it and said hello.

"Clara?"

The familiar voice caused her heart to thud. "Hello, Dr. Arno." Was he calling because the blood Carlo had drawn the other night showed her anemia was worse?

"It's good to hear your voice. How are you doing on the nightly dialysis?"

"Fine. I've been feeling better and better," she said while Valentino stood there watching her in a way that raised the hairs on the back of her neck.

"That's wonderful." After a distinct pause he said, "I have even more wonderful news for you."

As she continued to look at Valentino, pure revelation flowed through her. "You mean about my husband volunteering a kidney for me?" A softness had entered his eyes, too piercingly sweet for her to sustain. She turned away from him.

"Then Valentino told you. We both felt it would be better if the identity of your donor remained a secret until you came into the hospital for the transplant, but as long as you already know…"

Clara bowed her head, praying for the inspiration to make it through this phone call. "To say I'm in shock would be putting it mildly." All this time he'd been laying the groundwork… The extent of his self-sacrifice staggered her.

"The *best* kind of shock there is. You both need to check in the hospital as soon as you can get here."

"You're talking today?" The rhetorical question came out more for herself than for him.

"Preferably in the next two hours so the lab can run a few more tests on you. If all looks good, we'll do the transplant in the morning."

By now Valentino had walked around so she was forced to look at him. Clara closed her eyes tightly.

"I'm afraid we won't be coming, Dr. Arno."

"I don't understand."

"You see, we're on our way to Monaco for a few days so Valentino can talk to his sponsor face to face. He's already turned his home into a hospital and has given up his racing career for me. I won't allow him to give up one of his kidneys, too." Scalding tears ran their course down her cheeks. "That's carrying altruism to an extreme not even God would condone."

"*Piccola*—"

The endearment scorched her to the depths of her soul. She turned away from him again. "Please don't give up searching for a viable donor, Dr. Arno. I know *I* won't."

After hanging up, she walked into the bathroom to wash the moisture from her cheeks. When she came out again, an ashen-faced Valentino was still standing where she'd left him.

"I'm ready to leave for Monaco whenever you are. Our bags are packed."

His features looked chiseled. "We're driving to Rome."

An unnatural calm had come over her. "Father Orsini gave us one charge. To make the other person happy. It would make me very happy to see where you used to live. I'd like to meet your racing buddies. You have no idea how much I've looked forward to this trip."

He studied her for a long time. "We just got married. I don't want you to die. My idea of happiness trumps yours."

Valentino had a way with words and arguments that had always twisted her emotions until she was defeated, but not this time. "Not if it means your death, and it could… I'm not simply referring to the risk you take for undergoing an operation. There's the rest of your life to consider. If it were shortened because of this experience, I couldn't handle that along with everything else on my conscience."

"Then let me remind you of something Dr. Arno told me."

Clara saw the compassion in his eyes. It was too much. "I don't want to hear it."

She grabbed her purse and phone, then reached for her suitcase and started out of the bedroom. He followed with the bag she'd packed for him.

"You'll like it," he persisted after they'd reached the kitchen. "To quote him, 'At times like these, I always tell my patients to be thankful to God. In his wisdom, he gave everyone two kidneys, even though he knew we only needed one. That's so we could give the other one away.'"

She spun around. "I'm sorry, but that lovely little story doesn't make me feel better."

"It should," he fired back. "I don't need both of mine. By this time tomorrow you'll have a functioning kidney again. In four to five more days we'll be home from the hospital. With the medication he plans for you to take to minimize your body's rejection, you'll be ready to throw yourself into the limoncello business before you know it."

She lowered her suitcase to the floor. "The day could come when one of your kidneys won't work. Then you'll be thankful you still have the other one."

"If that moment should come, then I'll find me a donor."

He always had an answer. "What's the real reason for all this?" she demanded.

His eyes glittered. "The real reason? That covers a lot of territory, but I suppose it was something Father Orsini said that played into it."

Clara didn't know if she could tolerate hearing it, but she needed to know the whole truth now. "What was it?"

"He told me you could use a friend."

"I wish he hadn't said anything."

"How could he not? You're a favorite with everyone."

"That's not true," she cried softly.

"It's pointless to argue the fact. Needless to say his remark shot straight to my gut because I realized you'd always been my one abiding friend, the one person who continually built me up and made me believe in myself without asking anything in return."

The surprising explanation knocked the foundation out from under her.

Valentino moved closer. "I thought about it all the way back to the villa. You were the only reason my visit to Monta Correnti had sounded palatable. You know what happened when we saw each other on the stairs."

Yes. She knew. Her body trembled just remembering how he hadn't left her alone since.

"When I followed you to the clinic, I finally had a way to give you back something of myself for a change."

She felt her limbs dissolve when his hands slid to her shoulders. "You know me," he said in a husky tone. "I don't believe in what I can't see, but if my kidney could make you well, it would probably change my mind for me. Will you at least think about it while we're in Monaco?"

Once again he'd confounded her as only he could do. But even if he'd made her heart bleed, she would never let him go through that for her.

"Yes," she muttered. "Now can we please go?" She eased away, forcing him to relinquish his hold of her.

He carried their cases out the door and put them in the car

before helping her in the passenger side. "I'll be back with the machine."

In a few minutes they were ready and left the grounds. The gate closed behind them. "I've never been to the Costa Azzurra or Monaco."

"We'll stop several times along the way to eat and stretch so the drive won't be too much for you."

"Thank you." He never stopped thinking about her comfort for a second. "How close is your villa to the place where you drove in the Grand Prix?"

"Mine overlooks the main street."

"I know your sponsor has tapes, but it's sad you never got to stand on your own balcony and see yourself driving."

He broke into that male laughter she loved so much. "You're priceless, you know that? Wait till I tell the guys."

"At least you never crashed there."

"How do you know that?" His glance lingered on her profile.

"Bianca and I watched your races and saw every crash you were in." Each time she had almost died from fear.

"I didn't realize that," came the solemn admission. He reached out and grasped her hand to kiss it before letting it go again.

"It's a miracle you're still alive."

"Dr. Rimbaud told me the same thing every time he patched me back together."

She took a shaky breath. "Thank you for taking me on this trip."

"I've been looking forward to it, too, *piccola*."

"Even if there are other things you need to be doing?"

"Like what?" he demanded. "I'm your husband. This is where I need to be."

"I'm the most pampered wife I know." She was still so shaken by his plan to give her a kidney, she couldn't keep the tears out of her voice. "I loved this morning's balloon ride. How lucky was I to have the whole world at my feet?"

"I won't forget it either."

Her emotions were all over the place. "Tell me how it went with your father earlier, or didn't you get to see him?"

He let out a deep sigh. "He was there. Thanks to you, this morning we talked like we've never talked in our lives."

It was clear something monumental had happened. Without forethought she clutched his hard-muscled arm for a moment. "That's good."

"You have no idea."

Clara turned so she could watch him while he drove. She would never grow tired of looking at him. In profile or otherwise, his masculine beauty was stunning. "I want to hear all about it. Don't leave anything out."

Late afternoon of the following day, Valentino left his sponsor's office and walked out to the practice track. It surprised him the sun felt this hot. He was glad for it since he knew Clara welcomed the warmth.

He spotted half a dozen racers on his team surrounding his green-eyed wife seated in the middle of the bleachers. For the occasion she'd worn a wispy, periwinkle-colored blouse and white wraparound skirt with matching Italian sandals. Every color suited her.

Clara's knockout looks were only superseded by a feminine charm that came from someone grateful for life and interested in everyone. She projected that rare selflessness, guaranteed to melt the most cynical heart.

"So, Signora Casali?" He loved calling her that. It was a supreme moment for him to introduce her as his wife. When all this was a new experience for her, he was proud of her and the way she handled herself. "Are the guys giving you a hard time?"

"Oh, no." She flashed him one of her mysterious smiles.

"They've been entertaining me with unabridged stories about you." Jocular laughter ensued.

Roger, a three-time world Formula 1 champion, grinned at him, giving him the thumbs-up sign. "Your *belle épouse* has so many statistics in her head, she could write her own book on you. I'm jealous, *mon ami*. You have found yourself a *trésor*."

Valentino agreed with him and nodded before looking around. Most of the journalists who'd come to the track for a photo shoot had gone, but there were still a few left who'd been waiting to get last-minute pictures of him and Clara. They never gave up. Today had been his swan song.

Normally he would have hated the invasion of privacy, but having his wife with him made all the difference. He no longer felt defensive or uptight. In fact the cameramen scarcely impinged on his consciousness.

Pleased that she seemed to be taking it in her stride, he climbed the bleachers two at a time to hunker down behind her and put his arms around her neck. He kissed her tender nape where she smelled of flowers from her lotion. "What do you say we leave and enjoy dinner on the water?"

He felt the little tremor that ran through her body before she whispered, "I'd love it."

A few more pictures while he helped her off the bleachers and they headed for his car. Once inside, he drove them down the zigzag streets of Monaco City to the yacht harbor. Hand in hand they strolled toward the Quai des Savants. This was a local paparazzi hangout, but tonight he didn't care. "I thought you'd enjoy eating at a modern Parisian-style bistro."

The reflected lights off the water from the yachts created an illusion that her eyes were dancing. After they were seated, she smiled at him. "I don't speak French. You order for us."

"They serve a delicious veal escalope with mushroom sauce. I like a Madeira wine with it."

"It all sounds delicious, but will you tell them to leave the sauce off mine in case there's some dairy in it?"

He'd already anticipated doing it. After the waiter left with their order, Valentino got to his feet. "Let's dance."

"I haven't done it for a long time."

Once he'd pulled her from the chair, he drew her into his arms. "That excuse might have worked years ago, but you're my wife now. I don't care if you can't." He smiled down at her. "We'll just stand here and hold each other."

"Tino—"

He loved it when she blushed. While he was enjoying the moment, and her, and the night, she blew him away with some fantastic moves. They got lost in the music. He couldn't remember ever having this much fun dancing or anything else.

"Don't look now, but our dinner's waiting for us," she reminded him.

With reluctance, he guided her back to their table. "Next time, don't be so modest. You're a sensational dancer."

"Bianca and I used to practice."

Unable to resist, he pressed a kiss to her unsuspecting lips before seating her.

It didn't take long before she moaned. "I can't eat another bite."

"No dessert?"

She shook her head. "But don't let me stop you."

He had no intention of allowing that to happen, but the time wasn't yet...

As soon as they returned to the car, he took her past the Grimaldi Palace. At her request, he drove them around the Grand Prix racing circuit. She expressed a desire to visit the casino. He told her they'd do more sightseeing tomorrow. Though her energy seemed limitless, Valentino knew she had to be exhausted and finally pulled into the back of his empire-style villa for the night.

She hurried to their bedroom and got ready for bed fast.

"With you having to be up for my treatment tonight, we shouldn't have stayed out so late, Tino."

"I wanted to. We'll both sleep in tomorrow."

True to what she'd told him on their wedding night, she fell asleep within thirty seconds of her head touching the pillow. It worried him she'd overextended herself. He'd be more careful with her from now on. Unfortunately when she'd refused to go to Rome with him he'd been forced to pull out all the stops to get their marriage back on the right track.

For the last eight hours he'd purposely avoided any talk of kidney donors or her illness. His strategy had paid off. Tonight Clara had acted more relaxed and confident with him than he'd ever seen her.

Little by little they were settling into their marriage. From the moment he'd approached her parents, it had shocked him how right it had felt.

Once Valentino got her treatment started for the night, he pulled out his laptop. A dozen e-mails from Violetta Rapidita had been sent and needed replies. Isabella had written him, too. He opened it, wondering if this was bad news about their father.

Fratello mio, I didn't know how long you'd be in Monaco. In case you decided to stay there longer with Clara, I thought I'd better tell you what's happening. I don't want you to come back to Monta Correnti and be surprised in case you should run into Lizzie or Aunt Lisa and hear something you weren't aware of.

First off you need to know Lizzie and I have made up because we absolutely hate this war between Papa and Aunt Lisa. More than anything Papa wants the family to be reunited and we're in agreement.

Since the two of you talked the other day, he said he's done with secrets. After regretting that he kept quiet about the twins, he's told the cousins you're not his birth son, but he loves you as if you were. He doesn't want anyone hurting you later on.

Valentino rubbed a hand over his face.

Secondly, I know you're upset with me for getting in contact with the twins, but how can our family ever come together if things remain as they are? As you know, Lizzie and Jack are planning a June wedding, so she has sent invitations to Angelo and Alessandro.

The amazing twins were coming?

She's hoping everyone will show up. I do, too. Please don't be angry with me about this. Life's too short, don't you think?
Talk to you when you get back.
Love, Izzy

The penultimate line gave him pause because he found he couldn't disagree with his sister. Life *was* too short where Clara was concerned. Compared to doing everything to keep her alive, all else paled in significance, even his family's problems.

He stared into space. Before he answered his sister and told her his plans, he needed to send an e-mail to Dr. Arno, who deserved an explanation. The situation was bordering on desperate.

CHAPTER TEN

A WEEK later Clara drove to the farm early to spend the day with her family. She'd left her husband sleeping.

Since the morning she'd told Valentino she wouldn't let him give her a kidney, she'd noticed an alarming change in their relationship. It seemed that her refusal had killed his desire for the little amount of intimacy they'd shared.

On the surface he was the model husband and still affectionate with her, but in bed he didn't even try to hold her anymore. His behavior went beyond his fear that he might make her pregnant. They could have worked around that. To her sorrow he didn't leave himself open to discussion of their situation. For that matter he avoided any talk of her medical condition.

Since their return from Monaco, she'd had one conversation with Dr. Arno. He'd been understanding of the reasons she couldn't let Valentino be a donor, and he'd assured her everything was being done to find her one. Clara was trying to stay positive and stopped by the clinic for routine blood checks.

Because of Valentino's devoted service to her, he'd made it possible for her to lead what seemed like a normal life, but she was terrified he wasn't getting anything out of it. Not even a saint could go on like this much longer. Neither could she...

It all came down to one reality. Her husband was the source

of her joy and her pain, and this dichotomy of emotions was tearing her apart.

"I think you need to confront him," Bianca advised her some time later while she let Clara bathe Paolito. Her poor sister was still suffering horrible morning sickness. Until the advent of her nightly dialysis, Clara had lived with nausea and wouldn't wish it on her worst enemy.

She splashed water on the baby, who could sit up in the water if she propped him. "Any suggestions on how to do it?"

"Yes. When you drive back to town, buy yourself something sexy from that little lingerie shop on the Via Romana. Something black and filmy. You're gorgeous in black. Tomorrow morning fix your hair different and put on a different perfume. Be lying there next to him when he wakes up. Tell him it's time he had a treatment from you, then do what comes naturally."

Clara swallowed hard. "Then he'll know."

"You mean that you're madly in love with him?"

As she nodded their mother came in the bathroom. "Your cell phone rang while I was in the kitchen, Clara. I'll take over here with Paolito while you find out if it was important. If it's Valentino, tell him to come for dinner. I'm making his favorite cannelloni."

Clara and her sister shared a secret smile. "I'll tell him," she assured her mamma before hurrying downstairs. Just the thought that it might be her husband caused her heart to thud in anticipation.

She reached for her purse lying on the table and pulled out her phone to check the caller ID. It threw her off balance to discover Dr. Arno had phoned. He'd left a voice message.

"Clara? You need to come to the hospital as fast as you can. A kidney is suddenly available. Don't eat or drink anything. The nursing staff will alert me as soon as you've checked in and we'll go from there."

With hands trembling, she phoned Valentino. Pick up, Tino. Please pick up!

"*Piccola*?" he answered on the third ring. "Are you all right?" The concern in his voice was always there. How she loved him!

"Yes! Where are you?" she blurted.

"Getting ready to walk down to the restaurant. Why?"

"I'm coming for you. We have to drive to Rome immediately. I've got a donor!"

After a pregnant pause, "*Grazie a Dio.*" His voice throbbed. "I'll pack a bag for you and meet you below the gate. Whatever you do, don't have an accident on the way. My heart couldn't handle it."

Neither could hers. "I won't." Her voice shook. After she hung up, she shouted, "Mamma?"

"I'm right behind you and heard everything. Someone must have died, making it possible for my precious Clara to live." She wept. "Go, *bambina*! Every second counts! Your father and I will come to the hospital as soon as we can."

Whoever it was had to have signed a donor card while they were still living. As far as Clara was concerned, they were part angel.

Six hours later one of the nurses walked in Clara's hospital room. "They're ready for you, Signora Casali. You have two minutes before they come with the gurney to wheel you to the OR."

Clara nodded, overcome by the outpouring of love from her family. All the adults were here, gathered around her bed. Silvio hadn't left her side since his arrival with Maria. For once he didn't show his resentment of Valentino, which was a blessing in itself.

After her father kissed her one last time, her gaze finally fastened on her dashing husband, whose brown eyes were suspiciously bright.

He squeezed her hand. "This is it, my brave Clarissima."

"Oh, Tino—"

"I'll be with you every step of the way."

"I know that," she whispered in a tremulous voice.

"When you wake up, it will be to a new life." He lowered his mouth to hers in a kiss that felt more like a benediction than husbandly.

A new fear tore at her heart as she was wheeled out of the room.

The minute Clara was gone, Valentino turned to her family. "Dr. Arno says none of us can expect to see or talk to her until at least ten or eleven o'clock tonight. Do whatever you want until then. I'll be here the whole time and plan to catch up on some sleep while I wait."

Clara's mother hugged him. "You do that. No one deserves it more. We will see you tonight."

Once they'd all left the floor, he stepped across the hall to another room prepared for him where he quickly removed his clothes and put on a hospital gown. After he got in bed, a team of medical staff came in to prep him. Soon he was being wheeled out the door and down the hall to the OR.

Throughout his racing career he'd faced surgery several times for a bone to be set, but this was different. He loved the idea that one of his kidneys would be planted inside Clara. They'd had a connection since childhood. With this transplant, that connection would be indelible. Personal. Life-giving. Eternal. Belonging only to the two of them.

One day soon he hoped to plant something else inside her enticing body that would result in bringing both of them ineffable joy.

Clara kept waking up. Each time she did, she became more aware of her surroundings. Where was Valentino?

The next time she opened her eyes, she realized she was

back in a different room with a new nurse who was taking her vital signs.

"It's good to see you awake, Signora Casali."

"What time is it?"

"Midnight. You're in the transplant unit."

"I can't believe nine hours have passed."

"How are you feeling?"

"Strange."

"Strange is good."

"Where's my husband?"

"In time you'll be able to see everyone. Relax right now. Let the drugs do their job."

Between the anesthetic and other drugs being fed through the IV, she was feeling no pain, but the sight of the big machine next to her bed alarmed her.

"Did something go wrong with the transplant?"

The middle-aged woman smiled. "Don't you remember Dr. Arno telling you it went perfectly?"

"He did? Then why is the dialysis machine here?"

"In case your new kidney doesn't function right away. You probably don't remember him explaining that to you either." She gave Clara some pills to swallow. "Just take a few small sips."

"The water tastes good."

"Tomorrow you'll be able to drink liquids. Depending on how you're feeling, you'll probably be able to eat a little bit, too. Do you have any questions for me?"

"No, but I would like to see my husband."

"Tell you what. I'll go back to the desk and see how soon a visit is allowed."

"Thank you."

Before long she heard a familiar voice say her name. She opened her eyes. "Hi, Dr. Arno. The nurse told me everything went well."

A broad smile lit up his face. "It certainly did. You're a very lucky woman."

She nodded. "There are so many people I need to thank. You most of all."

"Not most of all. Without a donor, this wouldn't have been possible."

"I know."

"Before I let you talk to your husband, would you like to meet your donor?"

"Meet?" she cried softly. "But Mamma and I thought someone must have...died."

"No. In your case this altruistic donor is very much alive and came through the surgery beautifully, too. He wanted to see the person who received his kidney, but we'll only wheel him in for a moment."

Now that the transplant was over, the reality of the situation was overwhelming. She was about to meet the person who'd willingly given up a kidney for her? Clara couldn't comprehend that kind of sacrifice. Not really. What did you say to someone who'd just granted you a longer life?

Tears from too much emotion blurred her vision as she saw a woman pushing a man in a wheelchair. They came closer until she was able to make out his features.

It was the handsome face of her beloved husband.

She cried out his name on a sob. *"Why did you do it? Why?"*

"Don't you understand yet?" He was pushed as close to her as his wheelchair would allow. His intelligent brown eyes blazed with light. "I'm in love with you, darling. I think I was in love with you when we were children, but didn't know it."

To finally hear those words from that deep, silken voice...

More tears flowed down her cheeks. "I've been in love with you forever, but what if something happens one day and you'll need the kidney you gave me?"

"Then I'll give him one of mine."

Clara lifted her eyes to the woman who'd just spoken and received a second shock. "Isabella—" She hadn't realized.

"Yes." His sister smiled. "And if I find I need one, then Cristiano has pledged his to me. Because of you, Clara, our brother has found his happiness at last. This is what families are for, right? The Rossettis and the Casalis stick together."

On the fifth morning Valentino finished showering in preparation for leaving the hospital. Since their surgeries, he and Clara had been walking together, doing all kinds of exercises. They were more than ready to go.

Dr. Arno made his rounds after breakfast and released them. Within the hour a hospital van would be driving them back to Monta Correnti. This day seemed to have taken forever to get here.

As he was pulling on his tan chinos and a blue sport shirt he heard her call to him but it sounded muffled. He couldn't tell if she was excited or upset about something.

He emerged from his bathroom on a burst of adrenalin and found her standing by his bed.

"Look!" She turned around, giving him an eyeful of her womanly figure. All the tubes and catheters were gone. No more IV stand. She looked incredible and was dressed in the same outfit she'd worn to the track in Monaco. Those green eyes glowed as if they were on fire.

"Your kidney's been working inside me from the time it was transplanted. No more dialysis!"

It was the best news he'd ever heard. He took another step and wrapped his arms around her, careful not to apply too much pressure while their incisions were healing. "I'm glad I've been good for something around here," he teased to cover his emotions.

"Oh, Tino, I'm so happy and so terribly, terribly in love

with you!" She raised her hungry mouth for his kiss. They were starving for each other. Dr. Arno had told him they had to wait two weeks to make love. Valentino didn't know how he was going to hold out that long, not with a wife as passionate as Clara, but her comfort had to come first.

They had other rules to follow. Exercise every day. Walk. The longer the walks, the better. No driving a car or motor scooter for three weeks. No heavy lifting until after four weeks.

The fear that her body might reject his kidney had plagued both of them, but no longer. Naturally there was the possibility it might be rejected months or years later, but he refused to think about that right now. The different drugs she was taking were working.

"Signor Casali? Signora? When you're ready, the van is waiting for you at the south entrance downstairs."

Clara pulled away from him in embarrassment. Her face had gone a charming pink color. He would never tire of looking at her. Valentino had definitely come down with a serious case of love for his wife.

The nurse had brought two wheelchairs.

"Do we have to use them?" Clara asked her.

"It's hospital policy."

"Oh, all right," she grumbled and sat down in one. Valentino sank into the other one and reached for her hand. When she looked at him, they both saw the humor in their predicament and started to chuckle. Soon she was laughing. The sound filled him with an excitement he'd never known in his life.

After a short elevator ride, they were wheeled out to the van. The interior felt nice, comfortable. They thanked the staff for everything. Soon the attendant closed the sliding door and they were sealed off from the world for a while.

She darted Valentino a mischievous glance. "I feel like I did when we were little children. I would wait and wait for the end of school so I could run outside and hide from you. Somehow you always found me when nobody else could."

"It wasn't that hard." He grinned. "Whenever I got close, your laughter gave you away. I was attracted to it."

"My laugh?" she asked in an incredulous voice.

He nodded. "It has a happy quality. I liked being around you because of it. Don't ever stop. I couldn't take it."

"*Tino—*"

They were seated across from each other. He wanted to pull her onto his lap, but he didn't dare. After the hell she'd lived through, the thought of anything happening to her before they reached home was anathema to him.

Being a race-car pro, he had a problem letting anyone else drive him. The one hair-raising experience with his wife had been the exception because he adored her. At the moment he needed to have faith in the van driver's skill.

Since he couldn't hold her in his arms right now, he decided this would be a good time to tell her what Isabella had written in her e-mail. He already knew what Clara's response would be. She was a peacemaker. How else would she have survived from birth with a twin like Silvio?

Valentino's relationship with her brother still needed work. It would make her happy if he found a way to ease the tension. He'd have to think about that one.

"Tino?" she called out some time later. "Forgive me for interrupting you, but the driver's going the wrong way. He should have turned north."

"That's true, *if* we were headed for the villa."

"But we're not?"

"I thought we'd do something different."

For once she looked baffled. "Are you taking us to your old house on the lake?"

"No," he drawled.

She made a sound in her throat. "To the farm?"

"That depends on which one."

Silence fell between them before her gorgeous eyes rounded. "You bought the Brunello farm—"

His lips twitched. "Since the day we walked around the property, it's been known as the Casali place."

"Oh, darling—"

They were driving up to the farmhouse now. Her head swiveled around. "There must be a dozen trucks parked outside. My whole family's here! Whose car is that?"

"Isabella's. She brought Papa. He won't be able to stay long, but he came because he loves you."

"I feel the same way about him, Tino. He raised you as his own. I love him for that."

Valentino loved her for saying it and believed it. "They've all planned the celebration we couldn't have on our wedding day. Welcome home, *innamorata*."

She buried her face in her hands. In the next breath she'd broken down in quiet sobs from too much emotion. Valentino could relate.

He heard the van door open. Instead of the driver standing there, it was Silvio. His gaze shot to Clara, then passed to Valentino. For those few seconds he sensed her brother felt unsure of himself.

Taking advantage of the unexpected moment Valentino said, "Why don't you help her in the house while I talk to the driver?" He undid his seatbelt and climbed out of the van in order to give them some time alone.

Noise from the house reached his ears. Only the sounds of a big, gregarious family enjoying themselves could fill the air like that. By marrying Clara, he had entrée into their exclusive club. He'd never thought this kind of happiness could be his.

* * *

"Clara? This is for you." Bianca handed her a gaily wrapped gift.

"Another present? Thank you."

"Don't let Valentino open it," she whispered, kissing her cheek. "I'll call you in the morning."

Bianca, whose morning sickness seemed to be letting up, was the last of Clara's family to walk out the door. They'd brought the food and had done the dishes. Her mother had to be the one who'd made up their bed.

After her sister had gone, Clara, still seated on the couch, looked around the living room. She felt sated with food no longer forbidden to her. The wedding presents had been piled high on the coffee table. She couldn't wait to open them, but exhaustion had caught up with her. Tomorrow would be soon enough to dig in.

Seven o'clock wasn't late, but, having just gotten out of the hospital, she was ready for bed and knew Valentino was, too. A little while ago she'd seen him step outside with Silvio. She couldn't help but wonder how they were getting along. Maybe it was a good sign that her husband hadn't come back in yet, but it couldn't be good for him. He'd already been on his feet too long.

On her way to the bedroom with Bianca's gift, her gaze wandered around. Valentino had arranged for the interior of the house to be painted an off-white. He'd had it furnished with enough things for them to get by on. In a quiet aside he told her that, as soon as she was well enough, he expected her to decorate it the way she wanted. "Buy whatever else you want to make this *our* home, *piccola*."

Valentino was a rare man. It frightened her how much she loved him.

After she'd prepared for bed, she opened the present. Inside the tissue lay a black nightgown with lace straps. Definitely decadent.

When she'd asked Dr. Arno about that he'd said, "Two weeks and not before!" That was still nine days away. She smiled to herself before hiding it in the bottom of the drawer under some other clothes. Then she got in bed.

In a minute she saw Valentino's silhouette in the doorway. "We've got a slight problem, *piccola*."

Her heart skipped in worried reaction. "Silvio?"

"No. Amazingly enough he thanked me in a choked-up voice and we talked farming. I told him I would need his advice on how to go about getting started outside. He has offered his services. I never thought I'd see the day."

Contentment washed over her. She let out a relieved sigh. "Neither did I. Come to bed."

"That's the problem. In the hospital I would have sold my soul to be able to hold you. Now that I can in the privacy of our own bedroom, I'm telling you it wouldn't be a good idea."

"Yes, it would. We're both too tired."

"That's how much you know," he muttered.

"I'm wearing the same robe I wore at the villa."

"You think that protects you?" He started getting ready for bed. "Don't you realize how enticing you are when you're buttoned up from hem to neck?" he called out from the bathroom where he was brushing his teeth. "You might as well be wearing a sign that says 'warning—to proceed beyond this point could give you a heart attack'."

Clara laughed so hard it made her incision hurt.

When he finally climbed under the covers, they both lay on their backs. It was the most comfortable position for them. She reached out to touch his arm. He caressed hers. When his fingers came in contact with her graft, the movement stopped.

She heard Valentino suck in his breath. "Now I know why the good doctor left it in. He's a very wise man. You're safe from me for a while longer. *Ti amo*, Clarissima."

"*Ti amo*," she whispered back. It was liberating to be able to tell him *I love you*.

* * *

"What do you think, Papa? You're a connoisseur." Valentino had just dropped off Clara at the clinic for a checkup. Now was the perfect time to come to the apartment while he waited. He suggested the two of them sit at the dining-room table to enjoy a drink.

His father took another swallow. "It has a sweet bite. Very unusual."

"Do you feel it's good enough for your Rosa clientele to add it to the drinks menu?"

Luca eyed his son intently. "I didn't know you'd developed a taste for limoncello."

"In the last month I've developed a taste for several new things."

His father smiled at him. "Marriage obviously agrees with you. I knew it would once you found the right woman. That's the trick."

That *was* the trick.

"You're one of the lucky few who married your best friend and fell in love with her, too. That doesn't happen to everyone. I've a feeling it will last forever. It's a rare occurrence, just like this tangy liqueur." He lifted the wine glass and smelled the bouquet before emptying it.

"You've hit on the right word, Papa," Valentino mused aloud. Clara was like the drink she'd created. She had her own tang, her own flavor. His giving wife was no imitation of anyone else.

"Who makes it? This doesn't smell or taste like it came from Sorrento. It's sweeter."

"Your 'nose' never fails you. This comes from a local source."

"Ah… I knew it."

Among the traits he admired about his father was his insistence on sourcing local produce even if it was more expensive. He paid his staff more and gave them longer holidays.

These were the reasons he was in debt, but, on the other hand, these were the reasons the staff had stayed loyal to him. Giorgio had confided that Lisa had tried to bribe him several times to come and work for her restaurant, but she'd underestimated her brother's influence.

Luca stirred in his chair. "Do I know them?"

"Yes. Quite well, in fact."

He looked surprised. "They've never approached me."

Valentino smiled inwardly. "No. They wouldn't."

"What's their brand name?"

"Limoncello Clarissima."

His father blinked. "How unusual, yet beautiful... Reminds me of your wife. I hope she can one day give you a child because you'll have the most beautiful children around. But more importantly, I have to tell you that you'll make the best kind of father."

A lump lodged in Valentino's throat. "If such a miracle happens and it's a son, Clara has already decided we'll name him Valentino Casali in honor of your heritage."

"Well..." His father had to clear his throat several times. "Where did you say these people live?"

This was fun. "Right here in Monta Correnti."

"Why don't you bring them around to the restaurant tomorrow afternoon or the next afternoon and we'll talk about serving it for a trial period. I can't guarantee anything, of course."

"Of course," Valentino echoed.

He couldn't wait to get back to the farm to tell her. The long wait was finally over. Tonight would be their real wedding night. His papa had just made it possible for Valentino to give her a wedding present she'd never forget.

"About your idea for the tour-bus crowd. I think we should try it and see what happens."

Elated, he got up to kiss his father on both cheeks, then disappeared out the door with the bottle. There was only a little liqueur left. Enough to celebrate her return to life.

Once he took off in the Ferrari, it didn't take long to pull up outside the clinic where she was getting her post-op checkup. He hurried down the hall to the dialysis department. To his frustration she hadn't come out yet.

"She's not here," the receptionist called out. "She told me you were to meet her in the restaurant at the San Gallo hotel."

"*Grazie.*"

He had to fight his disappointment that they couldn't simply drive back to the farm. The San Gallo was the best five-star hotel in Monta Correnti and sat on a hill with its own lovely view. But it was always crowded, especially at this time of year when students and tourists were on spring break. Valentino didn't want to face hordes of people right now. All he wanted was Clara.

"*Buon giorno*, Signor Casali," the maître d' greeted him ten minutes later. "Congratulations on your marriage. I will give you a view table as soon as I can make the arrangements."

"Thank you, but that won't be necessary. I'm looking for my wife. She asked me to meet her in here."

He shook his head. "She hasn't come. No reservation was made."

Valentino took a deep breath. "I'll check with the concierge."

When he asked about her at the desk, the man said, "Signora Casali is in room 152. She'll be happy to know you've come. She was most anxious. Here's another key."

Filled with alarm that something had gone wrong at her checkup and she'd decided to tell him over their meal, he took the card key and raced across the foyer to the stairs. By the time he could let himself in the room on the next floor, his anxiety bordered on terror for fear her kidney had suddenly stopped functioning.

"Clara?" he cried out after flinging the door open.

"*Caro*—" she called from the bathroom "—I thought you would be at your father's longer."

"What's wrong?" he demanded.

"Nothing. I'm fine. I'll be out in a minute."

"You left the clinic without me. You're *not* fine! I know you're not." He raced across the room to open the door, but it was locked.

Frantic, he pressed his forehead against it. "*Piccola*? Don't shut me out."

"I would never do that."

He heard a click, then the door opened.

A barefooted woman stood before him. Except for her eyes that dazzled him with their green fire, nothing else was familiar. A new jasmine fragrance assailed him. Her dark hair was curly like a Gypsy's. She was a vision in sheer black lace over alabaster.

Her seductive smile captivated him.

"You have permission to discover for yourself that there's absolutely nothing wrong with me, *signore*." She wound her soft arms around him and gave him a kiss to die for. "But first, why don't you get out of these clothes? You've been my fantasy for years. Now I want the reality."

Valentino couldn't talk. He couldn't breathe.

"Is that going to be a problem for the famous Valentino Casali?" she teased. "Because if it is, you're in *real* trouble with your farmer wife."

* * * * *

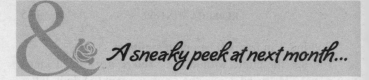
A sneaky peek at next month...

By Request

RELIVE THE ROMANCE WITH THE BEST OF THE BEST

My wish list for next month's titles...

In stores from 19th April 2013:

❏ Billionaires Galore! – Leanne Banks

❏ Bella Rosa Marriages – Fiona Harper,
Patricia Thayer & Jennie Adams

In stores from 3rd May 2013:

❏ Hearts of Gold
– Meredith Webber

*3 stories in
each book - only
£5.99!*

Available at WHSmith, Tesco, Asda, Eason, Amazon and Apple

Just can't wait?

*Visit us
Online*

You can buy our books online a month before
they hit the shops! **www.millsandboon.co.uk**

0413/05